USA Today bestse...
hot, happy contem...
humour and sensu...
the globe. She has ...
for the prestigious ...   ...omance
Writers of America and has won the award twice.

Sarah lives near London with her family. When she isn't writing she loves spending time outdoors. Visit her website at www.sarahmorgan.com.

Kim Lawrence lives on a farm in Anglesey with her university lecturer husband, assorted pets who arrived as strays and never left, and sometimes one or both of her boomerang sons. When she's not writing she loves to be outdoors gardening, or walking on one of the beaches for which the island is famous—along with being the place where Prince William and Catherine made their first home.

Tara Pammi can't remember a moment when she wasn't lost in a book—especially a romance, which was much more exciting than a mathematics textbook at school. Years later, Tara's wild imagination and love for the written word revealed what she really wanted to do. Now she pairs alpha males who think they know everything with strong women who knock that theory *and* them off their feet!

The Italian Mavericks

COLLECTION

January 2019

February 2019

March 2019

April 2019

May 2019

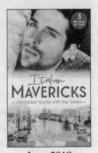

June 2019

**Watch out for the Greek Mavericks
collection coming soon!**

Italian Mavericks: Forbidden Nights with the Italian

SARAH MORGAN

KIM LAWRENCE

TARA PAMMI

MILLS & BOON

All rights reserved including the right of reproduction in whole or in part in any form. This edition is published by arrangement with Harlequin Books S.A.

This is a work of fiction. Names, characters, places, locations and incidents are purely fictional and bear no relationship to any real life individuals, living or dead, or to any actual places, business establishments, locations, events or incidents. Any resemblance is entirely coincidental.

This book is sold subject to the condition that it shall not, by way of trade or otherwise, be lent, resold, hired out or otherwise circulated without the prior consent of the publisher in any form of binding or cover other than that in which it is published and without a similar condition including this condition being imposed on the subsequent purchaser.

® and TM are trademarks owned and used by the trademark owner and/or its licensee. Trademarks marked with ® are registered with the United Kingdom Patent Office and/or the Office for Harmonisation in the Internal Market and in other countries.

First Published in Great Britain 2019
By Mills & Boon, an imprint of HarperCollins *Publishers*
1 London Bridge Street, London, SE1 9GF

ITALIAN MAVERICKS: FORBIDDEN NIGHTS
WITH THE ITALIAN © 2019 Harlequin Books S.A.

The Forbidden Ferrara © 2012 Sarah Morgan
Surrendering to the Italian's Command © 2016 Kim Lawrence
The Unwanted Conti Bride © 2016 Tara Pammi

ISBN: 978-0-263-27605-3

0619

MIX
Paper from
responsible sources
FSC® C007454

This book is produced from independently certified FSC™ paper to ensure responsible forest management.

For more information visit: www.harpercollins.co.uk/green

Printed and bound in Spain
by CPI, Barcelona

THE FORBIDDEN
FERRARA

SARAH MORGAN

For my editor Lucy Gilmour who is wise, clever
and always wears great shoes. Thank you.

CHAPTER ONE

THERE was a shocked silence round the boardroom table.

Amused by the reaction, Santo Ferrara sat back in his chair. 'I'm sure you'll all agree it's an exciting project,' he drawled. 'Thank you for your attention.'

'You've lost your mind.' It was his older brother who finally broke the silence. Cristiano, who had recently relinquished some of his responsibility in the company to spend more time with his young family. 'It can't be done.'

'Because you didn't succeed? Don't beat yourself up. It's fairly common for a man to lose his edge when he's distracted by a wife and kids.' Santo loaded his tone with sympathy, enjoying the brief interlude in what had been a long, punishing few weeks. And if he felt a slight twinge of envy that his brother had gone on to be as successful in his personal life as he was in business then he told himself that it was just a matter of time before he found the same thing himself. 'It's like seeing a great warrior fallen. Don't blame yourself. Living with three women can soften a man.'

The rest of the Board exchanged nervous glances but wisely chose to remain silent.

Cristiano's gaze locked on his. 'I am still chairman of this company.'

'Precisely. You've taken a back seat while you change nappies. Now leave the good ideas to the rest of us.' He was being deliberately combative and Cristiano gave a reluctant laugh.

'I'm not denying that your proposal is exciting. I can see the business potential in adapting the hotel to accommodate a wider range of sports and appeal to a younger demographic. I even agree that expanding on the West coast of Sicily has potential for a certain type of discerning traveller—' he paused and when he looked at Santo his eyes were deadly serious '—but the success of the project rests on you gaining the extra land from the Baracchi family and old man Baracchi would shoot you through the head before he sold to you.'

Good-natured banter gave way to tension. Those around the table kept their eyes down, everyone well aware of the history between the two families. The whole of Sicily knew the history.

'That is my problem to deal with,' Santo said in a cool tone and Cristiano made an impatient sound as he pushed back his chair and paced over to the expanse of glass that overlooked the glittering Mediterranean sea.

'Since you took over day-to-day running of the company you have more than proved yourself. You have done things I hadn't even thought of doing.' He turned. 'But you will not be able to do *this*. You will simply inflame a situation that has been simmering for almost three generations. You should let it die.'

'I am going to turn the Ferrara Beach Club into our most successful hotel.'

'You will fail.'

Santo smiled. 'Shall we bet on that?'

For once his brother didn't return the smile or take up the challenge. 'This goes deeper than sibling rivalry. You *cannot* do this.'

'Enough time has passed for us to put grievances aside.'

'That,' Cristiano said slowly, 'depends on the grievance.'

Santo felt the anger start to heat inside him but alongside the anger were darker, murkier emotions that sprang to life whenever the Baracchi name was mentioned. It was a visceral reaction, a conditioned response reinforced by a lifetime of animosity between the families. 'I was not responsible for what happened to Baracchi's grandson. You know the truth.'

'This is not about truth or reason, but about passion and prejudice. Deep-rooted prejudice. I have already approached him. Made him several more than generous offers. Baracchi would see his family starve before he sells his land to a Ferrara. Negotiations are closed.'

Santo rose to his feet. 'Then it's time they were reopened.'

A man cleared his throat. 'As your lawyer it's my duty to warn against—'

'Don't give me negatives—' Santo lifted his hand to silence the man, his eyes still fixed on his brother. 'So your objection isn't the commercial development which you concede makes sound business sense, but the interaction with the Baracchi family. Do you think I'm a coward?'

'No, and that is what troubles me. You use reason and courage but Baracchi has neither. You are my brother.' Cristiano's voice thickened. 'Guiseppe Baracchi hates you. He's always been an irascible old man. What makes you think he will listen to you before he loses that infamous temper of his?'

'He may be an irascible old man but he's also a frightened old man in financial trouble.'

'I'm willing to bet he's not in so much trouble he'll take money from a Ferrara. And frightened old men can be dangerous. We've maintained the hotel there because it would hurt our mother to sell our father's first hotel, but I've been talking to her recently and—'

'We're not going to sell. I'm going to turn it around but to do that I need the land. *All* of the land. The whole bay.' Santo saw the lawyer's agitation but he ignored him. 'I don't just want the land for watersports, I want the Beach Shack. That restaurant pulls in more custom than all our restaurants in the hotel. This is not about fuelling a feud, it's about protecting our business. While guests walk away from us to eat at the Beach Shack and watch the sunset, we are losing revenue.'

'Which brings us to the second problem in this ambitious scheme of yours. That restaurant is run by his granddaughter—a woman who very possibly hates you even more than her grandfather.' Cristiano looked him straight in the eye. 'How do you think Fia will greet the news that you intend to make an offer for the land?'

He didn't have to think. He knew.

She would fight him with everything she had.

They would clash. Tempers would burn hot.

And woven through the tension of the present would be the past.

Not just the long-standing feud over land, but their own personal history. Because he hadn't been entirely honest with his brother, had he? In a family where no one had secrets, he had a secret. A secret he'd buried deep enough to ensure it would never see the light of day.

The sudden rush of black emotion took him by surprise. With an impatient frown he glanced out of the window to the beach beyond but he didn't see sand or sea. Instead he saw Fiammetta Baracchi with her long legs and temper hotter than a red chilli pepper.

Cristiano was still watching him. 'She hates you.'

Was it hate?

They hadn't discussed feelings, he thought. They hadn't discussed anything at all. Not even when they'd ripped each other's clothes off, when his body had screamed for hers and hers for his, not once in the whole wild, erotic, out of control experience had they exchanged a single word.

And instinct told him she'd buried her secret as deeply as he'd buried his.

As far as he was concerned, that was the way it was staying.

The past had no place in this negotiation.

'Under her management the Shack has gone from a few rickety tables on the beach to the most talked about eatery in Sicily. Rumour has it that she's a talented chef.'

Cristiano shook his head slowly. 'You're walking into an explosive situation, Santo. At best it's going to be messy.'

Carlo, their lawyer, put his head in his hands.

Santo ignored both of them just as he ignored the elemental rush of heat and the dark memories that, now woken, refused to return to sleep. 'This feud has lasted too long. It's time to move on.'

'Not possible.' Cristiano's voice was harsh. 'Guiseppe Baracchi's grandson, his only male heir, died when he wrapped a car around a tree. *Your* car, Santo. And you expect him to shake your hand and sell you his land?'

'Guiseppe Baracchi is a businessman and this deal makes perfect business sense.'

'Are you going to tell him that before or after the old man shoots you?'

'He won't shoot me.'

'He probably won't need to.' Cristiano gave a grim smile. 'Knowing Fia, she'll shoot you first.'

And that, Santo thought without emotion, *was entirely possible.*

'This is the last snapper.' Fia lifted the fish from the grill and plated it up. The heat from the fire warmed her cheeks. 'Gina?'

'Gina is outside checking out the driver of a Lamborghini that just pulled into our car park. You know she has a taste for men who can keep her in the style of her dreams. I'll take those.' Ben scooped up the plates and balanced them. 'How is your grandfather tonight?'

'Tired. He's not himself. He doesn't even have the energy to snap at people.' Fia felt a ripple of worry and made a mental note to check on him next time she had a lull. 'Are you coping out there? Tell Gina to leave the customers alone and work.'

'You tell her. I'm too chicken.' Ben skilfully dodged the waitress, who came sprinting into the kitchen. 'Hey, be careful or we'll be sending you out on the boat for more snapper.'

'You'll *never* guess who just turned up—'

Fia shot a glance at Ben as she started on the next order. 'Serve the food or it will be cold and I don't serve cold food.' Aware that Gina was virtually trembling with excitement, Fia decided it would be quicker and more efficient just to let her gush. She added seasoning and olive oil to fresh scallops and dropped them onto the pan. They were so fresh they needed nothing but the best quality oil to bring out the flavour. 'It must be someone exciting because I've never known you starstruck before and we've had plenty of celebrities in here.' As far as she was concerned, a guest was a guest. They were here to eat and her job was to feed them. And she fed them well. Expertly she flipped the scallops and added fresh herbs and capers to the pan.

Gina sneaked a look over her shoulder to the restaurant. 'It's the first time I've seen him in person. He's stunning.'

'Whoever he is, I hope he booked because otherwise you're going to have to send him away.' Fia shook the pan constantly. 'It's a full house tonight.'

'You won't be sending him away.' Gina sounded awestruck. 'It's Santo Ferrara. In the flesh. Only sadly not showing anywhere near as much flesh as I'd like in an ideal world.'

Fia stopped breathing.

Weakness spread through her body and then she started to shake, as if she'd suddenly been injected with something deadly. The pan slid from her hand and crashed onto the flame, the precious scallops forgotten.

'He wouldn't come here.' *He wouldn't dare.* She was talking to herself. Reassuring herself. But there was no reassurance to be had.

Since when did she know anything about what motivated Santo Ferrara?

'Er—why wouldn't he come?' Gina looked intrigued. 'Seems logical enough to me. His company owns the hotel next door and you serve great food.'

Gina wasn't local, otherwise she would have known the history between the two families. Everyone knew. And Fia also knew that the Ferrara Beach Club, the hotel that shared her perfect curve of beach, was the smallest and least significant of the Ferrara hotel group. There was no earthly reason why Santo himself would choose to give it his personal attention.

Her concentration shot, Fia caught her elbow on the side of a hot pan. Pain seared through her and brought her back to the present. Furious with herself for forgetting the scallops, she plated them up with meticulous care and handed them to Gina, functioning on automatic. 'This is for the couple on the waterfront,' she croaked. 'It's their anniversary and they booked this six months ago so make sure you treat them with reverence. This is a big night for them. I don't want them disappointed.'

Gina gaped at her. 'Aren't you going to—'

'I'm fine! It's just burned flesh—' Fia spoke through her teeth '—I'll put it under cold water in a minute.'

'I wasn't thinking about your elbow. I was thinking about the fact that Santo Ferrara is standing in your restaurant and you don't seem to care,' Gina said faintly. 'You treat every

customer like royalty and when someone genuinely important turns up you ignore him. You do know who he is? *The*
Ferrara, yes? Ferrara Resorts. Five star all the way.'

'I know exactly who he is.'

'But Boss, if he's come here to eat—'

'He hasn't come here to eat.' A Ferrara would never sit
down at a Baracchi table for fear of being poisoned. She had
no idea why he was here and that lack of insight frustrated
her because she couldn't fight what she didn't understand.
And mingled in with the shock and anger was dread.

He'd walked boldly into her restaurant at peak time. Why?

Only something really, really important would make him
do that.

Terror rippled through her. *No*, she thought wildly, *it
couldn't possibly be that.*

He didn't know.

He *couldn't* know.

With a final curious glance, Gina hurried out of the kitchen
and Fia ran cold water over her burned elbow, trying to reassure herself that it was a routine visit. Another attempt by the
Ferrara family to hold out an olive branch. There had been
others, and her grandfather had taken each and every olive
branch and snapped it in two. Since her brother's death, there
had been nothing. No overtures. No contact.

Until now…

Functioning on automatic, she reached above her head
for a fresh bulb of garlic. She grew it herself in her garden,
along with vegetables and herbs and she enjoyed the growing almost as much as she enjoyed the cooking. It soothed
her. Gave her a feeling of home and family she'd never de-
rived from the people around her. Reaching for her favourite
knife, she started chopping, trying to think how she would
have reacted if the circumstances had been different. If the
terror wasn't involved. If the stakes weren't so high—

She would have been cold. Businesslike.

'*Buonasera*, Fia.'

A deep male voice came from the doorway and she turned, the knife turning from a kitchen implement to a weapon. The crazy thing was, she didn't know his voice. But she knew his eyes and they were looking at her now—two dark pools of dangerous black. They gleamed bright with intelligence and hard with ruthless purpose. They were the eyes of a man who thrived in a cut-throat business environment. A man who knew what he wanted and wasn't afraid to go after it. They were the same eyes that had glittered into hers in the darkness three years before as they'd ripped each other's clothes and slaked a fierce hunger.

Those three years had added a couple of inches to his broad shoulders and more bulk to muscles she remembered all too well. Apart from that he was exactly the same. Still the same 'born to rule' Ferrara self-confidence; the same innate sophistication, polished until it shone bright as the paintwork of his Lamborghini. He was six foot three of hard, sensual masculinity but Fia felt nothing a woman was supposed to feel when she laid eyes on Santo Ferrara. A normal woman wouldn't feel this searing anger, this almost uncontrollable urge to scratch his handsome face and thump that powerful chest. When she was near him, every feeling was exaggerated. She felt vulnerable and defenceless and those feelings brought out the worst in her. Usually she was warm and civil to everyone who stepped inside her kitchen. Reviews commended her hospitality and the intimate, friendly atmosphere of the restaurant. But she couldn't even bring herself to wish this man a good evening. And that was because she didn't want him to have a good evening.

She wanted him to go to hell and stay there.

He was her biggest mistake.

And judging from the cold, cynical glint in his eye, he considered her to be his.

'Well, this is a surprise. The Ferrara brothers don't usually step down from their ivory tower to mingle with us mortals. Checking out the competition?' She adopted her most businesslike tone, while all the time her anxiety was rising and the questions were pounding through her head.

Did he know?

Had he found out?

A faint smile touched his mouth and the movement distracted her. There was an almost deadly beauty in the sensual curve of those lips. Everything about the man was dark and sexual, as if he'd been designed for the express purpose of drawing women to their doom. If rumour were correct, he did that with appalling frequency.

Fia wasn't fooled by his apparently relaxed pose or his deceptively mild tone.

Santo Ferrara was the most dangerous man she'd ever met.

Without exchanging words, she'd fallen. Even now, years later, she didn't understand what had happened that night. One moment she'd been alone with her misery. The next, his hand had been on her shoulder and everything that had happened after that was a blur. Had it been about human comfort? Possibly, except that comfort implied gentle emotions and those had been in short supply that night.

He watched her now, his face giving no hint as to his thoughts. 'I've heard good things about your restaurant. I've come to find out if any of them are true.'

He didn't know, she thought. *If he knew, he wouldn't be toying with her.*

'They're all true, but I'm afraid I can't satisfy your curiosity. We're fully booked.' Her lips formed the words while her mind raced over the possible reasons for his visit. Was that really all this was? An idle visit to check out the competition? No, surely not. Santo Ferrara would delegate that task to a minion. Her brain throbbed with the strain of trying to second-guess him.

'We both know you can find me a table if you want to.'

'But I don't want to.' Her fingers tightened on the knife. 'Since when did a Ferrara dine at the same table as a Baracchi?'

His eyes locked on hers. Her heart beat just a little bit faster.

The searing look he sent her from under those dense, inky lashes reminded her that once they hadn't just dined; they'd hungered and they'd feasted. They'd devoured each other and taken until there was nothing left to take. And she could still remember the taste of him; feel the rippling power of his body against hers as they'd indulged in dark, forbidden pleasure, the memory of which had never left her.

In a crowded room she wouldn't have known his voice, but she knew how he'd feel and her palms grew hot and her knees weakened as her thoughts broke free of the restraints she'd imposed, liberating memories so vivid that for a moment she couldn't breathe.

He smiled.

Not the smile of a friend, but the smile of a conqueror contemplating the imminent surrender of a captive. 'Eat at my table, Fia.'

His casual use of her name suggested a familiarity that didn't exist and it unbalanced her, as he'd no doubt intended. He was a man who always had to be in control. He'd been in control on that night and there had been something terrifying about the force of passion he'd unleashed.

She'd taken him because she'd been in desperate need of human comfort.

He'd taken her because he could.

'This is *my* table we're talking about,' she said in a clear voice, 'and you're not invited.' She had to get rid of him. The longer he stayed, the bigger the risk to her. 'You have your own restaurant next door. If you're hungry then I'm sure they'd accommodate you, although I admit that neither the food nor the view is as good as mine so I can understand why you find both lacking.'

There was a stillness about him that made her uneasy. A watchfulness that she didn't trust.

'I need to speak to your grandfather. Tell me where he is.'

So that was why he was here. Another round of fruitless negotiations that would lead the same way as the others. Thanks goodness he'd made this visit at night, she thought numbly. No matter what happened, she had to ensure he didn't return during the day. 'You must have a death wish. You know how he feels about you.'

Those eyes were hooded as he watched her. 'And does he know how *you* feel about me?'

His oblique reference to that night shocked her because it was something that had never been mentioned before.

Was he threatening her? Was he about to expose her?

Relief had been replaced by sick panic as various avenues of horror opened up before her. Was that why he'd done it? To have a hold over her in the future? 'My grandfather is old and unwell. If you have something to say you can say it to me. If you want to talk business, then you'll talk to me. I run the restaurant.'

'But the land is his.' His soft voice was a million times more disturbing than an explosion of temper and that control of his worried her because she felt none where he was concerned. She thought about what she'd read—about Santo Ferrara more than filling his brother's large shoes in his running of their global corporation. And suddenly she realised how foolish she'd been to think that the Beach Club was too insignificant to be of interest to the big boss. It was precisely *because* it was too insignificant that it had caught his attention. He wanted to expand the Beach Club, and to do that he needed—

'You want our land?'

'It was once *our* land,' he said with lethal emphasis, 'until one of your unscrupulous relatives, of which there have been all too many, chose to use blackmail to extract half the beach from my great-grandfather. Unlike him, I am willing to propose a fair deal and pay you a generous price to regain that which should never have left my family.'

And it was all about money, of course. The Ferraras thought everything could be bought.

Which was what frightened her.

The initial feeling of relief that had flooded her had been replaced by trepidation. If he were intent on developing the land then she'd never be safe.

'My grandfather will never, ever sell to you so if that is what this visit is about you're wasting your time. You might as well go back to New York or Rome or wherever it is you live these days. Pick another project.'

'I live here.' His lip curled. 'And I am giving this project my personal attention.'

It was the worst news she could have had. 'He hasn't been well. I won't let you upset him.'

'Your grandfather is tough as boots. I doubt he is in need of your protection.' A few layers of 'civilized' had melted away and the dangerous edge to his tone told her that he meant business. 'Does he know that you're deliberately attracting my customers away from the hotel to your restaurant?'

He was six foot three of prime masculinity, the force of his nature barely leashed beneath that outward appearance of sophistication. And Fia knew just how much heat bubbled under the cool surface. She'd been burned by that heat.

His passion has shocked her, but nowhere near as much as her own.

'If by "deliberately" you mean that I'm cooking them good food in great surroundings, then I'm guilty as charged.'

'Those "great surroundings" are exactly the reason I'm here.'

So that was what had brought him back. Not the night they'd shared. Not concern for her welfare or anything that was personal.

Just business.

If she weren't so relieved that there wasn't a deeper reason, she would have been appalled by his insensitivity. Whatever else had happened, a death lay between them. Blood had been shed.

But one inconvenient death wouldn't be enough to stand in the way of a Ferrara on the path to acquisition, she thought numbly. It was all about empire building. 'This conversation is over. I need to cook. I'm in the middle of service.' The truth was she'd all but finished, but she'd wanted him out of here.

But of course he didn't leave because a Ferrara only ever did what a Ferrara wanted to do.

Instead of walking away he lounged against the door frame, sleek and confident, those eyes fixed on her. 'You feel so threatened by me you have to have a knife in your hand while we talk?'

'I'm not threatened. I'm working.'

'I could disarm you in under five seconds.'

'I could cut you to the bone in less.' It was bravado, of course, because not for one moment did she underestimate his strength.

'If this is the welcome you give your customers I'm surprised you have anyone here at all. Not exactly warm, is it?' The fringe of thick lashes made his eyes seem darker. Or maybe the darkness was something they created together.

She knew that the addition of just one ingredient could alter flavour. In this case it was the forbidden. They'd done the unforgivable. The unexplainable. The inexcusable.

'You're not a customer, Santo.'

'So feed me and then I will be. Cook me dinner.'

Cook me dinner. Just for a moment her hands shook.

He'd walked away without once glancing back. That, she could handle because, apart from one night of reckless sex, they'd shared nothing. The fact that he'd played a much bigger role in her dreams wasn't his fault. But for him to walk back in here and order her to cook him dinner, as if his return was something to celebrate…

The audacity of it took her breath away. 'Sorry. Fatted calf isn't on the menu tonight. Now get the hell out of my kitchen, Santo. Gina manages the bookings and tonight we're full. And tomorrow night. And any other night you wish to eat in my restaurant.'

'Gina is the pretty blonde? I noticed her on the way in.'

Of course he would have noticed her. Santo Ferrara not noticing a blonde, curvy woman would be like a lion not noticing a cute impala. That didn't surprise her. What surprised her was the ache in her chest. She didn't want to care who this man took to his bed. She'd never wanted to care and the fact that she did terrified her more than anything. She'd grown up witnessing that caring meant pain.

Never love a Sicilian man had been the last words her mother had flung at her eight-year-old daughter before she'd walked out of the door for ever.

Afraid of her own feelings, Fia turned her back and finished chopping garlic, but they were the ragged, uneven cuts of an amateur, not a professional.

'It's dangerous to handle a knife when your hands are shaking.' Suddenly he was right behind her, too close for comfort, and she felt her pulse sprint because even though he wasn't touching her she could feel the warmth of him, the power of him and feel her answering response. It was immediate and visceral and she almost screamed with frustration because it made no sense. It was like salivating over a food that she knew would make her ill.

'I'm not shaking.'

'No?' A strong, bronzed hand covered hers and immediately she was back in the darkness of that night, his mouth burning against hers, his skilled fingers showing her no mercy as he drove her wild. 'Do you think about it?'

She didn't need to ask what he meant.

Did she think about it? Oh, God, he had no idea. She'd tried everything, *everything*, to wipe the memory of that night from her mind but it was always with her. A sensual scar that was never going to heal. 'Take your hand off mine right now.'

His hand tightened, the strength in those fingers holding hers still. 'You finish serving food at ten. We'll talk after that.'

It was a command not an invitation and the sure confidence with which he issued that command licked at the flames of her anger. 'My work doesn't finish when the restaurant closes. I have hours of work and when that is done I go to bed.'

'With that puppy-eyed boy who works for you? Playing it safe now, Fia?'

She was so shocked by the question that she turned her head to look at him and the movement brought her physically closer. The light brush of her skin against the hardness of his thigh triggered a frightening response. It was as if her body *knew*. 'Who I invite into my bed is none of your business.'

Their eyes met briefly as they acknowledged privately what they'd never acknowledged publicly.

She watched, transfixed, as his gaze turned black.

A long dormant feeling slowly uncurled itself inside her, a response she didn't want to feel for this man.

What might have happened next she'd never know because Gina walked in and when Fia saw who she was carrying she wanted to shout out a warning. She wanted to tell the other girl to run and not look back. But it was too late. Her luck had run out. It was over. It was over because Santo was already turning to locate the source of the interruption, an irritated frown scoring the bronzed planes of his handsome face.

'He had a bad dream—' Gina cooed, stroking the sobbing toddler. 'I said I'd bring him to his mamma as you've finished cooking for the night.'

Fia stood, powerless to do anything except allow events to unfold.

Had circumstances been different she would have been pleased to see a Ferrara shocked out of his customary cool. As it was the stakes were so high she watched with the breath trapped in her lungs, reluctant witness to his rapidly changing emotions.

His initial irritation at the disturbance gave way to puzzlement as he looked at the miserable, hiccuping child now stretching out his little arms to Fia.

And she took him, of course, because his welfare mattered to her above all other things.

And two things happened.

Her son stared curiously at the tall, dark stranger in the kitchen and stopped crying instantly.

And the tall, dark stranger stared into black eyes almost identical to his own, and turned pale as death.

CHAPTER TWO

'Cristo—' His voice hoarse, Santo took a step backwards and crashed into some pans that had been neatly stacked ready to be put away. Startled by the sudden noise, the child flinched and hid his face in his mother's neck. Aware that he was the cause of that sudden display of anxiety, Santo struggled for control. Only by the most ruthless application of willpower did he succeed in hauling back the searing anger that threatened to erupt.

From the security of his mother's arms, the child peeped at him in terror, instinctively hiding from danger and yet intrigued by it.

And she would have been hiding, too, Santo thought grimly, if she had anywhere to hide. But she was right out in the open, all her secrets exposed.

He didn't even need to ask the obvious question.

Even without that instant moment of recognition he would have seen it in the way she held herself. That raw, undiluted anxiety was visible to the naked eye.

He'd come here to negotiate the purchase of the land. Not for one second had he anticipated *this*.

From the moment he'd walked into the kitchen she'd been in a hurry to get rid of him, and now he understood why. He'd assumed their past history was to blame for her response. And of course it was. But not in the way he'd thought.

There was a heaviness in his chest, as if his heart were being squeezed in a clenched fist.

Confronted by a situation he hadn't anticipated, he struggled with emotions that were new to him. Not just anger but a deep, primitive desire to protect.

The weight in his chest bloomed and grew into something so huge and powerful he felt the force of it right through his body.

I'm a father.

But even as he thought it, he also thought, *this is not how it was supposed to be.*

He'd always assumed that he would eventually fall in love, marry and then have children. He was a traditional guy, wasn't he? He'd seen his brother's joy and his sister's joy and he'd arrogantly assumed that the same experience awaited him.

He'd missed it all, he thought bitterly. The birth, first steps, first words—

Tormented by those thoughts, Santo gave a low growl.

The toddler's eyes widened with alarm as he sensed the change in the atmosphere. Or perhaps it was just that he detected his mother's panic. Either way, Santo knew enough about children to know that this one was about to dissolve into screams.

With another huge effort of will, he forced himself to suppress his feelings. It was the hardest thing he'd ever done. 'It is late for someone so young to be up.' He injected his voice with the right amount of gentleness, focusing on the child rather than the mother. Even looking at the boy sent a searing pain through his chest. It was a physical effort not to grab him, strap him into the seat of his Lamborghini and drive away with him. 'You must be very tired, *chicco*. You should be in bed.'

Fia stiffened, clearly taking that as criticism. 'He has bad dreams sometimes.'

The news that his son suffered from bad dreams did nothing to improve Santo's black, dangerous mood. What, he wondered darkly, had caused those dreams? Reminded of just how dysfunctional this family was, anger turned to cold dread.

'Gina—is it Gina?' He glanced at the pretty waitress and somehow managed to deliver the smile that had never failed him yet and it didn't fail him now as the girl beamed at him, visibly overwhelmed by his status.

'Signor Ferrara—'

'I really need to speak to Fia in private—'

'No!' Fia's voice bordered on desperate. 'Not now. Can't you see that this is a really bad time?'

'Oh, it's fine,' Gina gushed helpfully, blushing under Santo's warm, approving gaze. 'I can take him. I'm his nanny.'

'Nanny?' The word stuck in Santo's throat. No one in his family had ever employed outside help to care for their children. 'You look after him?' He didn't trust himself to use the words 'my son'. Not yet.

'It's a team approach,' Gina said cheerfully. 'We're like meerkats. We all look after the young. Only in this case there is only one young so he's horribly spoiled. I look after him when Fia is working, but I knew she'd finished cooking tonight so I thought I'd bring him for a cuddle. Now he's calmed down he's going to be just fine. He'll go straight off again the moment I put him in his bed. Come to Auntie Gina—' Cooing at the sleepy child, she drew him out of Fia's reluctant arms and snuggled him close.

'We still have customers—'

'They're virtually all finished,' Gina said helpfully. 'Just waiting for table two to pay the bill. Ben has it all under control. You have your chat, Boss.' Apparently oblivious to the tension crackling around them, Gina cast a final awestruck glance at Santo and melted from the room.

Silence reigned.

Fia stood, her cheeks pale against the fire of her hair, dark smudges under her eyes.

Words were some of the most deadly tools in his armoury. He used them to negotiate impossible deals, to smooth the most difficult of situations, to hire and fire, but suddenly, when he needed them more than ever before, they were absent. All he managed was a single word.

'Well?'

Despite his heightened emotional state, or perhaps because of it, Santo spoke softly but she flinched as if he'd raised his voice.

'Well, what?'

'Don't even think about giving me anything other than the truth. You'd be wasting your breath.'

'In that case why ask?'

He didn't know what to say to her. She didn't know what to say to him.

Their situation was painfully difficult.

Before tonight they'd never actually spoken. Even during that one turbulent encounter, they hadn't spoken. Not one word had been exchanged. Oh, there'd been sounds. The ripping of clothes, the slide of flesh against flesh, ragged breathing—but no words. Nothing coherent from either of them. He was a man confident in his sexuality, but he still didn't really understand what had happened that night.

Had the whole forbidden nature of their encounter acted as some sort of powerful aphrodisiac? Had the fact that their two families had been enemies for almost three generations added to the emotion that had brought them together like animals in the darkness?

Possibly. Either way, their relationship had been like a blast from a rocket engine, the sudden heat tearing through both of them, burning up common sense and reason. He should have known there would be a price. And clearly he'd been paying that price for the last three years.

'Why the hell didn't you tell me?' His tone was raw and ragged and he watched as her breathing grew shallow.

'For a supposedly clever man you ask stupid questions.'

'Nothing—*nothing*—that has happened between our two families should have prevented you from telling me *this*.' With a slice of his hand he gestured towards the open door. 'This' had vanished into the night with the accommodating Gina and letting him out of his sight was one of the hardest things Santo had ever done. Soon, he vowed. Soon, the child would never be out of his sight again. It was the only sure thing in this storm of uncertainty. 'You should have told me.'

'For what purpose? To have my son exposed to the same bitter feud that has coloured our entire lives? To have him used as some pawn in your power games? I have protected him from all of that.'

'*Our* son—' Santo spoke in a thickened tone '—he is my son, too. The product of both of us.'

'He is the product of one night when you and I were—'

'—were what?'

Her gaze didn't falter. 'We were foolish. Out of control. We did something stupid. Something we *never* should have done. I don't want to talk about it.'

'Well, tough, because you're going to talk about it. You should have talked about it three years ago when you first realised you were pregnant.'

'Oh, don't be so naive!' Her temper flared as hot as his. 'This was not some cosy romance that had unexpected consequences. It was complicated.'

'The decision whether or not to tell a man he's the father of your child is not complicated. *Cristo*—' Floored by the monumental issues facing them, he let out a long breath and dragged his hand over the back of his neck, seeking calm and not finding it anywhere within his grasp. 'I cannot believe this. I need time to think.' He knew that decisions made in the heat of anger were never good ones and he needed them to be good ones.

'There is nothing to think about.'

Santo cast his mind back to that night, a night he never allowed himself to think about because the good was irrevocably entwined with the really, really bad and it was impossible to unravel the two. 'How did it happen? I used—'

'Apparently there are some things even a Ferrara can't control,' she said coolly, 'and this was one of them.'

He looked at her blankly. The whole night had merged for him. Pulling out details was impossible. It had been crazy, wild and—she was right—ill-advised. But what they'd shared hadn't been the product of rational decision-making. It had been sheer animal lust, the like of which he'd never experienced before or since.

She'd been upset.

He'd put his hand on her shoulder.

She'd turned to him.

And that had been it—

Such a small spark to light such a raging fire.

And then, even before the heat had cooled, she'd had the call telling her that her brother had been killed. That single tragic phone call that had sliced through their loving like the blade of a guillotine. And after, the fallout. The recriminations and the speculation.

The young waiter appeared in the doorway, his eyes on Fia. 'Is everything OK? I saw Luca awake, which is always nice because I managed to snatch a lovely cuddle, but I heard raised voices.' He shot Santo a suspicious look, which Santo returned tenfold. The news that everyone appeared to be cuddling his son except him simply fuelled his already fiercely burning temper. An unfamiliar emotion streaked through him—the primal response of a man guarding his territory.

So his child was called Luca.

The fact that he'd learned the name from this man drove him to the edge of control.

What exactly was his relationship with Fia?

'This is a private conversation. Get out,' he said thickly and he heard Fia's soft intake of breath.

'It's OK, Ben. Just go.'

Apparently Ben didn't know what was good for him because he stood stubbornly in the doorway. 'I'm not leaving until I know you're all right.' It was like a spaniel challenging a Rottweiler. He glared at Santo, who would have given him points for courage had he not been way past admiring the qualities of another man. Especially a man who was making puppy eyes at the woman who, only moments earlier, had been clutching his child.

'I am giving you one more opportunity to leave and then I will remove you myself.'

'Go, Ben!' She sounded exasperated. 'You're just giving him another reason to throw his weight around.'

Ben gave her one last doubtful look and melted away into the darkness of the night, leaving the two of them alone.

Tension throbbed like a living force. The air was heavy with it. He could taste it on his tongue and feel the weight of it pressing down on his shoulders. And he knew she could feel it too.

His head was a mass of questions.

How had no one guessed? Had no one questioned the identity of the child's father? He didn't understand how she could have hidden such a thing.

'You knew you were pregnant and yet you cut me out of your life.'

'You were never in my life, Santo. And I was never in yours.'

'We made a child together.' His low growl came from somewhere deep inside him and he saw her recoil as if the reminder came as a physical blow.

'You need to calm down. In just ten minutes you've frightened my child, virtually seduced his nanny, bawled me out and been unforgivably rude to someone I care about.'

'I did *not* frighten our child.' That accusation angered him more than any of the others. 'You did that by creating this situation.' And he still didn't understand how she had kept her secret. His usually sharp mind refused to work. 'This is your grandfather's idea of revenge? Punishing the Ferraras by hiding the child?'

'No!' Her chest rose and fell, her breathing shallow. 'He adores Luca.'

Santo raised his eyebrows in disbelief. 'He adores a child who is half Ferrara? You expect me to believe that age has finally gifted a Baracchi with tolerance?' He broke off, alerted by something in her eyes, some instinct that went bone-deep. And suddenly it fell into place. Finally he understood the truth and the reality was another blow to his already aching gut. '*Cristo*, he doesn't know, does he?' It was the only possible explanation and one that was confirmed by the look in her eyes.

'Santo—'

'Answer me.' His voice didn't sound like his own and he saw her take a step backwards. 'You *will* tell me the truth. He doesn't know, does he? You haven't told him.'

'How could I tell him?' Underneath the desperation was a profound weariness, as if this issue were a heavy weight she'd been carrying for too long. 'He hates everything about your family, and he hates *you* more than any man on the planet. Not just because your surname is Ferrara, but because—' She didn't finish the sentence and he let it hang there because to get involved in a discussion about her brother's death would mean being sidetracked, and he refused to be sidetracked.

They had a child.

A child that was half Ferrara, half Baracchi. An unimaginable bloodline.

A child born out of one night that had ended in tragedy.

And the old man didn't know.

He wondered how her grandfather could not have seen what he himself had seen instantly.

White-faced, she stared at him. Santo was so shell-shocked by the enormity of the secret she'd been carrying, he was reeling from it. How had she done it? She must have lain there every morning wondering whether today would be the day she'd be found out. Whether today would be the day a Ferrara would come and claim their own.

'*Madre de Dio*, I cannot believe this. When the child is old enough to ask about his father, what did you intend to tell him? On second thought, don't answer that,' he said thickly, 'I am not ready to hear the answer.' He knew as well as anyone that life was no fairy story, but belief in the sanctity of family ran strong in his veins. Family was the raft that kept you afloat in stormy seas, the anchor that stopped you from drifting, the wind in the sail that propelled you forward. He was the product of his parents' happy marriage and both his brother and sister had found love and created their own families. He'd assumed that the same would happen to him. Not once had he considered that he would have to fight for the right to be a father to his own child. Nor had he dreamt of his child being raised in a family like the Baracchis. He wouldn't have wished it on anyone. It was a nightmare almost too painful to contemplate.

Her breathing was shallow. 'Please, you have to promise me that you will let me deal with this. My grandfather is old.

He isn't well.' Her voice shook but Santo felt no sympathy. He felt bitter and angry and *raw*.

'You have had three years to deal with it. Now it's my turn. Did you really think I'd allow my son to be raised in your family? And without a father in his life? The notion of family is alien to a Baracchi.' He jabbed his fingers into his hair, his stress levels turning supersonic. 'When I think what the child must have gone through—'

'Luca is happy and well cared for.'

'I saw your childhood.' Santo let his hand fall to his side. 'I saw how it was for you. You don't understand what a family should be.' And it broke his heart that his son had been raised in a family like that.

Her face was ghostly pale. 'Luca's childhood is nothing like mine. And if you know what mine was like then you should also know that I would never want that for my son. I don't blame you for your concern but you are wrong. I *do* understand what a family should be. I always have.'

'How? Where would you learn that? Certainly not in your own home.' Her home life had been fractured, messy and unbelievably insecure because the Baracchi family didn't just fight their neighbours, they fought amongst themselves. If family was a boat built to weather stormy seas, then hers was a shipwreck.

The first time they'd met properly she'd been eight years old and hiding on the far side of the beach. *His* side, where no Baracchi was supposed to tread. She'd taken refuge in the disused boathouse, amongst jagged planks of wood and the acrid smell of oil. He'd been fourteen years old and totally at a loss to know what to do with his wild-haired intruder. Was he supposed to hold her captive? Ask for a ransom? In the end he'd done neither. Nor had he blown her cover.

Instead, intrigued by her defiance, spurred on by the lure

of the forbidden, he'd let her hide there until she'd chosen to return home.

Weeks later he'd found out that the day she'd kept her solitary vigil in his boathouse had been the day her mother had walked out, leaving Fia's violent Sicilian father to cope with two children he'd never wanted. He remembered being surprised that she hadn't cried. It was years before he realised that Fia never cried. She kept all her emotions hidden inside and never expected comfort. Which was probably because she'd learned there was none to be had in her family.

Santo's mouth tightened.

Maybe she did shut people out, but there was no way in hell he'd let her shut him out. Not now. Not this time. 'You made your decision, by yourself with no reference to anyone else. Now I will make mine.' He cut her no slack. Didn't allow the beseeching look in her eyes to alter him from what he knew to be the right course of action.

'What do you mean?'

'When I'm ready to talk, I'll contact you. And don't even *think* of running because if you do I will hunt you down. There is nowhere you can hide. Nowhere on this planet you can take my son that I can't find you.'

'He is my son, too.'

Santo gave a humourless smile. 'And that presents us with an interesting challenge, doesn't it? He is possibly the first thing our two families have had in common. When I've decided what I'm going to do about that, I'll let you know.'

As the furious growl of the Lamborghini disturbed the silence of the night, Fia just made it to the bathroom and was violently sick. It could have been panic, fear, or some noxious combination of the two, but whatever it was it left her shaking and she hated the weakness and the feeling of vulnerability. Afterwards she sat on the floor with her eyes closed, trying to formulate a plan but there was no plan she could make that he couldn't sweep aside.

He would take control, the way the Ferraras always took control. His contempt for her family would drive his decision-making. And part of her didn't blame him for that. In his position she probably would have felt the same way because, now, she understood how it felt to want to protect a child.

Fia wrapped her arms around her knees and pulled them closer, tucking herself into as small a space as possible.

He hadn't listened when she'd tried to explain herself. He hadn't believed her when she'd told him that she'd made sure that Luca's childhood was nothing like her own.

His mission now was to rescue his son from the Baracchi family.

There would be no softness. No concessions. No compromise.

Instead of being raised in a calm, loving atmosphere, Luca would be subjected to the intolerable pressures of animosity and resentment. He'd be the rope in an emotional tug of war.

And that was precisely why she'd chosen this particular rocky, deadly path and she'd lived with the lies, the worry and the stress for three years in order to protect her son.

'Mamma sick.' Luca stood there, his favourite bear clutched in his arms, that dark hair rumpled. The harsh bathroom lights spotlighted every feature and for a moment she couldn't breathe because right there, in her son's face, she saw Santo. Their child had inherited those unforgettable eyes, that same glossy dark hair. Even the shape of his mouth reminded her of his father and she wasn't going to start thinking about his stubborn streak…

Realistically, it had only been a matter of time before her secret was out.

'I love you.' Impulsively she dragged him into her arms and kissed his head, letting the warmth of him flow into her.

'I'm always going to be here for you. And Gina, and Ben. You have people who love you. You won't ever be alone.' She held him tightly, as she had never been held. She kissed him, as she had never been kissed. Perhaps it wasn't fair to blame Santo Ferrara for assuming that his child was being raised in a toxic atmosphere. He had no idea how hard she'd worked to ensure that Luca's childhood was nothing like her own.

And as he snuggled against her, happy and content, she felt her eyes fill.

What had she lacked, she wondered, that her own mother hadn't felt this same powerful bond? Nothing, *nothing*, would induce her to walk away from her child. There was no price, no power, no promise that could make her do such a thing.

And there was no way she was going to let Santo take her son.

Blissfully ignorant of the fact that their lives were teetering on the edge of a dangerous chasm, he wriggled out of her arms.

'Bed.'

'Good idea,' she croaked, scooping him up and carrying him back to his bed. Whatever happened, she was going to protect him from the fallout of this. She wasn't going to let him be hurt.

'Man come back?'

Her insides churned again. 'Yes, he'll come back.' She was in no doubt about that. And when he returned he'd bring serious legal muscle. She had no doubt about that, either. Events had been set in motion and there was no stopping them. No stopping a Ferrara from getting what he wanted.

And Santo Ferrara wanted his son.

She sat on the bed, watching her son fall asleep, her love for him so huge that it filled every part of her. The strength of that bond made it all too easy for her to imagine Santo's feelings. Deep inside her, the guilt that she worked so hard to suppress awoke.

She'd never been comfortable with her decision. It had haunted her in the dark hours of the night when there were no distractions to occupy her mind. It wasn't that she regretted the choice she'd made. She didn't. But she'd learned that the right decision could feel completely wrong. And then there were the dreams. Dreams that distorted reality. Twisted the impossible into the possible. Dreams of a life that didn't exist.

Blocking out images of black, silky lashes and a hard, sensual mouth, Fia stayed until Luca was safely asleep and then returned to the kitchen to clear up. Because she'd sent the staff home she had to do it herself, but the mindless work helped calm the panicky knot in her stomach. She poured her anxiety into each swipe of her cloth until every surface in the kitchen shone, until sweat pricked her brow, until she was too bone-tired to feel anything except the physical ache of hard labour. And then she grabbed a cold beer from the fridge and took it to the small wooden jetty that butted out from the restaurant.

Fishing boats bobbed quietly in the darkness, waiting to be taken out onto the water.

Usually this was a time to be calm, but tonight her nightly ritual failed to produce the desired effect.

Fia kicked off her shoes and sat on the jetty, feet dangling in the cool water, her gaze sliding to the lights of the Ferrara Beach Club on the opposite side of the bay. Eighty per cent of her customers tonight had come from the hotel. She had reservations for plenty more, booked months ahead. Twisting off the cap, she lifted the bottle to her lips, realising that by being good at what she did, she'd inadvertently drawn the eye of the enemy.

Her success had brought her out from under the radar. Instead of being irrelevant to the all-powerful Ferraras, she'd made herself significant. This was all her fault, she thought miserably. In pursuing her goal of providing for her family, protecting her son, she'd inadvertently exposed him.

'Fiammetta!'

Her grandfather's bark made her jump and she sprang to her feet and walked back towards the stone house that had been in the family for six generations, a feeling of sick dread in her stomach. *'Come stai?'* She kept her voice light. 'You're up late, Nonno. How are you feeling?'

'I'm as well as a man can be when he sees his granddaughter working herself to the bone.' He scowled down at the bottle in her hand. 'A man doesn't like to see a woman drinking beer.'

'Then it's a good job I don't have a man I need to worry about.' She teased him lightly, relieved that he had the energy to spar with her. This was their relationship. This was Baracchi love. She told herself that just because he didn't express it didn't mean he didn't feel it. On some days she actually believed that. 'What are you doing up? You should be asleep in bed.'

'Luca was crying.'

'He had a dream. He just wanted a cuddle.'

'You should leave him to cry.' Her grandfather gave a grunt of disapproval. 'He'll never grow up to be a man the way you coddle him.'

'He's going to be a fine man. The best.'

'The boy is spoiled. Every time I see him, someone is hugging him or kissing him.'

'You can't give a child too much love.'

'Did I fuss over my son the way you fuss over yours?'

No, and look at how that turned out. 'I think you should go to bed, Nonno.'

'Can I cook for a few people? That's what you said to me—' he winced as he walked stiffly towards the waterfront

'—and before I know it my home is full of strangers and you are serving good Sicilian food on fancy plates and lighting candles for people who wouldn't know the difference between fresh food and fast food.'

'People travel a long way to taste my cooking. I'm running a successful business.'

'You shouldn't be running a business.' Her grandfather settled himself in his favourite chair at the water's edge. The chair he'd sat on when she was a child.

'I'm building a life for myself and a future for my child.' A life that was now overturned. A future that was threatened. Suddenly she didn't trust herself not to betray what she was feeling. 'I'll fetch you a drink. *Grappa*?'

She had to tell her grandfather about Santo, but first she had to work out how. How did you tell someone that the father of his precious great-grandchild was a man he hated above all others?

Fia walked back to the kitchen and grabbed the bottle and a glass. It was a long time since he'd mentioned the Ferraras. And that was because of her, of course. Concerned for Luca, she'd insisted that if he couldn't speak the name positively then he wasn't to speak the name at all.

At first she was just grateful that he'd taken her threat seriously, but now she was wondering whether it meant he'd actually softened over time.

Please. Please let him have softened—

Fia put the glass on the table in front of her grandfather and poured. 'So what's wrong?'

'You mean apart from the fact that you are here every night slaving in that kitchen while someone else looks after your child?'

'It's good for Luca to be with other people. Gina loves him.' She didn't have the family she wanted for her son, so she'd created it. Her son was never going to be lonely in the way she'd been lonely. He had people he could turn to. *People who would hug him when life threw rocks.*

'Love.' Her grandfather grunted with contempt. 'You are turning him into a girl. That's what happens when there is no father to teach a boy to be a man.'

It was the perfect opening for her to tell him what she needed to tell him. But Fia couldn't push the words past her dry throat. She needed time. *Time to discover what Santo intended to do.* 'Luca has male influences in his life.'

'If you're talking about that boy you employ in the restaurant, there's more testosterone in my finger than he has in his whole body. Luca needs a real man around.'

'You and I have very different ideas about what makes a real man.'

His bony shoulders slumped and the lines on his forehead were deep. In the past month he appeared to have aged a decade. 'This isn't what I wanted for you.'

'Life doesn't always turn out the way we plan it, Nonno. When life gives you olives, you make olive oil.'

'But you don't make olive oil!' He waved a hand in frustration. 'You send our olives to our neighbours and *they* make our oil.'

'Which I use in my restaurant. The restaurant that everyone in Sicily is talking about. I was in the paper last week.' But somehow the buzz that she'd got from that fleeting moment of success had gone. Recent events had diminished it to nothing. 'The week before I was mentioned in an important travel blog. The article was called "Sicilian Secrets". I'm doing well. I'm good at my work.'

'Work is what a woman does before she finds a husband.'

Fia put the bottle down on the table. 'Don't say that. Soon, Luca will be old enough to understand you and I don't want him growing up with that opinion.'

'Men ask you out! But do you say yes? No, you don't. Dark,

blond, tall, short—it's always "no". You shut everyone out and you have done since Luca's father.' He looked at her intently and Fia's fingers tightened on the bottle.

'When I meet a man I'm interested in, I'll say yes.' But she knew that wasn't going to happen. There had only ever been one man in her life and right now he despised her. And worse, he thought she was an unfit mother.

Barely able to think about that, she focused on her grandfather and felt a flicker of worry as she saw him absently rub his fingers across his chest. Impulsively, she reached across the table and touched his hand. When he immediately withdrew, she tried not to mind. Her grandfather wasn't tactile, was he? It was silly of her to even try. He didn't hug her and he didn't hug Luca. 'What's wrong? More pain?'

'Don't fuss.' There was a long silence while he glared at her and something in his gaze made her stomach clench.

Was it just her guilty conscience or did he—?

'You weren't going to tell me, were you?' The harshness of his voice shocked her and she felt as if the earth had shaken beneath her feet.

'Tell you what?' Her heart was suddenly pounding like a drum in a rock band.

'He was here tonight. Santo Ferrara.' He said it as if the name tasted bad on his tongue and Fia put the bottle down before it slipped from her hand.

'Nonno—'

'I know you banned me from mentioning his name but when a Ferrara walks onto my property, that gives me the right to talk about him. You should have told me he was here.'

How much did he know? How much had he heard?

'I didn't tell you because I knew this would be your reaction.'

He thumped his fist on the table. 'I warned that boy not to step onto my land again.'

Fia thought about the width and power of those shoulders. The haze of dark stubble accentuating that hard jaw. 'He's not a boy. He's a man.' A wealthy man who now ran a global corporation. A man with the power to shake up everything she loved about her life. A man who had gone off to talk to lawyers and think about the future of her son.

Their son.

Oh, God—

Her grandfather's eyes glowed bright with rage. 'That *man* walked into my home—*my home*—' he stabbed the air with his finger '—with no respect for my feelings.'

'Nonno—'

'Did he have the courage to face me?'

'*Calma*! Calm down.' Fia was on her feet; the emotion was a burning ball at the base of her ribs. If her grandfather was this upset now, how much worse was it going to be when he found out the truth? It was starting again, only this time Luca would be in the middle of it. 'I didn't want him to see you and this is why! You're getting upset.'

'Of course I am upset. How could I not be upset after what he has done?' His face was white in the flickering light from the candle and Fia was sure that hers was equally pale.

'You *promised* me when Luca was born that you would let the past go.'

He gave her a long, long look. 'Why are you defending him? Why is it that I'm not allowed to say a bad word about a Ferrara?'

Fia felt the heat pour into her cheeks. 'Because I don't want Luca growing up with that animosity. It's horrible.'

'I hate them.'

Fia breathed deeply. 'I know.' *Oh, yes, she knew.* And she'd thought about that every day since she'd felt the first fluttering low in her abdomen. She'd thought about it as she'd pushed her son from her body, when she'd first looked into his eyes and every time she kissed him goodnight. There were days when she felt as if she couldn't carry the weight of it any more.

Her grandfather's eyes were fierce. 'Because of Ferrara, you will be alone in the world when I'm gone. Who will look after you?'

'I will look after us.' She knew he blamed Santo for her brother's death. She also knew it was pointless to remind him that her brother had barely been able to look after himself, let alone another. It had been his own reckless irresponsibility that had killed him, not Santo Ferrara.

Her grandfather rose unsteadily to his feet. 'If Ferrara dares to come back here again and I'm not around you can give him a message from me—'

'Nonno—'

'—you can tell him I'm still waiting for him to act like a man and take responsibility for his actions. And if he dares set foot on my property again I'll make him pay.'

CHAPTER THREE

Santo sat and waited in his office at the Ferrara Beach Club—
an office hastily vacated in his honour by the manager of
the hotel. If he needed an indication as to why this hotel was
less successful than the others in the group it was right there
on the desk. Lack of discipline and organisation was visible
everywhere, from the scattered papers to the dying plant that
drooped sadly in the corner of the office. Later, he'd deal with
it. Right now he had other things on his mind. Mocking him
from the wall was an enlarged photograph of the hotel manager, posing with his wife and two smiling children.

A typical Sicilian family.

Santo stared moodily at that picture. Right now he felt like
tearing it down. He'd never considered himself idealistic, but
was it idealistic to assume that one day his family would look
much like the one in the picture?

Apparently it was.

He glanced at his watch.

Not for one moment did he doubt that she would come.
Not because he had faith in her sense of justice but because
she knew that if she didn't, he'd come and get her.

His face expressionless, he waited as darkness gave way to
the first fingers of dawn; as the sun rose over the sea, show-
ering light across the smooth glassy surface.

He'd sent the text in the early hours, at a time when most

people would have been asleep. It hadn't occurred to him to try and sleep. There had been no rest for him and he knew there would have been none for her, either.

Exhaustion fogged his mind and yet his thoughts were clear. As far as he was concerned the decision was clear. If only the emotions were as simple to deal with.

He checked his phone again and found a message from his brother, another person who had been frequenting the early hours. Just four words—

What do you need?

Unconditional support. Unquestioning loyalty. All those things that a family should offer, and which his did. He'd been raised with that support, surrounded by love. Unlike his son, who had spent his early years in the equivalent of a pit of vipers.

Sweat beaded on his brow. He could barely allow himself to think about what his son's life must have been like. What was the long-term impact of being raised in an emotional desert? And what if the abuse hadn't just been emotional? Although he'd been young, he still remembered the mutterings and the rumours about the Baracchi family. Remembered seeing Fia sporting bruises almost all the time.

The knock on the door was the most reluctant sound he'd ever heard.

His eyes narrowed and he felt a rush of adrenaline, but it was only a young chef from the kitchen, bringing him more coffee.

'Grazie—'

The rattle of the cup on the saucer and her nervous glance told him that his black mood was visible on his face although they'd probably all misinterpreted the cause. Everyone in the hotel from the top down was jumpy about his visit. Normally they'd have reason. They had no way of knowing that his current mood was caused by something different. That a reorganization of the hotel was the last thing on his mind right now.

She melted away but moments later there was another tap on the door and he knew instantly that this time it was her.

The door opened and Fia stood there, those fierce green eyes glittering like jewels in a face as pale as morning mist. One look at her white face told him that she hadn't had any more rest than he had.

She looked washed out and stressed. *And ready for a fight.*

Across the room their eyes clashed.

They'd been lovers.

They'd shared the ultimate intimacy, but that wasn't going to help them navigate the treacherous waters they now found themselves in because they'd shared nothing else. They had no relationship. Essentially they were strangers. All they'd had were a few chance encounters and one stolen night, one delicious taste of the forbidden. None of that was going to help them through this desperate situation. And it *was* desperate; even he could see that.

'Where is my son?' He snapped out the words and she leaned her back against the door and looked at him.

'Asleep in his bed. In his home. And if he wakes, Gina is there, and my grandfather.'

The anger rushed at him like a ravenous beast ready to snap through the last threads of his fragile self-control. 'And that is supposed to provide me with comfort?'

'He loves Luca.'

'I think we have a very different idea of what that word means.'

'No.' Her eyes were fierce. 'No, we don't.'

Santo's mouth tightened. 'And will he still "love" him when he discovers the identity of his father? I think we both know the answer to that.' He rose from his chair and saw her hand shoot towards the door handle. His mouth tightened and his eyes narrowed in a warning. 'If you leave this room then we will be having this conversation in public. Is that what you want?'

'What I want is for you to calm down and be rational.'

'Oh, I'm rational, *tesoro*. I have been thinking clearly from the moment I saw my child.'

The atmosphere thickened. The air grew overly warm.

'What do you want me to say? That I'm sorry? That I did the wrong thing?' Her voice was smoky-soft and that voice drew his eyes to the smooth column of her throat and then to her mouth. It had been just one night but the memory of it had left deep scars in his senses. He knew how she'd taste because he remembered it vividly. He knew how she'd feel because he remembered that too. Not just the smooth texture of her skin, but the softness of her gorgeous hair. Now released from the clips that had restrained it during cooking, it fell down her back like a dark flame, reflecting the sunrise back at him. He remembered the day her father had cut it short in a blaze of Baracchi temper, hacking with kitchen scissors until she'd been left with a jagged crop. A horrified Santo had witnessed the incident and had tried to intervene but the sight of him had simply inflamed the situation.

She'd sat still, he remembered, saying nothing as hunks of long hair had landed in her lap. Afterwards she'd hidden in the boathouse, her fierce glare challenging him to say one word about it and of course he hadn't because their relationship didn't encompass verbal exchanges.

And it had been in the boathouse, on that one night that had ended so tragically, that their relationship had shifted from nothing to everything.

Santo hauled in a deep breath, resisting that savage, elemental instinct that had him wanting to flatten her to the wall and drag the answers from her. 'When did you find out you were pregnant?'

'Why does that matter?'

'I'm the one asking the questions and right now you'll answer any question I choose to ask you.'

She closed her eyes and leaned her head back against the door. 'Not for ages. Afterwards…I can't really remember. It's all a blur. First there was the hospital. Then the funeral. And my grandfather…' Her sudden silence said more than words. Her breathing was fractured. 'It was chaos. The last thing I was thinking about was me.'

Yes, it had been chaos. Pandemonium. A huge tangled mess of blame, guilt, regret and raw emotion. The frantic rush to save a life that was already lost. A moment of intimacy lost in a sea of negative publicity and cruel gossip. Remembering it sent the tension flowing through his muscles and he knew she was feeling the same. In fact he was fairly sure that the only thing holding her upright was willpower.

'So when *did* you find out?'

'I don't know. I suppose it must have been a couple of months. Longer—' she rubbed her fingers over her forehead '—it was a very difficult time. I probably should have realised sooner but at the time I just thought that everything I was feeling was part of the shock. I felt sick the whole time but I thought that was grief. And when I did finally work it out it seemed like—'

'—one more problem?' His hands were clenched by his sides but her eyes flew to his, appalled.

'No!' She shook her head violently. 'I was going to say that it seemed like a miracle.' Her words dropped to a whisper. 'The best thing in my life came from the worst night of my life.'

It wasn't the response he'd expected and for a moment it threw him. 'When you realised, you should have contacted me.'

'For what purpose?' There was despair in her tone. 'So

that you and my grandfather could rip each other to pieces? Do you think I wanted Luca exposed to that? I made the decision that was best for my baby.'

'*Our* baby,' Santo corrected her with lethal emphasis. 'And from now on we'll be making those decisions together.' He saw the panic flicker across her face and knew that anxiety was responsible for those dark shadows under her eyes.

'Luca is happy. I can understand how you're feeling, but—'

'You do not understand how I'm feeling.' His voice was raw. Savage. He didn't know himself and he certainly didn't trust himself. 'This is my son we're talking about. Did you honestly believe I would want him to grow up a Baracchi?' He braced himself to ask the question that had robbed him of sleep. 'Has he ever hit him?'

'No!' Her denial was immediate and sincere. 'I would never, ever allow anyone to touch Luca.'

'And how do you defend him? You never defended yourself.' Perhaps it was low of him, but he told himself that his son's welfare was more important than her feelings. 'You just endured it.'

'I was eight years old!' Hurt and reproach flickered in her eyes and suddenly he felt like an animal for ripping into her. That was what people had done all their lives, wasn't it?

'I apologise for that remark,' he breathed and she shook her head.

'You don't need to. I don't blame you for being protective of your child.' She spoke quietly, as if she had long since resigned herself to the fact that no one had any concern for her. 'And yes, I was brought up in a violent family but that violence came from my father, not my grandfather. I assure you that Luca has never been at risk. He has had a warm, loving childhood.'

'Without a father in his life.'

She flinched as if he'd slapped her. 'Yes.'

'Naturally I am relieved that he has been safe, but that doesn't change the fundamental issue here. Family is the most important thing to me. I am a Ferrara and we look after our own. There are no circumstances—*none*—that would induce me to walk away from my own child.' His words struck another blow because of course her mother had done exactly that. She'd walked away when Fia was only eight years old.

Her face lost the last hint of colour and he wondered briefly how it must feel to watch a parent walk away, leaving you to cope with danger alone.

He knew the story, as did everyone else. Her mother had been an English tourist who had fallen for the charms of the smooth, good-looking Pietro Baracchi, only to discover after the wedding that he was an incurable womanizer with a dangerous temper. After one beating too many, she'd turned her back on Sicily and her two children and soon after that Fia's father had been killed in a drunken boating accident.

She watched him steadily. 'You are very quick to judge me, but did you bother to come back and find out if there were consequences to our night together?'

Her unexpected attack shook him. 'I used contraception.'

'And that worked out well, didn't it?' She tilted her head. 'Did you, at any point, wonder how I was doing after that night? How I was coping after the accident that killed my brother? Did you bother to come and find me?'

'I did not wish to inflame the situation.' But her words had kindled a nagging guilt. He should have contacted her. The thought was uncomfortable, like walking with a sharp stone in your shoe.

'So you're admitting your concern that having contact with me would escalate our problems.' Her voice was remarkably calm. 'How much more inflammatory would it have been if I'd told you there was a child?'

'The child changes everything.'

'It changes nothing. It just makes everything harder.' She pushed her hands into the pockets of her jeans. With a face free of make-up and her hair loose, she looked impossibly young. More like a teenager than a successful business-woman. 'It's a waste of time dwelling on what is already done so let's talk about the future. Of course you want to see him. I understand that. We can arrange something.'

Distracted by the length of her legs in those jeans, Santo frowned. 'What's that supposed to mean?'

'I'm saying that you can see Luca. We'll work something out, providing you agree to certain rules.'

She was giving *him* rules? Stunned, he could barely respond. 'What rules?'

'I will not at any time tolerate you speaking ill of my grandfather in front of Luca. Nor will you denigrate anyone else in my family, and that includes me. No matter how angry you are with me, you will not show it in front of Luca. As far as he is concerned, we are united. We might not be together, but I want him to believe we are on friendly terms. Providing you agree to that then I'll let you have full access.'

Genuinely shocked at the depth of her misunderstanding, Santo felt exasperation surge through him. 'Access? You think I am talking about visiting rights? You think this is about making polite arrangements to take my child on the occasional outing?'

'Don't you want that?'

'*Si*, I want access. Full access.' His tone was a perfect reflection of his mood. Grim. 'The sort of access that comes from being a full-time father. Access to tuck him in at night and get him up in the morning. Access to spend all the time I want to spend with him. Access to teach him what family is *truly* about. And that is what is going to happen. I have had lawyers working through the night drawing up the necessary paperwork to acknowledge him as my son. *My* son.'

There was a hideous silence.

For a moment she said nothing and then she exploded across the room like a wild thing and pounded his chest with her fists.

'You will *not* take him from me! I won't let you.' She was so furious and he was so shocked by the unexpected explosion of emotion it took him a few seconds to grasp those slender wrists, a few more seconds to free himself from a lock of that vivid hair that had wrapped itself around him.

'And yet you took him from me—' He enunciated every syllable, threw those words right into her shocked face and saw the exact moment reality sank home.

'I'm his mother—' her voice was hoarse '—I will not let you take him. I will find a way of stopping you. He needs me.'

Santo paused long enough to make her suffer a fraction of what he had suffered since he'd discovered the truth. Then he released her hands and stepped away from her. 'If you're trying to impress me with your maternal dedication then don't waste your time. Even if everything else you say is true, the fact is that you have employed a nanny.'

She stepped back from him, confusion on her face. 'What does Gina have to do with this?'

'You don't look after him yourself.'

'I do look after him—' her eyes were stricken '—and there are reasons I choose to have a nanny. I can—'

'You don't have to explain. Caring for a child full-time is a demanding experience. A young child is very restricting, as your mother discovered. She chose to walk away from it. I'm willing to give you the opportunity to do the same.'

Her eyes were huge. 'I don't understand what you're saying.'

'I'm saying that I will take full responsibility for him.'

'You're…threatening to take my son from me?'

'Offering,' Santo interjected smoothly, watching her face closely. 'Offering, not threatening. And if you want to see him then of course that can be arranged.'

Her breathing was shallow. 'You think I want to give him away?'

'You can have your life back. And given that I'm prepared to sweeten the deal with a significant financial incentive, it could be a very comfortable life. It's a generous offer. Take it. You'd never have to work again.'

She lifted her hands to her cheeks and gave a choked laugh. 'You really don't know anything about me, do you? I love my son, and if you truly believe for a moment that I'd give him to you on any terms then you have no idea who you're dealing with.' Her hands dropped to her sides. Clenched into fists. 'There's nothing I wouldn't do to protect my child.'

Unmoved by the anger in her eyes, Santo nodded. 'Your mother would have taken the money and run. It's to your credit that you didn't do the same.'

'So this was some sort of test?' She gave a moan of disgust. 'You're sick, do you know that?'

'Our child's future is at stake. There is nothing I wouldn't do to protect him. If protecting him means offending you, I'll do that too.' He threw her own words back at her and she wrapped her arms around herself.

'I am not my mother. I will never leave Luca.'

'In that case we will find another solution.' And there was only one that he could see. He consoled himself with the fact that at least she was making an effort to fight for her child.

'Do you think I haven't searched for one?' Her raw tone exposed layers of despair. 'There *is* no solution. I don't want him shuttled between us. I don't want him absorbing all the bad feeling that runs between our families. He's been brought up in an atmosphere of happiness and calm.'

'Knowing your grandfather, I find that impossible to believe.'

'My grandfather has stuck to my rules.'

Santo frowned. 'More rules?'

'Yes. From the moment Luca was born, I insisted that any mention of the name Ferrara in our house had to be positive. I didn't want my son growing up in the same poisonous atmosphere I experienced.'

Genuinely surprised, Santo lifted his eyebrows. 'And how did you achieve this miracle of good behaviour?'

'I threatened to take his grandson away unless he agreed to my terms.'

If he'd been surprised before, he was shocked now. *So she was stronger than she looked, then.* 'Ingenious.'

'You will abide by the same rule. You will not speak badly about my family in front of Luca. If you can't say anything nice, then you don't mention us. When he spends time with you I want to be confident that you are not denigrating my family and I *will* know because right now Luca is like a recording device. He repeats everything he hears.'

Fascinated that so much passion could be trapped in such a small package and reluctantly impressed at her steadfast refusal to involve herself in the Baracchi/Ferrara hostilities, Santo took his time to respond.

'Firstly,' he said softly, 'the bad feeling was all on your side. We made several overtures, all of which were rejected. Secondly, you will know what I am saying to Luca because you will be there to hear it in person. Thirdly, our families will be merged, so all this ceases to be relevant.'

'Merged?' Nervous, she pushed her hair back from her face. 'You mean because Luca belongs to both of us?'

'I mean because I intend to marry you.'

Silence spread across the room.

For a moment he wondered if she'd actually heard him.

Then she made a strange sound in her throat and took a step backwards.

'*Marry* you?' Her voice was barely audible. 'You have to be joking.'

'Relish the moment, *tesoro*. Up until now, women have waited in vain for a proposal of marriage from me.'

She looked as if she'd suffered a major shock. 'You're proposing.'

'In a practical sense, yes. In a romantic sense, no,' he drawled, 'so if you're expecting me to get down on one knee you can forget it.'

This, he thought, would be a real test of her devotion to their son.

She lifted her hand to her throat and looked at him as if he was mad. 'Apart from the fact that we haven't laid eyes on each other for three years and barely know each other, there is no way our families would accept this.'

'I presume you are talking about your side of the family, because my side will support me in whatever decision I make. That's what families do. The reaction of yours is of no interest to me.' He gave an indifferent shrug. 'And as for the fact that we barely know each other, that will be rectified quickly enough. You will get to know me fast enough because I don't intend to let you out of my sight.'

She sleepwalked to the window. 'I saw a picture of you just last week strolling along a red carpet with a woman on your arm—you have a million women chasing after you.'

'Then it's fortunate for you that I was waiting for that one special person and hadn't yet made that commitment.' His expectations mocked him. His brother and his sister both had strong, happy marriages. He'd had no reason to believe that his wouldn't be the same. His hopes for the future were undergoing a transformation so rapid that it left him reeling.

'I can't accept your proposal.' Her voice had lost some of its strength. 'I don't need to. I run a successful business and—'

'This isn't about you, it's about Luca. Or does your streak of selflessness only emerge when it suits you? If you truly have Luca's best interests at heart then you will do what is right for him.' He came right back at her, offering no soft words of reassurance and she shook her head frantically.

'It would be wrong for Luca, too.'

'What's "wrong" is my child growing up in a family that doesn't know the meaning of the word,' he said coldly. 'He is a Ferrara and he is entitled to all the love and security that comes with being a Ferrara. And I am going to use every means at my disposal to make sure he is given that right.'

'You're doing this to punish me.' Her eyes were horrified. She knew how much power he wielded. She knew exactly what he could achieve if he set his mind to it. He saw her mind going to all sorts of places and he let it happen because it suited his purpose to scare her.

'Luca deserves to be raised in a strong, solid family, not that I expect you to understand that.' Another low blow and to her credit she didn't flinch from it.

'I do understand that. I understand that an ideal family is a unit of people who love and support you unconditionally. I admit I didn't have that, so I created it. I wanted Luca to be surrounded by people who would love him and support him and in reality I did need help because I wanted to be able to support us financially and not rely on my grandfather.'

'That is the most convoluted justification for a nanny I've ever heard.'

'You are very disparaging about nannies, but that is because you have aunts and cousins who all help each other with childcare. I don't have that and so I found a warm, loving girl I trust. She's been with us since Luca was born, and so has Ben because I wanted him to have a good male role

model—' She bit her lower lip. 'I'm aware that my grandfather isn't soft or tactile. He never hugs and I wanted Luca
to be hugged. I wanted him surrounded by people who felt
like I did. People who would give him affection. I didn't have
a family like yours, but I tried to create one for him.'

She'd *created* a family?

Santo thought about what he'd seen. About the amount of
affection he'd witnessed in that short time with his son. 'If
that is true, then that is definitely a point in your favour, but
it is no longer necessary. Luca doesn't need a stand-in family. He can have the real thing.'

'You're not thinking straight.' Her voice was remarkably
strong. 'My father married my mother because he made her
pregnant. I was first-hand witness to the fact that approach
doesn't work. And now you are suggesting we do the same
thing?'

'*Not* the same thing.' He heard the chill in his own voice.
'Our marriage will be nothing like your parents', I can assure
you of that. They led separate lives and their children—*you*—
were the casualties of their selfish, hubristic existence, not to
mention the vicious Baracchi temper. Our marriage will not
be like that.'

She rubbed her fingers over her brow and gave him a desperate look. 'You are angry and I don't blame you for that,
but please, please think of Luca.'

'I have thought of nothing but Luca since I walked into
your kitchen last night.'

'How can he possibly benefit from you and I being together? You are being hasty—'

'Hasty?' Just thinking about how much of his son's life he'd
missed made him want to punch his fist through something.
'As far as I'm concerned we are long past "hasty". Luca has
an aunt and an uncle. Cousins to play with. He has a whole
family he knows nothing about.' Seeing the wistfulness in

her eyes, he drove his point home. 'As a Ferrara he will never feel lonely or unloved. He will never have to hide in an abandoned boathouse because his family is in crisis.'

'You bastard—' She whispered the words, her eyes two deep pools of pain, but Santo was impervious to any emotion but anger.

'You hid my child from me. You robbed him of the right to a warm, loving family and you robbed me of something that can never be returned. Do I intend to dictate terms from now on? Yes, I do. And if that makes me a bastard I'll happily live with that title. Think about it.' He strode towards the door. 'And while you're thinking, I have work to do.'

'You're going to *work*?'

'Of course. I have a company to run.'

She shook her head in disbelief. 'I…I need some time to decide what is best for Luca.'

Holding on to his temper, Santo yanked open the door. 'Having a father and joining the Ferrara family is what is best for Luca and even twisted Baracchi thinking will struggle to distort that fact. You have until tonight to see sense. And I suggest you tell your grandfather the truth, or I'll do it for you.'

CHAPTER FOUR

THERE was nothing quite so cruel as the distortion of a dream.

How many times had she stared across the bay and envied the family life of the close-knit Ferraras? How many times had she wished she were part of that? It was no coincidence that in times of trauma she'd chosen to hide in their boathouse, as if simply by being there she might soak up some residual warmth.

She'd crawled through the open window, grazing her leg on the rough wood of the window frame, covering herself in dust as she'd landed. Fia hadn't cared about any of that.

With the sea lapping at the door that conveniently faced away from the bay, she had no fear that someone would find her. Who would look for her here, in the enemy camp? So sure had she been of the seclusion of her hiding place that when she'd seen Santo standing on the rocks, watching her, she'd known a moment of pure terror. Too afraid even to breathe, she'd waited for him to blow her cover. Her family hated his. Even a mention of the Ferrara name was enough to sour the atmosphere in her house for days. The only thing the Baracchi family knew how to nurture was a grudge.

And so she'd waited for Santo Ferrara to blow her cover.

Not only had he not done that, but he'd left her alone, as if understanding her need for space.

To her eight-year-old eyes, he'd turned from a boy she'd

envied into something close to a god. The boathouse became her regular hiding place and from there she could observe the Ferraras and see the differences between their family and her own. Suspicion turned to wistful envy. She'd envied the family picnics, their games on the beach. It was from them she'd learned that a quarrel could be affectionate, that a father could embrace a child, that a sister and brother could be close, *that a family could be a unit*.

Some of the girls at school had joked about discovering that they were secretly a princess. Fia's childhood dream was to wake up one day and discover that she was secretly a Ferrara; that there had been some mix-up at the hospital and somehow she'd ended up in the wrong family. That one day they'd claim her.

Be careful what you wish for.

Her head throbbing from lack of sleep, her stomach churning from an encounter she'd found hideously stressful, Fia dragged her mind back to the present and tried to work out what to do next. She had until tonight to find a way to tell her grandfather that the man he hated above all other was Luca's father.

Once she'd negotiated that hurdle she'd move on to the next one. How to respond to Santo's 'proposal' of marriage.

The suggestion was utterly ridiculous.

What sane woman would agree to marry a man who felt the way Santo felt about her?

On the other hand she could hardly criticise him for fighting for his child when her whole life had been spent wishing that her parents had done that for her. How could she argue with his claim that her son deserved to be a Ferrara when she'd modelled her little family on them?

If she agreed to his terms then Luca would grow up a

Ferrara. He'd have the life she'd craved as a child. He would be cocooned in a warm and loving family, wrapped up in love.

And for that privilege she would have to pay a very high price.

She would have to join the family too, only unlike her son she would never truly be part of it. She would be tolerated, rather than welcomed. She'd be on the outside.

And she'd spend every day of her life with a man who didn't love her. Who was furious with the decision she'd made.

How was that good for Luca?

It wasn't.

Somehow she had to make Santo understand that no one would benefit from such an arrangement.

Mind made up, she arrived back at the Beach Shack to find the kitchen a hive of activity. Life was the only thing that could fall apart and yet still carry on, she thought numbly. She should have been relaxed, here in her tiny slice of paradise with the sparkling Mediterranean Sea lapping at the shore just steps away from her, but she'd never felt more stressed in her life.

'Hey, Boss, I wondered where you were. I met the boat this morning. Beat everyone to it. The *gamberi* look good—' Ben was hauling a box of supplies into the kitchen. 'I've put them on the menu. *Gamberi e limone con pasta*?' He caught her expression and frowned. 'But if you'd rather do something else then just tell me.'

'It's fine.' Functioning on automatic, she checked the quality of the fruit and vegetables that had been delivered by her local suppliers. It was as if nothing had changed, and yet everything had changed. 'Did the avocados arrive?'

'Yes. They look perfect. It was a good idea to switch.' He paused with a box clutched to his chest. 'So, are you OK?'

He wasn't really asking that, of course. He was asking

what had happened with Santo and she wasn't ready to discuss that with anyone. 'Where is my grandfather?'

'Still in the house, I think. Oh, and Luca has a new word—' he was grinning at her '—*gamberi*. Gina and I took him down to the quay this morning while they were unloading the boat. He was fascinated by the octopus. Wanted to take it home. Which we did. But we didn't tell him we'd be cooking it and serving it with wine later.'

She managed a smile. Luca had grown up surrounded by these people. He was happy and confident. He'd witnessed none of the emotional fireworks that had scorched her childhood. Her heart ached to think that the simplicity of his life had gone for ever.

And just as she had that thought, Ben frowned over her shoulder.

'He's early for lunch, isn't he? And overdressed.'

Fia looked round and saw a bulky man in a suit hovering at the edge of her restaurant.

Her temper flared. Santo had promised her until tonight but already he was making his presence felt. 'Carry on, Ben,' she said quickly. 'I'll deal with this.' She had her phone in her hand and was dialling as she walked. 'Put me through to Ferrara—I don't care if he's in a meeting—tell him it's Fia Baracchi. Do it now…' Adrenaline coursed around her veins and she was ready to stalk right over there and smash her way into his precious meeting if she had to but moments later she heard his smooth masculine voice on the phone.

'This had better be important.'

'I have a man who looks like something straight from some mob movie prowling around my restaurant.'

'Good. That means he is doing his job.'

'And what exactly is his job?'

'He's in charge of security for the Ferrara Group. He's conducting a risk assessment.'

'A risk assessment?'

'Use your brain, Fia.'

From his curt tone she assumed he had people in the office with him and had no wish to broadcast his personal business. Soon the whole world would know, she thought numbly. They'd all know that Santo Ferrara had a son. And when that happened—

She wondered how he could concentrate in a meeting. She was so distracted she could barely string a coherent sentence together.

'I want him out of here. He'll frighten my customers.'

'The welfare of your customers is not my concern.'

Fia eyed the physical bulk and intimidating presence of the man currently exploring the perimeter of the restaurant and played the one card that was likely to influence him. 'He is going to frighten Luca.'

'Luigi is a family man and brilliant with children. And he's part of our deal. Now go and fulfil your part. Tell your grandfather or I'll do it myself. And don't ring me again unless it's urgent.' He hung up and Fia stalked over to the man, temper boiling, feeling as helpless as a fish trapped in a net.

'In two hours my restaurant will be full of customers. I don't want them thinking there is a problem.'

'As long as I'm here, there won't be a problem.'

'I don't want you here. You stand out. My guests will worry that something is going on. Luca is—' The fight went out of her and she swallowed. 'He's led a very low-profile life. I don't want him frightened.' She'd expected him to argue with her, to show the same rigid inflexibility as his arrogant boss, but to her surprise his eyes were sympathetic.

'I'm only here for his protection. If we can find a way to keep that low-key, that's fine by me.'

He knew the history. She could see it in his eyes and she lifted her chin, prepared to fight the whole world if she had to.

'I can protect my own son.'

'I know you think you can.' His voice was gruff. 'But he isn't just *your* son.' The implication was that it was the other half of the gene pool that mattered. If Luca had truly just been her son, he wouldn't have needed protection. Unfortunately his father was one of the most powerful men in Sicily and that bloodline made him a potential target for all sorts of unscrupulous individuals. The thought made her want to be sick.

'Is there really a risk?'

'Not with the security that Santo Ferrara has in place. Give me a minute to think about this—' He looked around the restaurant. 'We can work something out that keeps everyone happy.' His response was so unexpected that Fia felt emotion well up inside her.

Horrified, she gulped it down. 'I… Why are you being kind?'

'You gave my niece a job last summer when she had some trouble at home.' His voice was neutral. 'She had no experience, but you took her on.'

'Sabina is your niece?'

'My sister's child.' He cleared his throat. 'Why don't you give me the chair at the corner of the restaurant? I'll move a table to a position that works for me and I'll linger over my meal. That way I can blend with your customers and everyone is happy.'

Fia stared at him. 'And if he finds out?' There was no need to spell out who 'he' was.

'The boss doesn't micromanage his staff. He employs people he trusts and then lets them do their job in the way that best suits them.' He gave a faint smile. 'I wouldn't work for him if he didn't.'

Right now she didn't need to hear admiration in anyone's voice when they talked about Santo. But at least Luigi appeared reasonable. More reasonable than his boss.

'You can take that table—' agreeing to the compromise, she gestured '—and it would be great if you could take off your jacket. We're pretty casual here, especially at lunchtime.'

'Mamma!' Luca came sprinting through the restaurant and she heard Luigi's sudden intake of breath as he had his first glimpse of the child he'd been assigned to protect.

'Madre di Dio—'

The likeness was that obvious? Fia scooped her son into her arms protectively but he gazed curiously at the big man in the suit. He hadn't learned fear, she thought numbly. He'd been brought up here, by the beach, surrounded by people who loved him and guests who thought he was a charming addition to this hidden Sicilian gem. But once people knew he was Santo Ferrara's son, there would always be a risk. Even she could see that.

'This is Luigi,' she said huskily, 'and he is going to be eating in our restaurant today. Aren't we lucky?' She looked at the reassuring power house that was Santo's head of security and gave a slight smile. 'Thank you.'

'Figurati. You're welcome.' He winked at the boy and went to rearrange tables while Fia returned to her job.

A busy lunchtime merged into a crazy evening where she hardly emerged from the kitchen. She had time to check on her grandfather briefly, but no time to embark on a difficult conversation. It hung over her as she tossed *gamberi* into fresh pasta, and served her speciality dessert, *Zuccotto al cioccolato.* And all the time she was aware that time was running out.

By the time Gina and Ben had left for the night and everywhere was quiet, she was a nervous wreck.

All day she'd been rehearsing the best way to tell her

grandfather, trying to work out which combination of words would cause the least shock.

I need to talk to you about Luca.

You've often asked me about Luca's father...

Bracing herself for major conflict, she walked into the kitchen to finish her preparations for the next day and saw the frail figure of her grandfather crumpled on the floor.

'Nonno! *Cristo*, please, no!' She was across the floor and down on her knees in seconds, hands shaking as she gave his shoulder a gentle shake and then grabbed his thin wrist and tried to find a pulse. 'Speak to me— Oh, God, don't do this—' She scrabbled in her pocket for her phone and then realised she'd left it in the house.

'Is he breathing?' Santo's voice came from behind her, calm and strong as he strode across the room. His phone was already in his hand and he was talking into it, issuing a string of instructions in rapid Italian.

It was a measure of her stress that she was relieved to see him. She didn't even question what he was doing here. 'Did you call the emergency services? How long?'

'They're sending a helicopter.' With no hesitation, he moved her grandfather and pressed his fingers to the old man's neck. 'No pulse.'

Why had she felt his wrist and not his neck? She *knew* she was supposed to feel his neck but all her basic first aid knowledge had apparently been driven from her brain by panic. Unable to think properly, Fia took her grandfather's hand and rubbed it. 'Nonno—'

'He can't hear you.' Santo's voice was firm and steady. 'You need to move to one side so I can start CPR.'

'I'm not going anywhere!'

She heard someone running and then Luigi appeared in the kitchen holding a small box. 'Here, Boss—' He handed it to Santo, who moved with swift purpose and lightning speed.

'Undo his shirt, Fia.'

'But—'

'Just do it!' He yanked open the box and hit a switch.

'What are you doing?' Her fingers fumbled on buttons that didn't want to undo and she heard Santo mutter something in Italian and then strong hands were pushing hers aside and he tore the fabric and exposed her grandfather's chest in a single movement.

'Move away from him. Get back.' He ripped off the protective backing from two sticky pads and pressed them onto her grandfather's chest.

He just took control, she thought numbly, the way the Ferraras always took control. Not once did he hesitate or fumble.

'Do you even know how to use that thing?'

'It's an AED. And yes, I know how to use it.' He didn't spare her a glance. All his attention was focused on her grandfather as a disembodied voice delivered instructions from the machine.

Anxiety flared. 'You're going to give him a shock? But what if that's not the right thing to do? You might kill him!' And for a moment her own heart almost stopped because she realised that her grandfather's life was in the hands of a man who had no love for him.

His exasperated glance told her that he'd read her mind. 'This device contains a sophisticated computer chip. As far as I know, they're not programmed to bear grudges. Now let go of his hand.'

Reluctantly she moved back.

The voice instructed them to stand clear of the patient and press the button and after that the emergency services arrived and everything blurred. There was a flurry of activity while they stabilised her grandfather and then they transferred him swiftly into the air ambulance. And through it all she was aware of Santo, cool and in control. Santo, calling a top cardiologist and ordering him to meet them at the hospital. Santo arranging to drive her there. And when she pointed out that she had to take Luca and his Lamborghini wouldn't accommodate a child's car seat, he helped himself to Luigi's sturdy four-by-four instead. And Luca didn't even stir as she transferred him from bed to car seat, completely oblivious to the drama being played out around him.

'Does he have a favourite toy or something?' Santo secured the belt. 'Something he can't be without?'

She looked at him blankly and he gave an impatient sigh. 'My niece can't sleep without her favourite blanket. Does he have something like that?'

She swallowed. 'He sleeps with a stuffed giraffe.'

'Fetch it. It will help when he wakes up in a strange place.'

Wondering why he had been the one to think of that and not her, she sprinted to fetch Luca's giraffe and quickly stuffed a change of clothes for him into a bag.

Santo drove her himself and for once she was grateful for the tendency of Sicilians to drive too fast. They made the journey in silence and when he pulled up outside the Emergency Department he sat for a moment, his hands gripping the wheel as he stared at the double doors that led inside.

Fia undid her seat belt.

'They won't let you near him at the moment so there's no point in rushing. You might as well sit here for a while.' Santo switched off the engine. His expression was grim and there were lines of fatigue around his eyes. 'The waiting is the worst part.'

She was about to ask how he knew that when she remembered that his father had died suddenly of a heart attack. Had he been brought to this hospital? Staring at Santo's white knuckles, she assumed the answer to that was positive.

'Are you all right?' Her voice faltered because even to her

it sounded like a ridiculous question. Her grandfather was lying in the hospital and she was asking him if he was all right. And why would he even tell her? In all ways but one he was a stranger, except that no stranger ever made her feel the way that being close to him made her feel.

Even now, in these direst of circumstances, she felt that dangerous heat spread through her body. That awareness that made her skin prickle and her stomach flip.

He didn't speak and his silence unsettled her more than his anger had.

'I owe you thanks.' Embarrassment made her rigidly polite. 'For the lift and…and for your first aid skills. I'm grateful you arrived when you did, although I've no idea what you were doing there—' And then suddenly she knew.

He'd arrived ready to carry out his threat to tell her grandfather.

The reminder that she still had to do that made her feel sick.

'I gather he didn't take the news well.' His tone was flat and it took her a moment to understand that he thought her grandfather's heart attack was somehow related to their situation.

'I hadn't told him. I was going to. I'd just walked in and he was lying there. I panicked—' And that made her angrier than anything. Angry with herself. 'I don't know how I could have been so useless. I've done a first aid course. I should have known what to do.'

'It's different when it's someone you love.'

Were his words intended as comfort or statement of fact? Statement of fact, obviously. They didn't have the sort of relationship that allowed comfort.

That didn't stop her knowing what she owed him. 'How come you had one of those machines?'

'The AED? We have them in all our hotels. One at reception, one in the health and fitness clubs. Sometimes one on the golf course. Our staff are trained in CPR as part of their induction programme. You never know when they could save a life.' There was something in his voice that made her look closely at him but his profile revealed no clues as to his thoughts.

'Santo—'

'On second thought, why don't we go and see if there is someone who can give us an update.' Cutting across her, he opened the car door and then frowned as he realised Luca was asleep. 'There is no sense in disturbing him. Luigi can stay with him and let us know the moment he wakes.' He strode over to the other car and, after a brief exchange, Luigi eased his muscular bulk into the seat beside Luca.

'Don't you worry. If the little one so much as moves a muscle, I'll call you. You concentrate on your grandfather.'

Torn by her responsibilities, Fia allowed Santo to lead her into the Emergency Department.

As they walked through the glass doors she heard the breath hiss through his teeth. Even a brief glance was enough for her to see the tension in those wide shoulders. And this time she was sure that he was thinking about his father.

Of course she knew none of the details. Just that it had been sudden and that it had devastated the close-knit Ferrara family. Santo had still been at school, his older brother Cristiano away at university in the US. She'd seen pictures of the funeral in the paper, but she hadn't attended. A Baracchi wouldn't have been allowed within the charmed perimeter of the Ferrara circle but that didn't mean she hadn't felt his pain. It had seemed grossly unfair to her young mind that such a perfect family could suffer such a loss. Their father adored his three children. How was it right that he should die before his time?

And now Santo was back here, forced into it by grim circumstances.

The sight of a Ferrara in the hospital was enough to throw the staff into a frenzy. The top cardiologist had summoned his team and it was obvious from the flurry of activity that no expense or effort was being spared in the drive to save her grandfather.

Her brother had been jealous of that, she remembered bleakly. The ability of the rich, powerful Ferrara brothers to open doors with just one look. He'd wanted that for himself. What he hadn't understood was that their wealth and status had been achieved by hard graft. They didn't demand the respect of others, they earned it.

And in this instance she was grateful for their power and influence. It meant she had the best people taking care of her grandfather.

The exchange with the cardiologist was brief, but it was enough to confirm what she'd suspected—that her grandfather was alive because Santo had shocked his heart back into normal rhythm. That knowledge added to the confusion in her brain. She didn't want to be in debt to him, but at the same time part of her was proud that her son's daddy was a man who could save a life.

They were shown to a small room reserved for relatives and something about those impersonal, clinical surroundings increased her feeling of desolation. And perhaps he felt it too because he didn't sit, but instead stood with his back to her, staring out of the window at the chaos of the city.

Fia waited for him to leave and when he didn't her good opinion started to fade. Resentment grew with each passing moment. 'You don't have to stay. Even if he recovers, he won't be in a position to listen to you for a while.'

He turned. 'You think I'm staying so that I can tell him

the news? You think I'm that inhumane?' The ferocity in his voice shocked her.

'I assumed... Then why are you here?'

Incredulous dark eyes swept her face. 'Do you have any other family to support you?'

He knew she didn't. Her family wasn't like his. Apart from her son, the sum total of her family was currently fighting for his life in the coronary care unit.

'I don't need support.'

'The man you have lived with all your life is through those doors struggling to stay alive and you don't need support? That is coping with hard times the Baracchi way. Or should I say the Fia way.' He dragged his hand over the back of his neck and met her gaze. 'Maybe that's how you've dealt with them in the past but that isn't how you're going to deal with them in the future, be sure of that. I'm not leaving you here alone. From now on I'm by your side for all life's major events—births, deaths, the graduation of our children. And for the minor events, too. That's how we Ferraras conduct ourselves in a relationship. That's how it's going to be in *our* relationship, *tesoro*. Everything I said to you this morning still stands.'

The word 'relationship' reminded her that if her grandfather lived, she still had to break the news to him. And if he didn't—

Her heart felt as if someone was twisting it.

'You being here isn't support, Santo. It's adding to the stress because I know that you're just waiting to pick your moment to tell him.' Suddenly she needed to get away from him. From the width of those powerful shoulders and the sheer force of his presence. He'd made it his mission to eject her from the comfortable safe place she inhabited and she felt as vulnerable as a small animal chased from its burrow. 'I need to check on Luca.'

'He is still asleep. If he wasn't, Luigi would have called me.'

'He might not want to bother you.'

'I would trust Luigi with my life.'

Fia thought about how kind his head of security had been earlier. He'd had a job to do and he'd done it, but he'd done it with a sensitivity that had surprised her. 'It's not about trust. It's about the fact Luca doesn't know him. I don't want him to wake up, find himself in a strange place and be scared.'

Those eyes frowned into hers and he was about to answer when the door opened and the consultant walked in.

Panic gripped her. 'My grandfather—?' Now that the moment had come she was almost too afraid to ask the question that had to be asked. As if by postponing it for a few seconds she could change reality. 'Is he—?'

'He had an occluded coronary artery. Without rapid treatment he would not be here now. It is without doubt your use of the AED that saved him in those first precious minutes.' The consultant carried on, talking about heart muscle, clots and drugs, angioplasty and future risk factors but all she heard was that her grandfather was still alive. The rest washed over her in a wave of jargon she didn't understand and didn't want to understand.

It was Santo who asked the relevant questions. Santo who discussed treatment options and truthfully she was grateful to him because once again her brain seemed to be working in slow motion.

Eventually all the questions were answered and the consultant nodded. 'He wants to see you. Normally I would refuse at this point because he needs rest but it's clear that something is causing him stress. He is very agitated and he needs to be reassured.'

'Of course.' Fia flew to the door but the consultant stopped her.

'It was Santo he asked for. He was quite specific about that. Your grandfather asked for Santo Ferrara.'

Fia felt her knees shake and she glanced at Santo in horror. 'No! Seeing you will upset him badly.'

'He is already upset. Apparently there are things he needs to say,' the consultant told them, 'so I think it might be helpful for him. But keep it brief and keep any stress to a minimum.'

Santo would tell him that Luca was his child.

How was that keeping stress to a minimum?

Apparently suffering from none of her doubts, Santo strode through the door. 'Let's do this.'

She shot after him. 'Please don't.' She kept her voice low. 'Whatever you think of me, don't do this. Please don't tell him yet. Wait until he's stronger.' She almost stumbled as she tried to keep up with him, panicking madly, unable to see a single way that this encounter was going to have a happy ending. Why was her grandfather asking to see him? At this stage he couldn't even know that it was Santo who had saved his life.

Reluctantly, she walked into the room and caught her breath at the sight of the machines and wires that dominated her grandfather's frail form.

For a moment she couldn't move and then she felt a warm strong hand close over hers and the reassuring squeeze of male fingers.

Shocked, Fia stood for a moment, distracted by the novel experience of being comforted.

And then she heard a sound from the bed and saw her grandfather's eyes open. And she realised Santo's touch wasn't about comfort, but manipulation.

Instantly she snatched her hand away. 'Nonno—' She tried to catch his eyes and reassure him but her grandfather wasn't looking at her. He was looking at Santo.

And Santo, being who he was, didn't flinch or look remotely discomfited.

'You gave us all a shock,' he drawled, approaching the bed with a confidence that suggested he was a welcome visitor.

'Ferrara—' her grandfather's voice was weak and shaky '—I want to know your intentions.'

There was a long pulsing silence and Fia shot Santo a pleading glance, but he wasn't looking at her. He dominated the room, the power of his athletic physique a cruel contrast to the fragility of the man in the bed.

'I intend to be a father to my son.'

Time stood still.

She couldn't believe he'd actually said that. 'I don't—'

'About time!' Her grandfather's eyes burned fiercely in his pale face. 'For years I have been waiting for you to do the right thing—not even allowed to mention your name in case she walked out—' He glared at Fia and then coughed weakly. 'What sort of a man makes a woman pregnant and then leaves her to cope alone?'

'The sort of man who didn't know,' Santo replied in a cool tone, 'but now intends to rectify that mistake.'

Fia barely heard his response. She was staring at her grandfather.

'What?' He snapped the words. 'You thought I didn't know? Why do you think I was so angry with him?'

She sank into the nearest chair. 'Well, because—'

'You thought it was because of a stupid piece of land. And because of your brother.' Her grandfather closed his eyes, his face pale against the hospital sheets. 'I don't blame him for your brother. I was wrong about a lot of things. Wrong. There. I said it. Does that make you happy?'

Fia's heart clenched. A lump formed in her throat. 'You shouldn't be talking about this now. It isn't the time.'

'Always trying to smooth things over. Always wanting

everyone to love each other and be friends. Keep an eye on her, Ferrara, or she'll turn your son into a wimp.' Her grandfather's frame was racked by a paroxysm of coughing and Fia fumbled for the buzzer. Within moments the room filled with staff but he waved them away impatiently, his eyes still on Santo. 'There's one thing I want to know before they pump me full of more drugs that are going to dull my mind—' his voice rasped '—I want to know what you're going to do now that you know.'

Santo didn't hesitate. 'I'm going to marry your grand-daughter.'

CHAPTER FIVE

HE HATED hospitals.

Santo scrunched the flimsy plastic cup in his hand and dropped it into the bin.

The smell of antiseptic reminded him of the night his father had died and just for a moment he was tempted to turn on his heel and walk right out again.

And then he thought of Fia, keeping vigil over her grand-father, hour after hour. His anger was still running hot. He was furious with her. But he couldn't accuse her of not show-ing loyalty to her family. And he couldn't leave her alone in this place.

Cursing softly, Santo strode back towards the coronary care unit that brought back nothing but bad memories.

She was sitting by the bed, her hair a livid streak of fire against her ashen skin. Those green eyes were fixed on the old man as if by sheer willpower and focus she might some-how transmit some of her youth and energy to him.

He'd never seen a lonelier figure in his life.

Or perhaps he had, he thought grimly, remembering the first time he'd seen her in his boathouse. Some people auto-matically sought human company when they were upset. Fia had taught herself to survive alone.

He compared that to his own big, noisy family. He knew from experience that had it been a Ferrara lying in the hos-

pital bed the room would have been bulging with concerned
relatives, not just his brother and sister but numerous aunts,
uncles and cousins all clucking and fussing.

'How's he doing?'

'They gave him a sedative and some other stuff. I don't
know what. They say the first twenty-four hours are crucial.'
Her slim fingers were curled around her grandfather's. 'If he
wakes up now he'll be angry that I'm holding his hand. He's
not great at the physical stuff. Never has been.'

Santo realised that this woman's whole life revolved around
the man currently lying in the bed and the child fast asleep
in his car.

'When did you last eat?' It was the automatic Ferrara response to all moments of crisis and he almost laughed at himself for being so predictable.

'I'm not hungry.' Her voice was husky and she didn't shift
her gaze from her grandfather. 'In a minute I'll go and check
on Luca.'

'I just checked him. He hasn't stirred. He and Luigi are
both asleep.'

'I'll bring him in here and tuck him up on the chair. Then
you can go home. Gina will come and I need to call Ben and
ask him to cover tomorrow.'

Santo felt an irrational surge of anger. 'He doesn't need
to. I've already sorted that out. My team will take over running the Beach Shack for the time being.'

Her spine tensed. 'You're taking advantage of this situation to take over my business?'

Santo held on to his own temper. 'You need to stop thinking like a Baracchi. This is not about revenge. I'm not taking over your business, just making sure you still have one to
come home to. I assumed you didn't want to leave your grandfather's bedside to cook *calamari* for a bunch of strangers.'

Her cheeks were pale. 'I'm sorry.' Her gaze skated back to her grandfather. 'I *am* grateful to you. I just assumed—'

'Well, stop assuming.' Her fragility unsettled him. And it wasn't the only thing that unsettled him. The response of his body was equally disturbing. His feelings were entirely inappropriate for the surroundings. 'You can do no more here tonight. Your grandfather is going to sleep and it's not going to help anyone if you collapse. We're leaving now. I've told the staff to call me if there is any change.'

'I can't leave. It's too far to get back here again if something happens.'

'My apartment is only ten minutes from here. If something happens, I'll drive you. If we leave now you can still get some rest and my son can wake up in a proper bed.' He'd been trying not to think about that side of things, putting his own emotions on hold in order to maintain the delicate balance of a situation that could only be described as difficult.

Perhaps it was the logic of his argument. Perhaps it was the words 'my son'. Either way, she ceased arguing and allowed him to lead her away from the bedside to the car.

Ten minutes later Luca was tucked up in the centre of an enormous double bed in one of his spare bedrooms.

Santo watched as she spread pillows on the floor next to the bed. 'What are you doing?'

'Sometimes he rolls. I don't want him to fall onto the tiled floor,' she muttered. 'Do you have a baby alarm?'

'No. Leave the door open a crack. Then we'll hear him if he wakes.' Santo strode out of the room and she followed, her eyes tracing every detail of his apartment.

'Do you live alone?'

'You think I'm hiding women under the sofa?'

'I just mean it's very big for one person.'

'I like the space and the views. The balconies face over

the old part of the town, not that I think Luca will be that discerning. What can I get you to eat?'

'Nothing, thank you.' Restless and tense, she walked over to the doors that led to the balcony and opened them. 'Don't you keep these locked?'

'You're worrying about my security?'

'I'm worrying about Luca's security.' Biting her lip, she stepped onto the small area and ran her finger along the iron railings. Then she gauged the height of the balcony. 'This is a real hazard. Luca is two years old. His favourite pastime is climbing. He climbs anything and everything he can find. We're going to have to lock the doors to the balconies and remove the keys.' She was brisk and practical, but then she walked past him and he caught the scent of her hair. Flowers. She always smelt like flowers.

Irritated with himself for being so easily distracted, Santo followed her back into the apartment. This time her eyes were on the large sunken living room that formed the centrepiece of his luxurious apartment. 'You're worrying about the welfare of my white sofas? Don't. My niece has already spilled something unmentionable on them. I don't care. People are more important than things.'

'I agree. And I'm not thinking about your sofas, I'm thinking of Luca. More particularly, I'm thinking about the step down to your living room.'

'It's an architectural feature.'

'It's a trap for a fearless toddler. He's going to fall.'

Santo digested that. 'He walks perfectly well. We will teach him to be careful.'

'He gets enthusiastic and excited. If he sees something he wants, he runs. If he does that here, he'll trip and smash his head on your priceless Italian tiles.'

Santo spread his hands in a gesture of surrender. 'So this

place is not exactly child-proofed; I accept that. I will deal with it.'

'How? You can't exactly remodel the apartment, can you?'

'If necessary. And in the meantime I will teach him to watch the step.' He tried to hide his exasperation. However angry he was, he was well aware that she'd been through the most stressful twenty-four hours of her life and yet, apart from her visible panic when she'd found her grandfather, she hadn't shown any emotion. She was frighteningly calm. The little girl who had refused to shed a tear had grown into a woman with the same emotional restraint. The only sign that she was suffering was the rigid tension in her narrow shoulders. 'Are you always like this? It's a wonder Luca isn't a bundle of nerves, living with you.'

'One minute you accuse me of not taking good care of your son and then you accuse me of taking too much care. Make up your mind.' She picked up a slender glass vase and transferred it to a high shelf.

'I was not accusing you of anything. Just pointing out that you're overreacting.'

'You have no idea what it's like, living with an active toddler.'

Her words snapped something inside him. 'And whose fault is that?' Bitterness welled up and threatened to spill over. Afraid he might say something he'd later regret, Santo strode towards the kitchen, struggling with the intensity of his own emotions.

'I'm sorry.' Her voice came from the doorway.

'What for?' He dragged open a cupboard. 'Keeping my son from me or casting doubt on my abilities as a father?'

'I wasn't casting doubt. Just pointing out the hazards of having an active toddler in a bachelor pad.' She looked impossibly fragile standing there with her hair pouring over her shoulders in soft waves of wicked temptation.

He didn't want to feel anything but anger yet he was suffi-
ciently self-aware to know that his feelings were much, much
more complicated than that. Yes, the anger was there and the
hurt, but mixed in with those emotions was a hefty dollop of
something far less easy to define but equally powerful.

The same thing that had brought them together that night.

'We'll do what needs to be done, Fia.' He left the statement purposefully ambiguous and pulled plates out of the
cupboard. 'We need to eat. What can I get you?'

'Nothing, thank you. I think I'll go to bed. I'll sleep with
Luca. That way, if he wakes up he won't be frightened.'

Santo thumped a fresh loaf of bread in the centre of the
table. 'Who is frightened, *tesoro*? You or him?' He sent her
a black look. 'You think if you don't sleep in his bed you'll
be sleeping in mine?'

Wide green eyes fixed on his face. Those eyes that said
everything her lips didn't. The first time he'd caught her in
the boathouse he'd seen misery and fear, but also defiance.
Even though she hadn't said a word, he'd had no trouble reading the message. *Go on and tell. See if I care.*

He hadn't told.

And he knew she would have cared.

She showed nothing, and yet he knew she was a woman
who felt everything deeply. He wouldn't have been able to
list her favourite colour or whether she liked to read, but he'd
never doubted the intensity of her emotions. He'd always
sensed the passion in her, simmering beneath the silent surface. And eventually, of course, he'd felt it. Touched it. Tasted
it. *Taken it.* He could clearly remember the feel of her bare
skin under his seeking fingers, the scent of her as he'd kissed
his way down her body, the flavour of her under his tongue.

Sexual arousal was instant and brutal.

He dragged his gaze from the wicked curve of her hips
back to her face.

Those green eyes had gone a shade darker and her cheeks were flushed.

Santo strode over to the fridge and yanked open the door. Maybe he should just thrust his whole body into it, he thought savagely. He had a feeling that was the only way of cooling himself down.

He was about to pull out a dish of *caponata* when another memory revealed itself. Frowning, he let go of the dish. It wasn't true to say he knew nothing about her, was it? There *was* something he knew. His mouth tightening, he put the *caponata* back and removed *pecorino* and olives instead. Putting them on the table next to the bread, he gestured. 'Eat.'

'I've told you I'm not hungry.'

'I make it a personal rule only to resuscitate one person a day so unless you want me to force-feed you, you'll eat.' He tore off a hunk of bread, added a slice of *pecorino* and some olives and pushed the plate towards her. 'And don't tell me you don't like it. The fact that you love *pecorino* is one of the few things I *do* know about you.'

A tiny frown touched her smooth brow as she stared at the plate and then back at him.

Santo sighed. 'When you hid in the boathouse you always brought the same food.' For a moment he thought she wasn't going to respond.

'I didn't want to have to go home to eat.'

'You didn't want to go home at all.'

'I know.' She gave a strangled laugh and pushed the plate away. 'You do know this is ridiculous, don't you? Just about the only thing you know about me is that I like *pecorino* and olives. And all I know about you is that you like really fast, flashy cars. And yet you're suggesting marriage.'

'I'm not suggesting marriage. I'm insisting on marriage. Your grandfather approved.'

'My grandfather is old-fashioned. I'm not.' Her eyes lifted

to his. 'I run a successful business. I can support my son. We would gain nothing from marriage.'

'Luca would gain a great deal.'

'He would live with two people who don't love each other. What would he gain from that? You're punishing me because you're angry, but in the end you will be the one who suffers. We are not compatible.'

'We know we're compatible in the one place that counts,' Santo said in a raw tone, 'or we wouldn't be in this position now.'

Colour darkened her cheekbones. 'You may be Sicilian, but you are far too intelligent to truly believe that all a marriage takes is good sex.'

Santo took the chair opposite her. 'I suppose I should be grateful you're at least admitting it was good sex.'

'You're impossible to talk to.'

'On the contrary, I'm easy to talk to. I say what I think, which is more than you do. I won't tolerate silence, Fia. Marriages are about sharing. Everything. I don't want a wife who locks away her feelings, so let's get that straight now. I want all of you. Everything you are, you're going to give it to me.' Clearly she hadn't expected that response from him because she turned white.

'If that's what you want, then you really do need a different wife.'

There was a certain satisfaction in having flustered her. 'You've taught yourself to be that way. That's how you've survived and protected yourself. But underneath, you're not like that. And I'm not interested in the ice maiden. I want the woman I had in my boathouse that night.'

'That was… It was…' she stumbled over the words '…that wasn't me.'

'Yes, it was. For a few wild hours you lost control of this

persona you've constructed. That was the real you, Fia. It's the rest of this that is an act.'

'Everything about that night was crazy—' her fingers were curled into her palms '—I don't know how it started, but I do know how it ended.'

'It ended when your brother stole my car and wrapped it around a tree.' He'd hoped the direct approach might shake her out of her rigid control but apparently even the shock of his blunt comment couldn't penetrate that wall she'd built around herself.

'It was too powerful for him. He'd never driven anything like it before.'

'Neither had I,' Santo said icily. 'I'd only received it two days earlier.'

'That is a monumentally tactless and unfeeling thing to say.'

Then show some emotion. 'About as tactless and unfeeling as the wordless implication that I was in some way responsible for his death.'

There was a throbbing silence. 'I have never said that.'

'No, but you've thought it. And your grandfather thought it. You say you don't know me, so learn this about me right now—I'm not good with undercurrents or people who hide what they're really thinking and I sure as hell am not going to feed this damn feud that we've both grown up with. It ends here, right now.' The fire burned hot inside him, strengthening his resolve. 'If what you said to me this morning is true then I presume you want that, too.'

'Of course. But we can kill the feud without getting married. There is more than one way of being a family.'

'Not for me. My child will not grow up being shuttled from one parent to another. We've never talked about that night, so let's do it now. Whatever you're thinking, I want it out in the open, not gnawing holes in that brain of yours. You blamed me for the fact that he took the car. And yet you know what happened that night. I was with you. And we had other things on our mind, didn't we, *bellissima*?'

'I never blamed you.'

'Really?' His sardonic tone made her lift her head and look at him.

'Yes, really.'

He waited for her to elaborate but of course she didn't and that failure to break through her defences exasperated him because he wasn't a man who liked to fail. Jaw tense, he breathed deeply, his emotions at war with each other. 'It's late and you've had a hell of a night. One thing I know about toddlers is that they don't lie in just because adult life is collapsing around them. What time does he wake up?'

'Five.'

His working day frequently began at the same hour. 'If you're not going to eat, then get to bed. I'll lend you one of my shirts to sleep in.'

A faint smile touched the soft curve of her mouth. 'So you don't have a wardrobe full of slinky nightwear for overnight guests? The world would be disappointed to discover that.'

'I don't encourage overnight guests. They can grow roots fast.' He watched her steadily. 'This once, I'll let you retreat. Make the most of it because once we're married there will be no hiding. Be sure of that.'

'We're not getting married, Santo.'

'We'll talk about it tomorrow. But everything I said in my office still stands.'

'No, it doesn't. You were concerned that Luca had been harmed, but you can see now that he has had a happy childhood.'

'I admire your efforts to create the family you didn't have, but my son doesn't need paid employees to fill that role. He has the real thing. A family ready and willing to welcome him. He's a Ferrara and the sooner we make that legal the better for everyone.'

'Is it?' Her voice suddenly seemed to gain strength. 'Is it really better for him to be brought up by parents who are strangers?'

Santo's mouth tightened. 'We're not going to be strangers, *tesoro*. We're going to be as intimate as it's possible for a man and a woman to be. I'm going to rip down those barriers you've built. When you're with me you might as well be naked because there is going to be no hiding. Now get some sleep. You're going to need it.'

As intimate as it's possible for a man and a woman to be.

What was intimate about that cold, emotionless statement? He was blisteringly angry. Furious. How did he think they could achieve intimacy under those circumstances?

She wasn't going to marry him. It would be wrong.

Once he calmed down, he'd see sense. They'd come to an agreement about how to share Luca. And perhaps the three of them would spend some time together. But there was no need to make it legally binding.

Worry about her grandfather mingled with worry for her son and herself and Fia curled up in the bed, but there was no rest to be found in sleep, the dreams racing over her in a dark, tangled rush of disturbing images. Her mother, huddled in a corner of the kitchen, trying to make herself as small as possible while her husband lost his temper. The sight of her walking away, leaving her eight-year-old daughter behind. *'If I take you, he'll come after me.'* Standing with her grandfather as they buried her father after the drunken boating accident that had taken his life, knowing that she was supposed to feel sad.

She awoke to find herself alone in the bed. A lurch of fear was followed by a brief moment of relief as she heard the sound of Luca giggling. And then she remembered that they weren't at home, but in Santo's deathtrap apartment.

Almost tripping in her haste to get to her child, she shot out of the bedroom and followed the sound, ready to drag him out of trouble.

Expecting to find an energetic Luca fearlessly scaling a cupboard or plunging his curious fingers into a piece of high-tech electrical equipment, she instead found him sitting on a chair in Santo's sleek, contemporary kitchen watching as his father deftly cut shapes out of *brioche*.

Weak with relief, Fia paused in the doorway, astonished by what she was seeing. Father or not, Santo was a stranger to Luca. A tall, powerfully built intimidating stranger who was in an undeniably dangerous mood since he'd made the unexpected discovery that he had a son. It was true that he'd helped and supported her the night before, but nothing in his demeanour had led her to believe that there was any softening in his attitude.

She'd assumed that some of his anger would reveal itself in his interaction with the child and yet Luca was clearly not only comfortable, but vastly entertained and delighted with the masculine attention he was receiving along with his breakfast.

Judging from his damp hair, Santo had not long left the shower and it was obvious from his bare feet and bare chest that he'd tugged on a pair of jeans in haste, unable to finish dressing before Luca had demanded his attention. But the real change wasn't in his dress—or lack of it—it was the way he carried himself. There was no sign of the forbidding, intimidating businessman who had called all the shots the day before. The man currently entertaining one small boy was warm and approachable, his smile indulgent as he wiped his son's buttery fingers. He looked as though he did this every day. As if this was part of their morning routine.

As she watched, Santo bent down and kissed Luca and when the child giggled, he kissed him again as if he couldn't get enough of him.

Tears sprang to her eyes and Fia leaned against the doorframe for support.

Watching them made her heart clench. Luca had never had that, had he? He'd never known a father's love. Yes, she'd surrounded him by 'family' but even she couldn't pretend that what she'd created came close to the real thing. One day Gina would move on, Ben would marry and Luca's 'family' would disband.

Yesterday she'd been so sure that marriage between her and Santo would be the wrong thing for her son. She'd seen no benefit to him in being forced to live with two people whose only connection was the child they'd made.

But of course there *was* benefit and she was staring at it right now.

If they married, Luca would have his father. Not at prearranged times, like single snapshots taken on a camera. But permanently.

Santo still hadn't noticed her and, as he spoke to their son in lilting Italian, Fia found that she was holding her breath. When Luca replied in the same language pride mingled with emotions she didn't even recognise.

She was normally the one who gave Luca his breakfast. It was their morning ritual. And yet here he was happily pursuing that ritual with his father as if the two of them had been doing it for ever.

There was a lump in her throat and the lump grew as Santo leaned forward and kissed his son again, indifferent to buttery fingers that grabbed at his hair. He blew bubbles into Luca's neck and made him giggle. He pulled faces and tickled him.

He had nieces, she remembered, so he was obviously used to children, but still—

She couldn't ever remember being kissed by her father and she'd certainly never been kissed by her grandfather. And yet here was Santo, openly demonstrative with his child.

'Mamma—' Luca saw her, wriggled off the chair and hurled himself at her, *brioche* squashed in his fist.

Across the top of his head, her gaze met Santo's.

As she scooped up her child, she swallowed down that lump that still threatened to choke her.

A quizzical gleam lit his eyes, as if he were asking himself how long she'd been standing there. And suddenly she was very conscious that she hadn't even paused to brush her hair before sprinting from the bedroom.

There was something inappropriately informal about greeting him with her hair spilling wildly over her shoulders while wearing nothing but the shirt he'd lent her. Their attire suggested an intimacy that didn't exist and she felt herself flush with mortification as his eyes slid down her body and lingered on her bare legs.

'*Buongiorno.*' He injected the word with familiarity. As if this was a scene they both woke up to every morning.

Even though he'd dragged on his jeans in a hurry he looked utterly spectacular. Indecently handsome and more masculine than any single member of the species had a right to look. He didn't need the handmade suits to look good, she thought numbly, her eyes tracing the smooth swell of muscle that shaped his broad shoulders and drifting to his board-flat abdomen.

'Fia?'

She was so distracted by his naked torso that she'd missed the question he'd asked her. 'Sorry?'

'I asked you which language you use when you speak to him. English or Italian?'

'English—' Thoroughly flustered, she sat Luca back down on the chair. 'My grandfather spoke to him in Italian. We thought that would be less confusing.' She braced herself for criticism of that approach but he gave a brief nod.

'Then we will do the same. You do the English. I'll do the Italian. That's what I did this morning and he seemed to understand. He's very bright.' Pride in his eyes as he looked at Luca, he rose to his feet with that easy grace guaranteed to draw the female eye. The fabric of his jeans clung to the hard length of his long legs and she saw the muscles in his back ripple as he reached into a cupboard for a mug. *She'd drawn blood*, she remembered. She'd been so driven out of her mind by him, she'd scratched the skin of that smooth, muscled back. The craving had been so intense, the pleasure so deliciously erotic that she'd dragged her nails down his flesh. Not that he'd been gentle. The recollection set her skin on fire. The whole thing had been a hot, hard, violent explosion of earthy animal instinct.

And now she was hyperaware of every move he made. Of the flex of muscle in his strong wrist as he made her coffee, of the dark hairs that shadowed his chest and then narrowed down and disappeared below the snap of his jeans. Everything about him was overtly, unapologetically male and everything about her response was overtly, unapologetically female.

He was the hottest guy she'd ever laid eyes on. Always had been. And that was what made this situation so much harder.

His gaze flicked to hers, those slumberous eyes darkening as he read her mind. Despite the presence of their child, the brief moment they shared was wholly adult.

Desperate to break the connection, Fia blurted out the first thing that came into her head. 'My phone battery has died. May I use yours to call the hospital?'

The sardonic curve of his mouth told her he knew she hadn't been thinking about phones or hospitals. And neither had he. Just being in the same room created something so intense that it was almost tangible. It crackled the air between them and snapped the atmosphere tight.

'I've already called.' He placed coffee on the table without asking her how she took it. 'Your grandfather had a good night. He's still asleep. The consultant will be at the hospital in half an hour. I've said we'll meet him there.'

We?

She watched as Luca slid off his chair and wrapped his arms around his father's legs. Santo scooped him up. 'I'm starting to understand why you were worried last night,' he drawled. 'He's extremely active.'

'But you're coping well,' she said quickly, 'so he can stay with you while I go to the hospital.' She needed respite from the unrelenting stress of being with him. Most of all she needed respite from the constant assault on her senses and the memories that kept replaying in her head. Her heart was going crazy. She was so conscious of him that she couldn't breathe properly.

He lowered Luca to the floor. 'I'm coming with you.'

'I'd rather go on my own.'

'Of course you would.' His eyes glinted with deadly mockery. 'You'd rather do everything on your own, but you're never going to learn differently if you don't practise, so you can start this morning. We'll go together. Say the word after me, Fia. *Together.*'

Fia stared at her coffee. 'Do you have milk? I like milk in my coffee. Not that I'd expect you to know that because you don't really know anything about me, do you? Just as I don't know anything about you. And that is why this is so ridiculous.' But the heat had gone out of her argument. Last night she'd been certain, now she was just confused.

'Stop trying to pick a fight. I'll win.'

She breathed, 'All right, we'll go together. But in that case I need to use a phone. I'll call Ben and ask him to pick up

Luca. He's too little to be in a place like that for more than a short time.'

The change in him was instantaneous. Any trace of humour was wiped out. It was like watching a cloud suddenly pass over the sun, darkening the land beneath. Those eyes went from burnished gold to deadly black, the threat in them unmistakable. 'You will *not* call Ben.'

'I don't want Luca at the hospital. It's exhausting for my grandfather and stressful for him.'

'I agree. Which is why I've arranged—' He broke off as they both heard a commotion at the entrance of his apartment.

'Santo?' a female voice sang out and then a beautiful dark-haired girl strode confidently into the room. Clearly familiar with the layout of the place, she kissed Santo soundly. 'You,' she purred, patting his cheek with her hand, 'are a *very* naughty boy.'

Fia sat still, frozen to the spot by the sight of this beautiful creature and the ease with which she interacted with Santo. And, to make her pain even worse, he didn't even have the gall to look embarrassed. Instead he simply unpeeled the woman, gave her a smile and kissed her on both cheeks.

'Ciao, bellissima.'

Wounded by his lack of sensitivity, Fia stood up abruptly and was about to snatch her son and leave them to it when the woman turned to look at her.

Braced for bared teeth and female jealousy, Fia found herself suddenly wrapped in a tight, effusive hug.

Apart from Luca, no one ever hugged her. The shock of it kept her rigid, but before she could work out who the woman was she'd released her and turned her attention to Luca.

First she covered her mouth with her hands as if she couldn't believe what she was seeing. Then she scooped an unsuspecting Luca up and showered him with kisses, talking in rapid Italian as she danced round the kitchen with him.

And, instead of howling, Luca seemed delighted by the attention, responding to the woman's infectious smile with gurgles
of laughter.

Fia wanted to snatch her son out of the woman's arms.

Which one of Santo's many women was she?

She racked her brain to recreate all those media images of
Santo she'd tried to obliterate from her mind. Santo Ferrara
and a lean brunette at the opening of the Taormina Filmfest,
dining out with a sleek blonde on his arm, leaving his private
jet at the airport with a redhead in tow. She'd tried to blot out
the female faces, not commit them to memory.

She was just about to make a taut comment when a small
girl, a little older than Luca, rocketed into the room and
slammed into Santo's legs.

'Up!'

'I think you mean, "up, please", but your wish is my command, of course.' His amused drawl suggesting that this was
a frequent request, Santo scooped the child up. 'You need to
put in some overtime on the manners here.' He glanced at the
woman and his expression softened. 'Thanks for coming.'

'Anything for you.' With a cheeky smile the brunette put
Luca down, dropped her bag on the chair and looked at Fia.
'I'm really sorry to hear about your grandfather. You must be
worried sick, but honestly the hospital is just brilliant. And
I expect Santo has them hopping around because he always
puts a bomb under them. And you're not to worry about Luca.
We'll keep him with us until you're ready to pick him up. I
can't wait to get to know him better.'

Fia felt a flash of fury. Santo expected her to leave her son
with one of his women? 'There is no way—'

'Dani is my sister, yes? Daniela Ferrara. Although techni-
cally she's no longer Ferrara since she married Raimondo.'
Interrupting smoothly, Santo put the little girl down on the
floor. 'This is Rosa, her daughter. Luca's cousin.'

Cousin?

Startled, Fia looked at Dani, who looked right back. 'Er... you didn't know I was Santo's sister?'

'I didn't recognise you.' Fia's voice was a croak and Dani's eyes widened in contrition.

'Oh, no! You must have thought—' Looking at her brother, she gave an exaggerated shudder. 'Nightmare. We'd kill each other in two minutes. I like to be in charge in my relationships. Talking of which, Raimondo is parking the car. We thought we'd take Luca back home with us because we have all Rosa's toys there so it's easier.' She caught Fia's anxious look and smiled. 'You're thinking you can't let him go with a stranger, I know you are because I'd be thinking the same thing in your position. But honestly, he's going to have a great time and better with us than in that vile hospital or here. Santo's apartment is a deathtrap. You two can spend as long as you need to at the hospital and then go out to dinner or something. Don't rush. Do something romantic.'

'*Cristo*, you are like a one-woman talk show. Breathe, Dani!' Santo cast his sister a look of raw exasperation. 'Give someone else the opportunity to speak! You accuse me of being controlling and then you steamroller people with words. Conversation is supposed to be a two-way thing.'

'Well, no one else is saying anything in this room!' Dani bristled and Santo ground his teeth.

'Was there an opportunity? *Accidenti!* I don't know how Raimondo puts up with you. I would strangle you within two minutes of being alone together.'

'I would have strangled you first.' Dani turned to Fia. 'Don't let him bully you. Stand up to him; it's the only way to handle Santo, especially when he does his threatening act. I used to see you sometimes on the beach but you've obviously forgotten me.'

No, she hadn't forgotten. She just hadn't recognised the

other woman and now she didn't know what to say. How much did Daniela know? What exactly had he told his family?

It should have been a horribly awkward moment but Dani clearly didn't tolerate 'awkward' in her life. She said something in Italian to her little girl, who eyed up Luca, clearly decided he looked like someone she could play with and promptly dragged him off towards Santo's living room, leaving the adults alone.

'There. See? They're friends already.' Oblivious to her brother's glowering disapproval, Dani followed them out of the room. 'I'll watch them. There is nothing you can teach me about intercepting toddler trouble.' At the doorway of the kitchen, she glanced over her shoulder. 'I'll leave you two to discuss wedding details. And Santo, it doesn't matter how rushed a wedding is, a woman still needs to look her best so you'd better take Fia shopping. Or, better still, give me your card and *I'll* take her shopping because we all know you hate it.'

Santo's expression went from irritated to dangerous. 'Your help with Luca is welcomed. Your interference in any other aspect of my life is not.'

'Just because you've done all this in the wrong order is no reason not to make it romantic,' Dani said tartly. 'A woman wants romance on her wedding day. Remember that.'

She vanished to supervise the children, leaving Fia with her face burning.

Romance?

Whatever was between them, it certainly wasn't romance. What was romantic about a man being forced to marry a woman he didn't even like?

Santo drained his coffee cup and thumped it down on the table. 'I apologise for my sister,' he breathed. 'She still hasn't learned the meaning of the word "boundary". But if she will take Luca for us today, it will make everything a lot easier.'

Nothing, absolutely nothing, would make this situation easier.

The tension between them was like a dark storm brewing in the room. She couldn't imagine ever being able to relax with him. She was wound so tight that every reaction and response was exaggerated. Her senses were heightened so that the slightest glance was all it took to set her heart pounding.

The look he sent her told her that he felt it too. 'It is good that she has taken Luca because we need to talk. Properly.'

Fia thought about Luca being hugged and kissed by his father.

Santo clearly interpreted her silence as refusal. 'You can throw as many obstacles as you like between us,' he said softly, 'and I will smash through all of them. Be sure of that. You can say no a thousand different ways and I will find a thousand different ways to tell you why you're wrong.'

'I'm not saying no.'

'Scusi?'

'I'm agreeing with you. You said that you thought marriage was the best thing for Luca, and I'm agreeing with you.' Her voice wasn't entirely steady. 'Last night I was sure that marriage wasn't in Luca's best interests but this morning...well, I saw the two of you together and...and, yes, I think it would be the right thing for Luca.' Oh, God, she'd said it. What if she were wrong?

Silence pulsed.

'So you're doing this because you think it's the right thing "for Luca"?'

'Of course. What else?'

He strode across the kitchen towards her.

Fia forced herself to stand still, expecting him to stop, but he didn't stop until he had her with her back against the wall and nowhere to go.

Jaw tight, he slammed a hand either side of her to block

her escape. She was boxed in by rock-hard muscle and testosterone and because she didn't want to look at him, she looked at his bare chest and that was a mistake too because everything about him made her think of that night. She didn't need a close-up of his physique to know how strong he was. She'd felt that strength. *Why the hell hadn't he pulled on a shirt?* The world around her seemed to fade. She forgot she was in his kitchen. She forgot about her grandfather in the hospital and the cheerful sounds of her child playing in the next room. She forgot everything.

Her world became this man.

'Look at me.' His thickened command told her that if she didn't, he'd make her and so she lifted her gaze and the look they shared unlocked something dark she'd buried deep inside herself. Something she hadn't dared examine because she was so afraid of it.

The way she felt about him.

Breathing shallow, she stared into those burnished dark eyes that changed colour according to his mood.

'This is not just about Luca and I need you to acknowledge that because I don't want some martyr in my bed.' He lowered his head, his mouth as close to hers as it was possible to be and yet not touch her. He spoke so softly that he couldn't possibly be overheard and yet each word was delivered with such force and power that she knew they'd be forever embedded in her memory. 'If we do this, then we do it properly.'

If she licked her lips now, she'd touch him. If she made that single move she'd be kissing him. And she knew how that would feel. Knew how *he'd* feel. Even after more than three years, she'd never forgotten it. 'Yes. We do it properly. We…get to know each other.'

'I already know a lot about you—' That wicked, sensual mouth held hers hostage. 'I may not know how you like your coffee, but I know other things about you. Want me to remind you?'

'No.' She didn't need reminding. She'd forgotten nothing. Not the way he tasted nor the way he touched her. And now those memories were unlocked and she could feel herself melting—feel the heat of her own arousal spread through her body and the hard pressure of his.

His hand came up to cup her face, those same fingers that knew how to drive her wild, now firm and determined as they forced her to look at him. 'Sure? Because if this is going to work for Luca, it has to work for us.' His mouth was just a breath away from hers, the heat of him a pulsing, throbbing force. 'I have to get to know all of you, particularly the bits you're hiding. And you have to get to know all of me, *tesoro*. Everything.'

CHAPTER SIX

OVER the next few days she experienced the full might and force of the Ferrara machine. Her grandfather was moved to a private room to convalesce, his near miraculous recovery attributed to Santo's prompt intervention but also an astonishing will to live. And that will, the staff believed, came from a determination to see his granddaughter marry. And Santo fed that determination by keeping him appraised of the wedding plans—plans in which Fia had little input.

'If you have any requests then let me know,' Santo said one morning as they drove back from the hospital. 'We'll marry at the Ferrara Spa Resort, our flagship hotel. It's licensed for weddings and it's a beautiful venue, right on the beach. I'm planning on keeping it as small as possible.'

Of course he was. This wedding wasn't something to broadcast, was it?

'I'd like to invite Ben and Gina.'

He tensed slightly at the mention of Ben's name and she fully expected him to refuse, but instead he nodded. 'Yes. They are an important part of Luca's life. They should be there. I will arrange it.'

He arranged everything, or rather his team did.

It was his insistence that one of his top chefs step in to run the Beach Shack that enabled her to spend as much time with her grandfather as she needed to in those early days. And the occasional phone call to Ben was all it took to reassure her that all was well with the restaurant and that the new chef was following Santo's orders to run the place exactly as Fia ran it.

She wanted to be angry that he'd taken over, but the truth was that Santo had taken a hideous, stressful situation and made it as smooth for her as he possibly could. Because of him, her grandfather was making a good recovery, her business was safe and her child was happy.

And every time she felt wobbly about her decision, she just had to look at how he was with Luca.

'My staff have interviewed and appointed three nurses with excellent qualifications who will provide round the clock care for your grandfather when he is discharged home.' Santo negotiated the thick traffic with the ease of a native Sicilian. 'They will work on a rota so that your grandfather will never be alone.'

For years her only mode of transport had been her dusty old moped. Now each journey was made in supercharged, superaccelerated, air-conditioned luxury. 'I can't afford that level of care.'

'But I can. And I am the one paying.'

'I don't want your money. I can look after him myself. I've been running a successful business since I was eighteen.'

'Even if you were not about to marry me, that would be an unsustainable proposition. You cannot raise a child, run a business and be a full-time carer.'

'Plenty of people do just that. You may have missed the press release because it was sent to "modern man" and you don't fall into that category, but it is possible to have it all.'

'In my experience "having it all" usually includes a nervous breakdown,' Santo drawled, leaning on his horn as the driver in front stopped to let out a passenger and blocked the road. 'I want a wife, not a basket case so we'll buy in the appropriate help, which should leave you with the energy for the important parts.'

'I presume you consider the "important parts" to take place in your bedroom.'

'Funnily enough, I didn't mean that. I was talking about the energy required to care for a young child but yes, sex is going to keep you busy too. I'm a demanding guy, *angelo mia*. I have needs.' The engine growled as he accelerated past the car, shifting gears smoothly. 'And if you're going to satisfy those needs, you're going to need your sleep.'

She had a feeling he was winding her up but she didn't know him well enough to be sure.

He was ferociously bright, that she *was* sure about, but he also made no apology for being a red-blooded male.

All he'd used were words and yet the desire came in a rush, the force of it shocking her because she'd never felt this way with any other man and she didn't want to feel it about this one. Beneath all the worry and the questions, she was woman enough to wonder whether everything she remembered from that night was real or whether she'd imagined it all.

Yes, he'd been demanding, but she'd been demanding, too. In fact she couldn't even remember who had made the first move in the thick sweltering darkness of that hot summer night. He'd slaked his appetite and she'd slaked hers. He'd taken and she'd taken right back.

Because she didn't want to think about sex, she went back to something he'd said earlier. 'There is one thing you've forgotten in all this. You've forgotten to make me sign a prenuptial agreement.'

He laughed. 'We're *not* going to need one of those.'

'Don't be so sure. You're a very rich guy. Aren't you afraid I'm going to take you for every penny you have?'

'A prenuptial agreement is only necessary in the event of a divorce. I'm very traditional. I believe that marriage is for ever. Once a Ferrara wife, always a Ferrara wife. We will *not* be getting a divorce.'

'Maybe you'll want one.' She didn't understand her need to goad him but she couldn't help herself. 'Maybe you won't find being married to me particularly entertaining.'

'As long as you focus on one particular type of entertainment, we'll be fine.'

She decided he was definitely winding her up and threw him a look. 'If you're so damn horny how can you be sure marriage is going to suit you? Being trapped with one woman might drive you mad.'

'Been reading my press coverage?' He threw her an amused glance and a sexy smile that travelled right through her body. 'I never said I wasn't going to keep you busy but you can relax. You have no reason to be jealous. I intend to focus all my attention on you. *All* of it, *tesoro*.' His husky voice teased her nerve-endings. Or maybe it was the words again. The way he managed to inject each phrase with lethal promise. Under that veneer of smooth control she sensed darker emotions that simmered beneath the surface he presented to the world. From the rocky base of her own family, she'd watched him grow from boy to man. She understood the volatility that was so much a part of his nature, but she'd also seen the drive. Unobserved, she'd watched as he'd learned to windsurf and to sail. She'd admired the sheer determination that never allowed him to give up on anything until it was mastered. And then there had been the women. Golden-haired girls who flocked to the beach in the hope of attracting the attention of one of the Ferrara brothers.

It was no wonder he was sure of himself, she thought numbly. No one had ever said no to him. No one had ever challenged his supremacy. And suddenly she couldn't help herself.

'Maybe *you* won't be enough for *me*,' she said calmly, deciding to play him at his own game. 'I have needs too. Needs every bit as powerful as yours. Maybe you won't be able to satisfy me.'

Dark eyebrows rose, but the faint gleam in his eyes suggested he appreciated the humour. 'You think not?'

'No. I don't see why men always think they have the monopoly on sexual needs. I'm just saying that perhaps I'll be the one looking elsewhere.'

He stopped the car so suddenly that the seat belt locked.

Oblivious to the cacophony of horns sounding behind them, he turned to face her and her heart raced away in a crazy rhythm under that glittering gaze because the humour was gone.

'I didn't mean it,' she muttered. She realised she'd been stupid to goad him in that way. 'You were winding me up and I was doing the same. For goodness' sake, Santo—my father was unfaithful to my mother for the whole of their marriage, do you really think I'd do that?'

He inhaled slowly. 'Not a good joke.'

'No, but—' she hesitated '—since this conversation has turned serious—I'm well aware that you're marrying me just because of Luca so we're not exactly glued together by love, are we? I'm not a meek, obedient girl who is going to sit in the corner while you go off with other women. What happens if you do fall in love?'

He stared at her for a long moment and then turned his attention back to the road and eased back into the horrendous traffic. 'I'd be bored silly in five minutes with meek and obedient. I don't want you to sit in a corner. As my wife you will inevitably have a high profile. And whatever happened in the past, I respect you as the mother of my child and that is enough to glue us together. And as for your father—' his voice hardened '—his behaviour was dishonourable and beneath contempt. I would never behave in such a way towards the mother of my children. You have no need to worry. And no need to be jealous.'

Humiliated that she'd revealed so much, she turned her head and looked out of the window but she was oblivious to everything except her own emotions. She realised that she didn't even know where they were. She'd been so wrapped up in her emotions she hadn't been watching the route. 'I'm not jealous.'

'Yes, you are. You're worried I'm going to cheat on you and I don't mind that because it proves you're committed—' He leaned on his horn and overtook a driver who he obviously considered to be going too slowly. 'If you'd told me to go ahead and have an affair, I would have been worried. You feel strong emotions and I'm comfortable with strong emotions. I just need to persuade you to express them. From now on "hiding in the boathouse" is banned. And I use that term figuratively as well as literally.'

She hadn't been back to the boathouse for years. Once, it had been her favourite hiding place, her sanctuary, but she hadn't been back there since that night.

Santo drove into the courtyard of a beautiful palazzo and Fia glanced around her in surprise.

'Where are we?'

'My brother Cristiano's town house. You're choosing your wedding dress. Dani is here and also Cristiano's wife, Laurel. You'll like her. She is calmer than Dani so hopefully she'll add some sense to the proceedings.'

'They separated—' she frowned, trying to remember '—I read something in the paper.'

'But now they are back together and stronger than ever. They have a daughter, Elena, who is the same age as Dani's Rosa, and an older daughter, Chiara, who they adopted a year ago.' He switched off the engine. 'So you see, Luca's family is expanding by the minute.'

'I read that they were getting a divorce.'

'Not any more.' He gave a gentle smile and released her seat belt. 'As I said, *angelo mia,* once a Ferrara wife, always a Ferrara wife. Remember that.'

She got through the wedding ceremony by telling herself that she was marrying for love. Not love for Santo, but love for her son. And any doubts she might have had were swept away by the sight of Luca being welcomed into the big, noisy Ferrara family. He thrived on the attention, adored playing with his cousins and wouldn't let his father out of his sight. And Fia couldn't help but warm to Santo's mother, who embraced her tightly as she welcomed her to the family. They never held anything back, she thought. They didn't ration love. They weren't afraid that too much was a bad thing.

The media, tired of the endless gloom of economic disaster, greedily devoured a happy story. Thanks to the few choice details fed to them by the Ferrara publicity machine, they'd pieced together a romantic tale that bore no resemblance to reality. According to the press, their relationship had been conducted in secret because of the long-standing feud between their families, but now it was out in the open and the headlines read 'Love conquers all'.

But perhaps the press were most charmed by the sight of her grandfather and Cristiano Ferrara shaking hands and talking together at length, finally putting an end to hostilities.

'I'm worried this is all too much for you, *Nonno.*' The tension a constant knot in her stomach, Fia sat down on the chair next to her grandfather. 'You should still be convalescing.'

'Don't fuss. Ferrara has half the hospital standing guard,' her grandfather grumbled. 'What can happen?'

But she could tell he was impressed by the care and attention Santo had paid to him and if her insides hadn't been churning so alarmingly at the thought of what was coming, she would have been grateful, too. As it was, she stole a glance at the handsome man who was now her husband and felt a flicker of trepidation. It was all very well for him to say that marriage was for ever but, apart from the moment they'd exchanged vows, he hadn't looked at her. Not once. It was as if he were trying to postpone the moment he had to confront reality. What would happen when the guests finally left and they were alone? Would there be stilted conversation? Would he suggest an early night?

Her grandfather gave a rare smile. 'Look at Luca. Now *that's* how a boy should play.'

Fia looked and saw her son shrieking with laughter as his father held him upside down by his ankles. She felt a lurch of anxiety.

'I hope he doesn't drop him on the terrace.'

Her grandfather gave her an impatient look. 'You fuss him to death.'

Did she fuss him to death? She'd tried so hard to make sure Luca knew he was loved. Had she overdone that?

'I just want him to be happy.'

'And what about you? Are you happy?' It was the first time her grandfather had ever asked her that question and she didn't know how to answer.

She should have been happy that Luca now had his father in his life and that the long-running feud between their two families had finally been put to rest.

But how happy could a marriage be when the only love involved was for a child?

Her father had made no secret of his resentment towards his children. He'd married because of pressure from his father—her grandfather—and four lives had been damaged as a result of his innate selfishness.

But Santo was nothing like her father, she reasoned. It was obvious that he felt nothing but unconditional love for his son and already Luca was being enveloped in the warm, protective blanket of the Ferrara family.

'I'm giving him the land as a wedding gift.' Her grandfather scowled at her. 'Satisfied?'

She gave a weak smile. 'Yes. Thank you.'

He hesitated and then squeezed her hand in an almost unprecedented show of affection. 'You did the right thing. Eventually.'

The right thing for Luca, yes. But for her?

She was less convinced.

Eventually the guests started to drift away. Her grandfather, tired but less grumpy than she'd seen him in a long time, was ushered away by concerned health staff and only a few close family remained.

Feeling alone in the crowd of Ferraras, Fia paced restlessly to the far side of the terrace where they had gathered to 'celebrate'.

'Here—' Dani thrust a glass of champagne into her hand '—you look as though you need it. Welcome to the family. You look stunning. That dress is perfect, if I say so myself.' She clinked her glass against Fia's. 'To your future, which is going to be good, despite what you're thinking right now this minute.'

Fia wondered how she knew. She wasn't used to confiding in people. On the other hand, she was grateful to Dani for at least making an effort to be friendly. 'Am I that easy to read?'

'Yes.' Dani stretched out a hand and brushed a strand of hair from Fia's shoulder. 'I know that you and Santo have your problems; I'm not fooled by this story he's spinning for the world. But it's going to be fine now you're married. You'll work it out. There's something strong between you. I sensed it that morning I arrived to help with Luca. You could barely keep your hands off each other.'

That was just sexual chemistry and Fia knew you couldn't build a marriage on that. 'He's angry with me.'

'He's Santo,' Dani said simply. 'He feels deeply. About everything, but most of all family. Cristiano is the same. But now you *are* family.'

'But he didn't really want to marry me.' The words came out in a rush. 'I'm irrelevant.'

'Irrelevant?' Dani looked at her for a long time and then smiled. 'Let me tell you something about my brother. Whatever you may have heard, he is very, *very* picky when it comes to women and he believes that marriage is for ever. He would not have married you if he didn't think the two of you could make a go of it.'

'I don't think he's thought about us at all. This is about Luca.'

'But you made Luca together,' Dani said gently, 'so there must have been something. And you're certainly not irrelevant. He's spent the whole evening trying not to look at you.'

'You noticed that?' Her humiliation deepened but Dani smiled.

'It's a good sign. I have a suspicion my very confident brother is feeling confused for the first time in his life. That *has* to be a good thing.'

'I took it as a sign that he's indifferent.'

'I don't know what he feels but it's not indifference.'

Fia had no chance to question her further because Dani was immediately dragged away to speak to a bunch of cousins and Fia was left alone again. She was now married to one of the wealthiest men in Italy, but she longed to be back at the Beach Shack, clearing up after evening service, with the prospect of an early-morning dip in the sea with her son.

It had been agreed that Luca would stay with Dani and her family for the night and the thought of being without him brought a lump to her throat. Suddenly she wanted to scoop up her son and run straight back into her old life where her emotions and feelings had been a steady, predictable thing. Instead she had to hug him goodbye and watch as he left with his new family. Was it selfish to wish he were just a little anxious about leaving her? Was it wrong of her to wish he'd clung just a little longer instead of smiling with excitement at the prospect of spending more time with his cousins? Was it cowardly to wish she had him here, because he formed the only effective barrier between herself and Santo?

'He'll be fine. Don't worry about him. Dani may seem scatty but she's a devoted mother.' Santo was by her side. Santo, who was now her husband, for richer, for poorer. And it was definitely richer, she thought numbly. Even knowing how wealthy the Ferrara family were, she was still stunned by the sheer luxury of her new life. This was their flagship hotel and their corporate headquarters and at the far side of the private beach was the Aphrodite Villa, the jewel in the Ferrara corporate crown. Occasionally the family rented it to rock stars and royalty, but for the next twenty-four hours it belonged to them and the thought of being alone with Santo in a place designed for lovers made her feel something close to panic.

Over the past week she'd been so busy taking care of Luca, shuttling backwards and forward to the hospital to be with her grandfather, she'd managed not to face up to the reality of their wedding night. But now—

Suddenly she longed for those distractions that had kept her from thinking about this moment. The moment she'd be on her own with Santo.

'He didn't need to be sent away.' She kept her eyes fixed on the distance, determined not to look at him. If he could ignore her, she would ignore him back. 'It isn't as if he's intruding on a romantic interlude. It's crazy to turn this into something it's not.'

Her observation was met with silence.

Unnerved by that silence, she glanced briefly at him and collided with night-black eyes that glittered bright with intent.

'You don't think he'd be intruding?' He slid his hand behind her head and brought her face close to his. 'You want him here while we finally let this thing between us go free? Is that what you want?' His voice was thickened with raw lust. 'Because I, for one, have no intention of holding back. I've been doing that for long enough and it's driving me insane.'

Shocked, Fia stared into those eyes. She could see the blaze of hunger. Feel the hard bite of his fingers as he buried them in her hair. And everything he felt, she felt too. How could she not? The chemistry was so powerful that she felt it shoot right through her. She burned up and melted. It might have ended right there on the terrace had not someone cleared their throat right next to them.

This time it was Cristiano, Santo's older brother. Unlike Dani, he'd been cool with her and Fia suspected he wasn't going to be so easily won over as his romantic sister.

Brotherly love, she thought numbly.

She'd never had that. Her brother had been selfish and irresponsible and any warmth in their relationship had existed only in her mind. Unlike the Ferraras, where warmth surrounded the family like a protective forcefield.

With visible reluctance, Santo let his hand drop from her neck. 'Back in a minute.' Relaxed and unflustered, he strolled away with his brother and Fia took advantage of the distraction to make an exit. She had no intention of waiting. The atmosphere was suffocating and anyway, what was he planning? A romantic walk on the sand? Hardly.

Solar-powered lights lit the path to the beach and she walked quickly, blotting out the thought that this place was perfect for a lovers' stroll. The setting sun sent a ruby glow over the darkening horizon and in the background she heard the rhythmic chirruping of cicadas and the soft swish of the sea on the sand.

It should have been an idyllic setting but the perfection jarred against the reality.

It felt as inappropriate as the cream silk wedding dress chosen by Dani.

She should have worn red, she thought. Red for danger.

She approached the villa, was momentarily checked by the sheer beauty of the infinity pool and then stopped dead at the sight that greeted her. It was obvious that the place had been lovingly prepared for a night of romance. The doors were open to the beach. Chilled champagne waited by the bed, candles flickered on every surface and rose petals had been scattered on the floor leading to the luxurious bedroom.

She could have coped with the champagne and the candles.

It was the sight of those rose petals that made her throat close.

Rose petals said romance, and that wasn't what was going on here.

Their relationship was *not* about romance.

Emotions that had been building since Santo had first strode into her kitchen exploded. Trying to destroy the atmosphere created by the candles, she flicked on harsh overhead lights and started to open doors, looking for a broom—looking for something that would help her remove that romantic symbol from the floor. When she failed to find anything remotely like cleaning equipment she dropped to her knees and started to scoop the petals up by hand, sweeping them into a pile by the bed.

'What the hell are you doing?' An incredulous male voice came from the doorway but Fia didn't even look up. She didn't dare look up in case everything she was feeling spilled over.

'What does it look like I'm doing? I'm clearing up the evidence of someone's warped sense of humour.' The mound was growing but before she could add any more she was lifted off her knees and planted on her feet.

'What's warped about it?'

'It's a mockery,' she croaked. 'Someone is being intentionally cruel. Making fun of our relationship.'

Dark brows locked together in an uncomprehending frown. '*I* gave the instruction to prepare it the way we do for honeymoons and romantic breaks. I just married you. Short though it may be, this is our honeymoon. There are certain expectations. I've projected this as a romance because I don't want any rumours that will hurt our son.'

So even the rose petals by the bed were for Luca. All of it was for Luca.

'But he's not here now, is he? And neither are the journalists. So we can lose the rose petals.' Her teeth were chattering and he made an impatient sound and his fingers tightened on her shoulders.

'What is the significance of a few rose petals?'

'Precisely! They have no significance! They have no place in our relationship, and if you can't see that—' She tugged herself away from him. 'I think you are the most insensitive man I've ever met. I've gone along with this whole white wedding charade although I would have been quite happy just to have kept it small—'

'That was small.'

Fia wasn't listening. 'I've bitten my tongue when the press have gone on about Romeo and Juliet which, by the way, isn't actually the best analogy given that both of them die at the end, I said my vows and I gave you my son. I did all that not because I have feelings for you but because I have feelings for *him* and I can see that already he loves you! I'm prepared to do all that for him and I'm prepared to be nice Mommy when we're all together but when we're alone—that's different.' Suddenly she felt exhausted and she pressed her fingers to her forehead, struggling to contain emotion that felt too big for her body. 'Do you know what? I actually respected you for not once pretending this was anything other than a marriage of convenience, mostly *your* convenience, by the way. But nowhere in our discussions have we ever pretended that what we share is about…about…' her breathing stuttered '…rose petals.'

'*Cristo*, will you stop obsessing about rose petals?'

'I just don't need rose petals in my life, OK?' She was right on the edge and the thought of losing it horrified her. 'It doesn't matter how many rose petals you arrange to have strewn on the floor, our marriage is still a sham. And now I'm going to bed. And if you have any sensitivity you'll sleep on the sofa.'

'I have it on good authority I'm an insensitive bastard, so I guess that clears up any questions over where I'll be sleeping,' he drawled. 'And don't even think about making a run for it because I'll just drag you back. Look at me.'

She looked, and if breathing had seemed hard before it was doubly hard now. As she looked into those dark sexy eyes a part of her she'd buried sprang to life. She was used to controlling her feelings. She'd learned the skill as a child. Only once in her life had she truly let herself go, and it had been with this man. That night in the darkness, the night they'd made Luca, it had been all about touch and taste, soft sounds and a wild, maddening desire. It had unnerved her then. And it unnerved her now.

Because she'd put on the lights, there was no missing the purposeful glitter in his eyes or his obvious arousal. And there was no disguising the instant response of her own body.

It had been brewing, of course, since that night he'd walked into her restaurant, but they'd both held it in check.

Now, there was nothing to snap that frighteningly powerful connection. It wasn't about candles or rose petals, but an elemental force that was stronger than both of them.

He stood absolutely still and the stillness simply raised the tension because she knew now how this was going to end.

They moved at the same time, coming together with a violence that came close to desperation. His hands cupped her face as he kissed her hard. Her hands were on the front of his shirt, ripping. And then her fingers were on his flesh and he groaned against her mouth and grabbed the hem of her dress and yanked it upwards. They stopped kissing just long enough for him to strip it over her head and then his mouth crushed hers again, his hands buried in the thickness of her hair, his powerful body pressed hard against hers as the two of them staggered backwards into the wall. Still they kissed, his tongue hot in her mouth, her hands fumbling frantically with the zip of his trousers. She yanked it down and closed her hand over the thickness of him. He gave a savage groan, his hands bold and sure as he stripped her naked.

Desire was an elemental savage rush of fire. It poured through her veins, heated her skin and weakened her limbs. It blasted all thought from her head until her most basic instincts were screaming. She was naked in front of him but she didn't even care. Her only thought was that now he could get on and do what they both needed him to do.

And he did.

His mouth found the pulse at the base of her throat and her head fell back, the excitement almost excruciating.

'*Cristo*, I want you—' His hand was between her legs and his skilled fingers slid into her, exploring her so intimately that she sobbed his name on each ragged breath.

'Please—'

'Yes—' Without hesitating, he lifted her so that she was forced to wrap her thighs around him and then he was kiss-

ing her again, his mouth feasting on hers as they yielded to
the madness.

Her hands were on his bare shoulders and she felt the rippling power of his body and the strength of him as he posi-
tioned her. Like this she was helpless, but she didn't care. She
was wild with the feelings they unleashed together, utterly
lost in the mind-blowing excitement of his touch. He kissed
her as if this moment would never, ever come again, as if the
crazy collision of their mouths was the breath of life.

They dispensed with foreplay, the wild urgency of it stam-
peding over thoughts of taking it slow. There was no slow.
Just hard, fast and desperate.

His fingers dug into her thighs and she felt the smooth
tip of his penis against her and then he was inside her, hot,
hard and all male. She cried out and arched, taking him deep,
her body yielding to the demands of his. And he demanded
everything, took everything, until her orgasm came screaming down on her and took him with her, soft, sensitive tissue
clamping down on each erotic juddering thrust until the experience became one wild, mad rush of exquisite pleasure.

Fia clung to him, eyes closed, struggling for breath.

He supported her with one arm while he planted his other
hand on the wall behind her in an attempt to steady himself.
Muttering something in Italian, he rested his forehead on his
arm and struggled for breath.

'*Madre de Dio*, that wasn't how I planned it.' He lifted his
head and looked at her, those impossibly sexy eyes darkened
to near black. 'Did I hurt you? You fell against the wall—'

'Don't remember that.' She felt dazed. Weak. 'I'm all in
one piece.'

Except for her heart. Did that count?

But she wasn't going to think about that now. Didn't have
time to think of it because he was lowering her to the floor
and the moment he released her, her knees buckled. He caught

her easily and dragged her against him, but that meant that they were touching again and what began as support quickly moved into seduction. They couldn't help themselves. He buried his mouth in her neck. She slid her arms around his shoulders and pressed closer. Even after that explosive climax he was still hard and she gave a soft gasp as she felt the heaviness of his erection brush against her.

'Santo—'

'You're driving me crazy—' He slid a hand behind her neck and brought his mouth down to hers. Kissed her with raw hunger. Then his other hand slid between her thighs and she stumbled against him.

'The bed—'

'Too far—' His mouth devouring hers, he tipped her off her feet, down onto the floor.

She was dimly aware of her neat pile of rose petals scattering and then he rolled onto his back so that she was the one straddling him. Strands of her hair brushed his chest and she leaned forward to kiss him, unwilling to relinquish that pleasure even for a moment. His hands sank into her hair and he crushed her mouth with his. His tongue played with hers. Teased. Tormented. Her hands grew bold and greedy, tracing his flat, muscled abdomen and moving lower to close around the thickness of his shaft. If he needed recovery time then there was no sign of it and when his hands locked on her hips and he lifted her onto him, she paused for a moment, teasing him and herself by delaying the moment. She felt the smooth probing heat of him against her and he watched her through eyes that glittered dark with barely restrained desire. There was something about that sexy, smouldering look that snapped her control and she moved her hips gracefully and took him deep.

'Cristo—' His jaw tightened and the muscles in his shoulders bulged as he drove himself into her. The power should have been hers but she felt the hard throb of him inside her and the bite of his fingers on her thighs and realised that all the power still lay with him. He controlled her. He controlled every second of the whole erotic experience and this time when her senses exploded she collapsed onto his chest and felt his arms come round her tightly.

They lay for a moment and then he winced.

'*Cristo*, this is uncomfortable. We should move.'

She didn't think she was capable of moving but he slowly eased himself onto one elbow and then frowned down at her.

'You're bleeding!'

She glanced down at her arm. 'It's a rose petal. They're stuck to you, too.'

He shifted her gently away from him and sat up, removing rose petals with an impatient hand. 'Why are rose petals considered romantic?'

'They just are—in certain circumstances.' But not these, of course. The petals had been part of the image he wanted to create.

But how could she be angry with him about that? He'd been thinking about their son. And she didn't want Luca to be the subject of gossip and speculation any more than he did.

He sprang to his feet, lean and lithe, his body at the peak of physical fitness. 'Intrigued though I am at the prospect of picking rose petals from your body all night, I think the shower might be quicker.' Taking her hand, he pulled her to her feet and drew her across the bedroom into the wetroom.

He was completely unselfconscious and relaxed as he prowled into the shower and hit a button on the wall.

Fia was still staring at the muscular perfection of his lean, bronzed back when he turned.

'Keep looking at me like that and we're not going to make it to the bed any time in the next two days,' he warned, hauling her against him and burying his hands in her hair.

Steaming jets of water covered her and she gasped as the water sluiced over her hair, her face, mingling with the heat of his kiss.

Her body was slick and damp against his.

He washed the rose petals away and she did the same with him.

Hands stroked. Mouths fused. Senses flared.

He pressed her back against the tiled wall of the shower out of the direct jets of the water and slowly kissed his way down her body. The skilled flick of his tongue across her nipples made her arch into him and he clasped her writhing hips in his hands and anchored her as he kissed his way down her body. He didn't speak and neither did she. The only sounds were the hiss of the water and her soft gasps as he boldly took every liberty he wanted to take, first with his fingers and then with his mouth. It felt too intimate, made her feel too vulnerable, and she closed her hands in his hair, intending to stop him, but then he used his tongue, teasing and tormenting until she was engulfed by a dark, erotic pleasure that threatened to overwhelm her. She wanted him to stop and carry on at the same time. She ached with wanting him and when she felt the knowing slide of his fingers deep inside her she sobbed his name and felt her body race towards completion.

'Please—' Desperate, she moved her hips and he rose to his feet, lifted her thigh to give himself access and drove himself deep into her quivering, excited body. He was hot, hard and unapologetically male, each skilful thrust so intensely arousing that she cried out and dug her fingers into his warm, naked shoulders.

She felt him throb inside her, felt him drive them both higher and higher with long, sure strokes until pleasure exploded and her muscles clenched around him, the pulsing contractions of her body propelling him to the same peak of sexual excitement.

Sated, Fia dropped her head to his damp, sleek shoulder, stunned by a pleasure she'd never known before. He pushed her wet hair away from her face, stroked her cheek with a gentle hand and muttered something in Italian that she didn't catch.

Just in that moment she felt closer to him than she ever had.

Maybe, she thought numbly, maybe it would be all right. That degree of sexual intimacy wasn't possible without some degree of feeling, was it? Maybe, if the sex was this good, the rest of it would eventually be good too.

The gentle touch of his fingers on her face made her insides melt in an entirely different way. She softened. That frozen part of herself that prevented her from allowing herself to be close to anyone thawed slightly. Feeling incredibly vulnerable, she lifted her head to look at him. She didn't know what to say, but presumably he did because if there was one thing Santo Ferrara was never short of it was smooth words. He used them in business to command and persuade and yes, he used them with women. He would know exactly the right thing to say to capture the moment.

Supporting her with one arm, he leaned across and killed the jet on the shower.

The hiss of water was silenced.

Fia held her breath and waited. She felt as if she was poised on the brink of something life-changing. As if whatever he said now would shift the direction of their relationship.

'Bed,' he said huskily, his lashes darkened and damp with water. 'This time we're going to make it to the bed, *tesoro*.'

This time we're going to make it to the bed.

Her fragile hope and expectations shattered, Fia paled. 'That's all you can say?'

Dark eyebrows rose in lazy appraisal. 'I was thinking of your comfort,' he drawled. 'So far we've had wall sex, floor sex and shower sex. I was thinking bed sex might be a progression but if you want to try something else I'm up for it. You are utterly incredible.'

'You—' Fia was so upset that she couldn't finish her sentence.

Plunged from hope into the depths of despair in the space of minutes, *furious* with herself for being so gullible as to think even for a second that he might have feelings for her, she lost her cool.

'I hate you, do you know that? Right now, this moment, Santo Ferrara, I really, *really* hate you.' But even as she said the words, she knew they weren't true. It was the very fact that they weren't true that made her so upset. She was completely confused about her feelings. She barely knew him and yet she'd allowed him to—

Fia closed her eyes, embarrassed, excited, humiliated, vulnerable—all of it. The thought of how close she'd come to revealing her feelings and making a monumental fool of herself was a dizzying experience.

His eyes were suddenly wary. 'Very intense sex can make women very emotional.'

'It's not the sex that's making me emotional, it's *you*! You're a heartless, cold hearted, arrogant…s…s…'

'—sex god?'

'Slime ball!' Her heart was pounding and her whole body was shaking. She sucked in deep breaths, trying to calm herself down and she might have succeeded had he not given a dismissive shrug of those wide shoulders.

'I was joking,' he said flatly, 'but suddenly you're very serious. The sexual chemistry between us is off the scale and you're obviously unsettled by that. Don't be. Instead, be grateful that at least one part of our relationship is a spectacular success. It gives us something to build on. Sex is important to me and we're clearly not going to have any problems in the bedroom. Or the bathroom. Or the floor—' His lazy humour was the final straw.

'You think not? I've got news for you—we're going to have *big* problems. Sex is just sex! You can't build on it. Especially not the type of Olympic sex you go in for. With you it's all about performance! That's not emotional, it's just physical.'

'"Just physical" has had you panting and begging for the past three hours.' Reaching past her, he grabbed a towel. 'If it was an Olympic performance you were looking for then between us I'd say we produced a gold for the team.'

'Get away from me.' She planted her hands on his bronzed chest and pushed, but he stood with his legs braced, all rock-solid muscle and glorious male nakedness. 'I don't want wall sex, floor sex or bed sex. I don't want any sex! In fact I never want you to touch me again!' She pushed past him and grabbed her own towel from the heated cabinet, noticing that the rose petals had been turned to mush by the water from the shower.

Finally, she thought wildly, something that was truly symbolic of their relationship.

Wrecked, ruined and a total mess.

CHAPTER SEVEN

'MAMMA!'

Unnoticed by all concerned, Santo watched as Luca wriggled his way out of Dani's hold and sprinted across the sand to Fia. She scooped him up and hugged him tightly, her smile illuminating her whole face as she lifted him and swung him round.

'Oh, I *missed* you so much! Have you been good?'

Observing that outpouring of love and affection, Santo ground his teeth. Only an hour earlier he'd sat across from her as she'd eaten her breakfast in frozen silence. Not once had she looked at him. Any attempt on his part to engage her in conversation had resulted in monosyllabic answers.

Unable to understand how she could be upset after a night of spectacular sex, Santo's mood had grown darker with each passing minute.

Clearly the night had fallen seriously short of her romantic expectations, but what had she been expecting? He wasn't such a hypocrite as to pretend that their marriage was a great love match. That was just the story he'd given to the press to lure them away from the truth and ensure that Luca was protected from gossip. Granted the whole rose petal thing hadn't been one of his better ideas, but he'd taken her mind off them fast enough. The sex had been nothing short of mind-blowing. How could utterly mind-blowing sex have such a negative impact? Surely she should have been delighted that they were so compatible? He'd felt energized and optimistic that his hastily arranged marriage might prove to be more satisfactory than he'd ever imagined. He'd been dragged kicking and screaming into that state by his principles and his overwhelming love for his son. If his wife ended up being a hot fantasy in bed then that was a bonus.

His thoughts interrupted by the delicious sound of Luca's giggles, he turned his head to search for the cause of such hilarity and saw the two of them engaged in a tickling match that had both of them rolling on the sand. Luca tickled Fia's neck clumsily and she produced the expected response, squealing with laughter and pretending to wriggle free of him, a reaction that earned her more giggles. Santo watched that tangle of golden limbs with mixed feelings. Whatever he thought of her behaviour, she loved their son, there was no doubt about that. And Luca brought out a side of her he'd never seen before.

She was a different woman. Warm, approachable and open as she shared all of herself with her child.

Their enjoyment of each other was infectious and, without even realising what he was doing, he strode forward to join them, leaning down to join in the tickle. His son chortled and twisted and Santo's hand brushed against the side of Fia's breast.

Instantly the warmth faded from her eyes and she sprang to her feet, her expression shifting from happy to hostile in the blink of an eye. 'I didn't see you arrive. I thought you were on the phone.'

The immediate change in her stoked his temper. Luca had stopped giggling and was staring between them, confused. Acting on instinct, Santo scooped the child into his arms and then leaned forward to deliver a slow, lingering kiss to Fia's soft mouth. Heat shot through him but he banked down his own needs and kept the kiss sweet and not sexual.

When he lifted his head, her cheeks were pink and her eyes every bit as confused as their son's had been.

Something flickered there, something he couldn't quite identify.

'Never,' he said softly, 'send me that angry look in front of our child again.'

'Mamma,' Luca said happily and Santo smiled at him even though he could feel the hot rays of fury burning from Fia.

'Sì, she is your mamma.' *And she is very angry with me.* 'And now it is time we went home.'

That announcement was greeted with the same enthusiasm as an imminent storm warning.

She extracted herself from his hold and took a step backwards. 'I'm not going back to your apartment. I'm going to my restaurant today. And Luca is coming with me.'

'I agree.' Santo put Luca down on the sand. 'You need to get back to your business, and so do I. And Luca clearly has a good relationship with Gina so I'm happy for her to provide additional care while you are working. That arrangement can stay.'

'You're happy—' The outrage in her response died as he covered her lips with his fingers.

'Later,' he purred softly, 'you can thank me for preventing you from saying what you wanted to say in front of our child. Your animosity is unsettling him, *tesoro,* so from now on you will moderate your emotions unless we are alone together. That was your rule, by the way. Console yourself with the knowledge that I'm more than happy to fight you on whatever level you wish, on whichever surface you prefer once he is in bed.' Her mouth was warm against his fingers. He wanted to dip his finger inside, then his tongue, and then—

Her eyes darkened. He saw her throat move as she swallowed. Then her gaze slid to Luca, who was watching both of them closely. 'Your apartment is not a suitable place to raise an active toddler. Don't eat that, *chicco*—' Her tone altering from cool to caring, she reached down and removed the sand from Luca's fist before scooping him up protectively.

'I happen to agree with you, which is why we will not be using the apartment.'

'You said we were going home.'

'I have five homes.' Santo wondered how he could still want her so badly after a night of cataclysmic sex. 'I agree that the apartment isn't suitable for our immediate needs so I'm moving us all into our house on the beach.'

'Your childhood home?'

'The position is perfect and the structure sound. I've been renovating it for the past six months and, with a few overnight adjustments, it's perfect for a family. It has many useful features which I know will appeal to you—' he paused '—including a boathouse.'

He'd expected her to be delighted. She'd spent half her childhood hiding out there, hadn't she? She obviously liked it.

But there was no sign of the gratitude he'd been expecting. Instead her cheeks lost the last of their colour. She seemed about to speak, but then clamped her mouth shut and stared over the bay, struggling for control.

When she finally spoke, she was perfectly composed but she didn't look at him. 'We'll live wherever you want us to live, of course.'

The implication being that she would be going under sufferance.

Having expected gratitude, Santo felt a rush of frustration. He'd grown up in a family that always said what they thought. Dani said what she thought so often he frequently wanted to throttle her. Family gatherings were noisy. Everyone had an opinion and didn't hesitate to express it, usually at high volume and invariably simultaneously. He wasn't used to having to read a female mind. 'I thought you'd be pleased,' he said tightly. 'Living there will allow you to continue to run your business, visit your grandfather and still sleep in my bed.' That comment brought the colour back into her cheeks but still she didn't look at him.

Conscious of Luca, Santo bit back the comment that tasted like acid on his tongue. 'We'll be leaving in twenty minutes. Be ready.'

Confused and unsettled, Fia threw herself back into her work. And if the memory of that tender kiss lingered, she tried to eradicate it by reminding herself that it had been for the benefit of her son. There was no tenderness in what she and Santo shared. There was heat—plenty of heat. It was physical. Nothing more.

Having tried to diminish it in her mind, it was doubly frustrating that she kept thinking about it. Relieved to have something to distract her, she didn't know whether to be pleased or disappointed to discover that the Beach Shack had flourished in her absence.

'That chef Ferrara sent over here was good. He kept the menus the same, Boss.' Ben put a basket of glossy purple aubergines down on the floor. 'These look good. We put *pasta con funghi e melanzane* on the lunch menu. Are you happy with that?'

'Yes.' It felt good to throw herself back into her job and frustrating to discover that work didn't provide the distraction she needed. It didn't matter what she did, her brain kept returning to the moment the two of them had slammed into the wall, so desperate for each other that they'd thought of nothing but the need to slake their mutual lust. For years she'd longed for an experience powerful enough to overshadow the memory of the night she'd got pregnant with Luca, and now she had it tenfold.

'Er…is something wrong?' Ben gave her a nudge. 'Because you don't look as if you're concentrating and that's a dangerous way to be around a naked flame. You might burn yourself.'

It was a perfect description of how she felt after the previous night. As if she'd been scorched by a naked flame. Her entire body was still smouldering from the heat they'd produced together. Fia squeezed her eyes shut for a moment, trying to blot out the vision of smooth, powerful shoulders encasing her as he drove them both hard towards a shattering climax.

'Boss?' Ben's voice intruded on the erotic vision. 'Er… Fia?'

She gulped and snapped herself back to the present. 'What?'

'You look…distracted.'

'I'm fine,' she croaked. 'I just want to get on with the job. Right?'

Ben looked at her oddly. 'Right.'

'I'm just a bit tired. I need to concentrate, that's all.' She stared at the basket of glossy aubergines and for a moment she couldn't remember what she was supposed to do with them. All she could think about was the sensual curve of Santo's mouth as he bent his head to kiss her, of the skill of his fingers and the way he—

Furious with herself, she muttered something rude in Italian under her breath and Ben wisely scooped up the meals she'd plated up and retreated to the safety of the restaurant.

Gina was less sensitive. Being a typical girl, she wanted details. 'I read that article that said the two of you had been secretly in love since you were young—' she sighed '—that's so romantic.'

No, Fia thought grimly, frying aubergine slices until they were brown and softened. It was PR on his part, but to tell the truth would be to subject Luca to gossip so she kept silent and went along with the 'long lost love' scenario that the whole country seemed to find so heart-warming.

Only she knew that the truth was very different.

Santo had married her not because he had feelings for her, but because he wanted their son. The irony didn't escape her. She was the envy of millions of women. She'd married a superrich, supersuccessful, super-sexy man. She'd married a Ferrara.

Her first glimpse of her new home had left her reeling. She wasn't used to living in such luxury. Santo's modifications had made the most of the villa's enviable position right on the bay. Acres of glass gave it a contemporary feel, while making the most of the spectacular views of the bay and the nature reserve that pressed up against their land. No one could fail to fall in love with the house, but Fia's favourite room was the large, airy kitchen. If she'd designed it herself, this was what she would have chosen. It wasn't just a room to cook in, it was a room to live in—the heart of the home, with glass doors opening onto a terrace bordered on one side by a fruit orchard, so that picking a fresh orange for breakfast meant simply stepping outdoors and pulling one from one of the many trees. It was a place for family celebrations, for cosy breakfasts and intimate dinners. It was perfect.

She took Luca back to the villa late that afternoon, gave him tea in the beautiful kitchen and allowed him to explore. His discovery of what was clearly intended to be his bedroom drew gasps of delight and excitement.

'Boat!' He clambered onto his new bed, built in the shape of a boat, complete with curtains as 'sails'.

'Yes, it's a boat.' Watching the delight on his face lifted

her spirits and she had to concede that the room was beautiful. A little boy's dream.

A window seat was padded with overstuffed, beautifully appliquéd cushions, each reflecting the nautical theme. Baskets overflowed with toys and shelves were stacked with more books than the average bookstore.

'Your daddy doesn't understand the word "moderation",' Fia muttered, and with that single thought her mind, which she'd managed to distract for all of five minutes, was right back in the night before. No, he certainly didn't understand moderation. But she'd been as bad, hadn't she? Wall, floor, shower—

'Mamma red—' Luca looked at her and she blinked and snapped herself back to the present.

'Mamma hot.' She took his hand and went next door to what was presumably intended as a guest bedroom. It was a pretty room, with a tiny balcony and a view overlooking the private cove beneath the villa.

'Mamma sleep here,' Luca said happily, crawling onto the bed and bouncing on it.

Fia stared at him for a long moment and then smiled. 'Yes,' she said slowly. 'Mamma sleep here. What an excellent idea.'

There was no earthly reason why they had to share a bed.

While Luca ran back to his bedroom and set about turning the place upside down, she removed her clothes from the master suite and transferred them to the spare bedroom. Then she bathed Luca, who now had his own nautical bathroom to match his nautical bedroom, read to him and then allowed Gina to take over so that she could return to the restaurant for evening service.

A hectic evening improved her mood. She hadn't seen or heard from Santo all day, presumably because he was equally busy with his project to bring the Beach Club up to the standard of the rest of the group. Maybe this could work, she thought. If she played it very, very carefully, she wouldn't even see him. And if she kept very, very busy she might even stop thinking about him every second of the day.

Testing that theory, she plunged herself into her work, creating dishes, talking to her customers, interacting with her staff. By the time she'd finished for the evening, it was late.

She walked across the sand back to the villa, pausing for a moment to look at the boathouse that had provided her with sanctuary on so many occasions when she was younger. It stood at the far end of their private beach, but Fia couldn't bring herself to go there. She couldn't bring herself to confront the memories. She'd known loneliness before but she was fast discovering that there was nothing quite as lonely as a cold, empty marriage. And hers was still in its infancy.

The villa was silent. Gina had clearly retired to bed in the staff apartment, which was situated in an annexe.

Of Santo there was no sign.

Relieved to avoid confrontation, Fia settled herself in the guest bedroom. She took a shower and slid into the large, comfortable bed, her legs aching with tiredness after a day on her feet.

She was already drifting off when the door crashed opened, flooding the room with light.

Santo stood silhouetted in the doorway, his eyes homing in on her like a hunter locating his escaped quarry. 'Just for the record,' he said smoothly, 'hide-and-seek is a game for children, not adults.'

'I wasn't playing hide and seek.'

'Then what the hell are you doing in here? When I come home from work I don't expect to have to search for you.' The combination of his lethal tone and the darkening of those eyes sent nerves fluttering through her.

'You were expecting me to wait up and bring you your slippers?' He was so extreme, she thought. Another man might have waited until morning, or just opened the door and had a civilized conversation. Not Santo. He virtually broke it down.

He prowled into the room, circling the bed like a dangerous animal gauging the best method of attack. 'Did you really think I'd let you sleep here?'

'It is my choice where I sleep,' Fia muttered, holding the silk sheets firmly around her, which was ridiculous, of course, because nothing so flimsy would protect her from a man like Santo.

'You made that choice when you married me. You'll sleep in my bed tonight and every other night.' Moving so swiftly she didn't have time to react, he ripped the sheet from her fist and scooped her into his arms.

'Get off me! Stop behaving like a caveman.' She twisted in his grip but he simply grasped her more tightly, his superior strength making it impossible for her to escape. 'You'll wake Luca!'

'Then stop yelling.'

'He'll see!'

'And what he will see is his father carrying his mother to bed,' Santo growled, as he strode towards the master suite, 'which is a perfectly acceptable scenario. I have no problems with him knowing his parents sleep together.' Kicking the door shut behind him, he walked over to the enormous bed and deposited her in the middle of it.

'For God's sake, Santo—'

'Let me give you some tips about how to make a marriage work. First, withholding sex is not going to improve my mood,' he said coldly. 'Second, I can have you flat on your back within five seconds of making the effort so let's cut the pretence. It's one of the few things we have in common.'

'You think you're so irresistible.' Fia shot upright, intending to run for the door, but he came down over her, flattening her to the bed with his superior weight, pinning her arms above her head with one hand.

She squirmed under the weight of him. 'What are you *doing*?'

'Bed sex,' he purred, his eyes glinting into hers, his mouth hovering just above hers. 'The one thing we haven't actually experienced yet. I'm a sucker for new experiences, aren't you?'

'I don't want bed sex.' She gritted her teeth and averted her face, ignoring the rush of heat in her pelvis. 'I don't want sex at all.'

'You are just making a scene because you are scared about the way I make you feel.'

'You make me feel like filleting you with my sharpest knife.'

He laughed.

Her hands were trapped by his and she tried to twist her head away from him but he caught her chin in his other hand and held her still as he slanted his mouth over hers.

The skilled brush of his lips sent shards of heat shooting through her. She moaned and writhed under him. 'I don't want to sleep in the same bed as you.'

'Don't worry about that. The sleeping part is going to come much, *much* later.' His free hand slid under her nightdress and she struggled to free her hands and defend herself from what was coming but he held her trapped.

Warmth flooded through her as she felt his hand move between her legs. 'Let me go!'

His answer to that was to slide his fingers inside her.

Heat exploded. Unable to free her hands, all she could do was try and move her hips but moving simply intensified the searing excitement caused by his intimate invasion.

'*Cristo*, I have thought about nothing but this all day,' he groaned, capturing her mouth with his and subjecting her to an explicit kiss. 'I haven't been able to concentrate. I've been talking rubbish and I couldn't make any decisions, something that has *never* happened to me before. Obviously you were the same.'

'I wasn't the same—' It was the frantic protest of a drowning person. 'I haven't thought about you once all day—'

'You're a terrible liar.'

She discovered that he could smile and kiss her at the same time and if anything that smile made the whole experience all the more erotic because it changed the way his lips moved on hers.

'I'm not a liar.' Squirming, she tried to get free of him. 'I have been too busy to give you a single thought. And why would I? It's not as if we've shared anything special.'

'No?' He released her hands and slid down the bed, sliding her thighs apart, exposing her to his darkened gaze.

Fia moaned and tried to close her legs but his hands held her firmly and her moan turned to a sob of pleasure as his tongue explored that part of her with lethal accuracy.

Her body on fire, she tried to move her hips to relieve the ache but he held her captive while his tongue subjected her to erotic torture.

Pleasure came in a dark, rushing force and she felt it build inside her to dangerous levels.

'You're so hot I can't even think when I'm with you—' His voice raw, Santo eased himself over her shifting, thoroughly excited body and thrust himself deep.

And then he stilled. He stayed like that, buried deep inside her, jaw clenched at the control needed not to move.

Fia gave a sob. 'What are you doing? Please—' Her hands scraped down his back as she urged him to move but he stayed still, his control stretched to the limit as he waited for her to come back from the edge.

'I don't want you to come yet,' he said tightly, his mouth brushing over hers in an explicit kiss. 'I want you desperate.'

She could feel the hard throb of him inside her, his erection silken smooth and powerful as the rest of him. Her breathing grew shallow. She gave a faint whimper. But still he didn't move. And she knew he was struggling too. The muscles of his shoulders were pumped up and hard, his own breathing ragged as he held on to control.

'Santo—' she raked her nails down that luscious golden skin, over those powerful muscles '—please.' Her body was burning up, nothing mattered, nothing, except this. 'Please—'

His response to her plea was to slide his hand beneath her bottom and bury himself deeper still. 'Did you think of me today?'

She barely managed to speak. 'Yes. All the time.'

'And did you find it hard to concentrate?' His voice was husky and thickened with desire and she gave a desperate moan.

'*Yes*. Santo, please—'

He held her there, just short of that place she wanted to go, until she would have done anything for the release she craved.

Just when she thought she couldn't take it any longer, he moved, slowly at first, controlling the rhythm with ruthless precision, knowing exactly how to give her maximum pleasure.

At his urging, Fia wrapped her legs around his hips, arched against him and lost herself in the madness of it. And he lost himself too. Somewhere in the swirling pleasure she was aware that control had left him and instinct had taken over.

Her climax exploded, ripping through her whole body like a storm and she heard him utter a throaty groan before the spasms of her body drew him over the same edge.

Fia had never known pleasure like it. The pulsing heat of

him accelerated her own excitement and she sobbed his name as she clung to him and rode out that storm.

Afterwards, he rolled onto his back, taking her with him. His eyes were closed. 'I like bed sex.'

Fia felt dazed and stupid. 'You made me beg.'

'I *made* you? How?' His eyes stayed closed. 'Did I threaten you?'

She covered her eyes with her hand. 'You know what I mean.'

'You mean I gave you unimaginable pleasure.' He tugged her hand away from her face, a wicked smile curving his sensuous mouth. 'You're welcome, *tesoro*.'

He was so sure of himself, so arrogantly confident in everything he did that it made her feel a thousand times worse. 'I don't want you to do that again,' she blurted out, her face hot. 'Sex is one thing, but when you do *that*—'

'Do what?'

His eyes laughed into hers and she would have looked away but he caught her chin in his fingers so all she could do was glare at him.

'You know what.'

'Oral sex?'

She burned from head to foot. 'I don't want you to do it.'

'Why? Because it makes you feel vulnerable? Good.' His voice was a soft purr. 'When you're in my bed, I want you vulnerable. And it's OK to tell me what you like, although if you're really uncomfortable with that, that's fine too because I don't need your help to know when I'm turning you on.'

'Because you're such an expert, of course.'

'You drew blood with your nails, *angelo mia*,' he said drily. 'That was a bit of a clue. And what is wrong with being an expert? You would prefer a man who fumbles?'

'I cannot believe we're having this conversation,' she mumbled and he laughed, and rolled her under him again.

'You are full of contradictions. Bold one moment and shy the next. Two women in one body.' His tone suggestive, he slid his hand lower. 'What more can a man ask for?'

Worn out by Santo's demands and the violence of her own response, she slept late and then woke and panicked about Luca.

She sprang out of bed and sprinted along to his bedroom, only to be told by a besotted Gina that Santo had got his son dressed and given him breakfast before leaving for work.

'He's the perfect man,' Gina said dreamily, 'and you are so lucky.'

Fia ground her teeth. She didn't feel lucky. She felt stupid and brainless. He only had to touch her and she turned into a quivering fool. True, he'd pinned her down so at the beginning she hadn't had much choice, but by the end he wasn't pinning her and had she slapped him? Had she told him to take his arrogant self and sleep somewhere else? No. She'd begged.

Returning to the bedroom, Fia sank back onto the tangled sheets and covered her face with her hands, utterly humiliated by the memory.

She'd begged. She'd fed his already overfed ego. She'd made him feel like a sex god.

Her phone rang. She picked it up. 'Yes?'

His dark drawl came down the phone. 'How are you feeling?'

Stupid? 'Fine, thanks.'

'You were wiped. I let you sleep in.'

Because he'd turned her into a mindless wreck. 'Thanks.' But she couldn't bring herself to hang up. Holding the phone tightly, she held her breath, hoping that he'd suggest taking her to lunch or something. A picnic on the beach? Anything that might indicate he was interested in developing a side of their relationship that wasn't about sex.

'Get some rest today. I will see you tonight.' That statement was clearly supposed to fill her with warmth and anticipation. Instead it filled her with despair.

He didn't have any feelings for her and yet she couldn't wait for him to come home.

Utterly miserable, she poured all her love and affection into her son. At least that relationship was good and it was some consolation to observe Luca's delight at the presence of his father. It was impossible to feel this had been a bad decision when she saw the two of them together.

And so a new routine started. A naturally early riser, Santo took to sharing breakfast with Luca, allowing Fia an extra hour in bed. And she needed it because whatever problems they might have, they had none in the bedroom. And she schooled herself to switch off that part of herself that craved emotional warmth. And if keeping the barrier up between them made it hard to interact with him on any other level, then that was made easier by the fact she hardly saw him during the day. He'd taken personal charge of the redevelopment of the hotel and spent each and every day there, overseeing everything. She cooked Luca an early lunch and ate with him before she started the madness of lunchtime service. Then she handed him over to Gina while she concentrated on the busiest time of her day. Her own business was flourishing. The chef who had helped out when her grandfather had been in hospital continued to help and she found it stimulating to work with someone who'd had formal training.

It was a Monday afternoon, two weeks after they'd moved into their new home, when Fia finally felt able to take a full afternoon off. Having finished lunchtime service and experimented with two new dishes, she left her team to finish the preparation for the evening and took Luca back to the villa. Confident that Santo would be fully occupied at work as he always was, she changed into a bikini and took Luca into the beautiful pool that she only ever used when Santo was safely out of the way.

Luca clung to her as she slid into the water. Kicking his legs in the water, he looked beyond her. 'Papà.'

'Papà's working,' Fia said happily, holding him firmly round the waist.

'Not any more he isn't.' Santo's cool drawl came from the edge of the pool and she spun round, horrified to find him standing there with his phone in his hand. From his polished handmade shoes to his beautifully cut suit, everything about him shrieked of spectacular success. But it wasn't the intimidating businessman that made her shiver, it was the raw sex appeal that lurked under the veneer of smooth sophistication. He dropped his phone onto the nearest sun lounger. 'That looks like a good thing to do on a hot afternoon. I'll join you.'

'Join us?' Self-conscious in her bikini, Fia held Luca in front of her. 'You're in a suit.'

A sardonic smile touched his mouth as he shrugged off his jacket and removed his tie with a few flicks of his fingers. 'Not for much longer.'

She had no intention of arguing with him. She didn't want him to stay around long enough to argue. What was he doing here? She never saw him in the middle of the day. Never. 'D-don't you need to go back to work?'

'I'm the boss.' The shirt followed the jacket. 'I decide when I work. And I always spend a few hours with Luca every afternoon before his nap. This is our time together.'

This was news to Fia. '*Every* afternoon?'

'Of course. Why are you surprised? I have no intention of being an absent father.'

She had no idea that he'd been spending every afternoon with their son. 'How do you find time for that? You have a punishing workload.'

'And a competent workforce who can manage while I play with my son for an hour.'

'You didn't tell me.'

'I have missed out on almost two and a half years of my son's life,' he said quietly. 'Is it wrong to want to catch up and spend quality time with my family?'

'No.' Guilt stabbed her. 'It's nice for Luca. Obviously I'll leave you together.' Trying not to mind that her afternoon with her son had been hijacked, she started to move towards the steps but Santo frowned.

'Where are you going?'

'You said you wanted to spend quality time with your family.'

'Which includes you.' His eyes lingered on her pink cheeks. 'Why would you think otherwise? You are too sensitive. I was stating a fact, *not* trying to make you feel guilty.'

'It will be nice for Luca to spend time with you.' It annoyed her that she felt so weak whenever he was near. Her legs trembled and her stomach fluttered with an excitement that never quite went away when he was around. 'But honestly the two of you should focus on each other and I'll just—'

'—you'll just stay right there or I'll throw you back into the pool myself.' Naked now apart from a pair of boxer shorts, he strolled over to the pool house and emerged moments later wearing a pair of swim shorts.

Fia's mouth dried.

His dark gaze clashed with hers for a moment and he gave a faint smile.

'We can do this,' he drawled, averting his eyes from her body as he walked to the edge of the pool. 'We can occupy the same space and not strip each other naked.'

'Nekkid—' Luca said happily, mimicking his father, and Fia winced.

'You have to be careful what you say. He copies everything.

Usually the words you don't want him to copy.' Holding Luca close, she backed into the shallow end, waiting for Santo to execute a flashy dive. She'd once spent an entire day watching while he and his brother had dived off the rocks further up the bay. She knew he had all the skills necessary to impress her so it came as a surprise when instead he slid into the water. And her surprise must have shown because he lifted an eyebrow in her direction. 'Given that children invariably detect tension in an adult, it might be advisable not to look at me as if a shark has just arrived in the pool.'

'I thought you were going to dive. I didn't want you to splash him.'

'This is water, *tesoro*. The idea is to get wet.'

'I don't want him to be scared and put off for ever.'

'Is that what happened to you? I've noticed that you never go in the sea.'

'My brother used to pull me under and hold me there.'

Something flickered in his eyes. Sympathy? Anger?

She waited for him to say something derogatory about her family but instead he ducked under the water and emerged right in front of her. 'Swimming is all about confidence. We need to build up your confidence. And in the meantime I will teach him that the water is fun. My brother and I spent hours swimming when we were young.' Clearing the water from his eyes, he peeled Luca away from her and switched to Italian, talking constantly to his son as he bounced him in the water, making a point of splashing him and getting the child's face wet. And Luca loved every second, including the moment his father dunked him under the water. He came up gasping and then splashed his father back, enjoying himself so much that Fia felt an agonizing pang of guilt.

She'd almost deprived him of this. She'd made a horrible, terrible misjudgement. 'I'm sorry,' she blurted out and Santo stilled, his hands firm on his son.

'Sorry for what?'

'I...I was wrong not to tell you. I thought I was doing the right thing. I thought I was protecting him because I didn't want him to have the sort of childhood I had. But now I can see—' she broke off '—you're really good with him. 'He loves being with you.'

'And that should be a cause for celebration, no? So why are you looking so gloomy?'

'Because you're never going to forgive me,' she said wearily. 'It's always going to be between us.'

He stared at her for a long moment and his mouth tightened. 'You are talking like a Baracchi, not a Ferrara. It is the Baracchi way to bear grudges and stew in a simmering broth of past discontentment. But you are now a Ferrara so you will solve this the Ferrara way and that means moving on. The past is only of relevance if we learn from it. If not, then it has no relevance in our future.'

But what *was* their future?

Could they really sustain a family based on what they had? She loved Luca. He loved Luca. They were only spending time together now because she'd inadvertently encroached on the time he spent with his son.

But even knowing that didn't change the fact that right now they felt like a family and the emotion hit her in the chest with brutal force. This was what she'd wanted as a child, and she wanted it no less now that she was an adult.

Transferring Luca to his shoulders, Santo watched her steadily. 'It's only fair to warn you that if you leave this pool now I'll just haul you back.'

'How did you know I was going to do that?'

'Because I can read the signals. You always have one eye on an escape route.'

'We both know this is your time with Luca.' She turned scarlet, wishing she'd never started this conversation. 'You never spend time with me during the day. You get up early to be with Luca, you spend time at work and then more time with him, and then you come to bed and have—' she glanced at Luca and moderated her language '—we sleep together. That's our relationship. I'm someone you spend time with in the dark.'

There was a long, tense silence.

Santo drew in a long breath. 'Firstly, I get up early and spend time with Luca because he is an early riser and I am trying to give you more rest because you work extremely hard and I respect that. Secondly, I spend time at work because I am in the middle of an important project, *not* because I am avoiding you and as you are also working hard I didn't see that as a problem. Thirdly, I come to bed and have sex with you because that is the only time of day our paths seem to cross. I don't see you as someone to have sex with in the dark, but as my wife. And if daylight sex is what it's going to take to prove to you that I'm serious about this relationship, then I have no problem with that.'

'Sex,' Luca said happily, tugging his father's hair, and Santo gave a murmur of contrition and threw her a look of exasperated apology.

'*Mi dispiace*—I'm sorry—'

'My fault. I started the conversation. He's like a sponge. Just don't say it again. With any luck he'll forget.'

What might have happened next she didn't know because Luca reached out his arms to her and almost toppled into the pool. Santo caught him deftly and scooped the child off his shoulders. 'Your mamma is planning to run and you are in charge of stopping her,' he drawled, handing the child to Fia. But, instead of releasing his father, Luca kept one arm around his shoulders and reached out the other to Fia.

Accepting the hug meant moving closer to Santo. His bare

leg brushed against hers. His eyes flicked to hers. Wry amusement danced there.

Her stomach flipped. 'He needs toys,' she blurted out. 'Toys for the pool.'

'Of course he does.' His eyes were still on hers, mocking her because he knew she was trying to change the subject. 'We will go shopping this afternoon.'

'He still has a sleep in the afternoon.'

As if to prove that statement, Luca, exhausted after such an energetic afternoon, flopped his head onto his father's bare bronzed shoulder and closed his eyes.

'I'll put him in his bed.' Somehow Santo managed to ease himself from the pool without waking the sleeping child.

Fia watched him cross the terrace and then left the pool herself and took a quick shower in the pool house.

She was just wrapped in a towel when Santo appeared behind her.

'He didn't even stir. I envy his ability to fall asleep so easily.'

He looked so impossibly gorgeous that Fia simply stared. 'Right. Well, I'll just go and—'

'You're not going anywhere.' His mouth came down on hers and he gave the towel a sharp tug.

She made an abortive grab for it as it slid to the floor. 'What are you doing?'

'Proving to you that our relationship isn't just about nighttime sex.' His voice was a sensual purr and his hands slid down the length of her spine and pressed her against him. 'You're about to experience daytime sex.'

'Santo—'

'Wall sex, floor sex—' he kissed her neck '—shower sex, bed sex—' his mouth trailed lower '—how do you feel about pool sex?'

'Absolutely not—' she moaned as his fingers found that

most sensitive part of her. 'I wouldn't be able to look the staff in the eye ever again.'

'So I'll fire them and then you won't have to.' A wicked glint in his eyes, he captured her mouth with his. 'Turn around.'

'What?'

'I have a better idea than pool sex. Sun lounger sex. Bend over.' He turned her and Fia gave a soft gasp as he bent her forward. Tipped off balance, she put her hands flat on the sun lounger, a movement that exposed her bare bottom. Feeling horribly vulnerable, she tried to stand but he pressed down on her spine and kept her there.

'I'm not going to hurt you,' he said softly. 'Just relax and trust me.'

'Santo…we can't…' she moaned, but his fingers were already stroking her there, teasing and exploring while showing a total disregard for her modesty. And within seconds she forgot about modesty. Just when she thought she'd go crazy, she felt the heat of his shaft against her and his strong hands grasped her hips and held her still as he slid deep. His throaty groan mingled with her soft gasp.

'*Cristo*, you feel incredible—'

Fia couldn't respond. Her shaking thighs were locked against the hardness of his, and he was all heat and power, each driving thrust sending her closer and closer to her own climax. It came in a rush of heat that engulfed them both simultaneously and she would have collapsed if he hadn't been holding her. With a rough laugh, he eased out of her, scooped up her quivering body and carried her into the shower. 'Great idea of yours,' he said huskily, lowering her to her feet and turning on the jet of water. 'Daytime sex. Yet another reason to leave my desk. At this rate I will not win my bet.'

'Bet?' Still dazed, she pushed her hair out of her face as the water cascaded over both of them. 'What bet?'

'That I can make the Ferrara Beach Club the most successful hotel in our group.' He squeezed shampoo into his palm
and gently massaged her hair. 'I would never admit this to
him, but my brother is a very hard act to follow. When he took
a back seat in the company a year ago everyone assumed I
would just hold the reins and not change anything, but care-
taking someone else's baby doesn't interest me. I have more
respect and admiration for my brother than any man alive,
but I want to prove that I, too, have something to add to this
company.'

Lulled by the gentle stroke of his fingers, Fia closed her
eyes. 'You're so competitive.'

'*Si*, it is partly that, but not entirely.' His voice soft, he
turned off the shower and reached for a towel. 'When our
father died it was Cristiano who took over. I was in my last
year of school. He was studying in the States. He gave up
everything, came home and took over as head of the family.
My father's business was always small, but Cristiano took it
and turned it into a global player. Because of him, Dani and
I stayed in school and finished our education. He sacrificed
a great deal for us. I want to do well, not because I am competitive, although of course I am, but because I love him and
want to make him proud.'

He said it so easily, Fia thought numbly, standing still as
he towelled the ends of her hair dry. No embarrassment. No
awkwardness or fear that such an admission might somehow
diminish his masculinity. Just a simple declaration of absolute family loyalty and commitment, as if that was normal.
And for him it was, of course. She'd seen that commitment
in all the Ferraras, but from a distance, not close up. They
supported each other. Their lives were woven together like
a piece of cloth, stronger as a whole than it would have been
as individual strands.

Only now was she understanding what a fundamentally

bad decision she'd made when she'd kept the news of her pregnancy from him. He was right, she thought miserably, that she'd thought like a Baracchi. She'd assumed that the rift between them was a scar that would never heal because that was the way her family had always dealt with things. No slight was forgiven.

It shamed her to remember how many times the Ferraras had made overtures towards her family. Always, her grandfather had taken it as an affront.

'I didn't know that about you.' She tipped her head back and rinsed her hair. 'I mean, I knew you were close to your brother, of course. But I didn't know that he'd made those sacrifices. I knew he'd built the company into something amazing but I thought that was because he just had a driven alpha personality.'

'That too.' There was humour in his eyes as he turned off the jet of water and draped a towel around her shoulders. 'But we are fortunate in that. It was Cristiano who grew the business and supported us all at a time when my family was devastated by the loss of my father. He held it all together. And now I am happy to be able to take over that role so that he can spend more time with his family.'

She remembered Cristiano at the wedding. Tall, dark and intimidating. 'He doesn't like me. He doesn't approve of the fact you married me.'

Santo hesitated. 'He doesn't approve of the fact you didn't tell me you were pregnant, but that is in the past now. He is protective of me, just as I am protective of him. I gave Laurel a hard time when they separated, mostly because I didn't understand what was going on. Truthfully a man never knows what is going on in another's marriage.'

She felt a twinge of envy. 'You're so close to your brother and sister.'

'Of course. We are a family.' He said it as a simple state-ment of fact. As if it couldn't possibly be in doubt.

'I like it when we talk,' she said impulsively. 'We've never really talked about normal things. Even that night—' She broke off and he frowned.

'What?'

'We didn't talk. We just…did crazy stuff and then the call came and—'

'—and your brother was dead.'

They'd never really talked about that either, had they?

'He stole your car. You could have told everyone that, but you didn't. I've never thanked you properly for not going pub-lic with that.'

'How would that have helped? I had no desire to make a bad situation worse.'

'It might have made you look better. Nonno told people you'd lent it to him. And to be honest I don't know why any-one believed that, given the history between our families—' She shrugged. 'He made you look like the reckless one and I feel really bad about that.'

'Don't. He did not want to admit that his grandson stole the car,' Santo said quietly. 'He was grief-stricken. He didn't want to see bad, only good, and I understood that.'

'People believed—'

'The people who mattered to me knew the truth. The opin-ion of the world in general is of no interest to me.'

And he'd been surrounded by supporters, protected by that web of family that was fundamental to who he was. Whereas she… 'It was the worst time of my life. Worse even than the day my mother left and the day my father died. I thought Nonno was going to die,' she confessed, drawing away from him and tightening the towel around her. 'For weeks he just cried. Then he blamed himself and the guilt was almost worse than the grief. And then when he couldn't bear the guilt any longer he blamed the Ferraras. He cursed your name with every breath he took. And that carried on for months after Roberto died. And then I discovered I was pregnant.'

Santo knotted a towel around his hips, dark brows locked together, eyes fixed on her face. 'It must have been very frightening. You must have felt so alone.'

'I *was* alone. I had no one to talk it through with. I didn't know what to do. Somehow, you'd become the focus of his blame. He blamed you for lending Roberto a car he couldn't handle. I told him Roberto took the keys, but he just didn't want to listen. He didn't want to believe it. Then he blamed you for driving a flashy car that was nothing but temptation for a young man like Roberto. It was frighteningly illogical. He was the only person I had left in the world and I was watching him fall apart in front of me. First his son, my father, and then his grandson.'

'It must have been an unbearable loss,' Santo breathed. 'I remember when we lost my father, it felt as if someone had ripped a hole in our family. But we had each other and you had no one.'

'After that night, I waited for you to contact me,' she confessed. 'I used to lie awake, dreaming that you'd come—'

He swore softly in Italian and gathered her against him. 'And I assumed that I was the last person you would want to see. We talked about it, Cristiano and I, and we decided that it would be more respectful to keep a distance.'

'But did you tell Cristiano about us?'

He was silent, his chin resting on her head. 'No,' he said quietly. 'I didn't tell him that part.'

'And yet you are close and tell him everything.'

'That night was—' He broke off and she nodded.

'Yes, it was. And that is why I couldn't tell you I was pregnant. If you and I had ever spoken—if we'd had any sort of friendship or relationship—maybe I would have contacted you, but I honestly wouldn't have known what to say. "Hey, do you remember that night when we had sex?"' She bit her lip and drew away slightly so that she could look at him. 'First I was so swamped in my grandfather's grief and my own I didn't even know I was pregnant, and once I found out… I honestly didn't know what to do. My grandfather wouldn't have your name spoken in the house. How was I to tell him you were the father of my child? I didn't have anyone to talk to.'

Releasing her, Santo dragged his hand over the back of his neck. 'Now I am the one feeling guilty,' he admitted in a raw tone. 'When I walked into your kitchen that day and saw Luca, I just exploded. I thought "mine", and that was all I thought. I gave no thought to your reasoning.'

'I don't blame you for that. I'm just saying that it isn't as simple as just not telling you. It was much, much more complicated than that.'

He reached out a hand and drew her towards him. 'I rushed you into this marriage—'

'"Propelled" would be a better word.' Fia leaned her forehead against his bare chest. 'It was less shotgun than supersonic. But I could have said no.'

'I wasn't prepared to hear no.' His hands stroked her shoulders and closed over her arms. 'I pushed you into it.'

'I still could have said no. I have a brain and a mouth. I didn't agree to marry you because you bullied me.'

'Then why did you?' His voice was rough. 'You were saying no and then all of a sudden you said yes. What changed your mind that day?'

Her heart was pounding. 'One of the things you said to me was that I didn't have a clue what a family should be like.'

'I had no right to say that.'

Fia gave a sad smile. 'You had every right to say that. You cared about your son. You saw my family and didn't want that for him. But what you didn't know was that I'd been studying your family and envying your family all my life. When Luca was born I did my best to create what *you* had, not what *I* had. I wanted him to have that same network of people who loved him. I found Ben and Gina who are both warm, expressive, good people. I banned my grandfather from saying bad things. I tried to give Luca that web of support that you Ferraras take for granted.'

'I see that now. And I also see that one of the reasons Luca is so friendly and trusting is because he has been surrounded by love since he was born. And to do that in such difficult circumstances…I do think that what you achieved was nothing short of amazing.' He cupped her face in his hands and kissed her gently. 'That still doesn't explain why you suddenly agreed to marry me.'

'You kissed him,' Fia said simply. 'That first morning in your apartment when you were giving him breakfast. I walked in, sure that marriage would be the wrong thing…and you were kissing Luca. And I realised that nothing I'd created could match that. I realised that what I'd been working to reproduce was right in front of me. You were his real family. And he has a right to that, and to his cousins, aunts and uncles.'

'And do you regret that decision?'

'No. Luca loves being with you. It's only been a few weeks but his life has changed so much for the better.'

'You are an incredible mother and Luca is lucky. And you? What about your life?' His tone was unsteady. 'How is this marriage working for you? How do you feel?'

How did she feel?

She felt slightly light-headed as she always did when she was with him. She felt warm inside at his unexpected compliment. She felt—

She felt glad that she was married to him. And not just because of Luca.

Seriously unsettled, she pulled away. 'I feel fine.'

'Fine? What does "fine" mean? That word tells me nothing of how you really feel.'

She loved him. Somehow, over the past few weeks, she'd fallen in love.

The sudden realisation was like a sharp blade twisting in her heart and for a moment she couldn't breathe. Oh, how stupid. *What a crazy, dangerous, reckless thing to do.*

His mouth tightened. 'The fact that you don't know how to answer tells me a lot. You are a very unselfish person. You married me because you thought it was the right thing for our son. And you should know that I am determined to make this marriage work. I truly want you to be happy. From now on we will do more together. Not just with Luca, but as a couple. I will make space in my day and so will you.'

He had misinterpreted her silence and she was grateful for that because the last thing she wanted was for him to know how she felt.

The downside was that now he felt he had to work extra hard to please her.

She was going on his 'to-do' list.

Spending time with her wasn't a pleasure, but a responsibility.

Her pride shattered, Fia pulled away. 'You're very busy—' she pulled her damp hair over one shoulder '—and I'm very busy. Let's just carry on as we were. Honestly, that suits me.'

'Well, that doesn't suit me. If this marriage is to work it has to be about us as well as Luca.'

He wanted the marriage to work for Luca's sake. He was spending time with her for Luca's sake.

Humiliation piled on humiliation.

Switching off her own emotions, Fia tried to work out how she'd react if she weren't in love with him.

What would she say if she'd entered this marriage purely for the good of her son?

Spending time with Santo wouldn't bother her, would it? In fact it would probably seem like a good idea to get to know each other better. It made sense.

'Sure,' she croaked. 'If you want to spend time together, that sounds great.'

CHAPTER EIGHT

THE following morning she was woken by a shaft of bright sunlight as Santo opened the blinds.

'*Buongiorno.*' Sickeningly alert and energetic, he ripped the covers from her and handed her a robe.

Still half asleep, Fia gave a whimper of protest and stuck her head under the pillow. 'What time is it?'

'Time to get up,' he said smugly. 'You mentioned that you never see me in daylight so we are rectifying that, *dormigliona.*'

'Are you calling me a sleepy-head? Because, if so, you are to blame. You shouldn't—'

'I shouldn't what? Make love to my wife for half the night?' He removed the pillow and scooped her into a sitting position. 'I can't believe how bad you are in the morning. How did you manage when you were the one who got up for Luca in the morning?'

'I was cranky, irritable and generally horrid,' she mumbled and he gave a wicked smile as he smoothed her tangled hair back from her face.

'Fortunately you weren't any of those things last night.'

Fia turned scarlet. 'Why are you here?'

'Normally I will do the early shift, and that is another benefit to our marriage. We can share the load. But today we are going to have a family breakfast.'

He was listing benefits, she thought numbly, as if he had to constantly remind himself of all the reasons this marriage was a good idea. She'd never thought of herself as romantic, but she was starting to realise she was nowhere near as practical as she would have liked to be. She would have given a lot for him to have just said he was glad he married her because he liked being with her.

He glanced at his watch. 'Breakfast first, and then I have one short meeting I can't get out of. After that we are going shopping.' Showered, shaved and dressed in a suit, he looked so indecently sexy that Fia immediately wanted to grab him and haul him back into the bed.

'I have lunchtime service.'

'Not today. I've rearranged your schedule. *Don't* be angry with me.' Anticipating her response, he dived in first. 'Normally I wouldn't dream of interfering with your business, but today is about us. I really want to spend time with you.'

No, he didn't want to. He thought he ought to. Not because he found her company addictive, but because he wanted to invest time in his marriage for Luca's sake.

That was item number four on his agenda. Spend quality daylight time with Fia.

Resigned to going along with that strategy, Fia forced herself out of bed. 'I need to take a shower.'

'No!' He moved away from her so fast he almost stumbled.

Fia stared at him in confusion. 'I can't take a shower?'

'Yes, *you* can take a shower,' he hissed through gritted teeth, 'but I'm not going to take one with you.' He retreated to the doorway. 'I promised myself that today is going to be spent out of the bedroom.'

'Right.'

'Meet us downstairs when you're dressed.' He fumbled

behind him for the door handle. 'I'll make you coffee. You take it white. I know that about you.'

'Thank you.' She probably should have been touched that he was trying so hard but instead it just depressed her to think he had to make such an effort. A relationship should be a natural thing, shouldn't it?

By the time she joined them on the terrace, Santo had removed his jacket and was engaged in conversation with his son. Warmth spread through her as it always did when she saw the two of them together.

'Mamma!' Luca's face brightened and Santo rose to his feet and pulled out her chair.

'Mamma is joining us for breakfast so we must both be on our best behaviour.'

Fia kissed Luca and lifted her eyebrows as she saw the traditional Sicilian breakfast of *brioche* and *granita*. 'You made this?'

'Not exactly.' A rueful smile crossed Santo's handsome face as he sat back down. 'I ordered breakfast from the Beach Club. I want your opinion. We're losing business to you. You're going to tell me why. Is it the food? Is it the surroundings? I want to know what we're doing wrong.'

Fia sat down. 'I don't know anything about running a hotel so I'll be no help to you at all.'

'But you know a great deal about food.' He passed her a plate. 'And given that my customers would rather eat yours than mine, I assume you're in a position to have an opinion on that. I brought the menus down for you to look at.'

Fia took the menus from him and scanned them, wondering how honest she was supposed to be. 'Your menu is too broad.'

'*Scusi?*' Santo's eyes narrowed. 'You are suggesting we don't offer a choice? But choice is good. It means we can cater to a wide range of tastes.'

'You asked for my opinion. If you don't want it, don't ask.'

He breathed deeply. '*Mi dispiace*. Carry on. You were saying—?'

'It's good to have a choice, but you don't want to offer so many things that people don't know what cuisine you're serving. This is Sicily. Serve Sicilian food and be proud of it. In the Beach Shack we rely totally on local seasonal produce. If it's not in season, we don't cook it. We buy our fish fresh from the boat in the morning so we don't even choose the evening menu until we've seen what is fresh.' She reached across and took an orange from the bowl on the table. The skin was dappled dark red and purple and she picked up her knife and peeled it deftly, exposing the scarlet flesh. 'It is the temperature variation that makes these blood oranges the best in the world. That and the soil, which is perfect for growth. Our customers can see them growing next to the restaurant. We pick them fresh and juice them and I guarantee that when our guests return home they will want to buy blood oranges, but they won't be able to find anything that tastes like this.'

'So you're saying fresh and local. I understand that. But we are catering for larger numbers than you, so that degree of flexibility isn't always possible.'

'It should be. And what I don't grow, I outsource from local producers. I'll talk to my suppliers. See if they can cope with a larger order.'

Santo poured coffee. 'I want you to look over the menu properly and make suggestions.'

'Isn't that going to hurt the feelings of your head chef?' Fia handed Luca a segment to suck.

'My concern is not the feelings of my head chef but the success of the business which, ultimately, is in everyone's best interests. At the moment most of our guests prefer to eat with you.' He handed her coffee. 'Congratulations. You've just been appointed as Executive Head Chef, overseeing both the Beach Shack and the Beach Club.'

Fia gave a disbelieving laugh. 'You're a very surprising person, do you know that? All macho one minute and surprisingly forward-thinking the next. When you first mentioned marriage I assumed you were going to insist I gave up work and stayed at home.'

'Do you want to stay at home?'

Fia picked up a napkin and wiped the sticky juice from Luca's fingers. 'I love being with him, but I enjoy my work, too. I like the flexibility of the life I have and I'm proud of the fact I can support my son without financial help from anyone. But I wouldn't want to work if it meant I couldn't see him. This is a perfect compromise and I admit it's nice to have your chef helping out. I like him.'

'Now you are working with me, which means you can take off as little or as much time as you like. But not until you've told me how to improve the restaurants. Try the food.'

Fia tore a piece of the warm, buttery *brioche*, automatically studying the texture. 'I thought you'd be very traditional about a woman's role.'

'I think we have already established that we don't know enough about each other,' he said softly, 'but that is slowly changing. Now tell me what you think of the *brioche*.'

'It's good. A little greasy, perhaps.' She nibbled the corner, testing the flavour, and felt a glow of satisfaction because she knew hers was infinitely superior. And it should be. She'd worked herself to the ground perfecting the recipe. She kneaded and baked and tested until she was satisfied that it couldn't get any better. 'As we're married and I have a vested interest in your success, I'll share my secret recipe with your chef.'

Aware that he was watching her, she picked up her spoon and tasted the *granita* from the tall glass. 'Elegant presentation.' She made a mental note to review the way she served hers in the restaurant. 'It's difficult to make the perfect *granita*.'

'It's just water, sugar and, in this case, coffee.'

'The Arabs first introduced it when they flavoured snow from Mount Etna with sugar syrup and jasmine water.' She took another spoonful. 'But if it isn't frozen to the right consistency then it tastes all wrong.'

'And does this taste wrong?'

'It's not bad—' This time she scooped *granita* up with the *brioche* and tasted both together. 'I've had worse.'

He winced. 'That is not the accolade I was hoping for. So when and where did you learn to cook?'

She put the spoon down slowly. 'I taught myself. When my mother left, I was surrounded by men who expected me to cook for them. Fortunately I loved it. I made lots of mistakes and plenty of food ended up in the bin, but after a while I started to get a lot of things right and when they turned out right I wrote them down. Why are you looking at me like that?'

'You had *no* formal training?'

'Of course not. When would I have had formal training?' She poured milk into Luca's cup. 'I would have loved to go to college, to travel and spend some time with other chefs, but that was never an option.'

He gave an incredulous laugh. 'The chef who made that *brioche* trained at two of the best restaurants in Italy.'

'He probably hasn't made as many bad batches of brioche as I have. It's about experimenting. And it isn't all about training. Sometimes it's about the quality of the raw ingredients and giving the customer what they want.'

'And what do you think my customers want?'

'I only know about my own.'

'Given that a high percentage of your customers come

from my hotel, they're one and the same thing,' he drawled. 'I'm surprised your grandfather let you run the restaurant. Cooking for him is one thing, but running a business is another. He is very traditional.'

She wished he'd remove his sunglasses. With those dark shades obscuring his eyes she couldn't tell what he was thinking. 'My grandmother always had a few tables on the water's edge. Nothing fancy, but the food was always fresh and local. I suppose because she cooked for others, he was more accepting of me doing the same thing. But he does complain. He thinks I've turned it into something fancy.'

'You have had a very difficult life,' he said quietly. 'Losing both your parents and then your brother…and yet you've managed to hold it all together. Not just hold it together, but you have a thriving business, a happy child and a more mellow grandfather. You didn't repeat the pattern you saw, you created your own pattern.'

'The way you live your life is a choice,' Fia said. 'I chose to copy your family, not mine.'

'And you did that without any support. I want you to know that I do have enormous respect for what you have achieved. And I owe you an enormous apology for being so hard on you when I found out about Luca.'

'You don't have to apologise,' she muttered. 'I understand. You're very, very focused on family. I've never really had that so we sort of came at the whole thing from a different place.'

His dark eyes raked her face. 'Yes. I think we did. But we're in the same place now and that is the way it's staying.' He stood up abruptly. 'I have a meeting that will last about an hour. Then I've asked Gina to take Luca so that we can have some time alone.'

Alone sounded terrifying to Fia. Alone meant concentrating really hard on not showing him how she felt. Respect, she could take, especially from a man like Santo who didn't give it readily. Pity didn't interest her.

'Why don't we take Luca with us? Make it a family day out?'

Santo paused in the process of putting on his jacket. 'I was thinking more along the lines of something more romantic.'

'Romantic?' She managed a light-hearted laugh. 'Really, you don't need to do that. I appreciate the thought but it isn't necessary.'

'It is necessary. Apart from your wedding dress, I haven't bought you a single thing since we got together. You're my wife. You deserve the best.'

Oh, God, she was an embarrassment to him.

Why hadn't that occurred to her before?

She was married to Santo Ferrara and she was dressing the same way she'd always dressed. Mortified that he'd had to broach the topic in such a way, she caved in and nodded quickly.

'Yes, of course. Let's go shopping. Whatever you think.'

'Finish your breakfast. I'll pick you up in an hour. It's important that we spend time alone together. And you—' he bent to kiss Luca's dark hair '—are having a day with Gina. Be good.'

With a final glance at Fia, he strode off the terrace towards the hotel, leaving her staring after him in despair.

'He wants to spend the day with me because he thinks he ought to. And he's going to buy me clothes so that I look right and don't embarrass him in public. Your Auntie Dani has already told me he hates shopping so the fact that he's determined to take me must mean I'm not just a bit embarrassing but extra embarrassing.' Fia handed Luca another piece of *brioche*. 'Name one good thing about our relationship apart from you. Go one. Just one.'

'Sex,' Luca chortled helpfully and Fia gave a moan of despair and dropped her head into her hands.

'You look stunning in that.' Expending every effort to please her, Santo layered on the compliments but the more he praised, the more withdrawn she became. Having never before known a female to treat an extravagant shopping expedition with so little enthusiasm, he racked his brain to work out what he was doing wrong.

Was she disappointed that they'd left Luca at home?

'You like this?' She stared listlessly at her reflection in the mirror. Truthfully Santo liked her best in nothing at all, but he assumed that to admit that would be unlikely to improve her mood so he dutifully studied the blue silk dress and nodded.

'The colour suits you. Let's add it to the pile.'

She disappeared into the changing room to take it off and then re-emerged clutching the blue dress.

Santo took it from her and handed it to the sales assistant along with his card. 'That dress will be perfect for our family party.'

'What family party?'

'It's Chiara's birthday party in a couple of weeks. Ferrara family gathering. Cristiano adores his girls—and that includes Laurel—so you can be sure a big fuss will be made.' Santo picked up the bags in one hand and led her back to the Lamborghini. 'I thought I'd mentioned it.'

'No. No, you didn't.' She stopped dead just outside the store and Santo had to clamp her against him to prevent her from being flattened by a group of overeager shoppers.

Instead of pulling away, she stayed still in the circle of his arm, her head resting against his chest.

He frowned.

There was something intensely vulnerable about the gesture and he felt a flicker of concern.

It was the first time they'd touched like this, he realised, and he felt another flash of guilt at the way he'd treated her. He'd rushed her into marriage without giving any thought to her feelings. All he'd thought about was his son's welfare. Not once had he thought about hers.

The scent of her hair wound itself around his senses. The curve of her breast brushed against his arm. Fire shot through his body but he ignored it and forced himself to deliver a chaste kiss to the top of her head.

From now on he was going to focus on her, he vowed. 'You'll enjoy the party. It's a chance for everyone to get together.' Gently, Santo eased her away from him and brushed her hair back from her face so that he could look at her. 'My family always makes an enormous fuss about birthdays. Chiara will be six. Brace yourself for balloons and an indecent quantity of cake.' Still holding her hand, he threw the bags into the back of the car. 'The party is in their home in Taormina so we'll fly there because there is no way I'm negotiating Friday night traffic.'

'We're staying with Laurel and Cristiano?'

'Is that a problem?' He opened the door for her, trying not to focus on her legs as she slid into the passenger seat. 'Your grandfather seems to have made a good recovery and we still have a nurse there at night. If you're worried about the day, I can arrange something.'

'I'm not worried. Gina will be around.'

But Santo could tell she was lying and he searched for the cause. 'Are you finding the whole Ferrara family thing overwhelming?'

'No. I think you're all very lucky. You have a wonderful family.' She spoke as if she wasn't part of that and Santo breathed deeply as she fastened her seat belt without looking at him.

'Fia—'

Horns blared, interrupting his attempt to question her further, and he scowled and paced around to his side of the car. 'Dani and her brood will be there, too. And Laurel, of course. She's looking forward to getting to know you better. But she'll really appreciate us coming. It helps Chiara. She's only been with them a year.'

'A year?'

'Chiara is adopted. And don't ask me to tell you her history because it makes me want to punch a hole through something.' Santo started the engine and pulled into the fast moving traffic, driving as only a Sicilian could. 'When she first came to live with them she wasn't really used to people. She certainly wasn't used to people being kind to her. They were very patient, but it was little Elena who broke through that wall she'd built. Try telling a two-year-old that her new big sister just wants to be left alone—it doesn't work. And now they're the best of friends, as siblings should be.' He spoke without thinking and then saw a flicker of something in her eyes and cursed himself. Here he was, talking about siblings, and her brother was dead. '*Mi dispiace. Cristo*, I'm truly sorry, Fia.' He reached across and curled his fingers over hers. 'That was unbelievably insensitive of me. Forgive me.'

'There's nothing to forgive. I didn't have that sort of relationship with my brother and there is no sense in pretending that I did. My family is nothing like yours. And I don't want you to feel you have to tread carefully around the topic.'

Without releasing her hand, Santo took a sharp right turn and pulled into a narrow street. His fingers tightened on hers. 'My family is your family, *tesoro*. You are a Ferrara now.'

She stared straight ahead. 'Yes.'

Maybe it was taking her time to accept that, he thought.

Maybe after a few family gatherings she'd realise that she was part of it.

'I could make Chiara's birthday cake.' She blurted the words out as if she wasn't sure the suggestion would be welcome. 'But if they'd rather do their own thing—'

'No. I think that would be very well received. If you're sure it isn't too much for you on top of everything else.' Maybe that was what was wrong, he mused. She was working hard in the restaurant as well as looking after Luca.

Santo let go of her hand and drove for a few minutes before pulling up outside a small restaurant that had been his favourite for years. 'Today you are going to eat food that someone else has cooked for you. This place is incredible. Even you will be impressed.'

He needed to spend more time with her, he realised. He needed to make sure that their relationship wasn't just about sex.

He chose a quiet table in the corner of the courtyard, shaded by the tangled leaves of a mature vine. The tantalizing aroma of garlic and spices drifted from the kitchen and the sounds of sizzling mingled with the hum of conversation and the occasional raised voices of the chefs.

They ordered a selection of dishes to share and Santo watched as she tasted each one. At one point she went into the kitchen to question the chef and then pulled a notebook out of her bag and scribbled in it.

She was an instinctive cook, he realised, finding it a pleasure to watch her sample flavours and textures.

'This is good. But I'd make it without the pine nuts—' she dissected the food with her fork to study the composition '—and possibly lighter on the spices because they're overwhelming the flavour of the fish. If we served it with a green salad it would be a perfect healthy lunch for the Beach Club. And I've been thinking about that—'

'About the menu at the Beach Club?'

'You want to attract a young, sports-mad crowd. So you should serve a mixture of light, healthy food and a few pasta dishes that deliver carbohydrate without thick calorie-rich sauces. Increase the fish and vegetables. The current menu looks like a homage to comfort food.' She scribbled more notes for herself and he watched, thinking how much he'd underestimated her.

'Would you be willing to review the menus for the whole Ferrara Group?'

Her cheeks turned pink. 'Would you want me to?'

'Definitely. Whenever we build a new hotel, Laurel oversees the development of each fitness centre. She advises us on equipment and she helps us find the right staff.'

She put her pen down and picked up her fork. 'Is that how Cristiano met Laurel? She worked for you?'

'She was Dani's best friend at college and I employed her as my personal trainer. Cristiano was so impressed he asked her to advise on all our fitness centres. I never thought I would see Cristiano fall crazily in love, but he did. When he and Laurel split for a while he was like a different person. It was a great relief to everyone when they got back together. They never stopped loving each other and it was their love that held them together.'

She stopped eating.

Slowly, she put her fork down on her plate as if she could no longer face the food.

All the happiness seemed to have drained out of her.

Santo rewound the conversation in an attempt to work out what he'd said. Maybe she'd misinterpreted his story. 'So basically Cristiano was not willing to entertain the idea of divorce because he loved her so much.'

'That's romantic.' Her face was horribly pale and she sat

back and gave up the pretence of eating. 'This is delicious but I'm not very hungry. I'm sorry.'

'There is no need to be so polite. But a moment ago you were chatting happily and now you look as if I delivered bad news.' She'd been fine until he mentioned Cristiano's name. Aware that Cristiano had been cool with her at the wedding, Santo made a mental note to warn his brother to lighten up. 'If something is wrong, I wish you would just tell me.'

'Nothing is wrong. I'm having a really nice day. Just a bit tired.'

If she was tired, then that was his fault, Santo thought as they left the restaurant. Guilt flashed through him. They spent a substantial chunk of every night making love. He'd thought she enjoyed the physical side of their relationship as much as he did, but now he was wondering whether she just saw that as another one of her duties. He made a mental note to let her sleep through the night instead of keeping her awake.

He was all too conscious that he was the one who had propelled her into this marriage.

She'd married him because she felt she had a responsibility towards Luca.

Was she regretting that now?

Their marriage limped along for another few weeks with Santo going out of his way to fulfil the role of perfect husband. He showered her with expensive gifts, took her on glamorous nights out, even flew her to Paris to sample the food in a restaurant she'd mentioned. But the harder he tried, the worse she felt. Santo took to coming to bed later and later and when he did eventually slide into the bed next to her, he didn't touch her.

For Fia, it was the final straw.

The one thing that had always been good about their marriage was the sex, and apparently he no longer even wanted that. She was well aware that, before he'd married her, Santo didn't have a history of long relationships. He had a short attention span when it came to women, was easily bored and had a ferocious sex drive. No matter what he'd said at the beginning, it was obvious to her that he'd had enough of sleeping with the same woman.

And as far as she could see, that could have only one outcome.

Hadn't he told her right at the beginning that sex was one of the most important things to him? Hadn't he had confidence in the success of their marriage because they'd been so compatible?

If that part was over, what did they have left?

No matter what he said, there was no way a Ferrara would endure a sexless marriage.

He would take a lover, and that would be harder to handle than anything she'd had to handle in her life before.

Lack of sex, and the implications behind that proved more of a sleep disturber than too much sex and Fia grew more and more tired.

During the day she threw herself into her work. She spent time at the Beach Club and made some suggestions for changes that she thought would increase the popularity of the restaurant. She increased the volume of seating outside and altered the menu. When Santo told her that bookings had doubled, she was happy because she wanted so badly to please him.

Only with Luca could she really relax and then only if Santo was too busy to join them.

She took to checking his schedule so that she could be sure to pick times when he was tied up in meetings.

But Chiara's birthday party was looming and there was no avoiding the big Ferrara family gathering. Fia knew that seeing Cristiano and Laurel together would simply emphasize the cracks in her own marriage. Cristiano and Laurel were bound together by love. She and Santo were bound together by Luca.

Perhaps going away as a family might be good for them, Fia thought bleakly.

The plan was that after the party in the afternoon, the adults were going out to dinner and she squashed down her nerves and told herself that this would be a chance to get to know his family. And an excuse to add some glamour to her life.

Conscious that she spent a large proportion of her day dressed in unflattering chef's whites, she decided that this would be the perfect opportunity to wear one of the dresses Santo had insisted on buying her. She tried to remember which one had attracted the most enthusiastic response from him and in the end decided to wear the blue silk.

When she tried it on it felt and looked so good that her spirits lifted. Maybe things weren't as bad as she thought.

No marriage was perfect all the time, was it?

Santo was under a lot of pressure at work and taking a few hours out every day to spend 'quality time' with her simply increased that pressure. It was no wonder he had to work late.

They flew by helicopter, much to Luca's excitement, landing in the grounds of Cristiano's luxury palazzo in the hills above the pretty town of Taormina. From here she could see Mount Etna, and beneath her the sparkling expanse of the Mediterranean.

'This is Laurel's favourite place.' Santo urged her towards the terrace, carefully carrying the box containing the cake Fia had made. 'She had a difficult childhood and was brought up in care so she'd never had a home of her own. Cristiano bought this for her as a surprise.'

He loved his wife so much he'd bought her the one thing she'd never had—a beautiful home.

What would it be like, Fia wondered, *to be loved like that*?

As they rounded the corner she felt daunted by the number of people. 'Who are they all?'

He scanned heads. 'The man by the tree is my uncle and the woman next to him is his wife. The two women supervising the pool are cousins of mine—they work in marketing for the company—' the list was endless and then he moved on to the children '—Rosa is the one in the pool, you already met her with Dani. Chiara and Elena are together under the tree and the rest are children of cousins, friends, people we know—' He shrugged dismissively and she thought again how different his life was from hers.

'Fia!' Looking as lean and fit as ever, Laurel walked up to her and kissed her on both cheeks. 'Welcome. Isn't it hot? I just want to go and lie down in the air-conditioning. Chiara is feeling a bit overwhelmed, I'm afraid. I'm starting to wish we'd kept it smaller.'

'Does smaller exist for a Ferrara?'

Laurel laughed. 'Good point. Are you finding this family overwhelming too? I know I did. Fortunately you get used to it.'

The difference was that Laurel had a husband who adored her.

'I made the cake. I hope it's all right.' Feeling ridiculously nervous, Fia removed the lid of the box and Laurel gasped as she saw the cake.

'Oh, my goodness, it's perfect! A fairy castle—' Delight spread across her face. 'How did you *do* that?'

'I used the picture you sent me of her favourite toy.'

'The fairies even have wands—' Laurel's tone was awed as she examined the detail '—and wings. How did you make the wings?' Her response was everything Fia had hoped for.

'Spun sugar. I broke quite a few trying to get them right.'

Santo pulled a face. 'I'm expected to eat a pink turret and

fairy wings?' But he smiled at Fia. 'Very clever. And now I'm going to put it down because I don't want to be the one who drops it.'

He put it in the centre of the table.

From a distance, Chiara saw the cake and her eyes grew huge with wonder.

'She's too shy to come and investigate,' Laurel said. 'It's because she doesn't know you.'

In the end it was bouncy little Elena who dragged her big sister across the terrace towards the amazing cake.

'Elena never lets her out of her sight,' Laurel told Fia. 'She has her own room, but she crawls into Chiara's bed every night. She just adores her big sister.'

And the affection was clearly returned, although Chiara was less openly demonstrative.

'This is only her second birthday with us,' Laurel murmured. 'She didn't even know what a birthday was before she came to us, so if she doesn't do or say the right thing, please forgive her.'

Fia's eyes filled. Mortified, she blinked back the tears but not before Laurel had noticed.

'I'm so sorry.' Embarrassed, Fia pulled herself together. 'I don't know what's wrong with me at the moment. Not enough sleep or something.'

'Don't apologise. I cry on a regular basis when I think how lonely her life was. It's hard not to just want to give her everything, but of course all she really needs is love and stability.'

And it was obvious that she had that.

Chiara thanked her shyly for the cake but the real thanks was the look on her face as she examined each part of her fairy castle.

Cristiano strode over to join them and scooped up both his

daughters, one on each arm. 'Which one of you is the birth-day girl?'

Holding tightly to the man who was now her father, Chiara blushed shyly. 'Me.'

'Then it's time to come and greet your guests and make them welcome in true Ferrara style, young lady. And then we can cut that fantastic cake.'

Chiara wrapped her arms tightly around his neck. 'Will you come too?'

Fia saw the emotion in Cristiano's eyes. 'Of course,' he said softly. 'I am your *papà*. Where else would I be but by your side?' He smiled at Fia with genuine warmth. 'Welcome. And thank you for that spectacular cake. It was very thought-ful of you to make her something so special.'

It was a crazy, happy afternoon and when it came to bed-time Luca chose to sleep in a room with Chiara, Elena and Rosa.

Laurel rolled her eyes in disbelief. 'I'm so sorry. Are you OK with that? We have ten bedrooms. Don't ask me why they choose to cram themselves into one.'

'I think it's fantastic.' Fia thought about how lonely she'd been as a child. What she wouldn't have given to be tucked into a cosy room with three giggling cousins.

'Truthfully? I think it's fantastic too. And you don't need to worry because Cristiano's aunt is staying the night and she has promised to watch them.' Laurel gave the children a stern look. 'Straight to sleep, no nonsense.'

Having issued that edict, they left the room and Fia caught her eye.

'They're going to be up all night.'

'I think you're right. But the upside is that they might sleep late. And now we need to get ready. This restaurant Cristiano has picked is very elegant. We're all dying to hear your opinion on the food, although I'm not sure I can eat anything after all that cake. It was the best thing I've ever tasted.'

Warmth rushed through her.

She was one of them, she thought.

She *was* a Ferrara now.

Maybe her marriage wasn't perfect, but it was still early days and Santo had been making a huge effort. Instead of wishing she could have more, she needed to make the most of what she did have. She needed to try harder. And the first thing she'd do was kick-start their sex life. In the beginning he'd found her irresistible. It was up to her to rekindle that side of their relationship.

Santo was on the terrace drinking with Cristiano and Raimondo, Dani's husband, so Fia was able to take her time getting ready.

The blue silk dress skimmed her curves and showed off her legs. Maybe she wasn't as toned as Laurel, she thought as she looked in the mirror, but she ate well and ran around all day so her figure wasn't bad.

Sliding her feet into stilettos, she picked up her purse and drew in a deep breath.

Not once so far in their relationship had she actually tried to seduce Santo. This was going to be a first.

There was a brief tap and then the door opened and Laurel and Dani stood there.

Dani tipped her head to one side and studied her. 'Oh, my poor unsuspecting brother. He doesn't stand a chance.'

With that confidence-boosting comment ringing in her ears, Fia joined them and the three women walked down to the terrace.

Santo had his back to her and nerves fluttered in her stomach as she stared at those broad shoulders.

Cristiano saw them first and immediately broke off the conversation to greet them. Although he was complimentary to all, his eyes were on his wife and Fia felt a stab of envy at the obvious depth of their love.

From the little Santo had told her, that love had held them together through dark times.

Doubt slithered its way into her happiness. What did she and Santo have? Their marriage wasn't based on anything so powerful, was it? What was going to save them if trouble came their way?

As Dani planted herself in front of Raimondo and waited for him to say the right thing, Santo turned towards Fia.

He was gorgeous, the physical attraction so powerful that Fia caught her breath. And then she noticed that those dark, sexy eyes looked tired.

He wasn't sleeping either.

'Hey—' Dani punched her brother on the arm. 'Doesn't Fia look stunning? She is Fia the fantastic. Fia the fabulous. If you don't say something nice she might just turn into Fia the ferocious so you'd better say the right thing fast. Here's a hint—something like "let's forget dinner and just go straight upstairs" would probably go down well.'

Santo rounded on her. 'You talk too much,' he snapped and Dani took a step backwards, visibly hurt by the unexpected attack.

Cristiano observed that exchange with narrowed eyes, looking first at his brother and then at Fia, who wanted to do nothing more than just go and join the cosy heap of children upstairs and hide under the covers.

So much for seducing him.

It was clear he just wasn't interested.

'We ought to go,' Laurel said quickly. 'The limo is waiting. And Fia, I want you to tell me how to cook *arancine*. Cristiano loves it and every time I try, it's a dismal failure. I swear his mother still can't work out why he married me.'

Because he loved her, Fia thought bleakly. And love filled

in all the other cracks, like rain on parched earth. She had nothing like that and the cracks in her own marriage were widening. The shaky foundations were splitting apart and soon the entire thing would collapse.

Dani slipped her arm into hers as they walked. 'I have no idea what's wrong with Santo,' she grumbled. 'I apologise for my brother. Ugh. Men! This is why a woman has to have girlfriends. Let's talk about something important. I have a party to go to next week. I'm wondering whether to try some of that magnetic nail varnish.' She chattered away and Fia was grateful for the change of subject and for the nonstop talk that didn't require her input.

The evening was a success because of the efforts of the others, but somehow those efforts made Fia all the more aware of those widening cracks.

Despite the time she'd taken to look her best, Santo barely glanced at her, instead choosing to talk business with his brother and brother-in-law while Fia felt invisible.

If she still didn't attract his interest then that was it, wasn't it?

And if that part of their relationship was over, then the rest of it was over, too.

Whatever he said about marriage being for ever, there was no way a physical guy like Santo would want to stay with a woman he was no longer attracted to.

She was going to be the first Ferrara in history to be granted a divorce.

CHAPTER NINE

'I'M sorry if you found the weekend overwhelming.' Santo was formal and polite as they arrived home the following day.

'I didn't. Your family is lovely and it was a treat for Luca to spend time with his cousins.' She kept her voice bright and breezy and was so grateful for Luca, who kept up a running commentary about his cousins.

When Santo's phone rang, she almost moaned with relief, a feeling that doubled as he told her he was going to have to go straight to his office at the hotel and do a few hours' work.

And if there was something slightly cagey about the way he was behaving, she told herself that it didn't matter anyway. Even if he was lying about the work part and was actually seeing a woman, it was irrelevant.

When she made no response, he sighed. 'I might be late. Don't wait up for me.'

Of course she wouldn't wait up for him. He'd made it clear enough that he didn't want her. 'No problem at all,' she said quickly. 'Luca and I will have a swim in the pool and an early night.'

His mouth tightened and he started to walk away when he appeared to change his mind. He turned, uncertainty flickering in his eyes.

'Fia—'

He was going to tell her that this wasn't working. He was

going to tell her that he wanted a divorce and she would make a fool of herself because she wasn't ready to hear it yet. She needed to get her head round it. She needed to make plans.

'Luca, don't do that!' Using their son as an excuse, she shot across the terrace and relieved a startled Luca of a toy that was offering no threat whatsoever.

She fussed over him for a few moments and then Luca looked past her and his face fell.

'Papà gone.'

'Yes,' Fia whispered. 'He's gone. I'm sorry. I don't know what else to do.'

'Sex,' Luca said stoutly and she pulled him into a hug.

'Tried that,' she croaked. 'Didn't work.'

Somehow she stumbled through the day. She and Luca spent some time with her grandfather and then Gina took him back to the villa while Fia worked late at the Beach Shack.

Knowing that all that was waiting for her at home was a huge, empty bed, she was in no hurry to return to the villa. Instead she did something she hadn't done for years. Not since the night when Luca was conceived.

She went to the boathouse.

The approach took her along the stretch of private beach that belonged to the Ferraras. As a child she would have been guilty of trespassing and she realised with a lurch that she was now walking on her own land.

The main doors opened straight onto the sea, and a side door allowed access from the land. Fia had always slid in through the window, but this time she paused with her hand on the door, wondering whether it was just going to make her feel worse to visit somewhere that held so many emotional memories. It wasn't an accident that she hadn't been back here. This had been her escape in bad times.

The moon sent shimmers of light across the calm sea,

providing sufficient illumination for her to see what she was doing.

It occurred to her that it would have been sensible to fetch a torch, but she reasoned that she didn't need a torch to just stare at a collapsing old pile of planks.

The boathouse had been in a state of disrepair for so long that there was always a risk of injury, but as she pulled open the door she noticed that it opened smoothly. No creaks. She slipped quietly inside. In the past her routine had been to simply sit on one of the old lobster pots that were stacked by the door and stare at the water.

Her foot slipped on something soft and she frowned down at the floor. Oil? Fabric of some sort?

She was about to bend down and investigate when the place was suddenly filled with light. Shocked to discover that the place now had electricity, she looked up to see what seemed to be hundreds of tiny fairy lights strung around the walls.

Enchanted, she was just wondering what it all meant when she heard a sound behind her.

Turning quickly, she saw Santo standing there. 'You weren't meant to arrive yet.' His thumbs were hooked into the pockets of his jeans and he looked lean, fit and more handsome than one man had a right to be. 'I hadn't quite finished.'

Finished? Confused, Fia glanced around the boathouse, seeing the changes for the first time.

The place had been transformed. Those oily, splintered planks of wood had been sanded and polished. An oil stove nestled in one corner, ready to provide heat for chilly winter evenings and in another corner was a sofa, heaped with cushions and a fur rug.

It was the cosiest, most decadent place she'd ever seen. The tiny lights twisted along the walls made the place feel like a magical grotto.

She took a step forward and again felt the softness underfoot. Glancing down, she saw rose petals. Rose petals that formed a red carpet, not towards the bed, but towards a little table. And on the table was a small, beautifully wrapped box.

Heart beating, she looked at that box and then at Santo.

'Open it.' He hadn't moved from the doorway, the expression in his eyes cautious, as if he weren't sure of his welcome.

'You've—' She looked around her, noticing a million thoughtful little touches, like the little seat that had been placed by the doors to the water. The place she'd always sat with her arms wrapped around her knees, watching the sea. Instead of an upturned box, there was a rocking chair. 'You did this?'

'I know how unhappy you are and I know that when you're unhappy you need somewhere to go and be by yourself. I'd rather you didn't feel the need to escape from me but if you do then I want you to be comfortable.'

Her eyes filled. 'Our marriage isn't working.'

'I know that, and I suppose it isn't surprising in the circumstances.' His voice was uncertain. 'I have so many things to apologise for I don't know where to start.'

It wasn't the response she'd expected. 'You could start by telling me why the place is covered in rose petals.'

He ran his hand over the back of his neck. 'Remembering the night of our wedding still shames me. As long as I live I will never be able to delete the image of you on your knees sweeping up rose petals I'd so thoughtlessly had put down. I hurt your feelings badly.'

'I just thought it was mocking our relationship. It wasn't romantic. It was never romantic.' The tears sat in her throat and didn't move. 'Those rose petals—'

'—were a manipulation on my part, I admit that. But I was manipulating the minds of those around us, not mocking you. That interpretation didn't occur to me until I walked in and found you on your knees clearing them up. You once accused me of being an insensitive bastard and I am thoroughly guilty of that charge. But it was insensitivity rooted in thoughtlessness, *not* in a conscious desire to hurt you. I put these down myself, by hand. That's why they're not even in a straight line. I've never done it before.'

'Why did you do it now?' He still didn't get it, she thought numbly. Rose petals were a romantic gesture.

'I was trying to make you happy. I wanted you to smile,' he said thickly, every plane of his body rigid with tension. 'You smile with Luca all the time and I love it when you laugh. You never do that with me. You're always jumpy and on edge and that is probably my fault.' He spread his hands in a gesture of frustration and despair. 'But I do want you to be happy. What do I have to do?'

Fia felt tears scald her eyes and this time they refused to retreat. She swallowed, but they kept coming, brimming in her eyes and then spilling over onto her cheeks.

Santo swore under his breath and strode forward, folding her in his arms so tightly that she couldn't breathe. '*Cristo*, I have never, ever seen you cry. If the petals are going to upset you that much I'll clear them up again. Please, please don't cry. I'm trying really hard to please you but if I'm still getting it wrong then just tell me and I'll fix it.'

The ache in Fia's chest increased. 'I appreciate it, honestly, but you don't have to try this hard. It's horribly, horribly humiliating when I know that we're heading for divorce.'

He paled. 'A divorce? No! I will *not* agree to a divorce, but I'll agree to anything else you want. I know you don't love me, but that doesn't mean we can't be happy.'

'It isn't me who wants a divorce, it's you! And I do love you, that's the problem.' The words broke from her like waves onto a rock, eroding the barriers she'd built between them. 'In a way I've always loved you. Part of me fell in love with you when I watched you teach your sister to swim. You were so patient with her. I had fantasies that Roberto would do that for me but all he ever did was hold me under the water. I loved you when you let me use the boathouse for a bolt-hole and didn't tell anyone. I loved you that night when you touched my shoulder because you knew I was upset and I still loved you when we made love.' The sobs made her almost incoherent. 'And I loved you when I married you. I have always loved you.'

For a moment there was no sound but his uneven breathing and the soft lap of the water against the wood of the boathouse.

'You love me? But…I forced you to marry me.' His voice was hoarse. Stunned and decidedly uncertain. 'I bullied you.'

'And that was when I loved you most of all,' she hiccuped. 'My mother gave birth to me but apparently that wasn't enough of a bond to stop her from leaving me. You didn't even *know* Luca but you knew he was your son and that was enough for you. You were willing to do anything for him simply because he was family. You have *no idea* how much I wish my parents had shown me even a fraction of that commitment. For your child's sake you were even prepared to marry a woman you didn't love, not just any woman but a Baracchi. And you were prepared to do anything to make it work.'

'Forget that—' his hands gripped her arms '—is it true that you love me? You're not just saying that for Luca's sake?'

'I wish I were, because then this would be easy instead of really, really hard.'

'Why is it hard?'

'Because it's so hard to love someone who doesn't love you back.'

He cursed softly and cupped her face in his hands. 'You think I don't love you? What do you think the past few weeks have been about? I've been falling over myself to please you.'

'I know. You were working really hard at it and that was actually quite crushing.'

'*Cristo*, you are making no sense at all.' He made an impatient sound and gave her a little shake. '*How* is it crushing that I worked hard to please you?'

'Because it didn't come naturally. You were doing it for Luca.'

His hands fell to his sides. He stared at her.

'Clearly we have misunderstood each other badly.'

'We have?'

'I had no idea you loved me. And you clearly have no idea how much I love you.'

Fia stared at him and her heart rate doubled. Hope bloomed as he slid his hands into her hair and took her mouth in a slow, erotic kiss. She wanted to ask him if she'd heard him correctly but it had been so long since he'd kissed her like this, she didn't want him to stop.

He lifted his mouth from hers with obvious reluctance. 'How could you ever *think* I'd want a divorce?'

'We stopped having sex.'

'I was so conscious that I'd forced you into this marriage and then you made those comments about me being insatiable—'

'I liked you being insatiable,' she muttered. 'When you stopped I assumed it was because you were bored with me, so I chose an especially sexy dress last night and you didn't even look at me.'

'And why do you think that was? In most things I am a very disciplined man but I've discovered that I have virtually no self-discipline where you are concerned.' His tone was raw. 'I'd promised myself that I wasn't going to make the first move. That I was going to let you come to me. You didn't.'

'I thought you didn't want me.'

He groaned and gathered her against him. 'We have both been blind and stupid. And we are going to start again from now.'

Fia closed her eyes for a moment, the feeling of relief so enormous that she couldn't speak. 'Do you really love me? This isn't to do with Luca?'

'This has nothing to do with Luca.' He murmured the words against her mouth. 'This has to do with you and me but I've made a total mess of things because now I can't make you believe me. Because I rushed you into this, you think it's all because of Luca. I love you, Fia. And if there were no Luca I would still love you.'

'If there were no Luca, we wouldn't have met again.'

'Yes, we would.' Lifting his hand, he stroked a finger over her jaw. 'I didn't even know about Luca when I came back. The chemistry between us is so powerful we would have ended up together sooner or later, you know we would.' He reached past her, picked up the box that had pride of place in the centre of the table. With a few flicks of his fingers he dispensed with the packaging and flicked it open.

Fia gasped. 'What's that?'

'It's an engagement ring. I'm proposing.'

She felt dizzy as she saw the size of the diamond. 'You already proposed, Santo. We're married. I have the ring.'

'You have a wedding ring. And, as I recall, I ordered you to marry me. Now I'm asking you to stay married to me. Always. Whatever life sends, good or bad, I want you by my side.' He breathed deeply, his eyes wary. 'Tell me honestly— would you *want* me to let you go?'

Warmth rushed through her, erasing all her doubts.

'Never. The fact that I know how committed you are to family is what makes me feel so secure,' she admitted. 'I know that no matter what happens we'll work it through.'

'*Ti amo tantissimo*, I love you so much,' he breathed, 'and

I'm sorry I've messed this up so badly.' He slipped the ring onto her finger, above the gold band he'd given her on their wedding day. It fitted perfectly.

Fia stared at the huge diamond, dazzled. 'I'll have to have twenty-four-hour security if I wear that.'

'Given that I don't intend to leave your side, that won't be a problem. I'll be your personal security.'

Overwhelmed, Fia flung her arms around him. 'I can't believe you love me.'

'Why? You are the strongest, most generous woman I've ever met. I cannot even bear to think about how it must have been for you to discover you were pregnant at a time when your whole world was collapsing. If I could put the clock back, I would, and I would never have left your side.'

'You did the right thing,' she said softly, sneaking another look at her ring. 'If you had come back that night it would simply have added more distress for my grandfather. You were being sensitive, and it was the right decision.'

'But it meant that you coped alone. Knowing what I do about you, I do not blame you for not telling me about Luca. I understand why you made the decision you did. Your childhood experience was so different to mine. And yet, even with that background you didn't repeat the pattern.' He slid his fingers gently through her hair. 'When you told me that you'd forbidden your grandfather to say a bad word about a Ferrara, I couldn't believe it.'

'Although he was shocked when he discovered I was pregnant, I think it actually gave him something to live for.'

'You married me believing that I didn't love you. That must have been incredibly hard.' He eased her away from him and she blushed.

'OK. Maybe it was a little. Do you know what's weird? I've always wanted to be a Ferrara. All my life, I wished I was in your family.'

'And now you are.' His hands cupped her face and his eyes gleamed with purpose. 'And once you're in the family, you're in it for ever.'

Smiling, she wrapped her arms around his neck. 'Once a Ferrara wife...'

'...always a Ferrara wife,' and he lowered his head to kiss her.

* * * * *

SURRENDERING TO THE ITALIAN'S COMMAND

KIM LAWRENCE

For Aunty Pat a gutsy lady.

CHAPTER ONE

TESS LEANED HER hot forehead against the fridge and struggled to inject a smile into her hoarse voice. 'I'm fine,' she lied. 'I feel a hundred times better.'

'You're a terrible liar,' Fiona retorted.

Tess straightened up and lifted a hand to her throbbing head, responding to the affection in her friend's voice with a weak smile. 'No, I'm a very good liar.'

Only yesterday she had sounded sincere when she'd told her mum's PA that she was *really* sorry she couldn't attend the community centre official opening where her mum was cutting the ribbon. Flu had its plus points—though in this case she wasn't lying, she really *was* feeling better; even so a hundred times better than utterly wretched was still pretty awful.

'I would have dropped in on my way home but I had to work late. You're not the only one with this flu—half the office is off sick. It's a nightmare. But I'll definitely stop by in the morning after I drop off Sally and the girls at the station. Is there anything you need?'

'You really don't need—'

'I'll be there.'

Tess applied a tissue to her red nose. She was too tired to argue.

'Well, don't blame me if you catch this thing,' she grumbled.

'I never get flu.'

'I think they call that tempting fate,' Tess muttered as she rested from the two steps she had taken, leaning heavily against the worktop counter. It was crazy but her knees were still shaking from the effort of walking from the bedroom to the kitchen.

Fiona cut across her. 'In the meantime make sure you get plenty of fluids—' Tess heard the sliver of sharp anxiety that slid into her friend's tone as she added, 'You did change all the locks?'

'I did everything the police suggested.'

Which amounted to becoming a prisoner in her own flat. She glanced over at the extra bolts that had been fitted to her front door when she'd had her locks changed.

'They should have arrested the disgusting sicko.'

'They raised the possibility of a restraining order—'

The admission drew a gasp from Fiona. 'Then why…?' Followed by an understanding groan. 'Oh, of course, *your mum*…?'

Tess said nothing; she didn't need to. Fiona was one of the only people who understood. She'd been there when, at ten, Tess had become the poster girl for her mum's crusade against school bullying. And Fiona had been there again when her mum had used a tearful image of her at her dad's funeral as part of her campaign to win a local council election.

'She *means* well,' Tess said, unable to resist the knee-jerk reaction to defend her parent. It was true that Beth Tracey—she had reverted to her maiden name after she was widowed—did have the best of intentions, and though she had a genius for self-promotion it was never herself she promoted, but her good causes.

'The rumour is that she's going to put herself forward as an independent candidate for mayor?'

'I heard that rumour too.' Lucky for her, Tess reflected grimly, that her ambitious parent had finally accepted the fact her only daughter was not a political asset, though that didn't stop her trying.

'Even if I had gone down that route there is no guarantee the court would have granted it. He comes across as very...well...harmless. And I had no *proof* he'd even been in the flat. After all, he didn't actually *t...take* anything.' Tess hated the quiver in her voice—she'd sworn not to be a victim.

'What he did was way worse, Tess. That creep invaded your home.'

Tess was glad her friend couldn't see her as her knees sagged and she slid down to the floor. The incident had been the turning point, the moment Tess had realised that ignoring the man, even feeling sorry for him, was not an option. He was dangerous!

Even a month after the event the memory still had the power to send a wave of nausea through her, powerful, but nothing like the sick disgust, the profound sense of violation she had experienced that evening. The rose petals on the bed and the champagne and glasses displayed on the bedside table had been terrifying enough, but it had been the open underwear drawer that had made her rush to the bathroom to throw up.

It was as if her stalker had *wanted* her to know, and yet he had taken great care not to leave any evidence of his identity.

'I know.' Tess cleared her throat and struggled to

steady her voice. 'I suppose from their point of view people *leaving* flowers and champagne isn't a major crime.'

'Stalking is these days. Did you tell them about the emails?'

'There was nothing threatening. The police were sympathetic.' Tess had been prepared not to be believed but the professionals had found it easier than she had to accept that the deep and meaningful relationship Ben Morgan believed he shared with Tess consisted only of the odd good morning they had exchanged at the bus stop.

'Well, sympathy is going to be really useful when he stabs you in your sleep one dark night!'

Alerted by Tess's audible gasp, Fiona stopped and hastily backtracked. 'Not that he would, of course. The man's a wimp, a total loser! Me and my big mouth. Are you all right, Tess?'

Teeth clenched, Tess stubbornly fought her way back from the place where Fiona's angry remark had sent her, ignoring the icy fist in her stomach. Her chin lifted. To feel fear meant the crazy had won.

'Nothing two aspirin and a cup of tea won't cure,' she said, struggling wearily to her feet.

'*Turn that thing down, you lot, or I'll switch off the cartoons...* Sorry about that,' Fiona continued, raising her voice above the din that Tess could now hear in the background. 'My dear sister is taking a bath and the twins are running rings around me. Under-fives and a white carpet are not a good combination...*who knew*?'

'You go and save your carpet, Fi.'

'Are you *sure* you're all right? You *sound* awful.'

Tess managed a hoarse chuckle. 'I look even worse.'

She pushed a strand of lank hair from her face and turned her back on her distorted reflection in the polished surface of the kettle. A glance in the mirror, when she'd dragged herself out of bed earlier, had already revealed her red nose, dark circled eyes and ghostly pallor. 'But I'm fine.'

A snort of exasperation echoed down the line.

'All right,' she admitted. 'I feel terrible but I'm going to make myself a cuppa and go back to bed.'

'Good plan. I'll see you tomorrow.'

Putting on the kettle, Tess opened the fridge and pulled out an open carton of milk. Her congested nose meant it wasn't until it landed in a congealed gloopy mess in the bottom of her mug that she realised it had soured.

Deprived of it, suddenly all Tess could think about was a cup of tea. The corner shop was less than two hundred yards from her front door…if she took the shortcut through the alley.

Tess, still in her pyjamas, left the flat huddled in the duffel coat that Fiona's boyfriend had left behind the last time he and Fi had come to supper. He was a slight man but the coat still swamped Tess's petite frame.

Slow and steady, she counselled her shaking knees. *Like I have a choice!* She had made it halfway down the alley when she heard the helpful policewoman's soothing voice in her head.

'Look, don't get paranoid. You've done right to remove your online presence—a pain, I know, but the anonymity makes people like this guy feel brave. As for the rest, just take a few common-sense precautions—if you're out stay with friends, and if you're alone keep to public places where there are plenty of people and the

lighting is good. Very often guys like this fasten onto someone else.'

Tess's heart gave an extra-hard thud as she stopped dead, suddenly very conscious of the oppressive darkness that seemed to press in on her.

She had put herself in exactly the sort of situation the police had suggested she avoid.

Teetering feverishly on the brink of panic, she took a couple of deep breaths that made her cough, not calm. The hacking sound echoed off the high walls on either side as she resisted the messages from her feverish brain that made her want to turn around and run. That was a bad idea on two counts: she wasn't capable of running and she was actually closer now to the other side—the main street, where there were lights and people and safety.

'You'll be fine…fine, totally fine, you are not a victim…not a victim…' Her mantra stalled as the figure appeared at the other end of the alley. He barely paused before he began to walk towards her.

Tess opened her mouth to scream and nothing came out. She was living a nightmare, the horribly familiar recurrent one where she was paralyzed. She couldn't breathe. As if something malevolent were sitting on her chest—*someone* malevolent.

'Relax, I'm here to look after you, darling—'

It was not a scream but it was a noise. Desperately she tried again to raise the alarm…

'Without knowing the details of your sister's case I can't be sure, but from what you tell me I doubt very much if she would be a suitable candidate for the treatment.'

Don't kill the messenger!

Danilo let his eyelids lower to hide his expression before letting the tense breath escape his lungs in a carefully managed exhalation.

'But if you would like me to see her…?'

Danilo's lashes lifted.

The man sitting opposite saw the question in the dark depths. 'Obviously you'll want to discuss it with her?'

'Who?'

'Your sister. I understand that she had already had several unsuccessful treatments?'

From somewhere the memory of the angry words of the kid he had warned off his sister the previous month came back to him. *'You don't want to see me here again, but what about what Nat wants? She wants to see me, and I want to see her. I love her. When are you going to let her live her own life?'*

'She wants to walk.'

The man's understanding expression aggravated Danilo, who got to his feet and tipped his head in acknowledgement. 'I will be in touch.'

Her own life.

A life. That was what he wanted for his sister. It was to that end he had taken her to every top spinal expert, he had made himself familiar with every new piece of research. He would not give up, but he would ask her and she would agree with him.

She always did.

Frowning at his annoying inner voice, he waved away the driver who had got out of the limo to open the door.

'I'll walk.'

As he strode, hands dug in his pockets, along the pavement shining from the recent shower, he was lost in his own thoughts so he barely registered the sting of unseasonal hail that began to fall again, quickly covering his hair in icy, white fragments that clung to the dark strands. It was a typical British summer.

There were moments in life where a man was forced to face up to his failings, his weaknesses. He'd been in London the night that he'd faced his, the night of the accident that had robbed his parents of their lives and left his teenage sister in a wheelchair.

He should have been there, he should have been at the wheel of the car, and if he had things might have been different. He'd never know because he'd had a better offer, a night with a beautiful blonde in London. The excuse had come so easily.

Self-disgust churned in Danilo's belly as he relived the moment when the police had finally tracked him down to the hotel room. By that point the city sky had been streaked with morning light and his little sister had been in a hospital bed in Rome fighting for her life for over seven hours. And she had been *alone* because their parents had been lying on a mortuary slab.

He'd put a night of casual sex ahead of duty to his family.

If he'd not been such a selfish bastard…well, who knew? Things *might* have turned out differently. Would his more youthful reflexes have made all the difference? He'd never know; that was his punishment. Compared to Nat, though, he'd got off pretty lightly and she'd done nothing to be punished for, but one thing he did know was that while he had breath in his body he would not stop searching for a cure for his sister.

It was the right thing to do, the *only* thing to do, he had no doubts. And yet…? His frowning contemplation of the wet pavement deepened as he trudged along it with the surgeon's words—*discuss it with her*—floating around in his head. He kept picturing Nat's face the *last* time her hopes had been raised by the promise of a miracle cure and then dashed. She'd looked so bleak.

He shook his head, refusing to acknowledge the doubts in his head. His little sister was the strongest person he knew and he had to stay strong for her, stay positive, and one day she would walk.

He was so deep in his own thoughts that he'd walked past the alley before he registered the sound: a woman's cry, filled with fear. His response was hard wired—there was no question of walking on and pretending he'd not heard. A few seconds later he was at the entrance to the cobbled alleyway; the overhead street light illuminated the scene and seconds told him all he needed to know.

The guy had hold of the woman and she was trying to escape.

Danilo struggled to hold back the red mist that threatened. Bullies were a species that always challenged the objectivity he prided himself on. He could spot one at fifty paces, and like muscle memory the sight of a bully in action always awoke the fifteen-year-old in him, the one who had yet to enjoy a spectacular growth spurt that had seen him grow twelve inches in as many months and the musculature that went with it putting him safely beyond the attention of those creeps in life who looked for victims who were seen as weaker or different.

The man didn't see him coming so he put up no resistance when Danilo took hold of his collar and physically dragged him away from the young woman. One glimpse of her pale face, too pale to be pretty—the cheekbones too sharp, the eyes too big, the mouth… actually the mouth was pretty good—cranked up his chivalrous levels several more notches.

She reminded him of Nat, not that there was any physical similarity. Nat was beautiful, not plain, and his sister was tall, not tiny. Still, he'd not been there for Nat when she'd needed him, but he was here now.

'What the hell…?'

The guy let out a frustrated bellow, flailing wildly, his arms windmilling as he was set down on his feet yards away from the cowering figure of the woman. Apart from her, he didn't look so big—and obviously he didn't feel it either, when he turned and saw Danilo standing between him and his victim.

The aggression in the man's face diminished significantly but the wariness in his eyes was mingled with calculation as he held out his hands and smiled.

'This is a misunderstanding…' He spoke while moving in a direction that would give him access to the woman now hidden from his view behind Danilo.

Danilo negated his ploy by shadowing the move before allowing his glance to linger on the scratch that was seeping blood on the guy's cheek. *Good for her,* he thought approvingly.

'I don't think so. Do you want me to call the police?' he asked the woman without taking his eyes off the other man.

'I just want to go home.'

The hoarse little whisper had a heartfelt sincerity that didn't help Danilo's struggle to resist the impulse to shake the guy until his teeth rattled. Then she sniffed and he almost lost it. Instead he moved to her side.

'Or a hospital?'

'She's fine. *Police...?*' The falseness in the laugh grated on Danilo. 'You've got it all wrong, mate. This was just a misunderstanding. You know how it is. Something and nothing—*sweetheart.*'

In a heartbeat Tess tipped from relief to outright panic. What if this man believed him? What if he left her alone with bonkers Ben?

'I am not your mate.'

It wasn't until her rescuer spoke in a voice that held a twenty-below chill that Tess realised she had grabbed his arm in a death grip. His words made her feel better, but just to be sure she didn't let go; instead she tightened her grip and moved in closer.

'And to answer your question, no, I do not *know how it is* to force myself on a woman.'

'She's mine...'

Ben's voice made Tess's skin crawl. She shook her head in mute rejection. The denial locked in her throat, all she could do was squeeze her eyes closed to avoid the stare of Ben's cold, creepy eyes, but not before it had loosened the lid on the box in her head marked *Don't deal—lose, bury, forget!*

The deeply buried memory that escaped was so clear that for one disorientating moment Tess was sixteen again, cornered by the man her mum was dating. Watching helplessly as he locked the door, his smile and his soft, oily voice making her skin crawl and her insides chill as he told her they could *have some fun.* Tess knew she was lucky she never found out what his idea of fun entailed because it turned out that sleazy creeps did not find it *fun* to have their victim throw up all over their expensive new shoes!

'You know, it's been a long day,' the man beside her drawled.

She clung to the sound of his voice, focusing on the faint attractive accent, letting it drag her free of the memories that even now made her feel unclean, but most of all angry because she had felt weak and helpless. 'And I am not interested in a debate. However, we could move this discussion to the nearest police station?'

There was a silence followed by footsteps. Tess focused on the clean male scent of the man beside her and let it wash away the memory of the sour scent—a combination of sweat and cheap fragrance—that had emanated from her stalker.

The sound of footsteps had faded before her rescuer spoke again. 'He's gone. You can open your eyes.'

Italian... Tess speculated as she tilted her head to look up at the tall stranger. He'd have looked beautiful to her if he'd had a bad case of acne, but he didn't. He was actually incredibly good-looking.

'I could kiss you!' Relief made her more painfully honest than normal, and saying what she was thinking always had been one of her faults. 'But don't worry, I won't. I have the flu.' She let go of his arm and patted the fabric and let out a long fluttering sigh. 'I'm awfully glad he didn't hit you.'

His crack of laughter made her smile too, and as their eyes brushed she realised that he wasn't just good-looking, he was *amazing*!

He had the olive skin tone that went with jet-black hair, an angular face, dramatic chiselled cheekbones, high forehead, his face bisected by a straight nose, yet the austerity of his strong features was offset by an incredibly sensuous mouth.

His smile was pretty incredible too. It made her feel dizzy. But then he wasn't smiling, he was frowning and she was still feeling dizzy; his dark features were swimming in and out of focus in a weird way.

'It's none of my business…'

So why are you making it your business? asked the exasperated voice in Danilo's head.

Appreciating the meaning of the phrase *weak with relief* for the first time, Tess turned her head too quickly and felt the world spin.

'But don't you think maybe you should be a little more careful in your choice of boyfriends?' he observed, tempering both his advice and his disapproval. He might feel he was speaking on behalf of a brother she might have somewhere, but he wasn't and thank goodness for that. One little sister was enough… *Two…?* He hadn't been able to keep the one he had safe.

At least this woman didn't laugh at him the way Nat had or doubt his qualifications when it came to relationship advice. What Natalia didn't understand was that actually he was perfectly qualified, because for a long time he'd *been* the man that brothers warned their sisters not to date.

This woman just looked at him blankly, eyes wide, as though he were speaking a foreign language. He allowed himself the luxury of cursing softly in his native tongue, relieved when he saw comprehension spread across her face.

'No, he is…never…not…'

Through the rushing sound in her ears Tess could hear her own voice, then there was just the rushing.

Guilt and alarm grabbed at Danilo and he swore again, low and fluently under this breath, as he placed a steadying hand across her shoulders. She sagged like a rag doll and he wrapped his other arm around her middle. It was then he realised several things: she was shaking and, despite her petite appearance underneath the massive coat, she had curves. Only one fact was relevant.

'You're not going to faint.'

He said it in a way that at any other time would have made her laugh. Macho men who thought just saying something made it so always made her laugh. They generally didn't know why she was laughing—alpha males so often had no sense of humour.

She didn't laugh now though. Instead she leaned against the hand that was now pressed between her shoulder blades and hoped like hell he was right.

'I'll be fine.' The world was swimming back into focus and, yes, he was still as impossibly good-looking.

It didn't seem a very realistic statement, considering the unhealthy sheen of perspiration on her pale skin, but he approved of positive thinking, especially when the option was having an unconscious female on his hands.

'Breathe deeply, in and out…no, not *too* deeply.' He steadied her violent sway and left his arm around her waist while he pulled out his phone. He wondered if his plan to fly directly back to Rome was still realistic. 'That's better…'

She'd thought his eyes were brown, and they were incredibly dark, but now as he captured and held her gaze she realised they were midnight blue, like the night sky, and flecked with tiny points of silver that glittered like stars. From nowhere the phrase *soul stripping* came into her head, though actually clinical was more accurate.

She moistened her dry, cracked lips with her tongue and nodded. 'I'm fine now.'

She looked a million miles from fine. 'My car is coming. Where do you live?'

Tess, her heart still pounding though now with relief and not terror, heard herself recite her address like some obedient lost child. 'I don't need a lift. It's just around the corner.' *What else was around the corner?* Bonkers Ben? She shuddered. The mocking nickname no longer worked in making him seem harmless and absurd. He'd been waiting for her…watching? Was he still watching?

The realisation he could extract himself from this little drama sooner rather than later sent a surge of relief through Danilo and for a split second he was sorely tempted to accept the rejection at face value.

Then she looked over her shoulder, the movement fear-filled and furtive—*hell!*

'It's on my way.'

'It is?' She suspected it was a lie but wasn't about to call him on it. The thought of meeting up with her stalker sent a shudder through her.

Concern roughened the edges of his voice as he said softly, 'You're safe now.'

His voice pulled her back from the brink of panic; the unexpected gentleness in it made her want to cry.

'Please don't be nice,' she begged. 'I'll cry. I know I'm being…' *Pathetic.* 'I'm not normally so—' Tess brought her teeth down on her wobbling lower lip and blinked back weak tears. 'He… Ben… He isn't my boyfriend. He just thinks he is.'

Danilo dismissed her explanation with a shrug of his broad shoulders. 'Not my business.' And he had no desire to make it his business, he reminded himself, turning his head as his sister's features superimposed themselves over the pale, pinched face of this young woman, producing a familiar knife thrust of guilt that he didn't try to evade.

'I have a sister not that much younger than you.' The woman was a little older than he had first assumed. 'And I hope if she ever needed—' His sister *had* needed and he hadn't been there.

The woman took a deep breath and Danilo's habitual objectivity slipped as he watched her attempt to regain control. The effort to straighten her slender shoulders sent a jerky convulsive ripple through her entire body; the air left her lungs in a long gusty sigh, but not the tension.

Heavy lids shadowing his stare, Danilo was torn between reluctant admiration and irritation, his irritation reserved for the protective instincts he felt shift and tighten in his chest as a solitary tear escaped the swimming eyes lifted to his. Things got tighter as he watched it slide slowly down her cheek. He had never seen eyes quite that shade of golden amber before.

Her eyes, almond-shaped and framed by thick, spiky black lashes, lifted her face from plain. They were extraordinary. Still, she was *not* his responsibility.

'Well, thank you. I'd be grateful if it's not out of your way, but I'll be fine now—really.'

The delivery started firm and slowly faded, ending on a definite wobble. She looked at him with eyes that made him think of the runt of the litter of golden retrievers his father's favourite dog had produced.

Danilo, promised first choice of the puppies, had, against all advice, chosen the sickly-looking one who everyone had warned would not survive. But that little animal had gnawed its way into his heart with those eyes.

The dog had survived and was still rewarding his decision with unconditional love, though her coat was less glossy than it had been before she'd got old and stiff.

'But if perhaps you could walk with me, if you're heading that way?' Tess was shaking again, her body seized by inner tremors she had no control over. She didn't shrug off the hand that came to rest gently against her shoulder blades. She was glad of the contact while recognising she was acting like the sort of woman she despised: weak, malleable and in need of male support. And this particular male had an attitude that normally would have got under her skin.

Cut yourself a break, Tess, you've got the flu and you've had a run-in with your unhinged stalker.

CHAPTER TWO

'I'M TESS.' IT SEEMED only good manners to tell the man who had saved her from a situation that could have ended up with her being a crime statistic her name.

'Raphael, Danilo Raphael.'

An angel's name. Appropriate given the circumstances, though her guardian angel had the physical appearance of the fallen variety.

They had reached the end of the alley, where she hesitated. Danilo walked past her and out onto the identical-Victorian-house-lined street. 'Right or left?'

Tess didn't immediately respond because she was doing yet another mental regrade of his position on the gorgeous scale! She pressed a hand to her chest to alleviate the breathless sensation.

There were a number of people who could look pretty good in subdued light but a lot less that could look good spotlighted by the artificially white blanching glare of a street lamp. Her fallen angel could take the unkind illumination, probably because there was not a plane or angle on his crushingly handsome face that didn't deserve to be lit up. It was flawless.

But he was not just a pretty face—the rest of him looked pretty awesome too. This was a man who didn't need good lighting or perfect tailoring to set him apart from his fellow men!

As she paused, mouth slightly ajar, he raised a darkly defined brow questioningly. A slither of liquid heat washed through her, the effects of the fever obviously, as she gave her head a tiny shake and, feeling embarrassed, she stepped out, glancing nervously over her shoulder before tilting her head back to reply to his question.

It struck her for the first time that if she were looking for danger, then in a line-up she would dismiss the mild-looking, bespectacled creep who had been stalking her for the past months. Raphael, on the other hand, was not a man anyone would dismiss. He was the living, breathing photofit image of dark, brooding and dangerous to know.

Not just because he was a hundred feet tall and hard—he'd lifted Bonkers Ben as though he were a rag doll! Her stomach gave a tiny flip as she recalled the tensile strength in the fingers that had curved around her upper arm. This man had a dangerous vibe.

Mum always had said don't judge a book by its cover, which had always struck Tess as ironic even when she was a kid considering how much trouble her parent went to to present the right image to the public. Today it was all about image. Was this rampantly male stranger the product of some image consultant's efforts or did all that come naturally?

'Right,' she said, gesturing vaguely in that direction. The fact was she was never likely to know anything about this enigmatic man with his intimidatingly perfect profile beyond the fact that he had appeared at the right moment, and for that she would always be grateful. 'It's the fourth house along. The one with the red door.'

'This is it.'

Danilo glanced at the row of names beside buttons on the door frame; either this building was larger than it looked or the homes within were the size of shoeboxes. 'I'll see you to your door.'

Tess had enough fight left in her to challenge his *not open for debate* attitude. 'That's really not necessary.'

As she spoke she realised that the long, low car she had been aware of in the periphery of her vision had stopped. Like the man himself, it looked expensive. She nodded in its direction. 'It looks like your lift is here.'

He turned and raised a hand.

'I'll only be a moment.'

Tess watched as he strode over to the car and spoke for a moment to the driver. She was tempted to slip inside but being caught before she had closed the door on him would have been embarrassing, not to mention ungrateful. And there was the fact it was not exactly hard work to watch him; not only was he supremely elegant, but every move he made suggested a physical power that was riveting.

He returned a moment later and nodded towards the door. 'After you.'

'Fine,' she sighed out as she stepped a little ahead of him into the hallway. 'I'm on the top floor.' The curved staircase and the encaustic tiles underfoot were about the only original features left in the building which had been unsympathetically 'modernised' back in the seventies.

'Where is the lift?'

'We don't have one.' The trick, she told her shaking

knees, was to take one step at a time—literally. *This might take some time!*

She had gone up the first three steps, the situation not made easier by the man behind her who was vibrating silent impatience, when she heard a soft growl.

His flight might not be an option now, but at this rate he'd be here half the night and she'd be on her knees by the time she got to the top floor. Sure, the woman was remarkably plucky, but he'd always thought *plucky* was another word for *stubborn*.

It was all a bit of a blur as one moment Tess was holding onto the bannister, and the next she was being casually lifted up into his arms. She grabbed the fabric of his jacket as he strode onwards and upwards.

'Quite unnecessary,' she gasped, sounding a bit like one of those heroines who fainted a lot and got rescued by dashing heroes—she gave a laugh. She was so *not* that girl!

'I was losing the will to live.'

Tess kept her eyes straight ahead, aware of the occasional waft of warm breath on her cheek, trying to retain as much dignity as possible—*a bit late for that!* The hardness of his chest, the warmth, the false intimacy of the situation—all lent another layer of disorientation to what had been a very disorientating experience!

Outside her door he put her back down on her feet.

'You're very kind.'

His jaw clenched. 'I am not kind.'

'Well, I think you are.' She fished in one of the deep pockets for her key. 'So thank you, and goodnight.'

For the first time Danilo noticed there was something quite stubborn about her rounded chin. He found his eyes sliding lower down the column of her neck, the swanlike curve exposed now as she unfastened the top button of her ridiculous coat. She was too pale and too thin but her skin had a flawless, almost translucent quality. He scrutinised her with casual curiosity, wondering what she'd look like if she didn't dress like a reject from a charity shop.

'Not that good a night for you.'

She gave a sigh. It looked as if he wasn't going until she was inside. Flipping her hair, which hung in wet rats' tails down her back, off her face, she made a frustrated sound through clenched teeth. Her hand was shaking so hard she couldn't fit the key in the lock. 'There's a knack,' she panted, her breathing almost as erratic as her heart rate while ironically the man who had just carried her up three flights of stairs was not even breathing hard. He might not be breathing hard but she could feel the impatience rolling off him in waves. It didn't help.

As her frustration built Tess resisted the impulse to kick the door. Instead she rested her forehead on the door and jiggled the key once more.

Her sigh was one of intense relief when it finally opened. She reached for the light switch and stepped inside before turning around. 'Thank you again. I'll be fine now.'

Danilo, his head ducked to avoid the low beams in what had presumably started off as the servants' quarters in the house, nodded, half turned and then lost the fight with his conscience.

He closed his eyes and sighed. He really *wanted* to walk away. He wanted to listen to the voice of common sense that was urging him not to get involved, the same voice reminding him that this was none of his business, that no good, as his English nanny years ago had been fond of darkly warning, would come of it!

But inevitably the tug of guilt was too strong to resist.

'You don't look fine.' That was a massive understatement. Under the strong electric light her face was the colour of paper, the shadows circling her eyes so dark they looked like bruises.

Well, I can't argue with that! Tess's own gaze collided with the critical stare of her dark-eyed rescuer— no man should be allowed eyelashes that long—and stopped. She had just had a close encounter with her own personal stalker, she was struggling to stay upright on knees that felt like cotton wool and she was worried about how she looked... Tess put it down to the temperature she was inevitably running.

'Can I call someone for you?' It was called passing the buck and seemed like a very good idea. 'You shouldn't be alone.'

Alone. The word echoed around in her head in an unpleasant way that made her glance for reassurance at the row of locks on the door. Of course she shouldn't be alone. She *should* and *would* have been enjoying her third day of a fortnight in the sun with Lily, the classroom assistant, and Rose, who taught the other reception class, if it hadn't been for this wretched flu bug.

Her wistful thoughts went to her friends enjoying sun, sea and maybe even a bit of romance and she felt a twist of envy. The only other person she could call on was Fiona, and though she knew her friend would drop everything if she knew what had happened Tess had no intention of spoiling Fiona's last night with her sister and nieces, who lived in Hong Kong. This much-anticipated visit was rare.

There was her mum, of course, and she'd come running. As ambitious as her parent was, she had always put her daughter's welfare ahead of her career, a fact Tess hadn't always appreciated, but if her mum knew what had happened and got the full Bonkers Ben story then by the morning Tess's story, and her name, would have gone viral and appear in every newspaper, while her mum, looking glamorous, caring and just the sort of person you'd *want* to vote into office, would be doing the rounds of the breakfast TV programmes. When she had a cause her mother was relentless and self-promotion came as naturally to her as breathing, neither of which in themselves was a bad thing, but Tess knew from experience what it felt like to be at the centre of one of her mum's campaigns, and maybe she was selfish but she hated the idea of being stigmatised as a victim almost as much as she hated the idea of the attention.

Tess squeezed her eyes shut, but remained aware of the dark, brooding presence. His height was emphasised by the sloping beams. She didn't need her macho guardian angel to tell her she'd have to deal with the Ben situation; she already knew that. But not tonight. If she thought any more her head might explode.

Tess opened her eyes. 'I think—' She blinked. She hadn't invited him and she hadn't been conscious of him moving, but he was standing in her hallway. The presence that earlier had felt comforting now, in the enclosed space, tipped over into disturbing.

'There isn't anyone,' she blurted, then, conscious that might have made her sound as if she had no friends, she added tiredly, 'All I need right now is to sleep off this flu.'

'So what happened back there, you're going to act like it didn't happen?'

His disapproval hit an exposed nerve. 'I'm trying,' she gritted, feeling a flash of irritation with him for hanging around asking questions and making it impossible for her to do just that. Close on the heels of irritation came guilt; he had rescued her.

Danilo's gaze travelled from her face to the row of locks on the door and his face hardened as he translated what he saw. He felt the hot fury rise in him and fought to damp it down to a low simmer. There were relationships that went sour and then there were people who... His fists clenched as he thought about what in a perfect world would happen to bullies and cowards.

'Your boyfriend from the alley?'

She nodded tiredly. '*Not* boyfriend,' she said without any real hope he'd believe her. His sardonic expression suggested she was correct in this assumption. She opened her mouth then closed it, shaking her head, trying to tell herself that it didn't matter what a total stranger thought.

Teeth gritted, she focused on unfastening the toggles of her man-sized duffel coat, though size was all a matter of perspective, and for that matter so were men, she mused tiredly. While Fiona's boyfriend, Matt, was an average-sized guy, she was lost inside his coat. She couldn't think of any circumstances where she'd be wearing any garment belonging to the man whose eyes she could feel on the back of her neck, but they'd have to send in a rescue team with tracker dogs to recover her if she ever did.

The visual dragged out a laugh between huffs of exhaustion as she struggled with the coat.

The gurgle brought a flash of angry incredulity to his eyes. Was Tess so used to having boyfriends rough her up that she could laugh about it? His jaw tightened. Tales of abusive relationships never failed to outrage Danilo. The men were easy to understand—they were inadequate bullies, and his contempt for them was absolute. But he could never understand why some women always seemed to go back to them, believing that things would change.

It is not your role, Danilo, to lecture this woman on self-respect and personal safety, but the reminder didn't lessen the knot of anger in his chest.

Tess continued to struggle with the coat that felt like a ton weight on her sore shoulders. In fact every inch of her hurt and his scrutiny wasn't helping. The man could communicate more with silences than most people could with a three-page speech, and this time it was disapproval she was getting. No doubt he was just willing her to get a move on so that he could get back to his own important life. Did he think she didn't want that too? She gave a sigh of relief when the last toggle gave and the coat landed on the floor with a thud. She made no attempt to pick it up as she turned back to her rescuer.

'Thought I might have to sleep in it. Look, thank you for what you did.' She stopped when she saw he was still staring at the door.

Danilo could feel the pressure in his head as the anger beating inside his skull reached critical level.

'You should not have to live like this!' He flicked one of the locks with a long finger and spun around to face her, conscious as he did so that he'd just missed his chance to walk away. 'It is outrageous! *Madre di Dio!* How long has this been going on?'

'Please, I've already had this conversation once tonight. Nothing as bad as this has happened before,' she added, feeling the irrational need to defend herself.

'But something has happened before?' He seized on the comment. 'Do you still have feelings for this man?'

The question astonished her. 'I've never had feelings for him. I barely know him.' Or you, she wanted to add, but she didn't because she wanted more for this to be over and for him to go away. Didn't he know that guardian angels appeared at the right moment and then slipped away, silently, without comment, without giving a person a headache—a *worse* headache?

'What are you wearing?'

In the middle of sliding off the scuffed running shoes she had slipped on as she'd left the flat, Tess stopped, a deep flush travelling over her pale skin as her eyes moved from the onesie, chosen for its comfort value and not glamour, to his face.

'Pyjamas!'

'Yes, pyjamas,' she said, beginning to get irritated now. 'Maybe you don't wear them but I do.' She stopped, the colour in her cheeks deepening—*you just suggested he slept naked.*

If only her embarrassment had stopped there but, no, now she'd said it she was thinking it too. Tess was seeing a total stranger naked!

'You deserve better!'

Danilo had no idea where the words came from as he stood there, his embarrassment concealed behind a stony mask—he could assume that his seeming inability to walk away, duty done, conscience salved, was down to that initial nebulous connection he had made between her and Nat. He couldn't save his sister, he had failed Nat, but he could save this woman, who seemed to have serious self-destructive issues.

It was a statement that Tess couldn't take issue with, though she was uncomfortably aware that people rarely got what they deserved.

'He really isn't my boyfriend, though, like you, he *thinks* he is, he even tells people that he is, but in reality he is just a guy who uses the same bus stop as me. There is nothing more between us than small talk.

'At first,' she admitted, 'I just thought he was sweet… then, it was all a bit insidious, really. He'd turn up places I was, outside school, and then there were the emails and the texts. I thought if I ignored him he would get fed up and go away, then last month I had a break-in. There's no proof it was him. He didn't take anything but he left roses and champagne and…well, I took advice and precautions.'

Danilo heard her out in silence, his anger towards the other man growing as she told her story. 'I should have throttled the guy!'

'Well, with any luck I gave him my flu!' The grimly vindictive wish was so out of sync with the wan, pathetic figure standing there that he laughed. The sound drew her attention back to him. 'I hope you don't catch it.'

'You should inform the police.'

'He didn't actually hurt me, or even threaten to, it's just that I panicked. If I hadn't—if I'd just talked—'

'You were not to blame for what happened.'

'I know that, I'm just saying that I could have handled it better.' Actually what was she saying? She pressed a hand to her aching head. 'I suppose I will contact the police, but not tonight.'

'*Suppose?*'

Tess squeezed her eyes closed. 'If you yell I warn you I will cry and it is not a pretty sight.' Bending forwards as she was convulsed by a loud sneeze, she raised her head and found a box of tissues extended to her. She took a bunch and blew her nose loudly then, looking at him through watery eyes, rasped, 'Thank you.'

'So what are you going to do now?' he asked, tuning out the voice in his head that said, *Not your business*.

With a sigh she turned her back and moved towards the kitchen area that was sectioned off by a breakfast bar. 'I never got my milk for my cup of tea so I'm going to improvise,' she informed him, pushing her hand to the back of the cupboard where a bottle of sherry and the cooking brandy lived.

Standing on the other side the breakfast bar, circa the nineteen seventies, like the rest of the place, he watched as she took the brandy bottle and glugged some in the bottom of one of the mugs that sat on the draining board. 'Sorry, where are my manners? Would you like some?'

He looked at the label, a flicker of amusement moving across his face. 'Thanks, but I'll pass. Are you sure you should?'

She had enough energy left to silence him with a red-nosed killer look but not enough to get herself to the comfy armchair. She collapsed instead onto the sofa, glass in hand. Then, head pushed back into the cushion, she closed her eyes and took a swallow, choking a little as the raw alcohol burned her sore throat.

'For a woman who is being stalked you are pretty trusting.'

Tess forced her heavy eyelids apart… *Trusting?* The point was she *wasn't*. In fact by some people's more relaxed standards she was paranoid, thanks in no small part to the long-ago incident with her mum's boyfriend. It didn't take therapy to figure out that the episode had left her with some trust issues. Though now was definitely *not* the moment for a forensic analysis of her nonexistent sex life.

But maybe, she mused, her eyes drawn almost against her will to the hard angles and planes of the dark lean face of a man who exuded raw sexuality like a force field, it was the moment to wonder why it had not crossed her mind at any point tonight to feel threatened by this total stranger. Down to the fever or plain stupidity?

'Wait, you're not about to tell me you're also some sort of freak who's fallen desperately in love with me?'

He laughed. 'No.'

She lifted a hand to find her ear torn, the blood already caking. So it wasn't just her ear-ring she'd lost but her sense of proportion too—his laugh hurt!

She let the amusement in his voice wash over her, not out of choice but because she had reached the point where stringing two words together was an effort. The dignified high ground was a place Tess aspired to occupy, but she'd never made it there.

On a good day—actually, any day but this one— she would now be informing him that she scrubbed up pretty well, as it happened, and that she had plenty of offers, which would have been childish, but true.

She had moved on a long way from the sixteen-year-old with the bad case of acne, braces and no discernible curves that had inspired the sleaze whom she had so conveniently thrown up over. He'd been less than happy about her obvious rejection of his unwanted advances, enough to issue a disgusted parting shot—*'You should be grateful I'd even look at you!'*

The voluptuous curves had never materialised but two years later her skin had cleared, she had lost her braces and boys her own age had started noticing her. The trouble was their interest rarely lasted long, or, for that matter, was mutual.

Tess had discovered she seemed destined to attract the sort of man who equated her appearance and her small frame with a fragility she did not possess either physically or mentally.

No matter how good-looking a man was, Tess found it a massive turn-off when he treated her as if she were a china doll that might break, and when they discovered she wasn't sweet and yielding, but actually quite tough, they tended to drift away disillusioned—all except Ben, of course.

The man who loved her for who she was turned out to be certifiably insane—maybe, she mused, that was what it took?

She fervently hoped not.

Tess didn't really know who her perfect man was, but she knew he wouldn't patronise her and he would treat her on equal terms. And if he could offer some mind-blowing sex that would definitely be a plus, but so far she had not come close to it!

Of course, while she was telling herself she was waiting for the right man and that she wasn't going to be pressurised into *settling*, it occurred to her that she

might be one of those women who were never going
to meet the man who pressed all the right buttons. The
women who blamed the men because they didn't want
to face the possibility it might be them? That they...
she didn't have it in her? A bubble of rebellion came to
the surface of her drifting thoughts: *no, I want passion!*

'I suppose you think that it was something I did?'

'You can't go through life worrying about what other
people think. Are you awake?'

'Unfortunately, yes.'

The dry comment made him smile. He could think
of few people who could retain a sense of humour after
the evening she had had. 'Did you hear what I said?'

'You don't love me—I'm still recovering.'

'Then that's a no. I have a suggestion.'

'Another lock? A remote cottage on the Outer Hebrides? Already thought of it.'

'Your door won't take another lock and it rains too
much in the Hebrides.'

When did this Englishwoman become your problem?

Obviously she wasn't his problem, except in the
sense she had evoked such a strong protective response
in him, which was as difficult to ignore as a kick in
the chest.

Try harder!

He responded to the suggestion from his dark side
with a thin smile, which morphed into a frown as his
dark veiled glance lifted from the tiny defenceless figure on the sofa and slid to the door with its rows of
locks. All he had to do was walk through it. He'd done
what anyone could expect of him and more.

So *why* was he still here?

Because he knew about the price of selfish actions,

he lived with guilt, it was a constant presence in his life and he didn't want any more.

And it wasn't about playing the hero. That would, he reflected, his lips forming a fleeting sardonic smile, have been a serious case of miscasting.

When he thought of heroes he thought of his little sister. She was the most heroic person he knew. Bleakness drifted to his eyes. Maybe, he speculated, that was why he felt such a strong compulsion now he couldn't save Natalia, but he had the opportunity to save *someone*... His lips twisted in a cynical smile—it helped that it required little or no effort on his part and no sacrifice.

'That stuff is actually quite good.' She leaned back, feeling quite mellow as the glow from the cooking brandy in her stomach began to spread. The floating feeling was pleasant.

'When are you back in college?'

'School,' she corrected sleepily, and yawned as she watched him through the mesh of her lowered eyelashes. At a purely aesthetic level he was well worth looking at. A few sleepy moments later she realised that he was looking at her, not lost in admiration, but because she hadn't answered his question—now, what was the question?

'I teach,' she slurred tiredly. The virus and the events of the last hours were catching up with her big time.

Danilo blinked. 'You're a teacher?'

'No, I'm an *excellent* teacher,' she rebutted with a half-smile, then yawned.

Danilo, still making the mental adjustment, didn't register her attempt at humour. 'So what do you teach?'

'After I graduated I did some supply teaching, then for a term I was a support classroom worker for a little boy with muscular dystrophy, now I teach reception class.' She gave a self-conscious little grimace, aware that she had given away more information than the casual question required.

'A teacher with experience of...' Encountering the puzzled, expectant gaze lifted to his face, he tipped his head slightly. 'Bear with me... This man tonight, he knows where you live?'

Tess closed her eyes. 'Thanks for that comforting parting shot. I'll sleep better for it.'

'I am not trying to be comforting.'

'Imagine my shock.'

'I am trying to offer a practical solution. The fact is he has broken in here once and I wouldn't put it past him to try a stunt like that again. So, as I see it you have two options. You can go down the legal route or—'

'Live in fear?' she interrupted with a bitter laugh. 'I hate to interrupt this little motivational speech, but—'

'Come to Italy. Your stalker won't find you there.'

She could only assume he was trying to lighten the mood. 'Why not Australia? I've always fancied a bit of surfing.' She opened one eye. 'Don't do comedy, it's not you.'

'My little sister, Natalia, lives at home with me, work takes me away often—'

'You're offering me a job as a childminder?'

'Natalia is almost nineteen.' His dark eyes moved in an assessing sweep over her face. 'How old are you?'

'Twenty-six.'

'There was an accident and my sister is temporarily in a wheelchair. Her life has been on hold, most of her school friends have moved on...away... I think she feels isolated sometimes.' His focus had been so much on pushing forwards with Nat's recovery that it could be argued he had virtually pushed her into the arms of that no-hoper Marco.

It could happen again, and he couldn't be there for her all the time, but if she had someone there her own age, another woman to confide in... 'I think it might help her.'

'I'm sorry.' The picture he painted touched her deeply. 'Your parents...?'

'Were killed in the same accident.'

A powerful wave of empathy swept through Tess, almost painful in its intensity. She squeezed her eyes tighter closed over the hot sting of unshed tears and cleared her throat before responding huskily.

'I'm so sorry.' It seemed lame but what else could she say?

He cut a sideways look at her before tipping his head in acknowledgement.

'But I couldn't.'

'Why not?'

Indignation gave her the strength to lift her heavy eyelids. 'Are you serious? I can't just up and leave—' She stopped and thought, *or could she?*

It would solve the immediate problem, give her a breathing space to decide what to do about Ben and she was missing out on her holiday. She'd always wanted to see Italy.

'The decision is yours,' he said, giving the impression that he'd lost interest in the subject. 'When you have decided...' He pulled a card from his breast pocket and looked around for an empty surface to put it on before handing it directly to Tess.

'This is the number of my assistant in London. She

will coordinate things on this end, flights and so forth. She will take up your references. I was thinking that you could travel at the end of the week, either Thursday or Friday, unless your cold doesn't clear up.'

'I have flu,' she countered automatically. 'You want references?'

'Is that a problem?'

'No, it is not a problem.'

'When I leave you will lock the door.' Slinging the edict over his shoulder, he walked through the door.

It was around two in the morning when Tess woke up on the sofa, the business card clutched in her hand. She glanced over to the unlocked door and shivered. Well, she'd slept a little at least, no doubt the result of combining the brandy with the cold and flu meds she'd been liberally popping in an attempt to feel better. She looked at the card again, reading out the name printed on it in bold italics.

Danilo Raphael.

She would consider his offer but only after she had locked the door.

CHAPTER THREE

WHEN SHE TOLD Fiona of her plan the next day her friend was horrified.

'You're mad, crazy. You have no idea who this man is!' She looked at the business card he had handed her. 'Anyone can get one of these printed. For all you know he could be a pervert—'

'Give me some credit, Fi, I'm not an idiot. I looked him up online. He's legitimate.' He was actually a bit of a legend in his own lifetime, but, afraid of being accused of exaggeration, Tess didn't share these details. Instead she picked up her phone, scrolled down on the screen and handed it to Fiona—it was simpler.

Her friend took it without looking and snorted. 'Online I'm *legitimately* a size ten. People make stuff up all the time—' She glanced down and took a deep breath, the expression of awe that spread across her face almost comical. 'Wow! *He* rescued you?'

'I like to think of it more that he happened along at the right moment.' And what would have happened if he hadn't? Tess pushed the question away. Some things it was better not to know and she already had enough problems sleeping.

Fiona couldn't take her eyes off the phone screen. 'He *really* looks like that? This photo's not airbrushed or anything?'

'Well, he looks a bit older.' Harder, would have been more accurate. In the flesh Danilo Raphael possessed a streamlined lean toughness that didn't come across in the photos online, and there had been a lot to compare and contrast, but most were of him looking younger though still dramatically good-looking. The camera really did love those cheekbones, and so, it seemed, did the wide selection of women pictured draped all over him.

'He's a hottie!'

Tess chose to ignore Fiona's comment and folded the last item in her case. She huffed gently as she closed the lid. 'I hate packing and I never take the right thing,' she complained.

'You look good in a bin sack,' her friend consoled. 'If I had your figure…well, never mind that. So,' she said, handing back the phone, 'what does *gorgeous* do when he's not rescuing women?'

'Makes money.'

'He's sounding better all the time.'

'It seems he buys failing companies and makes them work, or at least he used to. He took over the family firm when his parents died a couple of years ago, and they had pretty much a finger in any pie you care to mention…' Tess mentioned a few. 'After their death, though, he dropped off the party circuit—'

'Got married and had a few kids?'

Tess managed to conceal her reaction to the question and shrugged. She had no idea *why* the idea of Danilo Raphael enjoying domestic bliss shocked her so much, but her friend's analysis of the low public profile did work.

'Maybe?' The information she had about the accident online was sketchy. The headlines were lurid and, though there was little detail, she felt safe assuming that this was what had brought about the change in this ex-playboy's lifestyle.

'You do realise what you described is called asset stripping? And asset strippers are not a breed noted for their warmth and human kindness.'

'He said he wasn't kind,' she remembered. Strangely, despite the trauma and her fever she could remember every word he had said and the exact intonation of his husky voice. She caught Fiona looking at her and carefully wiped away whatever expression had been on her face that had made her friend stare. 'But I'm hired to be a companion to his sister, not hold hands with him.' An image floated into her head of his long brown fingers; she pushed it away. 'I doubt if I'll even see him.'

One step through the door and Danilo swung back, the expression on his lean face impatient as he gave a shrug and responded to Franco's question.

'She's petite, maybe even a little mousey, she's probably looking lost…big eyes in a small face.' His mouth quirked as the description brought a disappointed look to his cousin's face. 'What were you expecting, a supermodel?'

His cousin gave a grin. 'It wouldn't have hurt. So what do you want me to do with this mouse?'

'Drop her off at the house. Nat is expecting her.'

'You don't expect me to stay and babysit, then?

I'm meant to be meeting the event organiser later this morning.'

'Your cousin Angelica will look after her and introduce her to Nat.' The furrow between his dark brows deepened. 'More problems with the party?'

'Just a few tweaks. I want it to be perfect.'

'That is the general idea,' Danilo agreed, holding eye contact long enough to see his cousin squirm. The lie was obvious but Danilo, already late for a meeting, let it lie.

'So I can just dump her and run?'

Tess, who had adjusted her step to accommodate the slower pace of her travelling companion, was about the last person from the London flight to clear the customs checkpoint, and as they entered the arrivals lounge together the elderly Italian lady was immediately surrounded.

The size of her laughing family was equalled by the number of kisses being exchanged. The warmth and volume of their greeting was overwhelming, and for a moment Tess shared the warmth and was literally swept along by it, until a young man kissed her and then drew back, blushing with teenage embarrassment as he quickly apologised for his mistake.

'Signora, mi dispiace.'

The old lady, laughing, took Tess's hand and introduced her.

'This is Tess, who held my hand during take-off and landing.'

'It was a mutual thing. I was terrified too.'

'Is there someone here to meet you?' the man who

had identified himself as her travelling companion's son asked.

Tess nodded, her eyes sweeping the area, refusing to acknowledge the tiny blip of anticlimax that tightened in her stomach. It wasn't as if she had expected even for one moment to be met personally by Danilo Raphael.

'I think that might be him over there.' She nodded towards the only person remaining, a young man in a designer suit who stood with hands in his pockets scanning the room impatiently and glancing up at the arrivals board at intervals. 'Excuse me, and congratulations on the birth of your first grandchild,' she added with a smile.

'Excuse me?'

The scowl on Franco's face lifted a little as the petite woman with the long glossy hair, wearing a pair of spiky ankle boots and a swingy little skirt that showed off her slender, shapely legs, stopped right in front of him. For a moment it seemed less important that Danilo was going to blame him for the no show of the English mouse.

Franco swallowed, his heart beating a little faster as she smiled. It was a really great smile.

'By any chance are you looking for me?'

'All my life, *cara*.'

The extraordinary amber eyes continued to meet his with a directness he was beginning to find unnerving. One of the feathery dark brows rose. She gave a kind smile and observed, 'Which is not actually so very long, is it?'

Feeling like a schoolboy and not enjoying the novelty value—he might not be able to impress his older cousin but young females were normally putty in his hands—he felt his face colour.

'I'm sorry, but you seemed to be looking for someone, so I thought perhaps you'd been sent to meet me by Mr Raphael?' She blinked away the intrusive image of the Italian's dark, strongly sculptured features and focused on the handsome and far less disturbing face of the young man she was addressing.

'You're the m… Mou…' Franco shook his head and allowed his eyes to drift to the pink pouty lips. 'I think,' he said regretfully, 'there has been some mistake.'

The words echoed the thought that had been fighting to make itself heard in Tess's head ever since she had boarded the flight. Was she making a colossal mistake here? She gave her glossy head the slightest of shakes and straightened her slender shoulders, pushing away the doubt. Mad or not, she'd made her decision and she was going to make the best of it.

'I should have introduced myself. I'm Tess Jones.'

Franco's jaw dropped, before moments later a smile spread across his features. 'And I'm Franco. Danilo said… Sorry, I was expecting someone…not you,' he finished awkwardly. 'Danilo is my cousin.'

'Well, that's a relief.' She arched a curious brow. 'Who were you expecting?'

Franco sidestepped the question. 'I thought you were with your family?' Franco nodded towards the group who were gathered around the elderly lady that the stunning English girl had appeared with.

The curious pucker between her feathery brows smoothed as she accepted the explanation. 'Oh, the Padrones.' She lifted a hand and waved. 'No, I've never

met them before. Carlita and I just bonded over our fear
of flying. We got talking and she's quite a character and
so proud of her family. Her youngest daughter lives in
London—she'd just had her first child.' Tess tucked the
woman's address into her bag and waved once more to
the family who were moving towards the exit.

'Where exactly did Danilo find you?'

For the first time her candid gaze fell from his.

'Long story but he was very…kind.' Not sold on the
accuracy of her description, Tess absently rubbed the
frowning indent above the bridge of her small straight
nose as one of the jumble of memories that had imprinted strongly surfaced.

For a disorientating moment the weight of a muscled
arm draped across her shoulders was so real that she
inhaled, anticipating the spicy fragrance with minty
overtones she recalled.

She inhaled again, this time to focus, feeling irritated with herself. There was no point coming to Italy
to escape if you brought the bad memories with you.

Danilo? Kind? While his cousin was one of life's
good guys, he was not what most people would call
kind. Franco managed to maintain a bland expression
while his imagination went into overdrive.

It was midnight by the time Danilo drove his car past
the security cameras mounted on the gates that swung
open as he approached and closed behind him as he
drove down the familiar mile-long tree-lined driveway
that led to Palazzo Florentina, the Tuscan home that
had been in the Raphael family for generations now.
The home he had returned to after his parents' deaths.

The road split just as the distinctive building with

its central golden stone tower, spotlit in the darkness, came into view. He drove along the right-hand fork and through the arch into the well-lit courtyard, built from the same distinctive stone as the main house.

Once, when the place had been the summer home of a royal family who had built the place—there was a *tenuous* family link to the Raphaels—all of these buildings would have been the stable block. Nowadays only one wing housed horses. So far Danilo hadn't been able to bring himself to reduce the number of animals. His mother had been a keen horsewoman and had adored each and every one, so he justified his economically irrational action, or lack of it, by promising himself that he would ride more—when he had the time.

He approached the wing opposite where the horses were housed in luxury, heading for the garages that took up another wing. The rest had been converted into accommodation. The largest staff apartment was occupied by a distant cousin. Since the death of her husband, Angelica had taken on the role of housekeeper, and her apartment was the only one that had its own garden.

He didn't bother raising the automatic doors; instead he parked on the cobbles, glancing up as he got out at the section of the buildings where Franco had an apartment. No lights showed at the windows, but then his young cousin rarely spent a night there if he had a better offer, which he frequently did. He'd probably crawl into work late tomorrow looking like hell!

Danilo's lips quirked as he recognised the irony of his disapproval—or was that envy? He was hardly in a position to judge considering that there had been a time not so long ago when he'd been the guy who partied most nights and the photos still existed to prove it.

Not that he led the life of a monk now—he knew his limitations—but nowadays his sex life was more...*discreet*. Discreet and disposable. He smiled without humour to himself, liking the alliteration.

He was a changed man. Approval of senior family members who had once accused him of bringing disrepute to the family name might have meant more had he changed his lifestyle out of choice. His public face had changed, his life had changed, but had he? Deep down wasn't he still the same selfish bastard he had always been? Take today and the English mouse—he had outsourced her to his cousin without a second thought, but the world thought he was a responsible, upright and valued member of society.

His lips twisted into a parody of a smile in response to the kick of self-loathing in his belly. *Because isn't that what matters?* he thought to himself.

His smile died, but the tired lines bracketing his mouth remained as his lean face set in a cynical expression, which was in danger of becoming permanently engrained. The fact was he didn't give a damn what anyone thought of him. He wasn't out to garner good opinion. The only thing he wanted, the thing his entire life focused on, was seeing his sister walk again.

He strode on, his lean face set in lines of steely determination now as he pushed aside the guilt that was a distraction and an indulgence.

Leaving the keys in the low-slung sports car—the security on the estate was good—he cut through the avenue of cedars, glad to feel the soft evening air on his face. He'd been cooped up in an air-conditioned office half the day and well into the evening. Dinner had been more about securing a contract than socialising so it had been annoying that the senior manager of the firm he was dealing with had not seemed to realise this and had brought his wife along, which had meant the meal had dragged on and no decisions had been reached.

Maybe that wasn't just due to the presence of the charming wife, though. Danilo had allowed himself to be distracted today by the thought of a pair of big, scared, golden eyes.

Those damned eyes had been prodding his conscience all day and he resented it. Hiring the Englishwoman was one of those ideas that had seemed good at the time. It was only when you walked away that you saw the flaws. If he was honest, Danilo had been hoping that Tess would get cold feet. He'd *expected* her to get cold feet but inconveniently she hadn't so presumably she was in her room now, feeling lost and overawed by her surroundings, totally out of her depth.

He just hoped that Nat hadn't been too *off* with her. He really hadn't anticipated his sister's reaction. In retrospect he could see he'd been clumsy with the way he'd broached the subject of the new, if temporary, addition to their household. The car crash of a conversation drifted through his head as he let himself into the house.

'A companion?'

He hadn't immediately recognised the danger in Nat's tone. 'More a friend.'

'Do you think I'm so pathetic you have to buy me friends? You can't buy friends.'

'I'm not—'

'Do you think I'm so stupid that I can't see what you're trying to do? She's a guard dog, isn't she? A spy—your spy—reporting back to you. I agreed not to see Marco—do you really trust me so little?'

'I do trust you, Nat,' he'd promised while thinking, *no*, it was the kid she'd got involved with he didn't trust. And Nat's reaction earlier today was yet another example of the influence the boy had had on his sweet little sister, who would never previously have argued with him this way.

He'd hardened his heart against the tears on her face and the crack in her voice when she'd said the lad's name; he'd had no hesitation in dismissing him and his decision had been proved right. Not that his sister had seemed to care when he'd revealed her boyfriend had already had several run-ins with the law.

Her reaction—*I know about that; we have no secrets*—had really set the danger bells in his head ringing.

'If this woman doesn't work out, fine,' he'd soothed, trying to make up lost ground.

'Do you even know her name?'

'She is called Tess.'

Going over the conversation in his head now, Danilo swore. He hated scenes and it was rare for Nat to treat him to one, but she had changed and he didn't know how to deal with it.

Oh, well, at least he didn't have to deal with it tonight.

He was approaching the staircase, a monumental curved cantilevered structure that was illuminated by light set in the stained-glass cupola two storeys above, when the laugh derailed his depressing train of thought. It was an unrestrained husky sound. He paused and listened, aware as he did so of the sound of music and voices, then that laugh again.

'Damn you, Franco, I meant it!' he growled as he realised this was a repeat of the night when Franco had brought back a group of friends. On that occasion they'd managed to leave a trail of destruction behind, along with the half-dressed blonde Danilo had found fast asleep on the library floor.

A dishevelled and very hungover Franco had been suitably contrite after he had first sulkily thrown the accusation of jealousy at Danilo. His jaw tightened as he moved through the rooms searching out the party venue, knowing he had no choice but to follow through with his threat of sacking Franco—an action which would no doubt bring Franco's doting mother down on his head.

'You idiot, Franco, why do you always have to push it?'

He swore softly in two languages. He'd cut Franco a lot of slack but he'd made it clear after the last incident that the next time it happened would be the last.

It wasn't until he had opened and slammed several doors that Danilo realised the noise that he had assumed was a party in progress was actually coming from the cinema room in the basement.

Some of the tension slid from his shoulders; he smiled at his mistake.

The cinema room was one of those things that had seemed like a good idea at the time. He could count on the fingers of one hand how many times they had used it even though he'd had it installed at the same time the builders had been making the necessary adaptations to make the historical building suitable for a wheelchair, two years ago now.

The half-open door of the soundproofed room explained the noise. As he pushed it and stepped inside the noise got louder and so did the voices.

Against the background of the big screen that seemed

to be playing the closing credits of an old black-and-white movie, three people sat in a half-circle.

His eyes went immediately to his sister's wheelchair, drawn up beside a table that bore the remains of a bowl of popcorn. Looking at her carefree smile brought a tightness to his chest. It made him realise how long it was since he'd seen her look that way. It reminded him of a time… He looked away quickly before the pressure in his chest became crushing, moving his focus onto Franco. His young cousin was sitting on the floor, a bottle of beer in his hand, for once not trying to look like something out of a men's fashion magazine as he took a swallow then choked, spluttering unattractively as he let out a cry of protest as the third person in the room lobbed a handful of popcorn at him.

'You pig, Franco!' His sister sent a second handful of popcorn that made her cousin duck his head.

Danilo caught himself grinning, then stopped suddenly, feeling old, or at least like the only adult in the room, but then he probably was! His interest shifted to the stranger who was curled up, her face turned away from him, on one of the big leather sofas that faced the screen with her legs tucked up under her. It was hard to tell from this angle if the person for whose benefit he assumed the conversation was being conducted in English was eighteen or thirty-eight. Franco was going through an *older* woman stage just now!

With more curiosity than he usually felt for the women in his cousin's life—this one had made his sister smile—his gaze travelled from the flash of pink-painted toenails, moving upwards over what he could see of her slim, denim-clad legs and the tee shirt she wore tucked in at the waist. The logo emblazoned across

the white cotton encouraged readers to save a tree but
Danilo's attention was less captured by the sentiment
than the soft curves the cotton hinted at.

His libido gave a lazy kick. He recognised this as a
call to stop putting off pencilling in a space in his mental diary for some fun or at least sex, because the day he
felt even vaguely attracted to anyone his cousin dated
it was time to take action!

As he watched her, the girl's head fell back and her
face, hidden up until this point, was revealed. First just
her profile, clear cut and youthful, then, as she twisted
around a little, he got the full-face effect.

She was beautiful, or was that striking? A hard call
to make even if his brain had been functioning, which it
wasn't. The impact of that first glimpse had suspended
all but the most basic functions. It took him several suspended heartbeats to wrestle it into submission and the
effort brought a sheen of moisture to his skin.

He was back in control now, but struggling to get
to grips with the sheer mind-numbing strength of that
flash flood of raw lust that had ribboned like fiery
threads through his body. The feeling remained but
in a more manageable form, a knot of pulsing desire.
As he continued to stare the cause of the electrifying
moment pulled her knees up to her chin and, one arm
curved in a graceful arc above her head, gave a rich
chuckle of laughter, low and husky. Earlier, the earthy
sound had drawn him; closer up it had a nerve-tingling,
tactile quality.

He had no idea what she was laughing at. It didn't
really matter—the sound was genuinely infectious. The
corners of his own mouth lifted as he listened to the
warm and uninhibited sound.

He was still smiling as she lowered her arm and pushed a gleaming strand of the wavy golden-brown hair that fell in ripples down her back from her face while simultaneously pulling herself upright into a cross-legged sitting position. Both actions held a supple fluidity that was fascinating to watch. He studied her face, which was the visual equivalent of the uninhibited musical laughter, laughter that had a skin-tingling quality—as did that mouth!

Danilo felt the last remnants of the fatigue that he had felt lift as he gazed at the bold, passionate curve of her lips. Fighting the fascination the pink cushiony softness exerted on him, it took a few moments to drag his gaze free from them and take in the smooth curve of high cheeks, a pointy, stubborn chin and dark slanted brows angled above wide eyes. A fractional turn of her head brought him into direct contact with those eyes, revealing a startlingly golden gaze, the amber glow emphasised by the dark rim around the iris.

The colour triggered a buried memory, where had he seen…? He shrugged away the half-formed question. No matter how deeply buried, he wouldn't have forgotten a woman this striking, this sleek and sexy.

And sensual, he silently added as he watched the tilted heavy-lidded eyes widen…in recognition? Again the question surfaced in Danilo's head but he barely heard it above the blood pounding in his skull, sending testosterone-fuelled heat flooding through his hardening body.

Not in his hormone-fuelled teens, or his hedonistic playboy days, could he recall feeling anything even approaching the level of raw sexual attraction that had nailed him to the spot for the second time in as many minutes. He didn't have a clue how long he remained that way before he became aware of his dog nudging his leg with her nose.

Spell broken, he glanced down at the retriever at his feet, her devoted eyes on him, her tail thudding on the floor.

'Danilo!' They had parted on poor terms but his sister sounded happy to see him.

'Good girl.' He bent down to pat Goldie, offering her the treat he always carried in his pocket and letting her take it off his hand before responding to his sister's warm welcome. He continued to be aware, very aware, of Franco's date, but his social mask was fully functioning.

From his position on the floor Franco yelled, 'I want it on record that it was not my choice of film and my eyes were only watering.' With a grunt he got to his feet and held out a hand to the girl on the sofa.

She didn't need it.

She performed the action a lot more stylishly than his cousin, rising from her cross-legged pose with the natural grace he associated with a dancer. There was something about her that made him think of a Degas painting.

Something... He stopped dead, shock colliding with disbelief in his head. It was quite impossible, and for several stunned heartbeats Danilo's brain simply refused to accept it. Finally he had no choice. The proof was there in a wide-eyed amber stare that seemed to mock him.

The barefooted, glowing woman standing shoulder height to his cousin with the rippling mass of shiny hair, arrestingly vivid face and provocative dancer's body calmly returning his scrutiny was the red-nosed, needy creature who'd dragged a chivalrous response from him a week ago.

CHAPTER FOUR

THE GUILTY IMAGE of a lost, vulnerable creature rose up to mock him before vanishing. And in her place stood a woman straight from a man's sexual fantasy—or was that just his?

She dropped down into a crouch with unstudied feline grace to rub the ears of the animal who was staring up at her with longing before planting a wet doggy kiss on her nose.

'Goldie!' Danilo said sharply.

He watched, hot colour streaking his cheekbones, as Tess rose with balletic grace, rubbing her hands over invisible creases in the jeans that clung to her hips as she pulled herself up to her full height, which couldn't be much more than five-two. Her height was the *only* thing that had remained unchanged.

It *was* her, but he still couldn't believe it!

'I don't mind. She's a lovely dog,' Tess said. 'I always wanted one growing up, but my mum hates dog hairs on her clothes.'

A faithless hound, Danilo thought as the animal reacted with obvious reluctance to the click of his fingers and began to pad across the room to him.

While Danilo waited for the animal to reach him

the conflicting emotions in his chest built and built until finally solidifying into something he could deal with—anger!

He'd spent the day feeling guilty for, as he'd seen it, taking advantage of the woman, for pretending even to himself that his motives were altruistic. If he'd really wanted to help Tess, he'd have dragged her to the police or even reported the incident himself, not brought her somewhere the little mouse was bound to be unhappy and out of her depth.

Yet here Tess was, in his home, looking not out of place but relaxed, as if she belonged! The roles were reversed: *he* was the one who felt like a damned intruder, an intruder in his own home, he decided, feeding his sense of outrage.

'Good evening, Mr Raphael.' She smiled and pushed her far-from-lank hair off her face. Nothing in her manner suggested she needed looking after, certainly not carrying up the stairs. Though if she had he couldn't imagine there would be any lack of offers. In fact, if you looked at the situation from one angle this might, at least on the surface, have worked out better than he could have hoped, but Danilo just couldn't shake off that initial gut response, the feeling, the totally *irrational* feeling, that he had been cheated.

'Good evening. I hope you had a good flight, Miss Jones?'

Was every dialogue she had with him going to sound like something from a Jane Austen novel? Tess wondered, deciding to go along with the lie that he had known who she was from the outset. He'd been as shocked by her appearance as she had anticipated, but she'd not been in a position to enjoy it.

Before delivering her response she pressed a hand to cover the pulse that was still frantically beating at the base of her throat. *Focus on the positive, Tess, you didn't fall down, or drool.* 'Apart from the take-off and the landing it was perfect, thank you, Mr Raphael.'

He gave an uninterested nod and continued to look every inch the brooding hero, though a lot more Heathcliff than Mr Darcy.

His sister spun her chair around and sped across the room to him, no visible trace of the sulky, resentful young woman he had seen earlier that day. He had no idea how the change had been wrought in such a short space of time, he just wished that he'd been the one responsible for it.

'Come on,' Nat urged. 'Join us. We could watch another film.'

'It's after twelve.' Danilo watched his sister's face fall, silently kicking himself when her happy smile vanished and was replaced by an antagonistic expression.

'But I'm not a child, Danilo, and, unless you've moved the goalposts, I don't have a curfew.'

Tess's elaborate and loud yawn broke the tense silence, and as eyes swivelled her way she gave a rueful grimace and apologised. 'It's been a long day. I think if nobody minds I'm ready for my bed.'

'Do you remember the way or shall I show you to your room?'

'I'm sure Miss Jones is capable of finding her own way to her room, Franco.' Danilo wondered at what point his cousin had abandoned his *dump and run* policy. Probably after the first smile. 'But first a word, Miss Jones…?' He aimed his glance a safe inch or so to the right of her lovely face, but found his eyes irresistibly tugged towards her mouth.

His inability to fight the draw of the sensual outline fanned the flame of his growing sense of being the victim of some giant con. He felt like someone who had paid for a safe and solid family car and been conned into leaving the showroom with a powerful motorbike. Shiny, attractive, guaranteed to make his heart beat faster, but not what he'd signed up for. This woman was not what he had signed up for.

His sister, framed in the doorway in her chair, swung back. 'You can't call Tess "Miss Jones" like that. It's so stuffy.'

Tess was quite happy if relations between herself and Danilo remained stuffy! Far less distracting that way!

It had taken Tess about five minutes after arriving to pick up on the underlying resentment when Natalia spoke of her brother, but it was equally obvious she adored him. It didn't take a genius to see that the household's personal dynamics were strained and she was starting to see why. Danilo had the rare ability to walk into a room and drain the joy out of it.

'Your brother is my boss, Nat.' *For how long?* was the question. His attitude suggested she had messed up in his eyes before she had even opened her mouth, or she might be paranoid.

Tess slid a covert sideways glance under her lashes towards the tall figure, and her stomach sank a little farther. No, *not* paranoid! She could feel the waves of disapproval and antagonism rolling off him from across the room, a reality that made little or no sense but then, after *that* moment tonight when she had first seen him, her reasoning capacity was pretty limited.

A little shiver rose from her toes. *Before* she had turned her head she'd known he was there. She had felt his eyes, something she had previously heard people say and she wanted to roll her eyes, but she really had!

There was no time to analyse it now, which she was quite glad about. *Disturbing* didn't begin to describe the head-spinning, finger-in-a-socket moment when heat had sizzled through her body. She had breathed her way through it and not done anything crazy but it remained a shameful reminder in her core.

There *should* have been no shock involved. She'd spent the last two hours glancing at the door, imagining Danilo standing there, at intervals glancing casually over her shoulder.

The only shock she'd anticipated, if she was honest, was *his*.

She was well aware that the last time their paths had crossed she had rarely registered on his radar as a woman, let alone a passably attractive one. Her efforts tonight to repair the minor dent he had delivered to her ego had worked, but seriously, oh, *wow*, had they backfired!

She inhaled, living a second time through that mindblowing moment when their eyes had connected. The heat that had flashed along her nerve endings had meant that when the anticipated recognition finally came Tess had barely registered it, let alone taken any form of satisfaction from it.

She pressed a hand to the pulse still beating frantically at the base of her throat. It had been like watching her knee jump after someone struck the right spot with a patella hammer, a reflex she had no control over. Danilo Raphael's dark stare had touched a spot, one Tess hadn't

even known she had, and the resultant electrical charge
that zinged along her nerve endings had been equally
outside her control. Not an experience she enjoyed.

She might have been more prepared for this *weird-
ness* if she hadn't, up until now, worked on the assumption that everything about that evening had been
exaggerated by fear and the flu—only it hadn't! If anything, her memory had downplayed Danilo Raphael. He
was darker, taller; her memory recalled a man who was
obviously better looking than, in her opinion, any man
had a right to be, but it had not accurately recorded the
innate, earthy sensuality he projected.

'No, he just writes the cheques,' she heard Natalia rebut, and dragged her attention back to the pretty
young woman in the wheelchair. 'You work for me and
I say it's Tess.' She angled a look that was half teasing,
half challenging across the room at her brother.

'The trick, Nat,' Tess explained, 'is letting a man
think it's his idea.'

It was *my idea*, Danilo thought grimly. *I brought
this woman here*...and she was already creating ripples.

'We can leave the discussion until the morning if you
prefer, Miss… Tess?' Perhaps recognising the coldness
of his words or picking up on his cousin's puzzled looks,
he added, 'I hope you had a good journey and Franco—'

'Great journey,' she cut in. The effort of smiling was
starting to make her jaw ache. 'And everyone has been
very kind and so welcoming.' *Until now!* 'And I'd prefer
to get it over with now.' Flushing at the implication left
by her words, she hastily tried to soften her comment
by adding, 'That is, you're very kind, Mr Raphael, but
I'm fine to talk…so long as you don't read anything
into the odd yawn.' She turned towards Nat and smiled.

'See you in the morning. Goodnight, Franco. Admit it, you enjoyed the film.'

'I might have,' Franco conceded, reacting to the teasing light in her eyes with an enigmatic look that morphed into a grin as he went on to explain, 'But if I admitted that I'd have to kill you to save my reputation. *Buono notte*, Tess, it was a great night.' He gave her a hug, nodded in the direction of the tall, brooding presence of his cousin and left, closing the door behind him.

The sound threatened to trigger a nervous meltdown in Tess. Without anyone else around to dissipate it, the tangible physical charge Danilo exuded took on the form of an electrical buzz in the air. It seemed amazing that the last time she'd been alone with him she hadn't really registered it. Even more amazing was the fact his presence had made her feel safe and secure that night. She was starting to realise that that had been a one-off!

'Alone at last.' She winced as her nerves found an outlet in flippancy.

He didn't react. 'Take a seat, Miss Jones.'

Her eyes widened in a flicker of dismay. 'Why? Is this going to take long, Mr Raph...?' She left the retaliatory addition unfinished; one of them had to be a grown-up and it didn't look as if it was going to be him. 'Thanks but I feel like I've been sitting all day.'

'So how long are we to have the pleasure of your company?'

His tone was perfectly polite but somehow he managed to send the strong impression that five minutes would be too long. Tess fought the urge to ask him just what the hell she had done wrong and replied evenly.

'Your PA seemed to think me going back a week before the next school term starts would be all right. Is it?'

Danilo paused, thought of his sister's laughing face and tipped his head, unable to bring himself to ask how she had magicked the transformation in his sister he'd observed. 'You seem to be getting on well with Natalia?'

Tess ignored the fact his comment sounded more like an accusation than a compliment and responded with perfect honesty. 'That's not a big ask. Nat is a lovely girl. You must be so proud of her.'

'She tires easily.' He frowned because it sounded as if he was putting up obstacles, then continued to because he was!

'Helena filled me in on the basics.'

His glance, defying his fractured self-control, had begun to slide down her body but the mention of his PA brought his gaze back to her face.

'So what else did Helena fill you in on?'

'Not a lot. She mentioned the car accident. Though you'd already told me a bit about it. How it robbed you of your parents.' Did the perfect tailoring hide scars from the same incident? Did that explain his touchy reaction? Survivor's guilt? Or was his body marked by the tragedy that had put his sister in a wheelchair? It was the stab of painful empathy that speared through her that pushed Tess to question, 'Were you in the car?' She bit her lip, her eyes widening in dismay the moment the words were out. 'Sorry, that is none of my business.'

He elevated a dark sardonic brow, fooled not a jot by the down-bent head. She was about as meek as a tsunami! 'I am none of your business.'

She nodded, acknowledging she'd been firmly put in her place.

'But, no, I was not in the car. I was out of the country.'

His voice was flat. Too flat, she decided, wondering what nerve she had touched before she reminded herself that it was none of her business.

'If you're worried I'm too ancient to connect with your sister you shouldn't be. I can just about remember what it was like to be nineteen.'

'But you can't remember what it was like to be in a wheelchair,' he fired back, angry because that *hadn't* been his first thought. His first thought when she'd mentioned her age, typically selfish, had been that she was not too young for him.

Not that he was going to do anything about it, not while she was under his roof anyway. He might not have deliberately compartmentalised his life but it had happened and the results spoke for themselves.

'No, obviously not.'

'Of all the frustrations it involves, of having the life, the future you had planned torn away from you.'

The suddenness of it, the painful strength of the emotions that poured off Danilo, made her take an involuntary step back from him.

He might doubt her ability to emote but Tess no longer doubted his. She felt a stab of guilt, realising that she had been on the brink of labelling him an unimaginative, control-freak bully.

'I don't suppose that any of us can, but we can try…?'

Her soft response brought his haunted stare back to her face. 'I would change places with her in a heartbeat if I could.'

He had thought it so many times but never voiced it so why the hell had he now? He lowered his eyelids to conceal his struggle as he reasserted control.

'She would probably feel the same way if the roles were reversed.'

Danilo's jaw clenched as he fought the urge to lash out at her verbally.

'But,' he said, enunciating each word slowly, 'they are not.'

If he had to lose it, why had he done so in front of this woman, who seemed to be a bottomless well of teeth-aching understanding?

He had raised his barriers so completely that if she hadn't witnessed the moment with her own eyes Tess wouldn't have believed it had happened, but it had and she'd seen something of Danilo that he hid from the world. He'd probably never forgive her for that.

'So, your duties…'

'Duties?' she echoed. She hadn't been expecting that but she was fine with it; she could multitask with the best of them. She supposed that was how rich people stayed that way: they got value for money. Besides, busy was good. It stopped her thinking about what waited for her at home, the issues that being here was delaying not resolving.

'I worked for a housekeeping agency when I was at college and—'

'You think this interests me why, exactly?' he drawled.

'Well, if you want me to work some hours in the house or garden as well—'

He looked at her as though she was speaking a foreign language, which of course she was, though that was easy to forget in a household where virtually everyone she had met spoke excellent English.

When Danilo finally realised what she was talking about he gave a thin, scornful smile. 'I do not require you to scrub floors. We have staff for that. I am speaking of what I expect of you in regard to your duties for my sister.'

Embarrassed colour flooded Tess's face as she gnawed down on her lip, unwittingly drawing his gaze to the pink fullness.

'I misunderstood.' And felt pretty stupid. 'I guess I haven't got my head into the *palace* frame of mind yet.'

'Well, let's hope we have no more misunderstandings.'

Was she imagining things or had that been a warning? Maybe not. She was getting the impression that Danilo Raphael didn't give his victims warnings—he went straight for the jugular.

Her hand lifted to her exposed neck but the shiver that went through her wasn't fear.

'My sister recently had a…'

He paused and Tess, who had given a guilty start when he started speaking, adopted an attentive expression, pushing away the lingering image of his lips brushing her neck.

'There was,' he continued slowly, 'a…' He lifted his hands in a kind of *to hell with it* gesture and finished his explanation with an impatient rush. 'She's just split up with her boyfriend.' It went against the grain to call the kid that but it got his point across, which was the main thing, without going into detail.

And it did: the sympathy on Tess's face was instantaneous. 'Tough. Was it...' she hesitated to ask if Natalia had been dumped '...*her* idea?'

'No, it was my idea. The boy took advantage of her vulnerability to insinuate...' His jaw clenched as his anger threatened to resurface. 'He was bad news. He already had a criminal record. I was prepared to give him a chance but he abused my trust.'

'He works here?'

'He worked here,' Danilo corrected grimly.

'So your sister was all right with you sending him away?'

His glance dropped, the dark lashes that framed his incredible eyes hiding his expression momentarily. Tess was quite glad of a moment's release from that compelling dark stare.

'She will appreciate her lucky escape, in time.' And he was realising the absurdity of his compulsion to defend his actions right now. 'And in the meantime I would appreciate it if you informed me if this boy or any others try to—'

Tess held up her hand to stem the forceful flow of his words. 'Are you asking me to spy on your sister?'

His dark brows twitched into an irritated straight line above his masterful nose. 'I wouldn't call it that.'

'Well, I would,' she exclaimed. 'And the idea makes me uncomfortable.'

A look of astonishment crossed his lean features. 'You are saying you won't?' Such an eventuality had not even crossed his mind, any more than it would cross his mind that any employee would turn around and say no when he gave an instruction.

Her chin lifted, the gleam in her eyes contrasted with her calm delivery. 'That's right.'

'The boy abused my trust.'

'And I'd be abusing Natalia's trust if I agreed to do what you want. And maybe you shouldn't push it?' she ventured.

He sucked in an astonished breath. *She* was offering *him* advice? *'Push it?'*

'Quit while you're ahead?' she offered by way of further explanation. The moment the words had left her lips, even without his rapidly darkening expression, she knew she had gone too far, but for some reason she just couldn't stop herself. The words just kept coming! 'I mean, there are not many girls of Natalia's age who would accept their brother deciding who they should or shouldn't date. I wouldn't have…if I'd had a brother… which obviously I don't.'

'If you had a brother to watch out for you perhaps you wouldn't have to rely on a stranger to rescue you from your poor choice of men.'

His words were chosen to deliver the maximum hurt and when they clearly hit home Danilo promptly felt like an utter heel.

Even the reasonable defence that Tess could not expect to censure him that way and expect him not to retaliate did not lessen his level of guilt.

She probably didn't even think she'd done anything wrong; she was *just being honest*! It was a justification that never failed to make him see red.

He stared at her quivering lips and wondered how it was possible to want to throttle a woman one moment and comfort her the next.

Danilo did neither, but sitting on the fence was not a natural position for him. He had a black-and-white attitude to life. A decision was either right or wrong, a per-

son someone he wanted to know or one to be avoided.
A woman was one he desired or one who would drive
him insane. Yet Tess Jones combined both in one small
exquisite package!

'I did not choose him,' she quivered out finally. 'And
before you remind me, I know that running away is
never the answer but this will give me breathing space,'
she added, clearly dealing with the subject before he
used it as another offensive weapon.

'I wasn't going to say that, and I know what I did
say was untrue, and for that I apologise.' Even after the
rare *mea culpa* moment he continued to feel as guilty
as hell. 'And if there is any help or legal advice whatsoever I can offer you to resolve your *problem* at home—'

Tess was totally thrown by the unexpected apology.
Nevertheless she had to make it clear to Danilo that she
wasn't about to be pushed around by him, any more
than she wanted to be intimidated by Ben. 'I prefer to
resolve my own problems my way,' she announced as
though she had it all worked out.

'Fair enough.'

But he wasn't being fair. He'd been anything but! *So
tell him, don't just stand there taking it*, the impatient
voice in her head urged.

'Ever since you arrived I get the impression… Look,
have I done something wrong? Broken some rule, kept
Nat up too late? It was light beer and she is over eighteen. It's not my imagination, is it? You've been looking
at me as though…as though I was a fraud. I understand
that I'm not what you expected—or probably wanted.'

'I do not think you are a fraud.' He wasn't going
near the wanting…the *wanting* was the problem! He

couldn't look at her mouth without *wanting* to taste it. To feel her under him...

'If you're going to sack me I'd prefer you told me now, not kept me on as some sort of charity case.'

He dragged his eyes upwards.

'Do you want to leave?'

Did he want her to say yes or no? Danilo had no patience with people who did not know their own mind so recognising the ambivalence of his feelings drew a furrow in his brow.

'I like Natalia.'

The furrow smoothed.

'And I think I can be good for her.'

It wasn't relief he felt, just the satisfaction of having the decision made. 'I see you don't suffer from false modesty, but how about we give it a trial week?'

She tilted her head to one side and looked up at him, a half-smile tugging at her lips. The speed with which she had recovered amazed him. Most women he knew liked to drag out an argument until they had forgotten what it was about.

'Fine, I'll let you know if you pass the trial.'

The door had closed behind her before Danilo allowed himself to laugh.

CHAPTER FIVE

'FRANCO IS TAKING us out for a drink.'

'That's nice of him.' Nat sounded casual, but…? Tess had been here a week now. Long enough to recognise some signals. She angled a curious look at Natalia's face, wondering what she was missing this time. 'Does Franco know?'

The question drew a slightly forced laugh that suggested Tess's first instinct was right. 'Not yet,' Natalia admitted. 'But you've been here a week and it's time we showed you the action in Castelnuovo di Val di Cecina.'

'I already have,' Tess reminded Nat. She had been enchanted by the nearest small town to the estate, which itself was about midway between Florence and Pisa. It was a charming, picture-perfect medieval town surrounded by a forest of chestnut trees. Their visit had been short but she could have spent the day wandering the cobbled streets, catching glimpses of the valley below.

'At night it becomes a different place. Well, not really,' she added, with a grin. 'But there is this very nice bar. Danilo takes me there for lunch sometimes because it's so nice.'

'Franco might have other plans.'

'He might but he'll change them. He'll jump at the chance to take you out even if he has to bring me too. You must have noticed that he's got a crush on you?'

Tess had noticed but she thought it was harmless with a shelf life, she suspected, of a few days. Her half-smile faded, but what would happen if his cousin got the wrong idea? What if Danilo thought that she was encouraging Franco, or even using Franco to try to make Danilo feel jealous? *What are you doing, Tess?*

Tess brought the inner dialogue to an abrupt halt. There was a trap and she recognised it, which meant it was one dark hole she was not about to leap into. Oh, sure, she had observed how eager everyone was to defer to Danilo to change plans, but even while she felt removed from this collective rush for approval she had some sympathy.

Because despite his arrogance—or was that because of it?—and the ruthlessness that was often only just below the surface, Danilo could also be charming, when he wanted to be, and then there was his smile, which was knockout, and his charisma was off the scale!

Her immunity to the *please Danilo* disease had made her feel a little smug, but maybe this was how it happened? How did the medical books term it…*an insidious onset*?

Her chin lifted, concern slipping into her eyes when her amused laugh wouldn't come. She had never pretended to be something she wasn't for any man and she was not going to start now!

The wattage of her smile increased. 'Do I need to change?' She glanced down. It was the sixth night she had spent at the *palazzo* and the entire dressing-for-dinner thing was still new to her. She had assumed that as staff she would be eating in the kitchen or at least in her room but Nat had made it clear that this was not the case.

The first night, spent with Franco and Nat, dinner had been a relaxed affair, but the next…well, she could tell from the way Danilo had kept staring at her bare legs that she'd got it wrong.

The next night her skirt had been even shorter…to emphasise a point. Should the fact she felt the need to have worried her? Tess pushed away the thought. Even if she had it wouldn't have mattered: Danilo had not joined them for dinner that night or any since.

So she had dressed to please herself, quite enjoying the nightly ritual. Tonight she wore a simple, floaty, summer dress.

'You look great.'

'And if I may say so, so do you.' It was true. Nat was wearing a figure-hugging number in baby-blue silk that brought out the colour of her eyes and emphasised the voluptuous curves that Tess so envied.

There was plenty of room, but Alexandra was sitting close enough for their thighs to touch, not that many men would have complained. The designer—her company had been awarded the contract to furnish the latest luxury cruise ship that was being added to the expanding Raphael Cruise Line—looked exactly what she was: an ex-model. Topping six feet in her heels, she was slim with endless legs. Somewhat cynically he suspected that she already had her plastic surgeon of choice on speed dial for the day she didn't like what she saw when she looked in the mirror.

The rows of gold bracelets on her wrist jingled as she

leaned across the table to top up her glass, giving him a free view of her excellent cleavage. Mildly amused by the action—Alex was pulling out all the stops tonight—Danilo felt his half-smile fade. Whatever Alex tried, it wasn't working.

Maybe he shouldn't have made the trip to Pisa with her. Nor suggested she break the trip from Florence to Pisa here—the small town where he was instantly recognised lacked the comfortable anonymity he sought. But why require anonymity? It wasn't as if he were committing a crime!

He considered drinking the untouched wine in his glass. Since when had he needed alcohol to appreciate a sexy woman? He held his hand above his glass as she lifted the bottle, which was now two thirds empty, not that Alex was anywhere near drunk.

'How many times a day do you need to shave? Not that I'm complaining! I like a man to look like a man.'

She lifted a hand to his cheek, rubbing her fingers across the stubble. She was a beautiful woman, at least he'd always thought so, who had made it clear on their first meeting that she was available. She'd made the first move and waited for him to make the next. He doubted she'd lost any sleep when he hadn't—until tonight.

He saw her looking at him expectantly but it was only when he took hold of her hand and placed it on the table that he realised she'd said something and he'd missed it.

'Sorry?'

'I said are you ready to leave? I don't want to keep you up too late.'

She was gorgeous and he was badly in need of sex so

the question was, why wasn't he leaping to his feet and paying the cheque? This was *exactly* what he needed.

Alex leant back in her seat with a sigh. 'It's not happening for you?'

'I'm finding it hard to switch off at the moment,' he explained, unable to get the image of a pair of golden eyes out of his head.

'Don't worry, I won't take it personally.' Alex smiled and broke the connection of their thighs as she leaned over to kiss him. 'But just so you know what you're missing...'

He leaned back in his seat but she followed. Short of tipping her on the floor, he was going to have to sit there and take it like a man! Danilo doubted many would have sympathised with his dilemma. She was a good kisser, he recognised on an objective level. While on another, non-objective, totally irrational level he discovered that kissing one woman while thinking of another felt like cheating. Wrong word, wrong feeling and what the hell was wrong with a man just enjoying himself? And yet, wasn't he just going through the motions? Was he being *polite*?

The thoughts slid through his head while his half-opened eyes drifted across the room, scanning the occupants with a detached curiosity as he detachedly kissed her back. His eyes had made one sweep of the bar when quite suddenly they made contact with someone who was staring straight at him. His libido, dormant all night, roared into painful life.

He swore, pulled back and had half risen in his seat before he sank back down again. He swore again as the connection was broken and Tess's hair fell across her face. Belatedly remembering his companion, he turned his head.

'Sorry!'

The expression on Alex's beautiful face suggested that she *was* taking it personally and he couldn't blame her.

'It's just that my sister and cousin are here.'

She looked slightly mollified. 'I thought, from the way you reacted, it was your wife or something.' Automatically she followed the direction of the tilt of his head. 'I take it that the woman in the wheelchair is your sister. I heard…' She broke off, looking uncomfortable, and added, 'I've met Franco, through a mutual friend.' Curiosity slid into her eyes as she studied the second woman in the group. 'Who is his new girlfriend?'

'She is not Franco's girlfriend.' The amusement in his voice sounded forced even to his own ears. He should be laughing; it was funny—weird how the images playing in his head did not make him feel like laughing. Images that involved Franco doing the things to Tess he had been imagining doing to her all week.

'Do we have to go over?'

'No.'

Alex looked pleased. 'So, who is she?'

'She is…' Recovering a little, the heat that had streaked through his body when he had half risen in his seat coalescing in his groin, he lied coolly, 'A family friend.'

Everyone's friend in a matter of days. Tess Jones had won hearts and minds; he was the only person who had not fallen under her spell.

Ever heard of denial?

'She has gorgeous hair.' Alexandra lifted a hand to

her own sleek blonde head, her confident smile twisting into a spasm of annoyance when the compliment she was fishing for didn't arrive. 'Are you going to introduce me?'

'No.' Then, to soften the bluntness of his response, he added, 'I wouldn't want to cramp their style.'

Franco gave their order to the barman and, lowering his voice, added in a conversational tone, 'Don't look now but… I said don't look!'

'Danilo!' His sister jerkily turned away, the tension that Tess had sensed growing in Natalia since they'd set off for the evening crystallising into something close to panic. '*Dio*, he isn't supposed to be here. What if he sees us and comes over…? Wait, he already knows, doesn't he?'

He has already seen us, thought Tess, who didn't turn her head. She already knew he was sitting in a corner pressed up against a gorgeous blonde who had been stroking his face adoringly when they had walked in. Unlike Nat, she hadn't experienced panic when she'd seen them, just nausea. It looked as if Danilo was not quite the workaholic his family thought, she mused sourly.

'Knows what?' Tess asked, concerned by the younger girl's pallor.

Nat shook her head, not meeting Tess's eyes. 'Nothing.'

'Actually, I think he probably knows everything. What's the word for it? *Omniscient?*'

Tess shot Franco an irritated look. 'Not helping.' She turned to Nat. 'What if he does come over?' It didn't matter; his presence had already ruined the night for

Tess. 'We haven't broken any laws.' Except the unwritten one that said no one could do anything without asking him first! The man was a control freak, she decided. But her thought processes were suspended by a fresh wave of nausea as the couple on the other side of the room began to kiss.

Franco, who was watching them too, let out a low chuckle. 'I doubt if he will. It looks to me like they'll be leaving soon.' His observation was tinged with envy as he added, 'Talk about get a room.'

Tess's mind had already gone to the scene Franco's comment painted. 'Is that his girlfriend?' She was staring; she didn't want to but she couldn't stop.

Ignoring his own advice, Franco turned his head. 'Danilo doesn't have girlfriends...he just has *partners*.' He glanced down at his cousin with a grimace of apology. 'Sorry, Nat.'

'Do you really think I thought my brother was a monk?'

Not a mistake anyone who had looked at his mouth would have made! The thought materialised at exactly the moment his eyes connected with hers. A flood of mortified heat scorched through Tess's body as she looked away. He hadn't really seen her, not at that distance, it had just seemed like it—but she had been staring.

She picked up her glass of wine and willed herself not to look back, though if they didn't want people to look they should really have taken Franco's advice, she decided crossly. If anyone should be embarrassed it should be Danilo.

'I'm just going to the ladies' room,' Nat announced, swivelling her lightweight chair around.

'Hold on.' Tess moved to walk beside the chair. Her determination *not* to think about Danilo having sex, especially with the tall beautiful blonde, had the predictable result that that was pretty much *all* she could think of. 'I'll come with you.'

'No! It's fine. That's why I suggested this place. It's very wheelchair friendly.'

Tess, watching her move away, frowned. 'Has anything happened today? Natalia seems a bit distracted.'

'I thought she looked pretty good tonight.'

'Yes, I know, but don't you think—?'

'Danilo a monk? That's a laugh! Before the car accident there were lots of girls, lots of nightclubs and—'

Tess, who had seen the pictures, read the stories, cut him off. 'You mean you modelled yourself on him?'

'I wish! The *treat them mean keep them keen* thing doesn't work for me. Seriously though, since the accident he's changed.' He flashed the cool blonde a look. 'Though not in everything. She is definitely his type.'

'Look, do you mind if we talk about something that *isn't* your cousin's, and my boss's, sex life?'

She aimed for casually amused but from Franco's expression she knew she'd missed it by several shrill miles.

Before he could say anything she handed him her glass. 'I'm going to check on Nat. I'm sure something is wrong. I'll have the same again.'

'Who am I to argue with women's instinct?'

When Tess found the ladies' room it was empty but for a couple of women who were checking their already perfect make-up.

'Sorry but have you seen a woman…in a…' about to say 'blue dress', she stopped, and, remembering a

comment Nat had made about people noticing the chair
and never seeing her, she finished with '...wheelchair?'
The two looked blankly at her, not understanding a
word, and with a frustrated grimace she shook her head.
'Never mind.'

Had she somehow missed Nat? Back out in the carpeted passageway she retraced her footsteps, standing
by the doorway so she could scan the entire room. She
could see Franco at the bar where she'd left him; there
was no sign of either Nat or Danilo and his blonde.
Starting to get seriously worried now, she ran back towards the ladies' room. This was stupid. Nat had to be
somewhere; she couldn't just have vanished.

As she stood there telling herself not to panic a door
opened and a couple walked through. Before it closed
Tess got a glimpse of a few tables spread over what appeared to be a cobbled courtyard area.

She ran towards it, and took a deep breath. If Nat
wasn't here she was going to have to raise the alarm. She
pushed the door open. The space behind the door was a
lot smaller than it had seemed. Probably a sun trap during the daylight hours, now it was illuminated by fairy
lights strung along the wooden struts of the pergola arrangement overhead. All in all the effect was romantic
and intimate. The couple there obviously thought so!

'Nat!'

The couple broke apart, the young man who was
squatting beside the wheelchair rocking back on his
heels.

Natalia, her expression one of embarrassment mingled with defiance, shook her head and took one of the
young man's hands between both of hers. 'You can't
tell him!'

Tess didn't need to ask who the 'him' she was talking about was. *Oh, hell, just what she needed!*

'He'll kill Marco!' Nat pronounced dramatically.

'I don't think that it'll come to that, Nat.'

The young man got to his feet. 'I am not afraid of your brother.'

More fool you, Tess thought as he extended his hand.

'I'm Marco.'

Tess took the hand and realised she was between the proverbial rock and a very hard place. Unbidden an image of Danilo floated into her head. He was the living embodiment of hard. Hard in every sense of the word, she decided. Ashamed of the illicit shiver that trickled down her spine, she pushed the image away.

'I'm Tess.'

'She's a friend. She's on our side, aren't you, Tess?'

Her instinct told her to respond with a yes but her common sense told her that taking any *side* would be a major mistake, so she sidestepped the question.

'I take it that you didn't accidentally bump into one another?' She arched a brow and looked from one to the other. 'Which is why you panicked when you saw your brother?'

The young man's eyes widened. Tess didn't need to understand Italian to get the gist of what he was saying.

'He's gone.'

'I will protect you from him, *cara mia*.'

Nat touched his arm. 'He's not a monster, Marco.'

'You defend him?'

'No, but…he thinks I'm still a kid, and he thinks me being in this is somehow his fault.' She banged the chair with her hand. 'He won't stop looking for a miracle. I hope you won't tell him.' She gave a little sigh that tore at Tess's heart. 'But if you do, I'll understand.'

Tess really wished that Danilo could witness this display of maturity from Nat, and she *really* wished she had not discovered the young lovers' secret. This was definitely a lose-lose situation, and as much as she sympathised with the young couple she could also see where Danilo was coming from. She felt a surge of exasperation. If he hadn't waded in with his size twelves the affair would probably have died a natural death by now. There was no better fuel for young love than prohibition!

'I don't want to be part of a conspiracy of silence, but, all right, I won't tell him, but I think you should. He will find out at some point and it'll be much easier if you come clean now. Just explain to him how you feel, the way you just explained it to me.'

'You know what happened to the last person who told Danilo he was wrong?'

Tess shook her head.

Nat gave a high-pitched laugh. 'Right, because nobody does.' Without warning her anger dissolved and her eyes filled with tears. 'I love my brother and I don't want to make him unhappy, but I love Marco too.'

Tess felt a sharp stab of sympathy. She knew what it was like to try and please the person you loved and fail. For years she had tried to be the daughter her mother wanted; it was only when she'd stopped trying that she'd realised her mum loved her even if she was never going to be a political asset.

Nat's sob was cut off as the door opened and four young women in a party mood spilled out into the courtyard. The illusion of privacy vanished as their laughter and chatter filled the air.

'I think it's best if you go now, Marco.'

The young man appeared inclined to protest but Natalia backed up Tess's suggestion. 'I'll be fine.' She glanced at Tess and said defiantly, 'I'll call you tomorrow.'

CHAPTER SIX

THEY WERE BACK at the palazzo before eleven. On the journey home Natalia had closed her eyes and given a not very realistic impression of being asleep. Once they were inside, pleading a headache, Natalia announced her intention of going straight to her room.

Tess, whose own head was pounding, made sympathetic noises and managed to insert a softly spoken comment before the girl disappeared. 'You know you have to tell him, don't you? Or stop seeing Marco.'

Natalia lifted her chin and glared at Tess. 'That's up to me, isn't it, not you? I can't stop you telling Danilo but I don't have to listen to your advice, considering you're being paid to give it!' Her lips quivered and her eyes filled. 'I… I'm sorry. I know I've put you in a terrible position but I can't give him up.'

Tess stood there waiting until the sound of slamming doors stopped, but waiting for what?

To find someone I can't give up?

It hadn't happened yet.

And it never would, not while she… Tess sucked in a shocked breath through parted lips, and thought, *Not while I can carry on pretending the only men who are*

*attracted to me are the ones that ignited nothing inside
more dangerous than friendship and affection.*

Even while the echoes of this flash of insight reverberated around inside her skull, she began to push
it away.

Because burying something solves it?

She set her soft jaw. This was *not* about her mum's
sleazy boyfriend. He had faded away, out of their lives,
and she had not asked questions, just felt relief, relief
that she didn't have to tell her mum, knowing that her
parent would shoulder all the blame.

But what if she'd buried the memory but not the fear?
The fear of not being in control, of being helpless, went
so deep that at some subconscious level she'd discour-
aged the attention of any man she could imagine herself losing control with.

Was all this denial now catching up with her?

Was it coincidental that she found herself in a place
she had never even dreamt existed? Feeling things she
had never felt, never *wanted* to feel and unable to stop
imagining herself losing control with a man who was
not at all safe… Or was it fate?

The slamming of doors had interrupted Danilo's online
study of the statistical breakdown of surgical success
rates for the few surgeons who had so far attempted
the technique that in theory could give his sister some
mobility back.

He was glad of the interruption. The numbers did
not make easy reading, even with a glass of brandy in
his hand. He wasn't drunk but he'd had enough to blur
the edges a bit and lower the volume on the uncomfortable questions circling in his head.

When, glass in hand, he went to investigate the commotion he discovered one of the questions—*or should that be one of the answers?*—standing in the hallway, her face covered by her hands. Anything approaching mellow vanished as heat streaked through his body.

He lifted the glass and over the rim took the opportunity to study Tess unobserved. Under the shield of his long dark lashes his eyes made a slow, predatory, upwards sweep from her feet, in the heels that gave her an extra three inches. She looked fresh, gorgeous and very sexy. By the time he reached her glossy head he decided he had either drunk too much or not nearly enough.

'So, a bad night, then?'

The deep drawled comment made Tess leap like a startled deer and spin around.

About a dozen doors opened off the massive marble-floored central hallway. The one that was now open led to a room Tess had never before entered: Danilo's study.

Danilo himself, looking tall, sleek and panther like, stood framed there and the rush of hormones she experienced made her head spin and her knees sag. A wave of intense longing washed like a relentless tide over her until her autonomic responses kicked in to equal the pressure building in her chest. She took a deep, shuddering breath.

'What are you doing here?' she squeaked, her voice accusingly shrill in her own ears.

'I live here.' His voice was mild; his stare was not. The dark blaze in his eyes made her stomach muscles quiver.

'I know.' Even before he reacted with a sardonic look of amusement Tess flushed and felt stupid—she was recognising a theme here—and as the guilty conviction took hold that he could see into her head it was all she could do to stop herself blurting out the secret. *Which one?*

'Sorry.' *Act normally. He doesn't know. He can't know, you're being paranoid.* 'You startled me.' She managed an edgy smile; if only that were *all* he was doing to her! As if his dark stare acted like some sort of truth drug, she had to endure the relentless, hormonal urge that reacted indecently to his presence.

While she was wondering if he had this effect on all women a memory surfaced in her head of the text she had received from Fiona on her first night here. She'd been able to laugh about it then; now, days later, it would be a struggle even to raise a smile.

Well, you've met him in the flesh, so how gorgeous is he on a scale of one to ten and, more importantly— would you?

Tess had responded in a similarly jokey style—had it really been only six days ago?

If I said he's a fifteen he'd be the first to agree—and, no, definitely not!

Actually, since then she had noticed Danilo was surprisingly lacking in the vanity department, possibly because he seemed to be oblivious to the way women stared at him. The other part of her response held true. She took comfort in the blatant lie and more comfort from the knowledge that she was never likely to be called upon to prove it, not when there were blondes like the one he'd been with tonight.

Pity her hormones had simply not got the message. He did look sinfully sexy standing there, one shoulder wedged against the acanthus-carved door frame, his white shirt unbuttoned at the neck, not a lot but enough to reveal a deep vee of golden skin and a smattering of darkly curling chest hair, which was too much for her comfort.

Mouth dry, heart pounding, she was simultaneously ashamed and excited. Guilt added yet another layer of discomfort to the moment. Tess dampened down a spurt of panic. If he asked her outright would she lie? More to the point *should* she lie?

Wasn't her silence as bad as lying?

Her guilt made her see suspicion in his face, the planes and strong angles emphasised by the dark stubble on his jaw and lean cheeks enhancing the fallen-angel quality of his features. As he dragged his hand back and forth across his hair she noticed that he looked heavy-eyed, as though he'd just tumbled out of bed.

Maybe he had?

Her stomach gave a deep lurch as her agile mind made another leap—or not bed, she speculated as an image of the tall blonde flashed through her thoughts, the woman's red-painted nails pressed into his hard, golden flesh.

Perhaps, she thought sickly, they hadn't made it that far?

She took a deep breath, reminded herself that Danilo Raphael's sex life was none of her business. So what if the blonde, looking less cool and more mussed than earlier, *was* behind that door stretched out on a sofa waiting for…? She pressed a hand to her stomach. A vivid imagination was at times a curse.

'Sorry to disturb you,' she mumbled, her expression determinedly composed as she stared at the intricate carving on the wall frieze to his right as though it were the most fascinating thing she had ever seen. A glimpse of some half-dressed woman was *not* a memory she wanted, though her eyes seemed to have other ideas. 'I was on my way...' She stopped. He was barefoot; in her head the detail confirmed all her suspicions.

'Is something wrong?'

'Not a thing,' she said stonily.

'I'm having a nightcap.'

She lifted her eyes from his feet and saw that Danilo was holding a drink in one hand. The amber liquid in the heavy crystal glass caught the light from the central chandelier and made her blink. She met his eyes, suddenly picking up on details she'd missed: the almost feral gleam in his half-closed, heavy-lidded eyes, the almost combustible tension in his lean body. He was like a man who had started something and...?

Her eyes widened as her imagination once more went into manic overdrive mode. Had he and the blonde argued? They'd seemed pretty friendly when she'd seen them, Tess thought sourly. Maybe the woman had a high-powered career and had been called away leaving him frustrated...drowning his sorrows? Looking for a substitute?

'Would you like to join me?'

The husky invitation brought her speculation to a dead halt, though she'd been so caught up that it took her a few moments to focus on what he'd said.

'*Join...?*' Her eyes moved past him to the room where she could see a ceiling-high wall of bookshelves.

'I'm inviting you for a nightcap, not to join an orgy.'

He rolled the word around his tongue as though he were tasting it, seeming to take pleasure from her discomfort.

Discomfort was a massive understatement, Tess felt like a pawn and she didn't like the sensation. 'Now, there's a word you don't get to use every day.'

He arched a dark brow, a half-smile quivering. 'Nightcap?'

'You're alone?' The incautious words were out before she could censor them.

'Who do you think I have in there?' He nodded at the room behind him without taking his eyes from Tess's face.

'It isn't any of my business.'

He burst out laughing.

Tess didn't join in. It was hard when you knew you *were* the joke.

'Sorry, it's just that you look…' He paused, took a swallow of his drink and drawled, 'Like an outraged nun.' If nuns wore dresses that short! His eyes dropped to the outline of her hips and bare, smooth calves, and the ever-present lust developed claws and dug deep. 'I could feel your disapproval across the bar earlier.'

So he had seen them.

'I was simply surprised,' she managed with something that resembled cool. 'It was quite a coincidence we had… At least Nat had received the message that you were in Florence.'

'So you weren't stalking me?' He watched her expression freeze and swore, his teasing attitude vanishing in the blink of an eye as she bit down hard on her trembling lower lip. The sight of the pinpricks of blood sent his protective instincts into overdrive, shaking loose a need to comfort inside him.

'Sorry,' he roughed out, his face a mask of contrition. 'Bad choice of verb. You shouldn't worry, you know, I'm pretty sure that you'll have no problems with that guy in the future.'

His trip to Dublin two days earlier, where he had a team working around the clock to deliver a report on the viability of the plan to redevelop a derelict industrial area, had meant a stopover in London could barely be classed as an inconvenience.

The stalker, according to the detailed dossier that had landed on his desk, was a man who lived his life to a pretty rigid schedule. The 'query OCD' written in the margin had seemed a good call to Danilo—which had made locating him easy.

The rest had not been rocket science. Once he had convinced the crazy that he was dealing with someone who was actually crazier than he was, it had been easy. Fear was a great motivator.

Tess didn't share his confidence, but, unwilling to reveal just how much the situation awaiting her in London was preying on her mind, she managed a cautious, 'I hope so.' Then surprised herself by revealing a decision she had made the previous evening, but not the repeating nightmare that had inspired it. 'I might swallow my pride and ask my mum's advice when I get back.' She caught his questioning look and added, by way of explanation, 'She knows some people...'

'That sounds ominous. Should I watch my step?'

Her smile glimmered as she imagined her mother as part of a criminal gang. 'Not *those* sort of people. She has contacts, with some women's charities, among other things.'

'She sounds an interesting woman.'

'She is.'

'I am surprised you haven't called on her expertise before.'

'My mum's help comes at a price. Look, can we talk about something else?'

He lifted his brows a little at the tautness of her voice but complied with her request. 'I have noticed the change in Natalia since you arrived.'

She tensed, waiting for the invisible blade she could feel above her head to fall. Did she tell him that Nat's affair preceded her arrival or keep quiet?

'I can't remember the last time she went out.'

She had been so sure that he knew that the unexpected reprieve made her body sag with a relief that was short-lived, as she realised that the last time Nat went out was likely as not for a secret meeting with her boyfriend.

Tess didn't know for sure. She hadn't asked and she wasn't going to; she had enough secrets to guard.

'But I'm sorry you didn't have a good evening.'

'It was fine,' she lied, bringing her lashes down in a protective sweep. 'I have a headache.' That at least was not a lie.

'Well, I'm glad that you persuaded Nat to go out. However, I'd prefer it if in future you run such things past me.'

Tess stiffened at the casual addition. 'Let me get this straight. What are you saying exactly? That when Nat suggests we go for a drive I have to say, "Hold on a moment, I just have to go ask your brother"—which, incidentally, might be hard as you're never here! Good grief, Danilo, aren't the walls here high enough without you adding more restrictions?'

His expression had grown colder as she'd been speaking and by the end of her impassioned speech his eyes were ice chips. 'Natalia is free to come and go as she pleases. I simply—'

'I'm not your sister's nursemaid and I think I made it quite clear when you made that particular suggestion before that I'm not about to act as your spy.' *That would make me a double agent.*

He made a clicking sound of aggravation with his tongue, dug his hands into his pockets and levered his long, lean length away from the wall. 'You really do have a talent for drama. I didn't ask you to be a spy.'

His attitude, the male arrogance oozing out of his every perfect pore, just touched a nerve and made her reckless. 'It's small wonder, if you treat her like a prisoner, that she doesn't feel she can discuss things with you!'

'But she discusses them with you?'

Tess's outrage dissolved like a spoonful of sugar in an ocean. She faked a smile and reminded herself that guilt was making her paranoid. But the way he was looking at her, as though he knew…but he couldn't— could he?

So, suddenly she had nothing to say for herself? While this was a pleasant change it did not lessen Danilo's anger at the accusations she'd already made. The very real possibility she might be right intensified those feelings of outrage, and left the taste of failure in his mouth.

Oh, he could shrug off the claim that Nat was afraid of him, and obviously there were things that she didn't tell him, that was normal, but he hated the distance that had grown up between them recently and he hated that he didn't know how to fix it. And if Nat hating him was the price of her walking again it was one he was willing to pay, but it did not make the prospect any more palatable.

'While I admire confidence, is it *conceivable* after what…a week here that you can be considered an expert on my relationship with my sister? But who knows?' Hands thrust into his pockets, he lifted his broad shoulders in a contemptuous shrug and sketched a smile. 'If you had run tonight's plan past me I would have been able to explain that because my sister's treatment is ongoing we are scheduled to fly to London tomorrow to see a consultant. The trip will be tiring for her and, if asked,' he drawled, 'I would have advised an early night, if of course that would have met with your approval.'

With each successive sarcastic stab from his cruel tongue Tess felt as if she were getting smaller, shrinking, so that by the time he had finished with her she'd moved beyond mortified blushes, was as pale as paper and felt about six inches tall.

'If Nat had told me—' She closed her mouth, pretty sure that ignorance would be no defence in Danilo's eyes.

'Nat doesn't know.'

She stared, too bewildered by the admission to be tactful. 'Why? Was it a last-minute thing?'

It was a toss-up which he found more aggravating: being asked to explain his actions, or feeling the need to do so. 'No. I made the arrangements before I left London.' And he was not about to question his decision; it was the right one. 'If Nat had known she would have worked herself up, become…upset…' She was still going to get tense and tearful, but at least this way she would not have spent the last week in a state of nervous anticipation.

So instead of that, Natalia had met up with her secret lover and become…upset. If Danilo had known…? Even as Tess closed down that avenue of speculation she acknowledged that, as things stood, it was inevitable that at some point she'd find out *exactly* how Danilo would react—unless Nat gave up Marco, which did not seem likely.

'You see, while I may lack your expertise, *I* have done this before and I do know my sister.'

Not as well as you think. 'So you'll tell Nat tomorrow.'

He nodded. 'The appointment is in the afternoon.'

'How long will Natalia be in London?' And what, Tess wondered, was she meant to be doing while the woman she was being paid to be a companion to took a trip?

'Just overnight and it's *we*.'

Tess shrugged. She had taken it as read that Danilo would be accompanying his sister.

'Only a flying visit, it depends on what Nat wants, but we could stay overnight or fly straight back, so don't pack too much.'

'*Me?* You want me to come?'

He arched a brow and looked impatient. 'You can't be company for Nat when you're in another country.'

'So you've booked my ticket?'

He looked at her blankly and she immediately felt stupid. Unlike her own, Danilo Raphael's world did not involve last-minute bargain flights.

'Nat's physio session is when?'

'Eight-thirty.'

'I'll cancel. It might be a good idea if you were on hand…'

'To take the flak?'

'I am more than capable of taking the flak, but if you could be there to…' Head bent, he dragged a hand across his face, the gesture so revealing that Tess's heart ached.

'Just be there, I would be…' his eyes brushed hers and the pause lengthened before he added an abrupt and harsh '…grateful.'

In her head she could see the door closing with a decisive whoosh and a dismissive click and she felt something approaching panic. He couldn't go! She needed more from him.

'So what time?'

Hand on the study door handle, Danilo swung back, his stance tense as he failed to stop himself imagining a scenario where he didn't reply, he just took those two fatal steps, hauled her into him, felt the collision of her soft body into his and discovered if those lips tasted as good as they looked. They would and he would take his time, he would… The effort to drag his thoughts away from the fantasy spinning in his head drew an audible grunt of effort from his throat.

'I haven't decided yet.'

The door closed.

Hands clenched, she turned away. *How pathetic are you, Tess?*

The answer, disturbingly, was that where Danilo Raphael was concerned—very!

She discovered the next day just how different travelling Raphael style was when they had boarded the private jet. Natalia took the luxury for granted, but it reduced Tess to a state of wide-eyed wonder, which she pushed to one side as she attempted to make conversation with Natalia. She managed to coax a smile or two out of the other woman but in the end, despite all her efforts to distract her, she lapsed into moody silence.

Distracting hadn't worked so Tess decided to face the elephant in the room. It turned out not quite as she hoped.

'You must be excited.'

'Excited?'

'About the appointment, the possibility—'

'That I'll walk again? There have been other appointments, a lot of them, there will be more. Danilo will never give up. He believes in miracles.'

Tess's throat had closed up with emotion. Natalia's dry eyes, the bleak acceptance in her voice, was more affecting than floods of tears could ever have been.

The helplessness she was feeling, she realised, was something that Danilo must feel every day, only magnified by a thousand.

The limo that took them from the airport continued the style of travelling, which, if she was honest, Tess could easily become accustomed to. Not that she would have the opportunity. In a few weeks she would be making the same journey, but on her bargain, no-frills flight. The time she had spent with the Raphaels a dim and distant memory. It was disturbing how she had become involved in the family's life during such a short period of time, but she knew that the intimacy was an illusion, that it would be a mistake to forget that she was just the hired help.

Tess enjoyed the car journey a lot less than the plane partly because during the flight she had not seen Danilo, who had been closeted away working, but there was no escaping his sheer overpowering physicality in the enclosed space. There was no escaping; the accidental brush of his knee against hers was enough to send a rush of charged hormonal heat through her body. She had never experienced anything like this before!

It seemed unlikely that a man with his experience didn't know what he did to her, which made those little things he kept doing, like staring at her mouth when they were talking, or standing too close, just plain cruel. It was equally possible that she didn't even register on his radar as a woman. She wasn't sure which scenario was preferable.

While the tension between herself and Danilo might not have existed outside her imagination, the tension between brother and sister was very real. Every glance and comment Natalia made was double-edged and loaded as she shot down in flames everything Danilo said. He must have noticed but he didn't react to any of the jibes or snapped comments. Tess actually found her sympathies swinging his way until Nat suddenly looked at him, her eyes filled with tears, and whispered a broken, *'Sorry!'*

Danilo just squeezed his sister's hand and smiled. 'It's fine.'

Tess had to look out of the window to hide the tears that she struggled to blink away, only looking back when the limo pulled to a halt.

'We're early. I thought we'd stop for tea first. This is your favourite?'

Nat looked out of the limo window at the hotel they had drawn up at. 'Lovely.' The girl's attempt to inject some enthusiasm into her dead voice brought another lump of emotion to Tess's throat.

She glanced at Danilo but the expression on his face told her nothing about what he was feeling.

An hour later, she stood in the ladies' room running her hands under the cold-water tap. The tea-time treat had been agony, but then sitting around a table with two people who barely spoke was never going to be relaxing, especially if the silence played out to a background of nerve-stretching tension.

'And you thought *you* had problems,' she told her reflection in the mirror.

She didn't want to think about her cringe-worthy efforts to fill the silences. To say she'd overcompensated was putting it mildly! She'd sounded like—the memory of the steady flow of bright chatter she'd maintained made her wince. By the end of the afternoon tea the sound of her own voice was grating on her, and none of her jollity had rubbed off on her companions.

Delaying the moment she had to go back, Tess lingered in the perfume-scented room for as long as possible, but there were only so many times a girl could reapply her lipstick.

'Time to man up, Tess,' she told herself sternly before squaring her shoulders and stepping out into the lobby.

When she had entered the space had been empty but it was now packed with people, some holding microphones, others cameras, all being aimed at an elegant figure who was fielding questions being thrown at her.

Tess stopped dead, experienced a mind-blanking rabbit-in-the-headlight moment, though fortunately she unfroze before anyone noticed her. The thought of the attention shifting her way made her shudder.

Danilo, who had been tapping his foot with impatience and contemplating invading the sanctuary of the ladies' powder room, saw that Tess was overwhelmed by the crowd she encountered in the lobby. He watched her skirt round the very edges of it, doing her best not to look up or make any eye contact.

She was so intent, for some reason, on avoiding attention and the woman who was fielding questions like the pro she clearly was, that she didn't register his presence until he touched her shoulder, at which point she jumped guiltily.

'What took so long? Nat is in the car.'

'Sorry, sorry... I...well, I'm here now.' She stepped around him so that he was between her and the public interview, his body acting as an effective shield, and she stayed that way until they had safely exited the building.

In the car she sank into her seat with a sigh and closed her eyes, though she opened them again when Danilo, sitting opposite her, said casually, 'Did you know that woman?'

'What woman?' Nat asked, looking from one to the other. 'You mean, the one in the lobby...who was she?'

'Beth Tracey. She's running for mayor.'

Tess didn't know why his knowledge surprised her. 'She hasn't actually confirmed that yet.' Maybe that was what the media scrum had been about.

'So you do know her?' Danilo pushed.

'Sort of...' He elevated a brow and she revealed with a hiss of exasperation, 'She's my mother.'

For the first time since she'd met him she saw Danilo Raphael look shocked. She supposed that was a triumph of sorts but she was used to that reaction from strangers when they discovered her parentage.

'You don't have the same name.'

Tess forced a smile to respond to Nat's observation. 'She uses her maiden name.'

'And how does your father feel about that?'

The question came from Danilo, so she turned her head to look at him. 'He died when I was small. Mum raised me as a single parent.'

'Your mum is famous…cool,' Nat pronounced. 'So don't you get on?'

Well, at least her family dynamics were proving a distraction for Natalia, who obviously found the situation curious.

'We get on fine. It's just that we are not very alike—we live very separate lives. She is very busy. I am…' She paused, thinking, *a disappointment.* 'I'm very proud of her.'

'I didn't realise that you had family in London. If you'd like to stop over and fly back tomorrow…?'

Tess was surprised by the offer. 'No, that's fine. I doubt Mum could see me at this short a notice.'

'You have to make an appointment to see your mum?'

You could see that in Nat's world this was pretty freaky and the girl's amazement made Tess wish she hadn't been quite so literal in her response.

'No, of course not,' she said, laughing off the idea. 'But she's busy campaigning at the moment.'

'And won't you be called on to help?'

After fighting the urge to announce it was not anyone's business, Tess gave a terse, tight-lipped response to Danilo's continued probing. 'Mum accepted that I'm not a political asset years ago and she has plenty of people happy to leaflet drop.'

* * *

They got to the Harley Street office a few minutes later. Tess waited in the ground-floor waiting room, which looked more like a drawing-room illustration from a glossy homes magazine, while brother and sister were escorted to the lift that took them up to the consulting rooms.

Tess refused the tea on offer, leafed through a few magazines but eventually, as the tension built, had to get up and walk around the room. If she felt like this she could only imagine what Nat was feeling right now, and Danilo. After half an hour of pacing she made herself sit down.

Her bottom had barely touched the seat when Danilo walked in so she sprang to her feet.

It was hard to read anything in Danilo's expression. 'How—?'

'Natalia had some questions for the doctor.' It was the first time that his sister had asked for him to leave.

The expulsion had been a shock, and one he had not seen coming. For two years he had been the conduit between the medics and his sister; the rejection—and that was what it had felt like—had caught him on the raw. She was asserting her independence, he got that, he even had some sympathy with it, but the fact was he knew what questions to ask, he knew—'

Tess's voice interrupted his brooding reverie.

'What?'

Tess was relieved to hear him sound irritable, and even more relieved to see the blank look that had made her think the worst slide from his eyes. 'I said, did it go well?'

He flashed her a sardonic look. 'That depends on

your definition of well, but it did not go badly. This was just the first consult. There will be more.' He hesitated long enough to worry her again before adding, 'I know you are scheduled to have a day off tomorrow and if you have plans that is fine, but would you mind spending some time with Nat? The days after one of these… it can be hard for her.'

And you, Tess thought, sensing the unacknowledged distress behind his closed expression and wondering if Danilo ever allowed himself a moment's weakness. She fought down the urge to say something comforting, pretty sure it would be received with as much appreciation as a spontaneous hug would have been.

'Of course I can.' Tess did have plans but they involved Natalia.

He tipped his head, aware even at this moment of a hard throb of need as their glances connected. 'I am grateful.'

She didn't want his gratitude, but she wanted to see him smile, see him happy, see the lines of tension bracketing his mouth smooth out. The strength of these feelings shocked her and made her blurt out unthinkingly, 'So, things are good right now?' The words brought his sardonic gaze to her face. 'I mean, not as bad as they could be? My mum always says you should live for the moment.' She closed her eyes and muttered, 'That sounded better in my head. I just meant—look, if you ever want to talk about—'

She was looking up at him, all earnest concern and 'a pat on the head, a cup of tea will make you feel better.' Something inside Danilo snapped. He didn't *deserve* to feel better; maybe this was him being punished? Pity from this woman with that mouth, that body—the sort that a man could fall into and forget.

Tess's eyes blinked wide when without warning his big hand curved around the back of her head, the movement almost casual as he drew her closer. Too startled to react, Tess registered the driven gleam in his heavy-lidded eyes as he lowered his head until his mouth was a whisper away from hers, their foreheads almost touching.

She held her breath, the languid weakness that spread through her body infecting every cell. Time seemed to slow, though in retrospect when she thought of the incident she realised it only lasted moments before he pulled back.

Clearing her throat, Tess struggled to regain a semblance of composure, and tried to reboot her lust-battered brain. What was she meant to do? Pretend nothing had happened? Shrug away the moment? Probably the wisest option but nobody had ever accused her of being wise.

She lifted her chin. 'So, what was that about?'

'A lesson.' For him as much as her, he decided, hugging his self-loathing tight as he reflected darkly on his supreme selfishness. His sister was facing a decision that could give her back her life or close off that possibility for ever. What sort of man could think about sex at a time like this?

The man he was.

Tess Jones might not know she needed protecting from him but Danilo did, and the simplest way to extinguish that sympathetic glow in her eyes was to open them. 'I realise that you consider *feelings* your area of expertise, but men—'

'Do not have feelings?' she suggested, starting to feel angry.

'They do not talk about them obsessively,' he sneered.

'So what *do* men do?'

'To relieve stress? Speaking for myself I find that sex works, so unless you're offering, *cara*...?' he drawled.

Tess lowered her lashes as the carnal bluntness of his careless words sent an unexpected thrill of excitement through her. Shocked more by her response than his comment, she was trying to think of a suitable response when he continued.

'You are very curious about our lives, but not so eager to share when it comes to your own family.'

'I don't know what you mean.'

'You couldn't close down the subject of your mother fast enough.'

'That's—'

'None of my business?'

Tess flushed but was spared responding when Nat appeared.

'How—?'

Nat shook her head. 'Not now, Danilo, can we just go home...please?'

CHAPTER SEVEN

AFTER DRIVING HIS car from the helipad where he'd left it that morning, Danilo changed his mind and took a detour when he heard the distant sounds of activity coming from the direction of the indoor arena.

Change your mind? mocked the voice in his head. *Wasn't this always where you were going since you started imagining Tess in a pair of riding breeches?*

She'd caught up with him just before he'd driven off to the helipad that morning; her hair had still been wet from the shower and even though she had yelled her request from twenty feet away he had imagined he could smell the scent of her shampoo.

Twenty feet was pretty much the distance she had kept from him since the previous week's trip to London. It helped but not enough. Logic didn't enter into it so he had stopped trying to work out why, despite the fact her position in the household put her off limits. He wanted her on such a fundamental level.

Pushing away the image of her face as he walked, he slung his discarded jacket over his shoulder. The day was turning out to be another warm one. He glanced at the slim silver-banded watch on his wrist as he headed towards the building.

It was early, but freed from the relentless round of meetings for the first time in what felt like weeks he could, he had reasoned, as easily work at home this afternoon, which he would have explained to anyone who asked, not that they had. He was the boss—or, as his father would have said, the buck stopped with him.

'When that day comes, Danilo, for you to step into my shoes—' at the time he had wanted to be a fighter pilot or a rock star '—you'll understand that leadership can be lonely. You won't always know the answers, but—'

'You do.'

'Sometimes, to be a successful leader, *acting* as if you know what you're doing is as important as actually knowing, but follow your instincts, Danilo, and you won't go far wrong.'

At the time he'd been unable to get his head around the idea of his father not being omnipotent and actually winging it. As for instincts, he hadn't been very sure he had any, at least not the sort his father had been talking about.

He succeeded in pushing away the lingering echo of his father's voice but the sadness remained. That *time* his father had spoken of had come a lot sooner than either of them had expected, and Danilo hadn't stepped into his shoes but been propelled by tragic events. Others within the financial empire his father had presided over had worried about how the financial world would react to this transition, which had in the end been seamless.

At the time, Danilo's focus had been elsewhere. If anything the time he had spent learning his new role had actually felt more like relaxation, a form of escapism, something he could actually control while the thing that really mattered to him, his sister, he had no control over. All he could do was sit beside her hospital bed and now it seemed as though she didn't even want him there. The memories of a few days earlier were still fresh in his mind. His feelings of rejection were confusingly mangled with pride.

Nat had come to him the next morning and the first words out of her mouth were, 'I wasn't punishing you!'

Which made him pretty sure that she was. Nothing she said made it any clearer what he'd done but he reasoned he probably deserved punishment, if not for the mysterious sin he had committed recently, then for the very real and unforgivable piece of selfishness that had put her in the chair.

She had gone on to relay pretty much word for word what the doctor had said. There were no surprises and Nat seemed to have asked all the right questions. When he'd commented on it she'd smiled.

'I had a good teacher.'

He nodded pleasantly to one of the young grooms who looked surprised when he saw Danilo. His father would have remembered the man's name, he realised, thinking that despite the fact the financial world, which had waited for him to fail, had now decided he had filled his father's shoes more than adequately, Danilo knew better.

The moment he walked into the covered arena he saw her. The sight of her standing there dissolved the last shreds of any self-deception, leaving shock ricocheting around uncomfortably in his head.

He hadn't accidentally ended up in the place he knew Tess would be. *Fine, accepted...now move on.* He could have wasted hours trying to analyse a feeling that he couldn't put a name to, he could have let himself believe this woman had touched something inside him that no woman ever had, but that would have been an indulgence because there was no mystery involved. This was obviously about sex, or a lack of it; this was about the iron self-control he brought into play in his personal life failing him; this was about her being the most sensual, provocative creature he had ever encountered.

He wasn't happy about this situation, but pretending it didn't exist or making her feel uncomfortable to be in the same room as him provided no sort of solution, any more than applying a sticking plaster to a severed artery would prevent a victim bleeding out.

The question was what would?

There was a simple solution: he'd brought her here, an action he now privately likened to inviting an unexploded bomb into his home...his life, so he could send her away.

So obvious, so why wasn't he doing it?

Because this was about Nat, not him. Since Tess's arrival the change in his sister had been borderline miraculous. She had rediscovered some of her enthusiasm for life. The situation was still a work in progress and obviously there had been the London blip, there were still resentful silences and looks directed his way, but they were less and less frequent. Tess Jones might be making his life uncomfortable but her influence on Nat was all positive.

And it wasn't just Nat, and Franco, who acted like an attention-seeking puppy in her presence, but even his aunt, not a woman easily impressed, had referred to his sister's companion as a breath of fresh air, and a very sensible woman.

Jaw clenched, he ground his even white teeth over his mounting seething frustration, ashamed that he had ever considered snuffing out his sister's smile simply because he was frustrated.

The arena was dark after the sun outside and it took his eyes a few moments to adjust and for him to realise that there was a horse and rider in the far end of the area. He barely spared them a glance as he continued to stare at Tess. She was a spectator, watching not in the tiers of seats at the far end, but standing balanced in a pair of crazy spiky ankle boots on the bottom rung of the fence that surrounded the exercise area, her elbows resting on the top bar. Her chin was cushioned on top of her hands. Her hair was drawn back smoothly from her face, secured at the nape of her neck by a thin leather thong. It fell in soft silky waves almost to her waist.

The pattern on her shirt was strident, bold swirls of clashing red and orange tucked into a pair of snug-fitting jeans, her tiny waist emphasised by the wide leather belt. Oblivious to his presence, she lifted both hands to wave at the distant figure on the horse, letting out a husky laugh and clutching wildly when she almost fell from her perch.

Dragging his gaze off her bottom, Danilo closed his eyes and exhaled a slow measured hiss of breath through flared nostrils. *Self-control! Dio*, it was going to require a miracle to douse the fire she lit in him!

The impulse to pull her off the rail and into him quelled even though the arousing image of his hands curving over her breasts remained. He opened his eyes. Three more weeks of this, or bend his self-imposed rule of keeping his sex life away from his family?

Weren't rules meant to be broken?

The step he took towards her was involuntary; where it would have taken him he'd never know because at that moment there was a sound of laughter. He automatically turned his head towards it and froze.

'What the hell is going on here?'

The sound of his furious voice drew a shocked gasp from Tess. For once the inner radar that seemed to alert her to his presence had failed her. She stepped back awkwardly from the rail.

'Hello.' It sounded stupid—not that he seemed to hear her; he was striding towards the closed gate of the manège, his intention clear. Knowing she had to stop him, she raced to his side, for once forgetting her no-touch policy as she grabbed his arm.

'Please don't go and drag her off. She'll be so embarrassed and she's having such a good time.'

'My sister is on a horse.' Tearing his eyes from the figure just long enough to direct a killer look at Tess's face, he ground out, 'My *paralysed* sister is on a horse.' It was the most terrifying thing he had ever witnessed. Sweat broke out as he watched. She looked small and the ground looked so far away.

'Yes, and she's having a great time.' Tess's attempt to lighten the mood fell flat.

She watched as he visibly paled with anger then exploded, pinning her with a wrathful glare.

'This is all your doing. Without your influence Nat would not have dreamt of doing this.'

'Calm down.'

A few minutes earlier he had been telling himself she was good for his sister. The dark irony was not lost on him, though her appeal to *calm down* was.

'Calm down? My sister is riding!'

'You can thank me later.' *Too flippant, Tess*, she thought with an inner groan.

'*Dio!* I can understand that you get a kick out of thwarting me, I can tolerate that while you appear to make my sister happy, but you have put her in danger! You can pack your bags and stay the night in a hotel. I'll book a flight for you for tomorrow.'

Shock froze her to the spot, the colour seeping from her face as she stared up at him. 'You're *sacking* me?'

He raised a sardonic brow and turned away, his long fingers slipping the latch that led to the arena.

'But…but…' She tightened her grip on his forearm. Her stomach reacted to the contact as though she had just stepped off a tall building, but she didn't let the sensation distract her. This was too important.

'Please, Danilo!' she begged urgently.

His lips were curled in a silent snarl as he swung back.

'You can sack me if you like—'

'Good of you to give permission,' he sneered sarcastically.

'But please don't do this. It's a massive mistake and you'll regret it. It took a lot of courage for Nat to get on that horse and if you go over there now and embarrass her, Nat will—'

'Better embarrassed than injured.'

'She won't be—'

'How dare—?'

'I asked you. I asked and you said I could—I know it was a bit retrospective, I should have checked yesterday, but—'

'Make use of the stables, take out a horse—*you*, not

my sister.' He stopped. 'Yesterday! This isn't the first time?'

She fought the instinct to retreat from the arctic blast of his furious glare and brought her lashes down in a concealing curtain. 'You didn't stop long enough for me to explain,' she muttered, the resentment that she recognised as irrational slipping past her guard. Since London there had been several occasions when they were alone when he had cut off a conversation abruptly, acting as though he couldn't get out of the room fast enough. The only reason she cared, she told herself, was that she hated bad manners.

'You knew what I thought and you could have put me right but you didn't because you knew that I would put a stop to this.'

'*This,* as you put it, is your sister having a good time, and I didn't tell you because Nat asked me *not* to. She wanted to surprise you.' And she hadn't wanted her brother to see her fail. 'And yes, I did encourage her, but I would never endanger Nat. She is totally safe. I used to help out at a stable that specialised in riding for the disabled, and there were people there with a lot worse disabilities than your sister.'

'My sister is not disabled. She is going to walk again!'

The fingers curled around his arm tightened as the amber eyes lifted to his warmed with sympathy... *Dio*, he had sacked her and she was feeling sorry for him.

'But until then don't you think it would be good for her to enjoy the things she can still do? Look at her face, Danilo—sack me if you like but don't spoil it for her,' she begged anxiously.

He flashed a look at the distant figure, took in

the figures beside her and took a deep breath. 'If she falls—' he gritted through clenched teeth.

'They are walking,' Tess pointed out as at the same sedate pace the horse carrying Natalia began to move across the manège towards them. 'The horse is a pony. It has beautiful manners and she is being led.'

Danilo gave a grudging nod of stiff assent as the two grooms who walked either side of the pony brought the animal to a halt. The groom holding the leading rein moved closer to speak to his sister, her words indistinct at this distance.

'But the fact is even if it is a donkey you had no right to do this without discussing it with me.'

'I'm sorry.'

He gave a grunt. 'No, you're not.'

Tess shrugged and took advantage of the fact he seemed to be calming down. 'True, but there really is zero risk.' She pointed at the two girls walking alongside the horse and the third holding the leading rein. 'Please don't glower like that. It took a lot for Nat to get up there and in the end it was making you proud that swung it.'

'I am proud of her. I always am.'

'Then show it and smile.'

The admonishment drew a grunt of shock from Danilo. *Though God knows why*, he thought grimly. The woman could not open her mouth without telling him what he was doing wrong. What he needed was some time with a woman who appreciated him, not this witch with her talent for interfering and the innate conviction she knew what was good for everyone—or was that just him?

'I'm beginning to wonder how I survived before you arrived to tell me how to behave.'

'Oh, I expect you'll cope when I'm gone.'

He turned his head sharply. *'Gone!'*

'You sacked me.' A first, but it was not the humiliation of being sacked that bothered her, but the panic that had surged through her at the thought.

Panic that would have been understandable if it had been the fear of her stalker waiting for her at home that had caused it, but it wasn't. It was the idea of leaving, of never seeing Nat and...who was she kidding? The thing that had pressed her panic button was not seeing Danilo again.

A muscle in his lean cheek clenched as their eyes connected, the emotions swirling around them suddenly solidified into a tension that made it an effort for Tess to breathe.

'You make me—' The words seemed drawn out against his will and the effort of cutting them off showed in the tension in his face as he found relief in an explosive expletive.

'Angry, I know.' Her voice, breathy and strange, sounded as though it was coming from a long way off.

'You know that's not what I'm talking about.'

She shook her head, her courage for once deserting her. 'No—' Her denial was silenced by the brush of his thumb against her lips.

She stepped away from the contact with a gasp. 'What are you doing?'

Good question, Danilo, what are you doing?

His cobalt-blue stare had a hypnotic quality. Tess was suddenly fighting for breath as everything seemed to move into slow motion, everything but her heart that continued to batter against her ribcage.

'Danilo!'

The musical sound of his sister's happy voice made them both start. Tess pulled back first, her pale face flaming red, and, after staring at her for a moment longer, Danilo turned after, arranging his features in the requested smile. Behind him Tess began to clap. He could almost feel her relief when he joined in.

The beam of pride on his sister's face as she continued to approach at a snail's pace was worth gritting his teeth for.

Natalia laughed again. 'I'll get better. It was only my second time, but I can still do it, Danilo. I can still ride!'

For a split second before he responded his guard was fully down and Danilo looked almost vulnerable. The stark contrast between the pain and pride etched in the proud lines of his face sent a piercing stab of empathy she didn't want to feel through Tess, who stood silently watching.

Removing the hand she had instinctively reached out to cover a white-knuckled fist that hung at his side— the gesture, she knew, would not be appreciated—she pressed it instead to her throat where an emotional lump ached. Blinking hard, she turned her head sharply away, taking a moment to regain control before she trusted herself to speak.

'So I see.'

'We dismount over there. Wait here.'

He took an involuntary step forwards as the horse turned. Tess caught his arm.

'Let her, Danilo, don't spoil it,' she begged huskily.

'Is that what you think I do?' He tore his eyes from the smile on his sister's face, turning his attention to the heart-shaped face looking up at him. '*Spoil* things?' He felt as if he were walking around with a weight attached to his chest, but he knew naming his emotions would not make it easier. He didn't deserve easier.

'Smile, please. And don't blame Nat. This is my doing, so if you're going to be mad with anyone—'

'I never doubted who was to blame,' he ground out between clenched teeth as his sister, who was several yards away now on her stationary mount, yelled over.

'Don't watch me, Danilo, we have this covered. I don't need your help. You make me nervous. Wait over there—both of you.'

'You heard her, come on.'

Danilo had heard her and he'd heard the imperious tone he had almost forgotten about as he tipped his head in acknowledgement of the order, and with a glimmer of a smile he called out to her, '*Sì*, Principessa.'

With a tight hold on the pommel, Nat, and the horse responding to the urging of a groom, turned to face them. 'You haven't called me that for ages.'

'You haven't been bossy for ages,' he tossed back.

'It's quite nice looking down on you for a change.'

It only took him a couple of long-legged strides to catch up with Tess, who was walking towards the tier of seats that Natalia had banished them to. 'I suppose you want me to say you were right and I was wrong?'

'This isn't about being right, or being wrong, though you are. Actually I have no problem with you not being infallible, but you clearly do.' Beside her Danilo stopped and she carried on walking, missing the expression on his face.

A moment later he caught her up and fell into step beside her.

'I used to come here and watch our mother in the ring.'

'Nat said she was very good.'

He nodded. 'She gave up an international career in show-jumping and a place on the national equestrian team when she married.' They had reached the tier of spectator seats but Danilo didn't sit down; instead he turned and stared out at the empty ring.

'My mum says a woman doesn't have to give up anything. She didn't.'

'Everyone is different. Seeing our mother on a horse…it was special, but it was her choice.' Even though it had never seemed right to Danilo.

'I've always been scared of horses. They're unpredictable.' A bit like Danilo, she thought, as she took the end seat in the bottom row.

'Nat used to love riding. Seeing her there just now has made me realise that she is growing up to be very like our mother and not just in looks. I saw my mother fall once when I was a kid. She looked so white lying there.' He nodded to the ring. 'I thought she was dead. They airlifted her to hospital. The next day she was back in the saddle with a fractured collarbone strapped up.' He stopped. 'You're scared of horses?' And he had spent the morning imagining her on horseback.

'No, just of heights.'

He laughed. 'But you helped at a stable?'

'My feet firmly on the ground. Mum encouraged me to get involved with community projects. I didn't always enjoy them but the stables were different. It was really rewarding to see how much confidence people gained. Being on horseback is a great leveller.'

Natalia did look happy. He felt a slug of guilt. This was the way she should have looked every day if he had been there for her. The way she would look when she walked again.

'So are you all right with this? She can carry on with the lessons? I'm forgiven?'

The soft question brought his dark gaze zeroing in on Tess's face as he acknowledged that there was nothing to forgive her for. That moment of gut-wrenching fear he had experienced when he'd seen Nat on the horse had made him lash out at Tess. 'She can carry on with the lessons,' he said, struggling to detach himself from the heavy weight of guilt in his chest.

The omission might not have been significant but the stab of hurt Tess felt was!

She pushed away the recognition as Natalia brought her chair to a halt beside her brother.

CHAPTER EIGHT

'I DIDN'T BELIEVE I could do it, but Tess said.' She flashed silent Tess a beaming smile. 'She said I could.'

Danilo looked at Natalia's glowing face and found himself wishing that he'd been the one to put the happy shine in her eyes.

'So what do you think?'

Tess was worried to find she could identify so strongly with the need for approval that shone in the younger girl's eyes.

'You weren't meant to see me until I'd got better.'

'You were tremendous!'

She smiled happily and agreed. 'Yes, I was, wasn't I?' She performed an acrobatic one-hundred-and-eighty-degree turn in her chair that made Danilo wince, though he did manage to bite back a cautionary admonition to take care—*just*.

'Where are you off to now, conquering Everest?' He had no doubt that if Tess suggested it Nat would have a go.

'No, that's next week. I have physio and...' she glanced down at her watch '... I'm late. Come on, Tess.'

'Can I borrow Tess for a moment?'

'Sure, but what do you want with her?'

A veiled look slid into Danilo's eyes, though it was the heightened colour along his cheekbones that caught Tess's attention—on anyone else she would have called it a blush. But when he spoke he sounded casual enough. 'Your birthday is coming up and you should not ask too many questions.'

At this reminder the slight furrow that remained in her brow faded. Danilo was happy to see the sparkle rekindled in her eyes but less happy at the voice in his head that reminded him it was there *despite* him and because of Tess.

'Fine,' Nat tossed over her shoulder before she paused, reminding Tess, 'But remember, we need to be at the hairdresser's for three thirty.'

Danilo stiffened as the words killed off any softening of his attitude.

'Oh, we've bags of time,' Tess called back before the girl sped off in her chair.

Danilo waited for his sister to be out of earshot before he turned to Tess, saying flatly, 'Cancel!'

He watched her smile gutter as she blinked up at him in apparent bemusement, so he spelt it out. 'The hairdresser comes here.'

It was impossible to tell from her expression just how much his autocratic delivery had aggravated her. 'Half the fun of having your hair done is hearing the gossip and watching other people. You wouldn't understand. It's called being sociable.'

He refused to play her game and rise to the bait. He was not going to allow his little sister to endure the ordeal her last trip out had involved.

'You couldn't know,' he admitted, trying to be fair. Which was the only thing at that moment stopping him coming down on her really hard. 'But the last time Natalia went to a beauty salon there was an…incident—'

Tess nodded. 'When the bathroom doors at the place were not wide enough to accommodate her wheelchair?'

'She told you?' When he had raised the subject later his sister had said she never wanted to talk about it.

Tess nodded.

'And yet you…' He shook his head in an attitude of disbelief, recalling the mortified tears running down Nat's cheeks when she had relayed the incident. 'Unbelievable! If you had a shred of imagination or half the empathy you like to pretend…' Words seemed to fail him. 'You know what I think?' he gritted out.

Tess was fed up making excuses for his autocratic attitude, making allowances for *his* feelings. She shrugged, reminding herself that she *didn't* care what Danilo thought of her. 'Wild guess…you're going to tell me?'

'I don't think you give a damn about Nat. The only thing you care about is being proved right. You just have to meddle! Well, I suggest you get your own life in order before you start interfering in others'.' She flinched, and for a moment he almost wished the words unsaid—*almost*.

'Let me spell out the situation. *They* come to *her*.' Nat had picked out her season's wardrobe from the comfort of home, she had beauticians, hairdressers and the like on speed dial, and she was not to be fobbed off with a trainee.

'It's a trip to the hairdresser's,' Tess said in a small but determined voice. She didn't want to make an issue of this but she would.

He breathed out, the air hissing through his clenched

teeth. 'You would expose Nat to insult just to prove some point?'

'What point?' she echoed, bewildered. 'I'm not trying to prove any point.'

'You walk in here and…you can't keep your nose out of anything, can you?'

Tess's head came up with a jerk. 'This isn't about me.'

'Everything is about you, since you arrived.' He dragged a frustrated hand through his hair and glared down at her glossy head.

'I don't like to see people unhappy, and if I can—'

'Bring a little light into their lives? Well, I don't need a damn sunbeam.'

What do you need, Danilo?

Her head spun. He had covered the space between them in a couple of strides and stood there towering over her, but when he spoke his voice was soft and every syllable carried a warning that made her shiver. 'And for the record, *I* am not a nice person.'

She heard the warning in each soft syllable but stood her ground, not because she was brave or stupid, but because her feet felt as though they were literally nailed to the ground. Being this close to him felt like standing on the brink of a live volcano. Close enough to feel the heat of his body as he towered over her, Tess could feel the waves of frustrated anger rolling off him.

'You think that I would not do *anything* for my sister!' he rasped out.

'I think you'd do anything for your sister, including keeping her hidden away in her golden cage, never leaving in case someone looks at her the wrong way.'

The coiled tension in his bunched muscles didn't

lessen, but as she watched the dull colour run up under
his olive-toned skin she felt a stab of sympathy push
through her own hurt and anger. She worried at the
plump, soft flesh of her lower lip with her teeth. Hell,
it ought to be easy to dislike him but it wasn't. Danilo
was devoted to his sister and that was the problem. He
wanted to protect Nat from everything, and the poor
girl, who worshipped him, let him.

'That is a gross exaggeration,' he managed finally.

She responded with a shrug. 'If you say so.'

'I do,' Danilo gritted through clenched teeth.

'You can't protect her from everything,' Tess said
quietly. 'Obviously *that* salon won't be getting her
custom but you underestimate her, you know. She is a
fighter. She realises that the thing to do if people are
ignorant is not to hide away but to educate them.'

The fact that what Tess said made sense only increased Danilo's levels of seething frustration and resentment towards her. 'And is this little lesson intended
for me?'

She gave a rueful grimace and accompanied her response with an eloquent shrug of her slender shoulders. 'Sorry, you can take a teacher out of the classroom
but—'

Jaw clenched, he ignored the olive-branch apology.
'I am not one of your little five-year-olds, Miss Jones,
and I am not impressed by homespun fortune-cookie
philosophy.'

'Then it's just as well I'm not interested in impress-
ing you,' she snapped back, losing what sympathy she
felt in the face of his refusal to relinquish his control
over his sister—talk about tunnel vision!

Talking to this man was like banging her head against

a stone wall. 'I realise,' she continued with acid sweetness, 'it probably makes you feel big and strong to rush to the rescue of helpless maidens, but we're not *all* weak and helpless. Some of us, the ones who don't feel it necessary to consult the great Danilo Raphael before we decide what side of the bed to get out of in the morning, can actually look after ourselves!' she finished, breathless and struggling to hold on to her attitude of self-righteous scorn—he looked mad again, *extremely* mad!

Halfway in she had been regretting her impetuous words, born of sheer frustration, but they had just kept coming and now, as she stood there hands on hips refusing to give him the satisfaction of seeing her take refuge behind one of the large bales of hay, she was *really* wishing that she had kept to the safe moral high ground instead of sinking to his level.

Danilo allowed his eyelids to flicker downwards, giving himself time to recover from the scene that was playing inside his head. The mental image involved Tess getting out of bed naked. It was a distraction that even his strong mental control was unable to banish, but he was able to use the same control to think past it and ignore the physical responses that he had zero control over.

It was crazy. Tess was attractive, sure, but in no way his *type.* This was what happened to a man when he ignored basic needs: they came back to bite him! He should have spent the night with Alex even if that had meant closing his eyes and thinking of…

Of their own volition his eyes slid to Tess's mouth. Did she bi…? He stopped the thought. There were some things about Miss Jones he *didn't* need to know.

Who are you kidding, Danilo?

He forcibly dragged his gaze from her mouth and told himself the sooner the better that he did something about the desert his sex life had been of late. If not Alex, there were others who did not contradict him at every turn. It was a matter of carving some time into his hectic schedule or going quietly insane; he needed meaningless sex urgently. At the moment, he could not afford any other sort—not that the situation was proving a hardship for him.

In the past he'd had what could be loosely termed long-term—as in three or four months—relationships, and he knew they required more time and energy than he was prepared at the moment to devote to his sex life. And those sorts of relationships had a habit of spilling over into the other parts of his life, and he appreciated how much more smoothly life ran when you compartmentalised. Sex was necessary as food was necessary, but not while there were more important things to deal with, like filling his father's shoes, and seeing his sister walk. He had no space left for the inevitable emotional demands of a relationship when it moved on from being simple sex.

'I do not need women to be weak to feel like a man, and you were not coping so well alone.' He watched her pale at the below-the-belt hit and immediately felt like a total heel.

'Well, I walked into that one, didn't I?' She gave a crooked smile, a characteristic he had come to recognise was very much her own, and she spread her arms wide, causing the sleeveless blouse she was wearing to ride up and reveal a sliver of tummy.

Half an inch and it sent a flash of heat through Danilo's already overheated body. He reacted with anger.

'You never walk. You jump, you run, you'd throw yourself off a cliff if it felt like the right thing to do. And while you do the right thing the rest of us... Do you know what *I* felt like when I saw Nat sitting on the back of that damned horse?' He dragged a hand across the stubble that had erupted on his jaw since he had shaved that morning and watched her eyes soften with compassion. She just didn't seem to get that he was not a man who needed compassion, or sympathy, or anything else from her.

Nothing, Danilo?

He ignored the inner voice but couldn't stop the hungry journey of his eyes as they slid down her body and made the return trip a lot slower.

'I can see that. I know I should probably have run it by you.'

One dark brow lifted. 'You think?'

'But you heard Nat. She wanted to surprise you.'

'Job well done,' he said grimly.

'I thought you were all right with it now?'

'I am. It's you I'm not all right with!' he bellowed then without warning. 'I'm beginning to dread coming home.' It wasn't until he made the claim that Danilo realised that the opposite was true. 'You realise the position you've put me in, don't you? If I forbid Natalia to do it again I'm the monster. You like to turn me into a monster, don't you?'

She rolled her eyes, exasperated by his determination to misrepresent everything she said. 'I don't think you're a monster. I think you're—' His upheld hand stopped her.

'Don't tell me, please. I doubt my ego would survive.'

She arched a sceptical brow but her laugh was

strained. His lofty attitude of amused indifference made her want to stamp her foot but that really would have given him something to laugh at.

'I think your ego is armour plated.' She had never encountered anyone with arrogance and a sense of superiority so bred into the bone. *Beautiful bones.* She brought her lashes down in a concealing sweep, ignored the twisting sensation and counted silently to ten before lifting her gaze to the man towering over her.

'You can't wrap your sister up in cotton wool. Well, you can, because I suppose you can do pretty much what you like, and it's true she'll be safe, but what sort of life will that be for her, Danilo?'

The appeal in her eyes passed Danilo by. He was unable to think past her assumption that he was free to act on impulses. His eyes darkened as his gaze slid to her mouth. If that were true…

'You think I can do what I like?' Had she made the accusation a few years ago she'd have been right. Back then he'd done what he liked, he'd lived for the moment. His idea of responsibility had been remembering his mother's birthday and having Christmas dinner at home. Now he couldn't remember the last time he'd acted on impulse.

And then he remembered: he'd brought Tess Jones into their lives. His eyes slid to the upturned face of the woman standing there, hands on her slender hips, smiling that infuriating, damned condescending smile of hers. Hell, he'd spent a morning closeted with a bunch of powerful individuals who had treated him with respect and sought his approval and he'd come home to this little slip of a woman who showed him not a jot of

respect and had demonstrated on every occasion possible she didn't give a damn about pleasing him.

'Well, I don't see anyone telling *you* what to do,'
she replied.

'Except you! You go out of your way to disagree with
me, challenge my authority.'

'Maybe,' she countered, 'I don't recognise your authority. People say what they think you want to hear
because they're scared of you!' she threw back.

He flinched, the white line etched around his sensual
lips growing more defined as he lost the last remnants
of his air of amused indifference. 'Are you suggesting
my sister is scared of me?' he demanded, outraged by
the suggestion.

'Not in that way. She just likes to please you. Just because you're a benevolent tyrant, it doesn't mean you're
not a tyrant. It wouldn't do you any harm once in a while
to listen rather than dictate.'

'Any more words of wisdom you care to bestow?'

Well, why not? Tess thought. If she was going to be
shown the door there was no point biting her tongue.
She might as well get it all off her chest.

'You're not *always* right, Danilo, and you know it—'

'The only thing I know is—' There was a strong element of compulsion in his expression and his action
as he raised his hand and touched her cheek.

Totally unprepared for his touch, Tess startled, like
one of the highly strung thoroughbreds in the stables,
and took a hasty step back. She stood there, her breath
coming in a series of tiny uneven pants, her shimmer-
ing golden stare trained on his face as she slowly lifted
her hand to her cheek. Her skin still tingled from the
brief contact and her stomach was quivering violently.

'Wh-why…did you do that?'

'I didn't *want* to.' He shook his head, unwilling to admit even to himself that the *need* that had flared without warning inside him was stronger than sense or reason. His nostrils flared as his burning gaze remained trained on her face.

What he wasn't saying, what was glowing in his incredible eyes, excited Tess in a way she had never experienced before. She watched as he lifted a hand and dragged it across his hair, making the black strands stand up in sexy spikes.

'Ever since you arrived here—'

He stopped abruptly, as if he could not force the words past the thickening atmosphere that quivered with tension. It reminded her of that stillness before a storm.

Always overpoweringly conscious of his physical presence, his raw masculinity, she felt that awareness jump, reaching an almost cellular level.

Tess's pulses did some leaping of their own as she struggled to drag her eyes from the muscle that was clenching and unclenching in his cheek.

His voice was so deep it was barely more than a whisper. The driven expression made her want to run away, but for some reason by the time the message reached her brain it said something different. Her eyes didn't leave his face as she took a step towards him. As she moved closer his hands closed over her upper arms and he impatiently dragged her into him until their bodies were close enough for her to feel the heat of his body, feel the tension in his muscles, inhale the scent of his skin.

It was an unimaginable situation and yet she had pictured it; the knowledge came with a rush of head-spinning excitement. Somewhere in the back of her mind there lingered a small corner, a fragment of sanity that was telling her this was a bad idea, but she determinedly ignored it.

'Say my name.'

She swallowed, the emotions swirling inside her making her throat close.

'I want to hear you say it.'

Her head dropped but even with her eyes squeezed tight shut she could still see his eyes, the burn in the midnight depths that awoke a need in her she had never experienced.

His hand went under her chin. Tess resisted, not the strong fingers drawing her face to him, but the heavy drag of desire low in her belly, the heat that made her shiver and her oversensitised skin tingle. Even as she fought she recognised the futility of the attempt. What was happening, and she had no name for it, was happening at a primal level.

Her head tilted back, her neck suddenly not strong enough to support her but it didn't need to, because his hand had moved, his fingers providing a supportive cradle at the back of her head. Her heart was drumming so hard with anticipation that it drowned out her husky whisper.

'Danilo.'

He sighed and smiled a slow smile, made up of equal parts predatory intent and heart-stopping tenderness. The combination killed off any lingering resistance as lust, hot and hungry, cut through the dreamy desire.

As he bent his head she reached up her hands, linking them behind his neck. The slowness felt like torture as he bent his head until his mouth was a bare half-inch from hers. She could feel the warm waft of his breath on her skin before he brushed his lips over the corners of her mouth, and, holding her gaze, he ran his tongue along the quivering outline.

Tess whimpered, the sound lost inside the warmth of his mouth as it finally captured her own. As the slow, sensuous possession deepened it lost finesse and became rough, hungry and raw. The feelings tearing through her were like nothing she had ever experienced or imagined.

She was not conscious of walking backwards until her back made contact with the stone wall of the building. Still kissing her, he slid his hands down her body, one moving to cup the curve of her bottom. She instinctively arched her back, pushing into him, only pulling back slightly as she felt the imprint of his arousal against the softness of her belly.

He said something, she didn't know what, and she wound her arms around his neck, letting her head fall back as he trailed hot, damp kisses down her throat.

If anyone saw us now they'd assume we were making... She sucked in a startled breath. And they'd be right, or at least they would be if this didn't stop now.

Right now, Tess!

Digging deep into her reserves, she placed her hands flat on his chest and pushed back. After a moment he reacted to the pressure and let her go. Her knees felt so weak that if it hadn't been for the stone wall behind her she'd have slid to the floor.

'You're right. Not here, not now,' Danilo said, thinking more clearly than he had done in days. He could see now that he'd been looking at this problem from the wrong angle. Trying to keep Tess at arm's length was like trying to put out a forest fire with a watering can.

Lighting more fires seemed counter-intuitive but giving that initial conflagration no place to go was an acknowledged method to quench a wild fire. Let it burn itself out but keep it within boundaries.

This was the point where Tess knew she was meant to say, *not anywhere, not ever*, but she didn't. As she stared up at him all the feelings he aroused in her narrowed into one beam of white-hot desire that blasted away the image of a face that had haunted her for half her life. The sense of liberation made her feel lightheaded.

Acknowledging that the ugly incident from her past had not gone away but spread out ugly roots from the dark corner she had consigned it to had been half of the healing process. Losing her virginity would complete it.

She wanted to have sex with the most gorgeous man on the planet and if he ended up breaking her heart she would deal with that later. In the meantime she was going to enjoy it, and so what if all he wanted was her body? She could deal with it.

'Only don't carry on looking at me with those big hungry eyes or I'll...' He took a deep breath and dragged a hand across his hair, somehow managing to look totally normal seconds later, when he tipped his head her way as though they had just exchanged nothing more intimate than a good morning while she was shaking inside and out.

If that was good morning, imagine goodnight!

CHAPTER NINE

'WELL, WHAT DO you think?'

Tess blinked. 'Think?'

'You haven't heard a thing I've said, have you?' Natalia angled a speculative look at Tess's face. 'And you keep smiling.'

'Do I?'

'Is it that guy at the coffee bar? I saw him give you his number. He was hot!'

Tess, who had forgotten the crumpled piece of paper in her pocket, smiled and tried to look mysterious. 'Maybe.' She could hardly say, *I was thinking about your brother kissing me.* She frowned as she thought of Danilo walking away. *Not here, not now.*

She really wished she had asked for more details. That she'd pinned him down to a time and a place. Astonished at the way she was thinking, she took a deep breath and looked at Natalia, who was happily chatting away. She didn't have a clue what she'd been talking about; all she'd been fantasising about was being made love to by Danilo.

By that evening, it looked as if the fantasy was going to remain just that. Danilo was not at the *palazzo* when they returned and he was a no show at dinner. The meal was a nightmare! Tess smiled through gritted teeth listening to Franco's jokes about his cousin's workload being blonde and six feet in heels, then refused the suggestion of a film session. She really wasn't in the mood for watching a cool blonde Hitchcock heroine ensnare her man.

She felt like a total and complete idiot. She'd finally decided to give herself to a man and he'd lost interest, or had a better offer. Who knew...who cared?

Me, she thought miserably as she tipped half a flagon of bath oil into the copper tub that took centre stage in her massive en-suite bathroom.

The bath was running when she heard a knock on the door and she called out, 'Hold on!' as she paused to switch off the taps. A leak in the ceiling of the *palazzo* could destroy a priceless fresco.

She opened the door, expecting to see one of the maids who turned down her bed each night, and instead saw Danilo standing there looking cool. But that illusion vanished as soon as she met his eyes. The dark slow burn she saw there lit a fuse inside her in the time it took for her heart to take a lurching thud, all her earlier anger fading.

It was mad, it was crazy, it was utterly illogical but she wanted to be with him tonight, actually any night.

Without a word he stretched his hand towards her.

Tess looked at his long brown tapering fingers and imagined them on her skin. A second later she laid her hand in his.

She jogged to keep up with his pace.

'Where are we going?'

'Somewhere we can be private. This is it, my room.'

He walked ahead of her, through the door, and stood to one side as she entered.

Danilo's private apartment was in the north-facing wing of the *palazzo*. She'd never been here before though she'd often wondered what it was like, but as he closed the door behind her Tess felt no urge to study the decor.

Danilo was a work of art, she decided, making a covert study of him. The angle of his head, the strong line of his back, the strong musculature and power of his thighs hinted at by the well-cut linen trousers he wore.

The click of the key as he turned it in the lock broke her rapt concentration.

It's really happening, then, she thought as he turned to face her.

She didn't realise his intention when he caught her hand, turned it over until it was palm up and unfolded her fingers one by one to expose her palm.

She stared at the key he placed in it before he closed her fingers and his hand over it.

'To keep them out, not you in. You can walk through that door any time you want to, you know that?'

She swallowed, struggling to force the words past the aching occlusion in her throat, but there was no hesitation before she handed the key back to him.

'I don't need it. There's nowhere else I want to be right now.'

And right now was all that mattered, she told herself and waited for the flurry of panic to subside. It did. The now was all that mattered, all that she could *allow* to matter, and she refused to think beyond it, beyond to a future that didn't contain Danilo.

'You're sure?'

His voice had sounded not quite steady. By comparison, her response was. 'Totally.'

With a nod, he inhaled through flared nostrils. She watched as he slid the key back into the lock and turned back to face her, his dark eyes seeking out and fastening onto her exotic, wide-spaced amber eyes. The unvarnished carnality of his stare sent a deep shudder through her receptive body. Tess snatched in air through parted lips when, without breaking contact, he began to unbutton his shirt.

Tess swallowed, breathing hard, her eyelids fluttering as she fought the compulsion to watch. She lasted until he slipped the last button and then she couldn't *not* look.

A deep, tremulous sigh escaped her parted lips.

The shirt hung open to the waist revealing a section of his flat, muscle-ridged belly and the light dusting of body hair on his broad, powerful chest that narrowed into a directional arrow as it vanished under the belt that hung low on his narrow hips.

The image imprinted itself on her retina as her skin heated. She moistened her lips and thought about touching him, thought about unfastening the silver buckle and…her thoughts shocked and excited her.

'Now your turn.'

It took a few moments for her lust-soaked brain to work out what he had said, what he was asking her to do. Her eyes widened and from some primal corner of her mind the confidence to do what he asked, not just because he asked but because she *wanted* to, came.

Shoulders back, she lifted her chin, her stance challenging him as she walked slowly towards him. She didn't stop until she was close enough to feel the heat coming from his body.

His eyes were hot too, hot enough to singe her as she held them for a moment before she turned around presenting her slender back to him. She could hear the sound of his harsh, rapid breathing above the thud of her heartbeat as she gathered the long skein of her hair in one hand and lifted it off her neck in silent invitation.

Her breath came quick and shallow as he slowly pulled down the zip of the silk shift dress she was wearing. The light contact of his fingertips on the damp skin of her back sent little shivers of sensation across her skin as they moved downwards until her back and the dimple above the upper curve of her taut bottom were exposed.

She stood there for a moment, feeling his stare burning into her back, then, taking a deep breath, she retraced her steps until she reached the spot where she had begun and turned. Holding his eyes, she slid her loosened dress off one shoulder then the other.

Danilo watched, his eyes half shaded by his heavy lids and thick lashes leaving just a glittering slit visible. He was fighting for each breath like someone oxygen-deprived. Each laboured inhalation lifted his ribcage and pulled his flat belly concave, all the while his eyes remaining trained on her face.

It wasn't until she let the dress fall, jiggling her hips as it slipped in a silken slither to her ankles, that his glance dropped.

She heard his raw gasp of, *'Che Dio mi aiuti...'* as she stepped away from the silken pool at her feet, and, head tilted to one side, took a step towards him and stood there poised, reminding him of a deer not sure whether to run away or towards the light. She stood before him, an incredibly arousing combination of wantonness and innocence in her pose.

Perfect, he thought as he greedily absorbed every detail, every perfect inch of her as she stood there in her heels, tiny pants, a bra that consisted of little more than two triangles of silk, so fine he could see not just the outline of her prominent nipples through it but the darker shadow of the areola.

She was beautiful. More than beautiful. Skin that pale and perfect did not exist, he had thought, outside the airbrushed photo spreads in glossy magazines. But she represented everything that was female and desirable. He was unable to take his eyes off her, his restless gaze remaining riveted as he moved towards her.

Tess gave a tiny cry and ran, meeting him halfway.

The impact of their collision was softened when his arm, resembling a band of steel, wrapped around her waist before, almost casually, he lifted her off her feet and dragged her against him in one smooth, effortless motion.

The delicious shock of skin-to-skin contact vibrated along her nerve endings, and combined with the arousing power of his display of strength it made her head start to spin. She didn't even connect the low feral moan with her as she reached out greedily for him, her fingers digging into the thick glossy pelt of hair, pushing deeper and holding him there as he found her mouth.

The kiss, hard, hungry, seemed to go on for ever, or at least until the heat that unfurled in her belly had ribboned out throughout her entire body until she was aflame, her sensitised skin tingling, her insides liquid. The hunger his kiss had awoken was relentless, all consuming, something outside her experience or imagination.

As he continued the carnally creative kiss Tess twisted in his arms, her attempt to wrap her legs around him aided when he grunted and shifted her higher up without breaking contact.

When he finally lifted his head they were both breathing hard.

Her legs still secured around his waist, she held his face between her hands. 'I like that a lot,' she told him.

Her fierce declaration dragged a raw laugh from his throat as he stared into her passion-glazed eyes with a mixture of hunger and fascination. '*Madre di Dio, cara,* so do I. I have never met a woman like you.'

'You are perfect!'

'It will be perfect,' he promised thickly as he kissed her again. Tess's lips parted without pressure, inviting the carnal intrusion of his tongue and meeting it with her own.

They stumbled, bodies entwined, until Danilo's legs made contact with the bed. He turned as he looked down into her passion-flushed face, her golden eyes glowing, waiting… She was the living embodiment of temptation. His heartbeat slowed, leaving the impression that they were suspended in time.

The impression was fleeting; the moment passed but the pressure in his chest didn't. It grew; he felt he couldn't breathe. The unfamiliar feelings that broke loose inside him as he looked at her increased in intensity, stronger than anything he had ever experienced. A mingling of tenderness and passion, the combination was as contradictorily confusing as this woman was. As their eyes caught and held he felt a surge of possessiveness that drew a growl from his chest, as all the disparate feeling she evoked in him narrowed to one— passion! Hot and dark, like nothing he could remember feeling, it gripped him now as in his imagination. He felt her female warmth gripping him, holding him tight in a slick silken sheath.

Breathless, she blinked up at him, not sure how she came to be sitting on the edge of the bed, but she was. Danilo seemed a long way away looking down at her. She wanted him on top of her, inside her, not miles away, then as she opened her mouth to voice her complaint he dropped to his knees at her feet.

She stared at his dark head as he lifted first one, unhooking her shoe before he slid it off and flung it over his shoulder. Then he did the same to her right foot. A tiny shocked gasp left her lips as he raised her foot and ran a finger slowly along the delicate arch before lifting it to his lips and kissing it. She shuddered.

By the time he had applied the same methodology to her other foot she was shaking like someone with a fever, a heat that burned away the last shred of sanity she retained. There was nothing left but deep, drowning need.

'Please...'

A pulse throbbed in his temple, pounding with the effort it cost not to respond to the carnal, throaty plea.

Every instinct inside him screamed protest when, instead of pushing her down and falling on top of her the way they both wanted, he caught her hands and pulled her to her feet.

He couldn't stop his hands sliding down to her bottom, curling over the peachlike curves, drawing her into him until their bodies collided and he heard her gasp.

She was too weak with lust to hold her head up; it fell back but not before, through heavy, half-closed eyes, she saw the taut, almost feral expression on Danilo's face. The image of it imprinted on her retina and she felt herself sinking deeper into the sexual thrall that held her tight in its grip.

Suddenly, she found herself sprawled onto the bed, her heart thudding as he lowered himself until, one knee braced on the mattress and a hand under her head, he loomed over her.

In mute supplication she held up her hands to him, her face a mask of need as she slid them over the sweet, slick miles of his powerful shoulder and back.

But instead of finally feeling the weight of his body on her, which was what she wanted, what she needed, the mattress lifted as he stood up until only their fingertips were touching.

He had not meant to let things go this far. He needed— it was important to say this, be upfront, not... His focus slipped, the urgency faded as he looked at her mouth and, unable to resist the temptation, the soft pink lushness offered, he bent his head.

The kiss that started at one corner of her mouth was softer than the others and then it wasn't. Her lips parted as his body, supported on one elbow, leaned over her. As his tongue slid inside her mouth she met it with her own, the ache inside her now frantic and inarticulate, but Danilo was speaking. Half the things he said were in his native tongue so she didn't understand them, but it didn't seem to matter. It was all wildly exciting, his eyes, his touch, his mouth. They said the things that really mattered.

He slid his hands down her bare shoulders and pressed his lips to the hollow above her collarbone.

Tess's head fell back as the kisses trailed in the direction of the valley between her breasts and he groaned. 'Your skin is so soft.'

Her hands glided over the muscles of his back, each individually delineated. The beauty of the perfect formation was not blurred by an ounce of excess flesh. He was hard and lean.

'I can't believe this is happening. You're incredible.'

And then to her utter dismay he stepped back, stood up and held up his hands as though he was warding her off.

Confused, she sat up. 'Danilo...'

'No!'

Her expression as she crossed her hands across her chest, the hurt shining in her eyes, almost snapped his resolve. If she had been anyone else he would have said *to hell with it* right there and then.

'You need to know this is something I don't do.' He closed his eyes and huffed out a deep, long, steadying breath.

His face was taut with the effort it had cost him to pull back. The pain of it was etched deep into the lines of stress bracketing his mouth.

She would have been more hurt if it hadn't been for the driven need that glowed in his darkened eyes, the layer of moisture that glistened on his bronzed torso, and the fact that he was panting deep, gulping breaths, as though he'd just run a marathon.

That makes two of us, she thought, getting angry instead. 'Have sex?'

He ignored the comment. 'Bring my personal life into this house.'

'You mean sex life.' It amazed her that she could sound so calm.

He nodded. 'If this happens—'

If it didn't happen here and now whatever he was about to say wouldn't matter, couldn't matter, because she would die; she would die from sheer *wanting*. She would die a *virgin* of sheer wanting, which was even worse!

'It will not make us a couple. I have no time in my life at the moment to devote to a relationship.'

'But you have time for sex?'

'Tess, you are not making this...'

'Easy? It is easy. You don't have to agonise. I already know what you're working up towards—telling me that you don't want emotional entanglements, that you don't want your family, and I'm assuming anyone else, to know that we are sleeping together—if we ever actually get around to it. So, bottom line, it's a sort of "what happens behind closed doors stays there", which is fine by me. And outside the bedroom we carry on as normal, which shouldn't be too hard. I'll be leaving in three weeks, which is why I'm talking so fast.'

The last comment drew a sharp laugh from him.

She had mimed a ticking motion as she went through the list and now she threw the invisible list over her shoulder and rose to her feet, facing him, hands on hips.

'So far so good but in this same spirit of complete disclosure I need to tell you something. It might surprise you,' she warned.

It was Danilo who sat down on the bed this time. 'That will not be a first. You are not about to break the news that you started life as a man?'

'I'm a virgin.'

'No, joking aside.'

'Not a joke.'

The smile slipped from his face and was replaced by a guarded expression.

'Years ago something happened, well, it didn't, but it was scary and I think that every time I came near to… it got in the way—'

'What happened?'

'It doesn't matter. The important thing is I'm dealing with it now.'

'Yes, it does matter.'

She glanced at his face, took a deep breath and told him.

He sat and listened, not speaking, not moving until she had finished, his over-stillness at sharp variance with the emotions breaking loose inside him. Anger poured through him in a steady stream, mingled with outrage and a protective surge too strong to deny.

'So what did your mother do when you told her?'

'I didn't. There was no point—she would have felt so guilty and he never came back.'

'So who have you told?'

'Just you.'

Just you. The words echoed in his head.

'That's why I think that over the years it sort of grew into something more than it was.'

'It was what it was—an assault! Such men, I would…' He slid into his native tongue but Tess got the drift of his savage outpouring before, feelings vented, he held out a hand, ignoring the voice in his head that reminded him he'd wanted just sex and already it was more.

After the tiniest of pauses she laid her hand in his, only to pull back when he asked, 'Why now, and why me?'

She shrugged, not quite meeting his eyes. 'I don't know.' Or didn't want to know. 'Right time, the way we met? It was... You make me feel safe and at the same time...' She ran a tongue across her dry lips. 'I really like the way you make me feel and I think it helps that all you want from me is...well, sex, because—' She let out a light shriek as he reached out, grabbed her and pulled her on top of him.

As he rolled her beneath him, breathless, she arched up into him as, supporting himself on his elbows, he kissed his way up her body. 'Do you mind about, you know...?'

He had reached her chest and as he slid one breast from the silken covering and fitted his mouth to the rosy peak she let out a low keening cry, half pain, half pleasure.

'It's a responsibility, but only a problem if we let it be,' he growled out as he lowered himself down onto her. 'I just want to make it as special for you as possible.'

She moaned and grabbed him, her fingers sliding down the slick skin of his back under the loosened shirt.

He levered himself up and began to fight his way out and then they were both tearing off clothes, their own and each other's, with frantic breathless urgency that did not make for speed but definitely raised the excitement stakes as they touched and kissed and tasted their way to freedom.

Tess was pretty much mindless with need by the time they were both fully naked. She wanted to explore every inch of him. He was so beautiful but she wanted so much more.

Then, as she was lying there naked, breathless, her entire body burning up with need, she kissed his chest, sliding her hands lower over the flat, ridged muscle of his belly. As her fingers closed over the silky hardness of his erection he let out a low groan and rolled her under him in one smooth motion.

Teeth clenched, he looked down at her, the driven need in his face sending a fresh wave of lustful longing through her. 'It has to be now, *cara.*'

Face hot, flushed, she nodded and closed her eyes, letting them half open as she heard him reach for a condom and sheathe himself. Then she felt the heat of him against the curls at the apex of her legs and took one deep breath, relaxing in a long, sibilant sigh as he slid into her, increasing the pressure as her body rhythmically tightened around him.

Her legs lifted, locking around his waist as every thrust took her deeper into the warm darkness, deeper into herself. She was more aware of herself than she ever had been, while also conscious of all of him, not just the place inside her he was touching. But him, the hardness of him, the heat... Danilo! Until the two became indistinguishable, where he began and where she ended unimportant, and they arrived at the same place at the same moment; their cries became one.

Tess floated back from the place he had taken her and opened her eyes to find Danilo watching her.

He gave a wolfish grin, still stunned by their primal coupling made more amazing because she came to him a virgin. 'Are you all right? I didn't mean—'

'I found it pretty wonderful. I'm left wondering if all egomaniacs are equally good lovers.' She missed his answering frown. She was asleep.

CHAPTER TEN

'HAD A GOOD NIGHT?'

Natalia smiled. 'Perfect. The best birthday ever,' she said, stifling a yawn and adding a rueful, 'Sorry!'

'You're exhausted.'

'A bit tired, but I'm fine.'

'You're not fine, you should go to bed—'

'I can't. I have to thank people and say goodbye and—'

Danilo pressed a light kiss to her forehead. 'All things I think I can do on your behalf. You go to bed.'

'Well, if you're sure?'

'I am,' he said firmly. 'Consider it part of your birthday present.'

'Danilo, Tess looks lovely tonight, doesn't she?'

He tensed, and silently amended, Tess looked *spectacular*. 'Where is this leading?'

'She's been here five weeks, she's due to leave next week.'

Five weeks and the last couple had been spent in his bed. That fire showed no signs of burning itself out. He was beginning to wonder if there was a way for her to stay longer. 'Yes, I know.'

'Can't you say something that will make her stay? I just hate the idea of her not being here.'

His jaw clenched. 'What do you want me to do, kidnap her?'

He saw her expression and moderated his tone, adding lightly, 'Maybe you could visit her there? Take a trip to London?'

'It won't be the same.' Natalia sighed.

An hour later Danilo had performed the last of the formal farewells, a situation that had paid surprising dividends when a handshake from one of the last VIP guests to leave had closed a deal that he had not expected to be finalised for weeks yet, so the evening had been a triumph on more than one level.

Danilo was now standing on the empty helipad when the head of the security detail approached him. He arched a brow. 'Problem?'

The ex-army, suited figure shook his head. 'Nothing of note. Just to let you know we'll do one final sweep of the grounds and then wind things down.'

Danilo glanced towards the thin ribbon of silver light created by the last of the cars as they moved down the drive and nodded. 'Good job.' He loosened his tie as the man walked away, speaking into his earpiece, before setting off in the opposite direction. He had his own plans to wind down too.

Fuelled by urgency, Danilo strode back towards the *palazzo*, crossing the terrace, which earlier had been packed with people but was empty now, save for the catering staff who were piling empty glasses and discarded champagne bottles onto trays with quiet efficiency.

Conscious of a steady buzz of anticipation in his blood, Danilo entered the ballroom where the band were packing up their instruments. He paused, his eyes moving around the room, searching as he had been doing all night, only now he did not need to be covert about it. It was not a guilty pleasure—just a pleasure.

He no longer had to fight the tug. He *could* cross the room, he *could* breathe in her fragrance. Obviously he could not have spent the evening with her beside him, an indulgence that would have been misinterpreted or even been considered a public declaration of sorts; it would be unfair to expose her to that sort of speculation.

The knowledge had not lessened his sense of frustration as the evening had progressed and he had seen Tess dancing with other men, smiling at other men, laughing up at other men.

Which was good! He had *wanted* her to enjoy herself, not hide in a corner. Not that such a thing would have been possible in that eye-wateringly sexy green dress, but maybe he'd wanted her not to enjoy herself *that* much.

Dio, who was he kidding? He hadn't wanted her to enjoy herself at all without him, he had wanted her. Just wanted her, beside him, with him…for them to be an official couple—and it was not possible.

Why not?

The question, so unexpected that he had no set answer to fall back on, sent a vibration of shock through Danilo. He had put his personal life on hold after the accident to focus on Natalia. It had been a choice and perhaps there had, he realised, been an element of the hair shirt about it, a way to expiate his sins; he *deserved* to suffer, not that he would ever suffer as much as his sister had.

Even then, he thought contemptuously, his sacrifice

had not gone as far as abstinence. He had justified this by thinking of these disposable liaisons as a practical release valve that left him with nothing but an empty feeling. Had any of this not so *noble sacrifice* helped Natalia?

The only thing it had proved was that he was a shallow, selfish bastard.

When he had begun sleeping with Tess it had been meant to be more of the same, but she was a very different sort of woman. He had always known that, but it had felt safe because she would be out of his life very soon. She would be out of his life. His lips compressed, self-disgust a metallic taste in his mouth.

With a painful and uncomfortable flash of insight he suddenly saw tonight from her point of view. He had acted as though he were ashamed of her, that she wasn't good enough for his friends, whereas in reality she was too good for them, and too good for him.

The tightness in his chest increased as he stared at the woman he had fallen into a relationship with. The question was, had he fallen in love with her too?

Suddenly he saw the evening as fighting his instincts to prove to himself that he could, to prove to himself that nothing had happened, as something very different. But if he felt that putting her at a distance would have prevented the truth that was hammering away inside his skull he could not have been more wrong.

A young man carrying a tray neatly sidestepped to avoid a collision when Danilo stopped dead without warning. He stood there amid the detritus of the festivities, staring at the figure who stood beside the piano player, the internal conflict stamped on his lean features.

The pianist, a young man who'd had a crowd of admirers around him all night, a fact Danilo suspected was attributable as much to his blue eyes as his talent, was smiling up at her, laughing while his fingers moved casually across the keys.

This time Danilo did not fight any impulses. He crossed the room in seconds and slid his arm across her shoulders, pulling her into his side.

'I've been looking for you.'

'I've been right here.' She lowered her chin to hide the hurt she knew he would see in her eyes, then, turning her head into his chest, she let herself stay there, giving herself a moment before she tilted her head back to meet his eyes. 'Has everyone gone?'

Of course they had, or he wouldn't be here now talking to her, after ignoring her all evening. She pushed away the quiver of resentment.

You knew what you were getting into, Tess, so no point crying foul now. He had never pretended. Sometimes she wished he would, which probably made her weak, or an idiot, or both?

If she'd been asked to put their relationship into words it would have sounded furtive...even sordid and, yes, there were moments when she asked herself what she was doing. Asked herself what had happened to her pride. But those moments never outlasted his kiss. When they were together everything felt *right*.

But tonight, as she had watched him from a distance as he'd worked the room, as important and powerful people had vied for his attention, she'd realised that she had started to live for those moments when the door closed and the rest of the world went away.

The fear the knowledge brought with it went soul deep. She had always prided herself on facing the truth but tonight had made her realise how close she had come to reading more into his desire than was there, of convincing herself that their love-making could not be so perfect if there was no emotional connection underlying it. She had forgotten that simply wanting something to be didn't make it happen.

For Danilo what they shared was sex, great sex, but just sex. This was the reality; tonight was the reality. In bed they were lovers and outside she was nothing to him and next week she would be less than nothing, a memory.

'Not quite everyone, *cara*. We are here.' He half turned her as his warm hands slid down her shoulders, pulling her into him. 'And I have just realised that we have not had a dance.' He glanced towards the young pianist, who nodded, and a moment later the room was filled with the sad, sweet sound of a classic romantic ballad.

Danilo tipped his head, the formality of the gesture in sharp contrast to the sensual glow in his eyes, which stayed on her face. 'May I?'

Tess hesitated and pulled away a little.

Danilo frowned. 'Is something wrong?'

She could have said, *Yes, I've fallen in love with you and I have no pride left.* But she didn't. Tomorrow was soon enough…one last night and then tomorrow she'd walk through the door before it was closed in her face, salvaging at least a little pride.

Her throat thick with emotion, Tess shook her head.

The furrow between his dark brows relaxed as, holding her gaze, he took her hands and placed them on his shoulders. After covering one with his own he placed his free hand in the small of her back before beginning to move to the music.

'I can't dance,' she cautioned, struggling to hide the deep sadness inside her. 'I'll tread on your toes.'

'A price worth paying to hold you close, *cara*,' he whispered in her ear.

The combination of the husky sentiment and the waft of his warm breath on her ear made Tess shiver. Eyes closed, she leaned her face against his chest, aware of the strong, heavy thud of his heartbeat. A couple of bars in and she had forgotten about her two left feet. It was that rare thing—a *perfect* moment. Everything else vanished and there was only the man who held her and the music and them together as one.

The people still working in the room stopped what they were doing to watch the duo who circled the room and others, drawn by the sound of the virtuoso performance by the young man who was destined one day to headline at opera houses all over the world, appeared at doorways and stood watching as the couple circling the floor, oblivious to the audience and their surroundings, lost in the music and each other, continued to move as one.

'The music has stopped, Danilo.' It was still in her head. She would never forget the sound—they had a song but no relationship...how ironic was that?

'I know.'

'People are staring.'

'Let them.' They were still moving to the music playing in her head—could he hear it too? The silk of Tess's dress hissed against the marble floor as Danilo twirled her out through the doors and onto the terrace before finally stopping. It was totally deserted now; the extra tables had gone and the moonlit night was silent.

Danilo hooked a finger under her chin and forced her face up to his. As their eyes meshed he took a deep breath, struggling to identify the unfamiliar feeling that tightened his gut as nervousness.

'I have to check on Nat. She had a headache. Then…'

One last night, she added silently, *to remember.*

The emotional ache in her throat threatening to emerge as tears, Tess blinked hard to stop them spilling and raised herself on tiptoe. The glow in his eyes as their glances connected—she could have easily read more into it than simple lust but she wouldn't let herself—made her head spin.

'I'll be waiting,' she said simply before she brushed her lips lightly over his.

The tantalising contact drew a groan from his throat. He hooked a hand behind her head and kissed her back with a hunger that made her knees sag. She clung to him for a moment after he pulled back.

'Don't be too long.'

Desire flared hotly in his eyes at the plea. 'I won't be.' Urgency made his voice raw as his soul-stripping scrutiny slid over the curves of her body, outlined in clinging green silk. 'Don't take it off. I want to.'

He was in the lift that gave direct access to his sister's suite when his phone rang. A glance at the number drew his brow into a frown.

'I'm sorry, I've just realised what time it is… I'll ring back tomorrow.'

Danilo cut across the British consultant's apology. 'Now is fine.'

'I know your sister cancelled her last appointment

but I just wanted to be sure—does she want to re-schedule?'

The lift drew to a smooth halt but Danilo did not move. 'My sister cancelled her appointment?'

'I assumed…' The other man's discomfort was obvious in his voice as he added quickly, 'No matter. I will discuss it with her tomorrow. It's just her phone was off. Don't worry, I'll speak with her tomorrow.'

Danilo slid the phone back into his pocket and stood there staring at the blank wall. Natalia had cancelled an appointment? He did not know that she had even had an appointment, and now she had cancelled?

He flinched as guilt hit him in the gut with the force of a sledgehammer blow. This was what happened when he took his eye off the ball, when he forgot where his priorities, his duty lay. This had happened because for the past couple of weeks he had spent his days thinking about nights with Tess.

Why was he even asking himself if he loved her? The question was irrelevant. He couldn't afford to be in love. Besides, Tess deserved a man who could give her more than he was able to offer.

He straightened his shoulders, prepared for what was to come, but as the doors slid silently open he realised that actually he wasn't!

Despite the promise Danilo made, the ice in the bucket that held the unopened bottle of champagne Tess had carried up to her room had dissolved into water by the time her bedroom door finally opened.

Normally Danilo slipped quietly into her room. This time there was nothing furtive about his appearance, but Tess, who was sitting on the bed at the time, did not make the mistake of reading anything good into the fact, as he'd wrenched the door open so hard the solid oak had rattled on its hinges.

When he slammed it behind him with equal force and turned his cold, contemptuous stare on her face the moment stretched and her dismayed confusion increased.

She'd seen Danilo frustrated and snappy, she had seen him irritated, she thought she'd seen him angry. Now she realised that she was wrong. She hadn't.

The Danilo standing there, his body clenched, every sinew taut, the golden skin blanched of colour as it stretched tight across his razor-sharp cheekbones that were scored with dull dark colour—now, *this* was angry. This was *furious*!

And all that fury was aimed at her, Tess realised, struggling to think past the shocked bemusement in her befuddled brain.

His taut body was literally quivering with outrage. Standing there, he managed to look simultaneously magnificent and scary, but most of all *furious*!

She pressed her lips together, tasting the strawberry gloss she had coated them with several times while she'd waited, trying to work out what was happening and more importantly why.

In contrast to his actions and rigid stance, Danilo's voice was lethally soft when he finally spoke. 'So, what are we celebrating?'

She watched as, without another word, he walked across to the ice bucket, pulled out the bottle and, with a sharp twist, popped the cork. The champagne exploded in a fountain, leaving barely enough to cover the bottom of the two glasses. He picked up one and raised it.

'A toast. To lies and liars everywhere, and especially to those we know and love.'

Tess ignored the glass. Her head was spinning in confusion. The anxiety in her stomach was making her feel sick. 'What has happened?'

'Oh, you know—same old, same old. Oh, and I have just walked in on my sister with her boyfriend, my sister who has cancelled her appointment with the consultant.'

'Oh, no!' Tess closed her eyes and when she opened them again sympathy glowed in them. 'I'm so sorry, Danilo.'

His jaw clenched as he fought to regain some level of control. He had been a fool but he would not fall for her soft sympathy again. 'And this comes as such a shock to you?' he drawled. 'Any of it?'

'No,' she admitted. 'I knew that she'd been seeing Marco. She cares for him, Danilo, and I really think that he cares for her. Where is the harm? She's a grown woman, Danilo. She has to make her own mistakes.'

'Easy enough for someone who isn't going to be around to pick up the pieces after those mistakes to say,' he sneered, refusing to acknowledge the hurt in her eyes. 'You wreak damage like some blasted tsunami.'

Her chin came up. 'It's not my fault and I'm sick and tired of you blaming me when anything goes wrong!'

Her protest was drowned out by the sound of the glass he was holding splintering in his hand.

'Danilo! You're bleeding! Let me…'

He looked at the blood dripping from his hand without interest and snapped, 'Leave it!'

She gave a shrug. 'Fine. Bleed to death!' she tossed back childishly. 'What exactly is wrong with your sister having a boyfriend? And don't try and tell me this is about Marco. You'd be the same about any man she dated. Has it even crossed your mind that Marco's feelings are genuine?'

'She is in a wheelchair.'

Her patience snapped—talk about tunnel vision! 'Well, maybe Marco can see beyond the wheelchair. Unlike you!' She watched him pale with anger at the accusation and her own anger drained away. 'You're not protecting her, Danilo,' she said softly. 'You're—' She stopped, shaking her head.

'I'm what?'

'You're smothering her.' There was no accusation in the words, just deep sadness.

'I will get her out of the wheelchair—' And yet he hadn't. All his life he had achieved whatever he set out to and now the only thing he wanted to do was eluding him.

'And what if you can't?' she countered quietly. 'What if—?'

'How long have you been filling Natalia's head with this sort of defeatist attitude?'

'Nat is the least defeatist person I have ever met. She is brave and strong and upbeat. I haven't brainwashed Nat. I couldn't. She is as stubborn and pig-headed as you are.'

'How long have you known?'

'Does it matter?' she asked wearily.

'Did you think it was amusing to plot behind my back?'

Her eyes blinked wide at the accusation. 'There was no plotting, there was no—'

'And you knew my feelings on the subject.'

The sweep of his cold eyes made her shiver.

'I found out by accident and what was I meant to do? She—' Aware that her explanation could seem as if she wasn't taking responsibility for her actions, she bit her lip and, shaking her head, lowered her chin to her chest.

'You were meant,' he ground out, 'to tell me. It's my job to protect her. She is vulnerable, an easy target. It's my fault she is in that chair, the least I can do is—'

As he broke off, swearing, Tess's chin came up. 'How is it your fault? It was a car accident. Weren't you in another country at the time?'

'I was in bed at the time.'

'Not yours?' she said, knowing the answer even before she read his expression.

He half turned, presenting his classical profile to her. Even at this distance she could see the tense quiver of fine muscles beneath his golden-toned skin. 'I was meant to join my family for a birthday celebration, but I had a better offer.'

The hollow sound of his laugh made her wince.

'If I had been there that night I would have been at the wheel and who knows? My reflexes are forty years younger than my father's were, but we never will know.' He dragged a hand across his dark hair and turned back to her. 'Because I put sex with a woman whose name I can't remember ahead of a promise. I will not do that again.' And yet he almost had; his innate selfishness had reasserted itself again. 'I made a promise to Natalia that she would walk again and nothing or...no one will get in the way of that.' Certainly not an affair with a woman he could not trust. Well, at least, he thought heavily, he had found out in time before he made a total fool of himself.

Well, at least she knew now and nothing she could

have done or not done would have altered the situation. Tess unfolded her legs from under her and slid off the bed where she had sat frozen since he had walked in. The swishing sound of the green silk on the floor sounded loud as she walked barefoot towards him.

Avoiding her eyes, his glance was snagged and caught by the thin spaghetti strap that had slid down one smooth shoulder.

'So this is really all about you and your guilt, your redemption, and not about Nat at all. You were not responsible for the accident because it was just that. If you'd been there that night you might be the one in a wheelchair.' Her eyes darkened. 'Or worse.'

'There is no worse,' he countered grimly.

Suddenly she felt very angry.

'How long will it take you to forget my name, Danilo?' She had gone beyond anger; there was just intense sadness in her soft voice.

'It was only ever sex. What the hell are you doing?'

Tess lifted her chin. 'Liar!' she charged. 'And I'm packing. I'm leaving because I'm sick of taking the blame for everything bad that happens in your life. I'm sick of it always being about *your* feelings, *your* needs. I'm sick of being our dirty secret because I thought the sex is good, but, you know, it's not that good!' she finished on a breathless note of antagonism.

The anger and fight suddenly drained out of her.

'Do you even think you've done anything wrong?' Without pause for her response, Danilo continued his ruthless and unfair analysis of the situation, answering his own question in a voice that was harsh with condemnation. 'Of course you did. You're not stupid, and I think that you didn't just *know*, I think you lent your assistance to the affair. You know Nat's vulnerable, but that didn't matter to you, did it? You are so damned convinced that you know what is best...you just can't resist meddling...'

Hands clenched, he leaned his head against the wall and, chest heaving, took several deep breaths as he pressed his fingers against his temples where anger pulsed and pounded.

'I think that without you there would not have been an affair.'

'It had been going on long before I arrived.'

He brushed aside the irrelevant detail with a wave of his hand. 'You knew that I wanted to keep that boy away from Nat.'

'Like I said, Danilo, it's not always about what *you* want.' She slammed the lid closed on the case with a bang.

'You planning on travelling like that?'

Without a word she stepped out of her dress.

Danilo swore and swung away. The hell of it was he *wanted*...he just *wanted*. Arms folded across his chest, he continued to stare out of the window.

'Does anyone live up to your standards, Danilo?' she wondered.

Nostrils flared, he turned back, Tess was standing there zipping up her jeans. She gave a loud sniff. Acknowledging that part of him still couldn't hear that sniff without wanting to comfort her only intensified the levels of his outrage.

'Well, you sure as hell don't!'

'You really are an obnoxious son of a...' She picked up her case and stalked to the door and he didn't make a move to stop her.

CHAPTER ELEVEN

WHEN TESS ARRIVED back in London she got in a taxi and went straight to her flat. For the first time in her life the take-off and landing had not bothered her. The entire flight was a blur. She had felt numb and strangely disconnected from what was happening around her as she sat in the back of the taxi listening to the driver chat.

She felt as though she had been holding her breath since she had walked out of her bedroom, and it wasn't until she closed the door of her flat behind her that she gave herself permission to breathe.

And feel. It was like walking into a wall of pain: unbearable!

With a cry she fell to her knees and, forehead pressed to the ground, began to weep. Keening sobs that seemed dragged from a place deep inside her.

She had no idea how long the storm lasted but when it was over she didn't have the strength to get up so she lay where she was and fell asleep. It was the middle of the night when she woke up. She got to her feet, stepped over her case, which still lay where she had dropped it, and walked into the bedroom. Not pausing to remove her clothes, she flung herself on the bed and slept again.

That set the pattern for the next forty-eight hours:

sleep punctuated by crying bouts. On the third day she looked at her dull-eyed reflection in the mirror and felt a wave of self-disgust.

What the hell am I doing? she asked herself. *Other than acting like a total and complete gutless wonder?*

She took a deep breath and literally and mentally squared her shoulders. At twenty-six, most people she knew had loved and lost at least once. It wasn't as if what she was feeling was unique—no, that was Danilo. Teeth clenched, she pushed away the image of his face but not before the ache inside her had intensified to the point where she rocked her body to ease it.

Did the feeling ever go away? she wondered, feeling a retrospective stab of admiration for the people who had their hearts broken and didn't fall apart.

It wasn't even as if she had started out thinking there was any future between them. From Danilo's side it had never been anything more than a sort of holiday romance, without much romance. The place that had existed was in her head.

She had known it would end, she had prepared herself for it, she just hadn't expected the end to be so acrimonious.

She could take Danilo not loving her back but the idea of him out there somewhere hating her was almost unbearable. She lifted her chin and exhaled, pushing her hair behind her ears as she struggled to push past that pain. She *would* bear it because she hadn't been raised to feel sorry for herself; she hadn't been raised to quit.

She showered and realised she hadn't eaten for days and checked out her store cupboard. A can of soup was about the only instant food she could find, so after she had eaten it she went out to shop. All so normal but so not normal.

Tess began to wonder if actually *anything* would ever be the same again. Would she be stuck in this cycle for ever? Her mood swinging wildly between deep despair, self-pity and anger?

That night she woke up at two in the morning wanting Danilo's touch so much that the pain made her think she was having a heart attack.

When it had passed, she lay there thinking, *If this is love, they can keep it.*

She'd been home a week before she felt able to ring Fiona without falling apart. She gave her friend an expurgated version of the summer's events and half an hour later Fiona landed on the doorstep with a bottle of wine in one hand, a carrier bag of chocolate bars in the other.

'Let's get drunk and fat.'

Tess appreciated the thought but the smell of the wine made her feel nauseous, so she passed. Not that it lessened the enjoyment of the evening, which came from being able to step away from her sadness for at least a few hours. It gave her some hope that one day she would be able to step away from it permanently, that she wasn't doomed to walk around feeling as though she had a large weight attached to her chest for ever.

She rang her mum the next day, expecting a lecture on self-reliance and toughness. Only to be surprised when her parent reacted with sympathy, and when Tess admitted she had spent the last week wallowing, instead of her mum telling her to man up she shocked Tess by saying, 'It was probably the best thing but maybe it's time to move on now?'

Later, she turned up at Tess's door, though her therapy was slightly different—a stack of election leaflets. She made Tess laugh when she suggested that pushing them through doors might be therapeutic.

Actually she was right—it was…weirdly.

Tess was glad when the first day of term finally arrived—the days that preceded it had felt like a lifetime—but as she stepped into the classroom and saw all the fresh, eager faces it felt like a clean-slate start.

She was going to look forwards, not sit in a corner and cry for what she'd lost because the things she was weeping for were things she'd never really had. She was lucky, she told herself, to be doing something she loved. Something that was fulfilling and challenging.

The start of a new school year was always hectic and this year particularly so. At the end of the first week Tess was feeling tired and drained, but she didn't read anything into it, not until the following Monday when, before the lunch bell rang, she felt so faint and dizzy that she had to sit down with her head between her knees to wait for it to pass. While she sat there, her classroom assistant, Lily had called an ambulance.

Luckily, she recovered enough to cancel the ambulance that was being dispatched, but it was still a very embarrassing incident. Even though it seemed a waste of time to her, she agreed when the deputy head made her promise to make an appointment to see her doctor.

Quite willing and fully expecting to wait for an appointment—she could not be classed as an emergency—Tess was surprised when they said they had a cancellation if she could come right away. The deputy head, who was standing there listening in, commandeered the phone and spoke. 'Yes, she can.'

'But I feel fine now.'

Tess said the same thing when she explained what had happened to the doctor.

She walked out of the surgery half an hour later not feeling fine at all. Her legs felt like cotton wool, her knees were shaking and her brain had shut down.

It wasn't until she found herself standing, looking in a shop window just around the corner from her flat, repeating what she had said to the doctor out loud— *But I feel fine*—that she realised two things. She probably wasn't fine and she had left her car in the surgery car park.

She decided to leave her car until the morning and walk the rest of the way home. She was so dazed that she didn't immediately see the person waiting outside her building for her until her name had been called out twice.

Her initial thought was, *So I'm not pregnant, just mad.*

'Tess, are you all right?'

Tess blinked. *Am I all right?* Natalia Raphael was sitting ten feet away, a suitcase on her knee and a wary look on her face.

'Nat, what are you doing here?'

Natalia gave a loud sniff. 'I have left home.' She then began to sob in earnest. 'Since you left Danilo has been totally impossible and when I said that if he wouldn't let me see Marco I would leave, he did that looking-down-his-nose thing…you know what I mean.'

Tess felt a pang of envy; she did.

'And I told him that Marco graduated top of his class, even though he was working two jobs, and he was the

best thing that ever happened to me and you know what
he did then?'

'Before or after he stopped swearing?'

'He didn't even do that so obviously I left. I said I
would.'

In other words Danilo had pushed her into a corner.
Oh, but he was going to be frantic!

'So Danilo doesn't know where you are?'

'No and you can't tell him ever. Can I stay with you?'

'I thought you'd want to be with Marco?'

'Marco is as bad as Danilo. He said that I was being
impulsive and I should go talk with my brother. *Talk*—
I ask you!'

'Oh, dear.'

'Can I?'

'I'd love to have you stay with me but…' she glanced
over her shoulder '…my flat is on the top floor and there
isn't a lift.' She took a deep breath. 'But don't worry—
I have an idea.'

Her mum arrived at the café when she and Nat were
on their second cup of coffee, or at least Nat was. Tess
had felt queasy after the first sip and spent the rest of
the time stirring it.

Tess made the introductions. She had already given
her mum the bare bones of the situation on the phone.
'Mum has a ground-floor flat and she has plenty of
room.' She left the two to chat while she excused herself.

Tess hissed in frustration as she struggled to get a
signal on her phone from the ladies' room, and when
she finally managed to get through to Danilo's mobile
number it went straight to the messaging service.

She really couldn't bear the thought of his frantic

reaction when he discovered his sister missing. Tess backed up her voice message with a text, just in case.

Danilo might hate her, but if she had learnt anything over the past few hellish weeks it was that, regardless of what he thought of her, she would always love him. She would never have him but she would have his baby. She glanced down, a wondering smile flickering across her mouth as she pressed a hand to her stomach as the reality finally penetrated the blank fog of panic and denial that had been her initial reaction.

She felt oddly calm, which was not rational. Her life was about to change and there was the task of telling Danilo. She had literally no idea what his reaction would be.

She wasn't even sure she would see him when he came for his sister—she had included her mum's number in the message—but if she did was now the right time to tell him? Or should she get used to the idea herself first?

Was there ever a right time?

Pushing the question away, she went back into the café, stifling a stab of guilt when she saw Nat deep in conversation with her mum.

She doubted it would matter to Natalia that Tess had not actually made any promises, but even if she had Tess had no intention of repeating her mistake. Not that doing the right thing on this occasion would mitigate what she had done in Danilo's eyes previously, but just as Tess felt she had acted in Nat's best interests last time, she felt she was doing so this time too—but then *right*, she thought sadly, was very much a subjective thing.

'Did you know that your mum knows Dame Eva

Black?' Natalia said the name of the famous visually impaired athlete with awe.

'Name-dropping again, Mum?'

'Don't be rude, and ungrateful. Eva sent you those tickets for your school auction.'

'That's great. Please thank my godmother for me.'

'Godmother? Wow!'

'Right, we are sorted. Nat and I are getting a taxi back to my place. Give her time to settle in and then you can join us for supper.' Beth leaned in a little closer and, under cover of kissing her daughter's cheek, whispered, 'Have you contacted her brother?'

Tess gave an imperceptible nod and her mother mouthed *good* before turning back to her house guest.

Once she'd seen them safely into a cab, Tess walked the short distance to her flat where for the second time that day she found a Raphael waiting for her on her doorstep.

Her heart stopped beating for a second and then compensated by climbing into her throat, beating so hard she could barely breathe.

He looked so familiar. Tall, sleek, unbelievably elegant and yet there were differences too. He was thinner, the body fat had burned off him—not that he had ever carried much—making him look harder and more...*hungry*. It showed in his face, the skin stretched tighter emphasising the angle and prominence of his cheekbones. She stood there absorbing the details with the hunger of an addict deprived of her drug of choice for too long.

He read the note that Marco had brought him for the second time and laughed.

There was a dark irony to it. He had told himself that

he was doing the right thing, the noble thing. He had put his life on hold for his sister. He had walked away from love, and did she appreciate this *noble* sacrifice? No! She wrote a note, in which he was labelled as a control freak, and ran away.

He inhaled, closing his eyes as he screwed up the paper in his hand. The situation forced his hand...he'd wanted everything to be perfect, but then life was not perfect.

Noble. Who was he kidding? Not himself any longer at any rate. He wasn't taking the noble route, he was taking the easy route. Pride had stopped him calling her back and cowardice had made him push her away.

Tess had been right when she'd accused him of using her as a scapegoat, whereas in reality she had brought only good into their lives. Deep inside he'd always known that; he had struggled not to love her because he didn't think he deserved to be happy while Nat sat in a wheelchair. Tess had said it was always about him and she was right... Had he ever once asked her what she wanted?

It was time he did.

He levered himself off the wall, the speech he had practised on the flight vanishing when he saw her. 'Hello, *cara mia.*'

Was he trying to be deliberately cruel?

Before he could say anything she rushed headlong into an explanatory speech. 'She is safe with my mum. I tried to contact you. I left messages. This was not my doing, and I didn't put her up to this, Danilo, and I'm not in the mood for one of your rants so please just go away!'

'I never thought you did…' But he had known where Nat would run. 'With *your mother*?'

She nodded, not quite sure what to make of this Danilo, who wasn't shouting or flinging accusations. The stillness about him confused her. 'The stairs.'

'Of course. I remember.' He remembered everything.

'How,' she puzzled, 'are you here now?'

'She left Marco a note, and to his credit he brought it to me as soon as he found it. He… We were pretty sure if she was going to run it would be to you.'

It was a compulsion that he understood well.

'It seems that I might—' He broke off, his heart contracting painfully as he took in the dark shadows smudged beneath her spectacular eyes. Her skin was so pale it seemed almost transparent. He fought down the urge to run his fingers over it, knowing it would be smooth and satiny to the touch. She looked fragile, breakable; he struggled past the need to wrap her in his arms.

'Might?' she prompted.

'I might have misjudged him. But everyone deserves a second chance, don't you think?'

The intensity of his stare made her nervous. His being here at all made her nervous! Thinking about how to tell him, when to tell him…the words, the tone to take…made her nervous. 'I…yes, I suppose. You must be anxious to see Nat. I can give you the address. I have a piece of paper here somewhere.' She began to search the deep pockets of the light belted trench coat she was wearing over her skirt and blouse.

'She is safe?'

Tess nodded. 'She might be wielding a protest banner when you see her next but she is fine.'

'Then no, I am not anxious to see her.'

She searched his face, seeking a clue that would explain the way he was behaving. 'You're not angry with her, are you?' Her jaw set. 'Because if you plan to yell at her the way—'

'No, I am not angry with *her*.' Only himself for being an utter imbecile. He had had paradise within his grasp and he'd walked in the opposite direction.

She heard the emphasis and thought, *So he's angry with me.* Pulling her hands from her pockets, she crossed them in front of her in an unconsciously self-protective gesture. No change there, then!

'Oh, hell, does it even matter?'

'Does what even matter?'

What's the point? It doesn't matter how you say it, or when, he's going to be furious.

'Danilo, I'm pregnant.'

His reaction to the blunt pronouncement was slow but when the look of shock appeared it was total. 'Pregnant?'

Her chin lifted to a challenging angle. 'Yes, and before you ask it's yours.'

'I never thought otherwise.'

'I suppose there hasn't been much time for it to be anyone else's.'

'Were you looking?' he growled out, the image of Tess falling into bed with another man seriously testing his determination to let her see that he was a changed man capable of calm control, the sort of man she deserved.

His comment released a fresh burst of anger inside her as the many, many *low* lights of the past few hellish weeks passed before her eyes. 'Sure, Danilo, it's been party, party all the way, what between throwing up and fainting in work. What the *hell* do you think I've been doing for the last few weeks, Danilo?' she demanded, as, hands on hips, she advanced until she was standing a foot away from him. 'Well?' she charged in a furious growl.

'I appreciate that it must have been hard for you, discovering you're pregnant…'

'I didn't even know I was until a few hours ago and that is the one *good* thing that has happened to me.'

'Good?' Freed from the self-imposed restraints—the effort of containing his delight and noisily expressing it had been a strain—he released a long sigh. He no longer had to hide his feelings in an effort to be sensitive to the anger and bitterness she might have been feeling, had every right to be feeling. An unplanned pregnancy was not every woman's idea of good.

A baby. He closed his eyes and let the warmth flow through him.

He couldn't even look at her! Tess ignored the hurt and embraced her anger as she lifted her chin and stood there in an attitude of angry defiance. 'Yes, I am, and—'

When Danilo opened his eyes he could see how paper thin her attitude was. In a way it emphasised how fragile she was. 'I will look after you…both.'

'Look after? I don't want looking after,' she choked out while the voice inside her head screamed, *I don't want looking after, I want* loving*!*

Danilo did not let the rejection deter him. 'Nonetheless, it is going to happen.'

She lifted both hands to her head, grabbing a handful of hair. 'Do you ever listen to anyone? I don't need you!' The lie emerged as a plaintive wail of despair.

'Fine, but I need you and, as you know, I am a self-ish man.'

She stopped, the tears she struggled to blink away trembling on her eyelashes as she stared up at him, suspicion warring with hope in her face. 'You need me?'

He tipped his head. 'Yes, in a need oxygen, need water sort of way. You are one of the essentials to life for me.' He spoke with the total certainty of someone who had imagined a life without Tess in it and knew that breathing was not the same as being alive.

The journey to self-awareness had been slow and painful, speeded by the truths jolted free when he'd discovered Nat's disappearance, but before he had reached this point it had taken Danilo a week of raging against the fate that had brought Tess into his life, alternating between anger and self-pity while he congratulated himself on being rid of her.

He hadn't asked to fall in love, he'd *wanted* to be punished, so when it had happened to him he had rejected it. He had rejected her and at the first excuse that had come he had pushed her away. But not the feelings she had awoken in him; they, he realised, would stay for ever. Love was as permanent as his fingerprints.

He had had everything a man could want and he had turned his back on it. Yes, he was an idiot and a coward!

His first instinct had been to get on a plane, but at the last moment he had paused. Tess had given him everything and in return... Self-disgust churned in his belly when he thought of the way he had treated her. He had never given her a word of tenderness, no romance, but he would!

He'd planned the proposal down to the smallest detail. The restaurant was booked, the singer he knew was her favourite was performing just for them and the chef he'd shipped in from New York. The only thing he was waiting for was the ring, which was still in the jeweller's—the one he had finally settled on had been far too big for her tiny fingers.

He had thought of everything except the unexpected, so here he was no ring, no romantic music, not even a straggly bunch of flowers…and definitely no script. That had gone out of the window the moment she had made her stunning revelation.

'What did you say?'

He couldn't think of any prettier way to say it so he just said what was in his heart. 'I love you.'

She tried to react with her head to the declaration, but she struggled to tune out the contribution of her hopeful heart, which was thudding like a wild thing in her chest. 'Is this about the baby?'

'I suppose everything from now on will be about the baby, but, no, irrespective of a baby or ten babies, I love you. I have loved you, and I would have been there to ask you—look, this isn't the way I planned it but, please, will you marry me, Tess? I don't know if you can ever forgive me for being such a total fool, because I am, but I'm a fool that loves you and I can change—'

'Oh, Danilo!' The cry came directly from her heart as she hit him like a heat-seeking missile, forcing the breath out of his lungs in a soft hiss.

'So does this mean you do forgive me?'

'I'll be your lover, your mistress, your wife. I'll be anything if I can be with you and I don't want you to change. I fell in love with you the way you are.'

Danilo swallowed, emotion thickening his voice as he responded to her emotional declaration. 'You are the most all-or-nothing person I have ever met and I'll settle for all: lover, mistress and wife.'

Oblivious to the stares of several passers-by and the honking of a few horns the couple kissed and carried on kissing until a remark from someone in a car brought Danilo's head up.

'Get a room,' he repeated. 'He has a point.'

'I have a room,' she pointed out. 'I can walk now,' she protested as he swept her up.

'Just let me pretend I'm boss, at least in public, *cara mia*, for the sake of my fragile male ego. In private I will be whatever you want.'

EPILOGUE

Three years later

EVERY EYE IN the place was on the bride, all except one pair. Danilo's eyes were trained on his wife's face. Tears were running down her cheeks as she stood there in the silliest hat he had ever seen, looking more beautiful than any woman who had ever breathed. That she loved him still filled him with wonder, pride was mingled with that wonder as his gaze slid down her body. Her outfit had not been designed to hide the swelling of her belly that made him so proud.

The baby due in three months had been planned this time. A little brother or sister for their son, who walked proudly, bearing the bride's train in his chubby hands, the determination not to trip over it as he had done in the rehearsal clear in his face.

He heard Tess release a relieved sigh as the bride reached the altar where the groom, Marco, who had finally accepted Danilo's offer to join their legal team after being persuaded nepotism had nothing to do with it, was standing.

'She made it,' Tess whispered, tears in her eyes.

'Of course she did,' Danilo said as he rested the

crutches he had held just in case the bride, who had been determined to walk down the aisle unaided, had needed them.

It had been Nat's decision in the end to go through with the experimental surgery, two more had followed and the physical therapy that had followed would have tested the resilience of a hardened soldier, but Nat had come through. The day she took her first step had been the day the young couple had announced their engagement.

There wasn't a dry eye in the house as the bride made her responses in a clear, confident voice. There were tears in Tess's eyes when she turned to look at Danilo. He knew what she was thinking about because so was he: the moment that *they* had stood in that very spot and exchanged the same vows.

He had told her, later that night, that it had been the first day of the rest of his life. His new life, he thought as her fingers tightened in understanding around his, was very, very good!

* * * * *

THE UNWANTED CONTI BRIDE

TARA PAMMI

CHAPTER ONE

TONIGHT, SOPHIA ROSSI decided with mounting desperation, her spirit animal would be a skunk.

Because desperation had a particularly pungent stink. It probably clung to her pores, spraying whiffs of it over pitying and curious bystanders, betraying her panic.

She had never belonged in the uber-rich Milanese society that her stepfather and mother dwelled in, was only a Rossi because Salvatore had adopted her after marrying her mother when Sophia had been thirteen. Facts of her life she'd never been allowed to forget by the crowd around her.

She'd somehow weathered the end of her engagement to Leandro Conti.

But this latest rumor—her supposed affair with her one real friend, Kairos Constantinou, who was Leandro's sister's new husband—had made her an object of gossip and even malice. If she'd known what a spectacle it made of her, she'd have refused Leandro's invite to his brother Luca's birthday party, which had been extended weeks ago. The invite was only driven by his guilt at breaking their engagement.

Her fingers tightening over the fragile champagne flute, she made a casual, painted-smile-in-place round around the curving, wide balcony of the Villa de Conti.

Somehow they'd made her into this temperamental shrew, this marriage-wrecking wanton that had become a liability to her family rather than an asset.

How had she, despite all her hard work, jeopardized the most important goal of her life—to support her stepfather, Salvatore, and rebuild Rossi Leather until her half brothers were old enough to take over?

Antonio Conti, the patriarch of the Conti family, reached her just as Sophia deflected another barbed insult. Glassy and brittle it might be, but she didn't let the smile drop from her face.

Silver threaded abundantly through his black hair. Antonio reminded her of a wolf—cunning, wily and quick to gobble up unsuspecting prey.

"Tell me, Sophia," he said, neatly cornering her near a white pillar, "whose idea was it to propose a marriage between my grandson and you?"

Swallowing her shock, Sophia stared at him. No one should have even guessed. "Our engagement is irrelevant now that Leandro is married."

"Your stepfather is ambitious but not clever," Antonio continued as if Sophia hadn't even spoken. "Hardworking but no vision. Even knowing of my desperation to find a bride for my grandsons, Salvatore would have never thought to offer you.

"He has no use for women."

The words were curt, even cruel in their efficient summation. But true.

Sophia had been trying for a decade to get Sal to see the value she could provide for the company, with zero progress. He gave her small projects, refused to listen to her ideas for Rossi Leather.

All he cared about was leaving a legacy for her half brothers, Bruno and Carlo.

"It was mine," she admitted. What did she have to lose at this point? "There was advantage to your family and mine in that match."

Sal could hold grudges on Leandro Conti and the Conti family for breaking the engagement, but Sophia was nothing if not practical.

Rossi Leather couldn't tide over their latest financial setback by alienating the powerful Contis. Antonio still held much sway over the older generation in the leather industry and Leandro Conti, his eldest grandson and CEO of Conti Luxury Goods, held the younger, more heated generation.

Antonio's second grandson, Luca Conti, however... had no clout or morals. Probably no talent. Just oodles of charm, sexuality and utter self-indulgence.

Even thinking about him made her cross. And bitter. And her knees weak.

She'd spent nights pacing her bedroom, sleepless, panicky, when the idea of marrying Leandro had presented itself to her. She'd made herself sick. She'd had nightmares about her past and present morphing into a distasteful, torturous future.

But the welfare of her family had precedence over naive decade-old dreams.

Antonio didn't look surprised. But then he'd known to ask that question, hadn't he? His silvery brows rose. "You're a curiously resourceful young woman, Sophia."

Sophia's cheeks heated up. "Even for a half-Italian bastard girl with a broken engagement behind her, you mean?"

He continued looking at her.

If she hadn't lost her finer sensibilities a long time ago, if she hadn't developed elephant-thick skin, she'd have been insulted by the purely assessing look the old man cast her, from the top of her dark hair in an efficient knot to the soles of her black Conti pumps, her only nod to fashion, with leisurely stops at her face and several other areas of her body.

"I'm not a cow to be assessed," she added with a glare. The flash of something in his gaze gave her the creeps. "I'm not in the market for an alliance anymore, either." There was only so much she could stomach, apparently, even for her family. "Of any kind," she added for good measure.

Amusement shifted the rigid lines of his face. Flashes of a similar set of features sent a flutter down her spine. "You're not only dedicated to your family but you're also sharp and fearless. I like you, Sophia."

Rarely did the opposite sex, except for her ten-year old brothers, say something that wasn't condescending or insulting to her. "I wish I could say the same. But I've seen you use everyone's shortcomings to your own advantage, including Sal's."

His smile lingered. "Then why not advise your stepfather?"

She remained silent, frustration a quiet snarl inside her. Because Sal never listened to her. He loved her, but not enough to trust her judgment or intelligence when it came to Rossi Leather. All of which she was aware the cunning wolf knew.

"I can give you a way to help Salvatore, Sophia. Without throwing yourself at a married man."

Stinging anger burned Sophia's cheeks but she stayed still. He'd baited her well and he knew it. She was going to throttle whoever had started that distasteful rumor.

"I will pour capital into Salvatore's business," Antonio continued, "create new contracts for him, bring him back into the old class, so to speak. After his string of poor business decisions, he certainly needs the help."

"I'm not for sale," Sophia retorted, a slow panic building inside. She felt like a donkey with a carrot visible but just out of reach. "I suggested marriage to Leandro as a way to help Sal, but I'd have kept every vow I made to him. I would've been a good wife."

"You believe I did not realize that? You believe I would let Salvatore...*persuade* me into letting you marry my grandson without learning all about you? It is exactly why I make this proposal."

Her pulse sped up. "What is your proposal?" she forced herself to say.

"I do have another grandson, *si*? Bring Luca to the altar, marry him and I will take a firm handle on Rossi financial matters. Your mother, your brothers, their futures will never be in peril."

"No!" Her sharp reply turned heads toward them.

Marry Luca, the Conti Devil?

The very idea was like walking on shards of glass for the rest of her life. *Bare feet and with a lead weight over her head.* "I don't want to spend an evening with the Conti Devil, much less marry him."

As though invoked by their discussion, Luca Conti appeared in the midst of the perfectly manicured lawn before them, a tall, gorgeous blonde following him like a faithful puppy.

A woman on his arm, as always.

The rage in those languid, smoky eyes the night of her engagement to his brother had haunted her. But he'd avoided her as she'd done for a decade.

His dark, wavy hair was in that same stylish cut. Low on the sides and piled high on his head, making his angular face even narrower. Sophistication and grace oozed from his every stride. But any kind of austerity ended with his hair.

Because Luca Conti was the most beautiful man she'd ever seen.

His face, now visible only in flashes as he moved

through the crowd with that loose-limbed stride had such perfect lines that her breath caught even from this distance.

Broad shoulders lovingly hugged by gray silk, narrowing to a tapered waist and muscular thighs honed to pure steel by hours and hours of swimming. He moved sinuously through the crowd, the tall woman a beautiful accessory around his lean and wiry body, a little on the thin side.

But who could remember all that after one glance at his face?

Wide-set, jet-black eyes, with dark blue smudges underneath, always the shadows underneath his eyes as if the man never slept, a steel blade of a nose and a wide mouth made of plump, lush lips that invited one, two… oh, a hundred glances.

Collagen had nothing on this man's mouth…

A mouth that invited sin with one word… A mouth he knew how to use every which way…

Sharp cheekbones created planes and grooves, in concert with the high forehead, as if every inch of it had been painstakingly designed and carved to render him breathtaking.

Those features should have been effeminate, too beautiful, yet something in his gaze, in his will, immediately imposed his fierce masculinity on the onlooker, as if the space around him had to become an extension of him.

And the devil was aware of his exquisite beauty, and the effect it had on the female sex, whether they were seventeen or seventy.

It was clear, from even up there, that Luca was sloshed if not drunk and so was the disreputable beauty, who also happened to be the Italian Finance minister's *almost* ex-wife, Mariana.

Had she thrown away her powerful husband for Luca?

Did she know that Luca would dispose of her like a toddler did last week's toys?

Sophia could almost, *only almost*, feel pity for the woman.

The hiss of a curse falling from Antonio's mouth by her
side punctured her obsessively greedy perusal.

Luca, as usual, was creating a ruckus. Heads turned toward him, including Kairos and Valentina. A stiff-lipped
Leandro cast a hand on Luca to stop him but his younger
brother pushed it away.

Whispers abounded, like the drone of insects.

As indulgent as his family and friends were of his usual
escapades, it seemed an open lovers' spat—for Luca and
the lady's argument was becoming clear now—with another man's wife was too scandalous for them to overlook.

"This is the man you want me to wed? The man who
shamelessly shows off his affair with another man's wife
with no thought to his family or hers? The man who thinks
every woman is a challenge to be conquered, a bet to win?"
The memory of her own humiliation at his hands was like
acid in her throat. "One who tramples hearts like they were
little pieces of glass? I wouldn't touch Luca if he were the
last man on earth."

Antonio turned toward her slowly, as if that small movement cost him a great effort. One look into his eyes and
Sophia knew he was going in for the kill. Now she was
the deer caught in the wolf's sights.

"Are you aware, Sophia, that the bank is ready to call
Salvatore's loan in? Or that he has no way to meet the next
production per schedule?"

Her heart sank to her toes. "That's not true. He applied
for an extension—"

"And was denied."

Sunken eyes peered at her with a cunning that sent
chills down her spine. He'd done this, she knew.

Oh, Salvatore had paved the way to their financial ruin with his own faulty decisions but this latest setback—the bank's refusal for an extension—was Antonio's doing.

Apparently, Antonio was just as desperate as she was. "Even if I were to agree to your outrageous proposal—" her entire life tied to that reckless playboy who had made her so weak once "—how do you think I can accomplish this? Even I, desperate that I am, can't drag a man to the altar. And definitely not the Conti Devil, who cares for nothing except his own pursuits."

Drunk as he was, Luca had somehow managed to steer the clinging woman away from the crowd. But her husky laughter and frantic begging in Italian could be heard from where they were standing, behind and beneath the balcony.

Heat tightened Sophia's cheeks as she understood the gist of the woman's phrases in Italian. Instead of distaste and fury, she felt pity.

The woman was in love with Luca.

Antonio dragged his gaze away from Luca, his mouth a tight line. His frail body seemed to vibrate with distaste, rage and, Sophia sensed with mounting shock, grief. Antonio Conti was grief-stricken over his grandson Luca. *Why?*

The image of the manipulative old man shifted in her mind, even as he took a deep breath, as if to push away the emotion. "No, my grandson cares for nothing in this world. His parents are long dead and Leandro, too, has washed his hands of Luca now.

"But to protect Valentina and her happiness, Luca will do anything. He will make a bargain with anyone to keep her birth a secret from the world."

Sophia gasped, unable to believe what she was hearing. "Her birth? This is not right. I want no part of it—"

"Valentina is not my son's daughter. She is the product of an affair their mother had with her driver. And if this comes out, it will ruin Valentina's standing in society and even her marriage to your friend Kairos.

"So use it to bind Luca to you. He will bend for Valentina's happiness."

No words came to her as Sophia stared at Antonio.

The idea of blackmailing the Conti Devil didn't bother her so much as using Valentina's secret. Dear God, she didn't want to hurt anyone.

An acidic taste lingered in her mouth. "There are too many innocent people involved in this. I won't hurt one of them just because—"

"Just because Salvatore might lose the company? Just because your mother and brothers might have to leave their estate, give up their cars, their place in this society? And what will you do, Sophia? Take up the project manager job your Greek friend offers you to support them? Quietly stand by as Salvatore watches chunks of his company broken down and auctioned off?"

"Why me? Why can't you find a willing woman and force *him* to marry her? Why—"

"Because you're tough and you do what needs to be done. You don't have silly ideas of love in your head. Only you will do for the Conti Devil."

Only you...

Antonio Conti's words reverberated through Sophia.

Oh, how she wished she'd not come tonight... Now she had a possible way to dig their finances out of the ruin but it would only be achieved by selling her soul to the devil...

She wasn't considering it, Sophia told herself, as she walked through the unending corridor of Villa de Conti. The black-and-white-checkered floor gave the mounting nausea within a physical bent.

Surely Antonio deluded himself that his devil-may-care, womanizing grandson could care about his sister. But she had to try. She had to see if there was a chance of salvaging their finances, if there was even a small sliver of hope that her mother, Salvatore and the twins wouldn't be driven to the road.

She reached a wide, circular veranda at the back of the villa.

Jacket discarded, shirt open to reveal a dark olive chest, cuffs folded back, Luca stood leaning against the wall. A foot propped up against it, eyes closed, face turned to the sky. The curving shadows his long eyelashes cast on his cheekbones were like scythes.

Scythes and blades. Her usually nonviolent thoughts revolved around weapons when it came to Luca.

Moonlight caressed the planes of his face, shadows diluting the magnificent symmetry of his features. Rendering him a little less gorgeous.

A little less captivating.

A little less devilish.

Almost vulnerable and…strangely lonely.

Slowly, Sophia became aware of her own reaction. Damp palms. Skittering heartbeat. Pit in her stomach. Even after a decade, her body went into some kind of meltdown mode near him.

She must have made a sound because his eyes opened slowly. Only his eyes were visible in the silvery light. They fell on her, widened for an infinitesimal fraction of a second, searched her face and then assumed that laid-back, casual, infuriatingly annoying expression that she hated.

"Sophia Rossi, of steel balls and tough skin and icy heart." Whatever alcohol he'd imbibed, his speech didn't slur. Mocking and precise, it arrowed past her defenses. "Did you lose your way, *cara*?"

His sultry voice thickened the air around them so much

that Sophia wondered if she could breathe through it. "Stop calling me..." No, that was way too personal. If she was going to do this, Sophia had to enclose herself in steel, lock away even the slightest vulnerability she had, not that she had any. She'd do this for her family, but she wasn't going to be the Conti Devil's amusement. Not this time.

He pushed himself from the wall while she formed and disposed words. When she looked up again, he'd moved close enough for her to smell the crisply masculine scent of him. The light from the hall caressed his features.

Breath was lost. Nerves fluttered. A sigh built and ballooned inside her chest. That small scar under his chin. The sweeping arch of his eyebrows. The razor-sharp lines of his cheekbones. Darkly angelic features that masked a cruel devil.

Jet-black eyes glinted with sardonic amusement at her mute appraisal. He propped a bent hand on the wall she was leaning against, sticking his other hip out. A pose full of grace and languor. Of feigned interest and wretched playfulness. "Tell me, how did you end up in the farthest reaches of the house, away from all the wheelings and dealings of your business friends? Did Little Bo Peep lose track of her sheep and wander into big bad wolf's way?"

Sophia tried to command every cell in her body to keep it together, wrenched herself into a tight ball so that all that touched her was the man's whispery breath. "You're getting your fairy tales mixed up."

"But my point got through to you, *si*?" He ran the heel of his hand over his tired-looking eyes while Sophia stared hungrily, cataloging every gesture, every shift. "What do you want, Sophia?"

"Your...*situation* looked like it needed rescuing."

The slight tug of his mouth transformed into that full-blown grin that always seemed to be waiting for an invite.

Evenly set teeth gleamed in an altogether wicked face. "Ahh…and so Sophia Rossi, the righteous and the pure, decided to come to my aid."

"Where is your lover? I can have one of our chauffeurs drive her home."

His gaze held hers, a thousand whispers in it. "She's in my bed, thoroughly lost to the world." It dipped to her mouth. Snaky tendrils of heat erupted over her skin. "I believe I wore her out."

Nausea hit Sophia with the force of a gardening hose, the images of a sweaty and ravished Mariana burning her retinas as if she could see the leggy blonde amidst a cloud of soft, white sheets.

Luca's bedroom—pure white sheets, gleaming black marble, black-and-white portraits all around… It was like being transported into your worst nightmare and your darkest fantasy, all rolled into one. While being naked and blindfolded and without any defense.

She let all the disgust she felt seep to the surface and stepped back.

"Don't you think this is too far even for you? They are not even divorced yet. And you're advertising it for all and sundry to see."

"But that's the fun, *si*? Tangling with the dangerous? Riling up her husband into one of his awful tempers?"

"And then you walk away?" *Like you did from me.* "Her life will be in ruins in terms of the society, while you latch on to the next willing v—"

His mouth curved into a snarl and his hand covered her mouth. Opal fire burned in his eyes. "Is that what you tell yourself, *cara*? That you were a victim all those years ago? Have you convinced yourself that I forced you?"

She pushed away his hand and glared at him, all the while pretending that her lips still didn't tingle from the

heat of his touch. That she didn't burn at the memory...
"I didn't mean that you take them without their... Damn
it, Luca, you and I both know he will ruin her over this."

"Maybe ruin is exactly what Mariana wants. Maybe
to be utterly debauched by me is her only salvation." The
words were silky, casual, and yet...for the first time in her
life, Sophia saw more than the hauntingly beautiful face,
the wicked grin, even the seductive charm. "You would
not understand her, Sophia."

"I just don't think—"

Sophia watched that lazy face swallow away that fury,
saw the emotion blank out of his eyes as easily as if someone had taken an eraser and wiped it away. "I don't give a
damn about your opinions, so, *per carita*, stop expressing
them." He bent toward her, diminutive as she was to his
own lean six-two. "What is it that suddenly interests you
about me, Sophia? Have you finally decided you need another orgasm to sustain you for the next decade?"

Flames scorched her skin; that was how hot she felt. *Yes*
floated to her lips, as if every cell in her had conspired to
form that word without her permission.

This was easy for him, too easy—riling her up, sinking under her skin. Even knowing what he was, still she
reacted like a moth venturing to a flame. "Not everything
has to have a sexual connotation in life."

"Says the woman who needs to be utterly and thoroughly—"

This time her hand clamped his mouth. Sophia glared
at him. His breath kissed her sensitive palm.

Long, elegant fingers traced the tender skin of her
wrists, leaving brands on her sensitive flesh. Slowly, as if
savoring every second of touching her, he pulled her hand.
"What did you think I was going to say, Sophia?"

She pursed her mouth and took a deep breath. "I have

a proposal I'd like to make to you, one that is mutually beneficial."

"There is nothing that you can offer me—" his gaze flicked over her, dismissal and insult in that look "—that I won't get from another woman, Sophia."

"You haven't even heard it."

"Not interested—"

"I want to marry you."

CHAPTER TWO

Not "will you marry me, Luca?"

Not "I think it makes sense for me to marry you now even though I've hated you for a decade and chose your brother over you just a few months ago."

Not "I need you to save my stepfather from sure financial ruin, so, *please, oh, pleas*e, won't you make me your wife?"

No, Sophia Rossi proposed marriage as she did everything else.

Like a charging bull and with the confidence that she could bend, twist or generally command him into doing her bidding. Probably with an adoring smile on his face, and the marble digging into his knees if she could manage it.

Dio, where did the woman's strength come from?

Luca Conti swallowed his astonishment. Her loyalty in considering this for her family's sake, when he knew how much she hated him—and with good reason—was admirable. He ignored the thudding slam of his heart against his rib cage—she was a weakness and a regret he'd never quite forgotten—and gave free rein to the riding emotion.

Amusement. Sheer hilarity.

It burst out of him like an engulfing wave of the ocean, like a rising crescendo of music, punching the air out of his throat with its force. There was a knot in his gut. Hand shaking, he wiped his wet cheeks.

What merciful God had granted him this wonderful moment?

For reasons all too Freudian, Luca hated his birthday. Loathed, despised with the hatred of a thousand exploding supernovas. But his self-loathing, as brightly as it flared from time to time, to his brother Leandro's eternal gratitude, had never overtaken his respect for life.

Over the years he had become better at handling his birthday. There was even a memorable threesome sprinkled through a couple of them. But not one of those miserable thirty birthdays had presented him with a gift like this one.

Just months ago Sophia had chosen Leandro over him to marry.

To see the one woman he had given up years ago— granted, after thoroughly breaking her heart—as his brother's wife every day would have been the straw that broke the camel's back. In other words, destination Hell on a direct flight.

He would have had to let the engagement go forward. The wedding itself, probably not.

He'd have seduced her, for sure. He'd have had to do it before the wedding, he remembered telling himself in a drunken haze. Luckily, his—now—sister-in-law Alex had shown up, turned Leandro's life inside out and spun Luca away from that necessary but destructive course.

And here Sophia was now…proposing marriage to *him* this time. The woman had balls. He loved her for that if nothing else. "I believe this is the best birthday present I've ever received, *bella*. How the mighty fall. Wait till I—"

He heard the outraged snarl before a filthy word fell from her stiff-lined mouth, and it was like a violin had joined the piano in his head. "If you tell anyone, I'll cut off—"

He burst out laughing again.

"Go to hell," she whispered, her petite frame radiating fury. Most of it self-directed, he knew, for Sophia hated betraying any emotion that made her weak.

He caught her wrist and pulled her inside the large, and thankfully empty, lounge behind them. Backing her into the wall, he pulled her arms above her.

The disdain in her eyes, the arrogant jut of her chin... It was like pouring petrol over a spark. Jerked at every primal instinct he had carefully banished from his life. Her breasts heaved as she fought him, as if they too fought against being confined.

"You thought you would propose marriage and walk away? You did not think I would find it entertaining?"

"You're a remorseless bastard." It was the first time she'd hinted at their past.

Regret was a faint pang in Luca's chest. Only faint.

Did he regret that he had hurt her ten years ago? *Si*.

So much that if given the chance he wouldn't do it again? *Non*.

He was far too selfish to willingly deny himself the true joy he'd found with her in those few weeks. "And you love playing the uptight shrew far too much."

Outrage, and most improbably, hurt, transformed her muddy brown eyes into a thousand hues of golds and bronzes.

Her stubborn, too-prominent nose flared. Incongruously wide mouth in a small face flushed a deep pink. The hourglass figure swathed in the most horrific black dress rubbed against him, bringing him to painful arousal.

In front of his eyes, she became something else.

She became the Sophia he'd known once and hadn't been able to resist, the Sophia he'd kissed with wonder, the Sophia she'd been before he had beat all the softness out of her.

She grunted and gave herself away, seconds before she raised her knee to his groin.

"How would this marriage of ours...*prosper and proliferate* if you turn me into a castrato, Sophia?"

Dancing his lower body away from her kick, he used the momentum to slam her harder into his hip. Her soft belly pressed and flushed into the lines of his body, his hip bone digging into it, as if it meant to make a groove for itself against her.

A softer gasp escaped her this time, throaty and wrenched away from the part of her she hid so well. So well that he had often wondered if he had known her so intimately once. That short huff for breath stroked Luca's nerves. Like strings of a violin...

Thick, wavy locks of hair fell from the ugly knot at the back of her head, touching the strong planes of her face with softness. The floral scent of her shampoo, something so incongruous with the woman she was, *or pretended to be*, fluttered under his nose. Luca pressed his nose into the thick, wavy mass. Kneaded the tense planes of her upper back as if he could calm himself by calming her.

He had never forgotten his amazement at the fire that had flared between them, how easily his plan had gone utterly wrong ten years ago. How, even for his jaded palate, Sophia had proved to be too much of a temptation.

Dio, suggesting marriage to him, of all men... Hadn't she learned her lesson? Why was she tempting the devil in him?

He *was* tempted. What man wouldn't want to muss up those ugly dresses and that shrewish facade and want to find the soft woman beneath? What man wouldn't want a claim on that kind of loyalty, on that steely core of her?

He set her away from him, none too gently. Lust riding him hard, he drew one rattling breath after another.

He controlled the pursuit of pleasure and the pleasure itself. Without shame or scruples, he used his charm, his looks, to draw women to him, amused himself for a time and then walked away.

He'd carefully built his life to be that and nothing more. He'd trampled her innocence even when he'd intended to do the right thing once. But in the end, he'd left. He would walk away again.

After having a small taste. She really expected it of him—to behave abominably, to torture her with his lascivious words and deeds. He couldn't disappoint her.

His humor restored, he eased his grip on her. Instantly she shoved at him. He didn't budge. "I can think of an infinitely more pleasurable *and* mature way to vent your frustration."

"It's hard to be mature when you laugh in my face like this."

"Your dignity is that fragile? The Sophia I keep hearing about in boardrooms and business mergers is apparently nothing short of Goddess Diana."

He curved his mouth into his trademark smile. Her glare didn't dim one bit. If anything, she stiffened even more.

Dio, when was the last time he had had such fun? And they hadn't even shed their clothes yet. "I was right, it is I that gets under your skin."

Her eyelids fell slowly. A second to restore her quaking defenses. Right on cue, she looked up, her fiery glare renewed. "I forgot that it's all a big joke to you."

"Being a debauched playboy who cares for nothing is hard work."

"I was stupid to think we could have a mature conversation. All you—"

"Then persuade me."

"What?"

Surprise in her gaze filled him with a strange satisfaction. Shocking, needling, generally startling Sophia out of that hard shell could become addictive. "Persuade me. Indulge me. Make me an irresistible offer."

Make herself irresistible to the most beautiful man on the face of the planet? A man who held nothing sacred?

"I have a better chance of finding treasure in my backyard," she said softly. Wistfulness snuck into her voice and she cringed.

"Kiss me, then."

"What?" She rubbed her temples, dismayed at how he reduced her to a mumbling idiot.

"Put your lips on mine and pucker them up. Your hands can go on my shoulders or my hips or if you're feeling bold, you can grab my ass—"

"What? Why?" Years of oratory at debate club evaporated, her brain only offering whats and whys.

"That should be the first step for a couple considering marriage, *si*? I could never marry a woman who didn't know how to kiss."

Don't. Look. At. His. Mouth. "It's obvious you're only torturing me and will never really consider it and you..." She looked and the contoured lushness of it made her lick her own lips, which made him grin and prompted her to raise her gaze. "Your lover is lying in your bed and you're—"

"If you'd been paying attention and not mooning over me—" Sophia fisted her hands, just fighting the urge to wipe that satisfied smile off his face, for he was right, damned devil "—then you would know that Mariana and I are over."

"You just said you wore her out!" Her brow cleared. "You said that just to rile me up, didn't you? There was hardly any time between when you left and I found you for you to...to—" She couldn't believe what her logic led her to say. If only she could stop blushing! "—*wear her out.*"

"I actually don't need that much time to get my lover off—"

"Where is she?" Sophia cut him off.

"She's a lightweight and I kept plying her with drinks. Her husband's divorcing her, which is what she wanted, but she's a little emotional about it. I couldn't just...throw her out of the party when she was in such a state."

"No, of course, not. They all adore you even when you're done with them."

Except her, Luca thought with something akin to a pang in his chest.

"You're free to adore me, too, *cara.* No one will have to know."

She snorted. That inelegant movement of that sharp, stubborn nose made him chuckle. *"God,* really, you don't need any more admirers, secret or otherwise. *And* I'm not kissing you."

Pink and wide, her mouth was like a long bow, the only feature in her face that was soft and vulnerable. A pillow of lushness. It betrayed that tough-as-nails, no-nonsense persona of hers.

He desperately wanted to feel it under his own, wanted to taste all that pent-up passion. One kiss wouldn't hurt. She was the one who'd cornered him, the one throwing outrageous ideas at him, the one looking all delectably confined and uptight in that dress. "How do you expect me to believe you're not playing a joke on me with this proposal? Maybe this is revenge? Maybe you intend to make me fall in love with you, and then leave me at the altar pining for you? Maybe…"

Brown eyes glittering, wide mouth mobile, she laughed. It was a full-throttled laugh, deep and husky. The kind that came all the way from your stomach, burned through your lungs, leaving you a little dizzy. Her body shook all over.

The sound stole into Luca, filling every hungry crevice inside him. It was one that could cut through the darkest space, filling it with light. "What is so funny?"

"You, falling in love. *With me.*"

He said it softly. "The whole world assumes Sophia Rossi is tough, brave, the conqueror of every challenge. Decimator of men. Only I know what a coward you are."

It fell in the space between them like a weapon, and he waited, breath balling up in his lungs. Anger and apprehension vied in her face until she covered the distance between them. He didn't know if she was going to slap him or kiss him or castrate him. No woman could create that mystery except Sophia. No woman had ever filled his veins with this heady anticipation.

Fingers on the lapels of his shirt, she jerked him close. "No one calls me a coward, *you manipulative bastard.*"

Throaty and tart, growly and yet with a deep vein of need pulsing beneath, it was Sophia to the end. Brave Sophia accepting facts and meeting them head-on. Dutiful Sophia kissing the man she hated just to hear him out.

Short and curvy, she barely came up to his chest. Hands on his shoulders, she pulled herself up, as if to elongate herself. Like a vine clinging to a cement wall.

That pressed every inch of her to him. Lush breasts, followed by such a thin waist that he wondered how it held up those glorious curves, then flaring into rounded hips, hips a man would anchor himself on while he thrust inside her. Shapely thighs that would clutch a man tight as he jerked in pleasure within her velvet heat.

Again and again, until he forgot what or who he was.

Such heat rolled over his skin that Luca's fingers dug into her soft flesh.

With a protesting moan, she stilled her mouth on his. The tips of their noses collided and a soft sigh left her. Hot breath kissed his hungry lips. Then she moved that mouth again. Testing and trying. This way and that. Halting thoughtfully and then hurrying along urgently when she liked the fit.

Brown eyes met his. And the world stilled. Time and space narrowed to this minute, this space around them. Never breaking his gaze, she slanted her head and dragged a kiss from one corner of his mouth to the other.

She took control of the kiss like she did everything else.

And Luca let her take over. Let the scent and taste of her fill every hungry crevice. Let her imprint herself on him.

Flames of fire raced along his veins when she licked the seam of his lips and probed for entry. Desperate, Luca opened his mouth under hers. The throaty sound of her gasp shivered down his spine. Never had he been waiting like this for pleasure. Never had he been the recipient.

Suppressing every instinct to take over the reins of the kiss—he'd never waited to be pleasured—he let her seduce him. She obliged, stroking the inside of his mouth with bold flicks, teasing and incinerating. Took his mouth with a carnality that left him shaking to the very marrow.

Christo, he'd never been so aroused by just a kiss.

The sound of footsteps behind them brought Sophia back to earth with a thud.

Her mouth stung with the taste of Luca, her body

thrumming with unsatisfied desire. The crisp hair on his wrists teased her palms.

But she felt anything but exultant. She wanted to cry. She wanted to ask him to take her to his bedroom, turn off the lights and—no, not his bedroom. Not the place where he'd probably made love to a horde of lovers, each more stunning and thin and wispier than the next. Maybe they could slip away into that veranda, hide under the moonlight and he could kiss her a little more.

She could pretend that he'd never broken her heart and that he wanted her just as much as she did him.

Because when Luca kissed her, Sophia was always carried off to some faraway land. A land where she could be strong enough to be weak, where she could let someone care for her, where she didn't worry about her family, where she was not mocked for who she was.

Where a man like Luca didn't have to be induced into seducing a woman like her...

She hid her face in his chest. His heartbeat thundered against her cheek. He was warm and male, both exciting and comforting, something she hadn't realized until this moment she missed.

Sophia couldn't dredge up anger for that kiss. Toward him or herself.

His fingers wandered up and down her hips, questing and caressing. "I'd rather we kissed again, but I keep my word." Deep and hoarse, his voice pinged over her heated skin. "So tell me, why do you wish to..."

Suddenly, a hand on her shoulder pulled her from his arms, turned her around.

"Tina, *non*!" she heard Luca shout dimly.

Sophia didn't see it coming. Someone slapped her. Hard. Her head went back, pain radiating up her jaw and through her ear. Tears blurred her vision and she blinked to clear them away. Pulling in a shuddering breath, she looked up.

Valentina—Luca's sister and Kairos's wife, stood before her, her lithe, willowy body shaking with rage. Her entire face was mobile with emotion, turning her into a volatile beauty. "You...*you tart!*"

Sophia raised a brow, refusing to show her dismay. "Tart, really?"

Her composure seemed to only rile the younger woman more. "You're determined to go through all the men in my family, aren't you? First Kairos, and now Luca? And to think I felt sorry for you when Leandro broke your engagement."

"Basta, Tina!" Luca again. His arm around Sophia's shoulders, he was a wall of lean strength against her. A dark scowl framed his features, his fingers rubbing against her arm in unconscious comfort.

Against every rational warning, Sophia felt her body leaning into his.

"You know the rumors about Kairos and her?" Tina screeched, her eyes filling with tears.

"If there's truth to them, confront your husband, Tina."

"Fall into her clutches, then. Maybe she will leave my husband alone." Her black gaze raked over Sophia in a sneer. "Although I do not see the appeal."

Valentina left with the same fierceness as she had come in. Like a storm, leaving a minefield of awkward silence behind.

Sophia untangled herself from Luca's side and ran her fingers tentatively over her cheek. She thought she might be a little sick but it could be because of how much dessert she'd eaten in her anxiety tonight after the strict diet of the last two weeks.

Luca pulled her to him; she tried to swat him away.

He won in the fight for possession of her. She swallowed hard. Fingers on her chin, he examined her cheek. "I apologize. She had no right to behave like that." His mouth became a hard line. All the charm, the wicked laughter, was gone.

She waited for the inevitable question about her and Kairos, but it never came. But then, the one thing Luca had never been was a hypocrite.

"Marriage to Kairos is not good for her."

She frowned but he didn't elaborate. "Kairos can be hard to—" he raised a brow and she realized she'd jumped to her supposed lover's defense "—understand."

"You feel sorry for her?" he said, amazement in his eyes.

Sophia shrugged. Despite the sting in her cheek and the burn in her stomach at the comment on her looks, something inside Sophia recoiled at the vulnerability in Valentina's eyes. A palette of emotions for Kairos, who was as hard-hearted as hell, to see. And everything was acted upon, too...

No man was worth that self-doubt, that haunting sense of inadequacy, Sophia wanted to tell Valentina.

Swift anger rose through her at Kairos; he was supposed to be her friend. Couldn't he have reassured Valentina instead of using Sophia to keep his own wife at a distance?

"It's obvious that what I suggested is a disastrous idea." She chanced a glance at Luca, greedy to the last second. She'd make sure it was another decade before she saw him again. Something in her clenched tight. "Forget what I suggested."

Without waiting for his answer, Sophia turned and walked away.

And in that moment she hated all men.

Antonio, for planting that horrible idea in her head, for using her desperation to promote his own agenda.

Kairos, for using their friendship as a barrier against his own wife.

Salvatore, for never giving her a chance in the company, even though he called her his daughter.

And the man behind her, more than anyone else, for kissing her like he meant it. Now and ten years ago. For making her want him so much, for making her weak and foolish, for making her imagine, even for a second, that she was all the things she could never be.

CHAPTER THREE

LUCA SPENT THAT Monday morning with Huang from the design team of Conti Luxury Goods, studying the prototype for new heels that would be released the coming spring.

Huang and he had worked together for almost ten years now, since Leandro had convinced Luca to take a small part in Conti Luxury Goods. Luca interacted only with Huang, and Huang worked with the rest of the design team.

He picked up a royal blue pump, tracing the aerodynamic sole with his fingers. The success of these pieces didn't worry him. As always, anything he designed, from pumps to handbags, became instantly covetous among the fanatically fashionable.

Seeing something raw and shapeless transform into something so pleasing, that was success to him. But this particular design run had come to fruition and he felt the loss of it keenly. It had been quite a challenge—the design of the new heel. Now the production team would take over.

Familiar restlessness slithered through his veins. What to work on next? Sophia's outrageous proposal from Friday night winked at him.

Dio, but that had challenge and fun and all kinds of things written into it. She hated him—had every right to, but she was still attracted to him. When his looks tripped Sophia into that kind of a kiss, he couldn't quite hate them. It should have been one of a hundred kisses, she one of numerous, interchangeable faces he filled his life with and yet, the taste of her lips lingered, the passion with which she had taken him lingered, filling him with a restless craving for more.

Since he had no intention of following that up with Sophia, he needed a woman. To forget her and her kisses and that he had no place in her life. *Soon.*

He was at the door when Huang said, "You're not going to wait?"

"For what?"

"You don't even know, do you? Your brother—" Huang's smile dimmed for the rift between Leandro and him, the first in their life, was fodder for office gossip "—is at the board meeting today. The one that's going on now."

"Well, he's the CEO of CLG, Huang." His mind ran over the next few days. He couldn't disappear without checking on Tina first.

"There are rumors that he's making a big announcement today."

Luca stilled.

His brother claimed to have changed, that he regretted ruthlessly arranging Tina's marriage to Kairos, pulling such deception over their sister, even if he intended it for her own good. But Leandro did nothing without reason. Needing to control everyone and everything around him was an itch in his brother's blood.

A lot of fates depended on Leandro's decision. Including Salvatore's. And Sophia's.

Her problems are not yours.

No warning could curb his thoughts, though. The poor state of the Rossi finances was common knowledge now. What would be her next move? Who would she propose marriage to next?

Curiosity was wildfire in his gut, eating away at that

restlessness that never deserted him. Her expression when she had walked away, defeated yet resolute, stayed with him.

If nothing, it would be amusing to see what Sophia would do next. So Luca waited, for Sophia was a breath of fresh air, cold and yet invigorating, in his predestined life.

Leandro was stepping down as the CEO of the CLG Board.

Two hours and a million thoughts later, Luca still hadn't recovered from the shock. For years Leandro's life had been CLG. Kairos, his brother-in-law, would be the front-runner for CEO.

What use would his sister, Tina, then be to the ruthlessly ambitious Kairos once he had that?

His thoughts in a tangle, Luca walked past the alarmed secretary and pushed the door open to his brother's office.

Kairos was in Leandro's office, his hands on Sophia's shoulders.

Jealousy twisted Luca's gut, his blood singing with that same possessive fury again. *Dio*, only Sophia reduced him to this. Willing control over his emotions, he stayed by the door. The question he'd refused to ask, because he'd believed that Sophia was above such disgusting behavior as him, even after Tina's accusations gnawed at him now.

How well did Sophia know him?

Sophia's quick shake to Kairos's whisper, the intimacy their very stance betrayed…suggested something more than an affair, something far more dangerous.

He couldn't be the only man in the world who realized Sophia's worth, the only man who wanted to claim her in every way. Did Kairos want more, too?

Even if they weren't having an affair, it was clear Sophia had something with Kairos that Tina could never reach.

He'd hated this match between Tina and Kairos from the beginning, but seeing the stars in his sister's eyes, he had stayed out of it. Even now, every instinct in him wanted to let Kairos have the CEO position he'd pursued with such cunning and ruthlessness, to let their marriage reach that destructive conclusion.

Only the tears he'd seen in Tina's eyes at that party stayed his hand now.

It had been Leandro who had brought Tina to live with them after their mother's death but it was Luca who'd made her laugh. Luca who'd gained her trust first; Luca she laughed with over all these years.

With her smile and generous heart, Tina loved Luca unconditionally, provided as much an anchor in his life as Leandro had.

Smarting at the direction of his thoughts, Luca ran a hand through his hair.

If there was a chance that Tina's marriage to Kairos could be saved, he had to take it. He had to trust in Leandro's belief that Kairos was the right man for Tina.

And to give Tina a running chance, he'd take away what stood between his sister and Kairos—the CEO position of CLG and Sophia Rossi. Luca's seat on the board, which he'd have to claim for the first time in his life, would see to the first.

The second...

The solution that appeared released a panic in his gut, as if a noose were tightening around his neck.

Of all the women in the world, Sophia was the last woman he should be contemplating marriage to. She had proved to be dangerous to his peace of mind even as a chubby, composed nineteen-year-old. Now she was a force to be reckoned with.

"Can we borrow...*your office, Kairos*?" Luca interrupted the sweetly nauseating scene. "Sophia and I have something important to discuss."

"I won't let you bully Sophia."

"How about you show that concern for my sister? Your wife, remember?" Luca retorted.

Another squeeze of Sophia's shoulders and Kairos left.

"That looked like a very cozy scene, very tender," Luca said, leaning against the closed door, batting away at the ugly emotion festering in his gut. "I gather he knows what Tina did."

He saw her spine stiffen, making her look like an angry crow in her black dress. "I didn't tell him. And I came by to tell him that he should clear this misunderstanding with Valentina."

As always, the black linen was unadorned with the skirt falling demurely past her knees, high necked and severely cut. Yet the very cut and the way it enfolded all of her emphasized the very voluptuousness of the woman's curves. If her intentions were to cover up that exquisitely luscious body with those painfully severe dresses, then she was an abysmal failure.

The only thing her horribly dowdy dresses showed was her rejection of style and fashion. Of her femininity. That she found herself not worthy enough of even trying.

He wanted to tear the ugly fabric off her and dress her in slithery silks, discover that satiny soft skin that he'd tasted once thoroughly, make her—

"Luca?"

Christo, two minutes in the same room and he could imagine only one scenario. The easy way she unmanned his control made Luca's tone uncharacteristically harsh and bitter. "How did he receive *your mutually beneficial proposal*? Should I be flattered that you asked me first?"

Disgustingly shameful words, he realized the moment he spoke.

She stilled, dismay pouring out of her entire frame. That she was hurt by his callous remark, that she could be pushed to some reaction by him, any reaction, elated Luca. *He was truly a twisted devil.*

"No," she said, boldly meeting his eyes, only the shadows in her own betraying her emotions, "you're the only one I've proposed marriage to. And before you ask another disgustingly hypocritical question, no, I've not propositioned Kairos into some sort of illicit affair, either.

"I do not sleep with married men. Much less a close married friend. Much less a man who already asked me to marry him and I refused."

Shock stole coherence from Luca. Suddenly, he saw it.

Ruthlessly ambitious, Kairos had first wanted Sophia and Rossi Leather. When she'd refused, he'd set his sights on Tina and the Conti Board instead, with Leandro's blessing.

And now his dear brother-in-law probably wanted to eat his cake, too...

Dio, now he couldn't undo knowing that Tina's marriage was in trouble.

Sophia hitched her handbag over her shoulder, knuckles white, and glanced at her watch. "If you'll excuse me, I have several other men I have to proposition, blackmail, extort so that I can save my family's livelihood. If you've had enough fun at my expense, I'd like to get started."

"I want to talk about your proposal."

Her hands stilled on her desk. "No." Fury bristled from her. "I used to think you still possessed some notion of decency. But no. You are every horrible thing I thought of you all these years."

"I'm serious, Sophia."

Something shone in her eyes. He'd never met a woman who worked as hard as Sophia did, one who dusted herself off even after being denied every opportunity she deserved.

Such strength, such endurance and yet he knew, like no one else did, that she was vulnerable, too. Was it any wonder she fascinated him?

Sophia stared at Luca, trying to gauge his mood. Trying to banish the taste of him from her mouth.

Even as she knew that she had a better chance of forgetting how to breathe. For a week, she'd lain flushed and restless in her bed, touching her lips, as if she could invoke that feeling again.

Ran a hand over her breasts and down low, where she'd been already damp. Just imagining his fingers down there, his mouth on her heavy breasts, she'd been aching all night. Reaching for something only he could give and she could never ever want again.

Today, he was wearing a V-necked gray sweater and black jeans. With a bristly beard and dark shadows beneath his eyes, he looked exactly the man he was—a recklessly gorgeous playboy with a long night behind him.

"Sophia?"

She came to with a startle, her cheeks on fire. He was serious? He wanted to hear her proposal? "I've heard that Leandro and you are on the outs now?"

"Si." One long finger traced the edge of the desk, and Sophia could tell this was something that bothered him— this rift with his brother.

"With Leandro stepping down, your vote could become the deciding factor on a lot of things."

"Like whether Rossi Leather should be cut for pieces and distributed among everyone."

She nodded, hiding her shock. For a self-indulgent, in-dolent playboy, Luca grasped the situation far too quickly. "You enjoy the extravagant lifestyle being a Conti affords you. I mean, you're used to those custom designed Armani suits, that flat in downtown Milan, that Maserati and all those women, yes?" she said spitefully, knowing full well that Luca could be a pauper and women would still strip for him in the middle of a birthday party.

He sighed, even as deep amusement glinted in his eyes. "You know I do. I dread losing any of it. I didn't realize Leandro was serious about letting it all go to hell."

"If you give me the required rights, I will do everything Leandro has done for you all these years. Represent you on the board and take care of your interests in CLG. You won't have to lift a finger."

"I see you've used your superior knowledge of my likes and tastes to reel me in." If there was any justice in the world, her glare should have turned him into dust.

"What do you get in return?"

"If we marry, my stepfather could be convinced to bring Rossi's under the umbrella of CLG. He's been resisting it because he thinks his legacy would be swallowed up."

"*Dio*, controlling old men and their obsession with their legacies. So this agenda is not driven by Kairos, then."

"What?"

He shrugged. "You have to admit it's a good theory. Kairos decides you'll marry me, can have me by the balls and consequently, has my vote in his bid to be CEO."

"That is too ruthless even for him. Not forgetting the obvious flaw in the plan that I, of all women, could have your ba—" She gasped; it was like there was her own personal furnace inside her, and the rogue grinned as she cleared her throat. "Could have you under my control, in any manner."

"I could never marry a woman who lacks in feminine wiles."

She gritted her teeth. He had to pick the most uncomfortable aspect of that. "Another fantastic reason for why it's a crazy idea."

He gave her a considering look. "If you have such faith in that bastard Kairos, then why not accept his help?"

"Luca, what is your problem with Kairos?"

"He's too hungry for power. Which means he'll do anything in his hunt for it."

"Yes, how infinitely atrocious that Kairos is so ambitious when he could be chasing woman after woman in eternal pursuit of pleasure."

"Why isn't he helping you with Rossi's?"

"He offered but I don't like his solution. Everyone, including Kairos, has an agenda for Rossi Leather without considering what's actually best for the company or my family. And the problems we have aren't going to be solved by a simple influx of cash. Salvatore will bring us back here into this same situation in a year again. No one can help us."

Not even Antonio.

The minute she didn't toe the line—which would probably include some impossible task like domesticating the devil in front of her—Antonio would tighten the screws on her. Threaten their company or withdraw his support.

"The only way to ensure we don't fall into this hole again," she said, with a mounting sense of defeat, "is if I take the reins myself."

"You think Leandro would have recognized how smart and efficient you are and given you the reins. That's why you were so eager to marry him."

"He always struck me as a fair, principled man."

Her unshakeable trust, the admiration in Leandro's implacable nature, rubbed Luca raw.

He had never bemoaned the fact that only he, and not Leandro, had inherited every despicable thing from their father—his good looks, his brilliance and maybe his madness. But in that moment he envied his brother the freedom to be his own man, the right to his own mind that made Sophia admire him so much.

"You would have married him, shared his bed?" Fury threaded his tone, which shocked her as much as him. "After the history we have?"

Color mounted her cheeks. "Rossi's needs a complete rehaul, five years to build it to a stable position again. Leandro would have given me that chance."

Her stepfather's damned company… It always came back to that. "I've no doubt that you will do it in three. You'll make Rossi's better than it has ever been."

Shock rooted Sophia to the floor, a faint whooshing in her ears making her dizzy. She ran a shaking hand over her brow. "What?"

"*Dio*, you sang this same song even a decade ago. You went into raptures, *non, you almost climaxed* with anticipation every time you talked about your plans for your Rossi Leather. Extension, branching away from leather production completely, focusing on accessory design… Just do it already, Sophia."

He stared at her, brows raised in question while Sophia processed those words slowly. Dear God, he remembered all of her naive, hopeful, detailed plans for Rossi's.

Heat pricked her eyes. Her head hurt as if under some great liquid weight; even her nose felt thick. Or rough. Or something very close to tears.

Did he know what a gift he gave her?

He didn't give the compliment grudgingly like Kairos,

who recognized talent and hunted it with a ruthless will. He didn't give the compliment insidiously, as if her intellect and smart business sense were odd, distorting it into some sort of stain on her femininity. As if somehow they minimized her as a woman.

He didn't give it to placate her, like her mother. Even her mother, she knew, wished Sophia was different. Wished *Sophia made it easy on herself*; wished *Sophia didn't feel like she had to prove herself in a man's world*.

Wished *Sophia wasn't still fighting, even after all these years*.

No, Luca stated it as a matter of fact. With the same tone as if to say: people need oxygen to live.

Given the chance, Sophia Rossi could make Rossi's better than it has ever been before.

Simply that.

Just that.

Joy bloomed from her chest, spreading like warm honey through every cell, stretching her mouth into a wide smile.

He came to stand before her, and for once, Sophia couldn't step back. It seemed as if he had thoroughly bypassed all her defense mechanisms. "Sophia?"

"Hmmm?"

"You have a blank look in your eyes, and I'm not sure you've breathed in the last ten seconds. Also…you're smiling at me like I'm your favorite person in the world. *Dio*, you're not dying, are you?" He tilted her chin up, raked her face over with that searing gaze. "Now that I think about it, you look like you've lost weight and there are dark shadows under your eyes."

Her hands drifted to her hips and his gaze followed it eagerly. She pulled them up as if burned. The scent of him stroked over her senses. Just a little dip at her waist and her breasts would graze his chest. Her legs would tangle with his. And then she could—

"This is not some pathetic, last-minute attempt to have some good sex before you die, is it?" Something glittered in his gaze as he gently ran a finger over her cheek. "Because, *cara mia*, we don't have to marry for that. All you have to do is ask and I will *gladly* show you how fun it is on this side."

When was the last time she'd had fun? "I'm not dying."

"As much as that would solve a lot of problems for me, that is good to know. Now, I will give you three months of marriage."

Sophia couldn't believe he was agreeing to a proposal she'd made in sheer desperation. He seemed to decide as easily as he'd decide which party to go to. *Or which woman to take home on a given night.* Worse, she couldn't believe the way every cell in her leaped at the chance to be near him. Three months as his wife… *Lord*, it was both her salvation *and* utter ruin. "Why are you helping?"

"One, I want to throw a small hitch in my brother-in-law's plans. Two, I hate working, as you neatly pointed out."

Her heart sank to the floor. "You're doing this to drive a wedge between Kairos and me? I told you I'm not sleeping with him."

"A little distance wouldn't hurt, then. Especially if it is provided by me. Leandro has washed his hands of me. I'll have to claim my seat on the board. And like you said, who better than my own wife to watch out for my interests and work in my stead? We both get what we want."

"What is it that you're promising exactly?"

"You can't turn Rossi's around in three months but it's a start in digging it out of that hole, *si*?" He tucked an errant curl behind her cheek, a wicked smile on his mouth.

"I want to give you what you want, Sophia. And a couple of things you are too stubborn to ask for."

Her cheeks heated up. If it beat any faster, her heart was going to burst out of her chest. Her gaze lowered to his mouth, cinders lighting up her blood. *Don't. Ask. Don't—*

"Your arrogance in yourself is breathtaking."

"Arrogance, *bella mia*? I state fact. You know where you're going to end up."

Memories and sensations rushed through her—rough breaths, the slide of hot, damp skin like velvet over hers, pain giving way to incredible pleasure...every other sense amplified in the darkness that she'd insisted on...

Heat poured through her, like lava spewing out. Her skin felt tight, parched, her pulse ringing through her. "No...I don't want to sleep with you ever again."

"Who mentioned anything about sleep? Just don't fall in love with me," he added with a grin.

"I'm not a naive idiot anymore," Sophia replied, confident that she'd avoid that trap.

Luca was irresistible but she was walking into this with her eyes wide open.

Love wasn't for her; he'd helped her see that firsthand. She'd hated the loss of control over her own happiness, over her mood, over her sense of self-worth. In a moment Luca had stripped her of everything.

She despised the hollow feeling it had left in her gut. The haunting ache that she lacked something. She never wanted to be that vulnerable ever again.

He reached the door, turned the handle and looked back at her. "Do you have protection?"

He couldn't mean what she thought he did. *No way.* "Like a bodyguard?"

He grinned and Sophia wanted to wipe that grin off his pretty face with her bare hands. "No, like a contraceptive."

"That's none of your..." He moved so fast and so smoothly that Sophia blinked. The heat from his body was a tantalizing caress on her skin, beckoning her closer. She answered only to stop him from coming closer. "Yes, fine. I'm on the pill. Not that it's relevant to you."

He pushed a tendril of hair away from her temple. That stubborn lock that never stayed back. "Good." His warm breath raised the little hairs on her neck.

Knowing that he was saying it to shock her didn't stop a pulse of throbbing need between her legs. It took every ounce of her energy not to press her thighs close. She needed something distasteful, something to snap herself out of that sensual web he weaved... "You...I... You've had numerous lovers. I won't just—"

The glittering hunger in his eyes told her she'd already betrayed herself by talking as though she was considering it. *Damn!* "I'm clean."

Like a dream, feverish and hot and full of some elusive subtext, he left.

Sophia stared at the door for a long time, her knees shaking. Covering her face with her hands, she sank back against the desk.

Luca Conti was going to marry her. Of all the men in the world, that unpredictable, recklessly indulgent playboy was giving her the chance no one else would. It was going to tangle up everything with everyone horribly. Three months of her life would change the course of the rest of her life. Even after his reckless cruelty ten years ago, she was still affected by him.

But Sophia could only obsess over one thing.

That, for three months, she could kiss him all she wanted.

CHAPTER FOUR

LUCA HAD KNOWN rejection from his mother when he'd been seven. He'd suffered debilitating headaches, insomnia and worse before he hit puberty.

The first time he'd had sex, he had been seventeen, with a woman a decade older. He hadn't really wanted the sex; he'd wanted to be held by the woman, to be less lonely for one night. Messed up as he'd been, he'd still realized what he'd done.

He'd whored himself—his looks, his charm, his body, for a bit of affection.

One didn't need a degree in psychiatry to realize that.

When Leandro had finally discovered him—his brother had always come after him no matter the time of the day, no matter how devious Luca tried to be—sitting on the floor of the hotel room with his head in his hands, and looked at him with nothing but understanding and patience and that all-consuming love that his brother used to justify arranging his siblings' lives, Luca had thrown up all over the floor. And promised himself never again.

Never again would he sink that low.

Never again would he succumb to that cavernous craving within.

Never again would he be without control.

For the most part, he was sure he'd succeeded.

Instead of fighting the sudden bouts of insomnia and crazy energy, he poured himself into everything and anything he could get his hands on. He studied like a madman, inhaling and conquering every subject he touched. He'd become a human sponge.

Leandro would sigh and smile when Luca said he wanted to try something new.

Arts and history. Mathematics and astronomy. He'd dabbled in all of them, but moved on, nothing calming the restlessness within. Only music—the relentless, endless chords churning in his head released onto paper, played until he achieved every single note—could soothe it.

It was both his release and his curse. He'd fashioned a wooden doll for Tina after she'd come to live with them, and realized he loved creating things, designing things, too. So he'd started working with Lin Huang, the creative head of Conti Luxury Goods' design department.

Through the years he'd achieved a kind of balance, a normal—for him. He wrote music for hours on end when in that grip, worked at CLG and other projects of his own, surviving on an hour or more of sleep for days. Then he had those carefree days where he got drunk, partied, took endless women to his bed. And had uproarious fun at the expense of others.

Fortunately for him, he'd discovered he liked sex, just for itself. That he could enjoy it without whoring himself for something else. He'd slipped up only once from the happy path he was forging for himself.

Ten years ago, with Sophia. She'd been the first real thing in his life and he had let himself be carried away.

Sophia was the only one who'd ever made him forget himself, who had shredded his control so effortlessly.

For all his reputation as a self-indulgent playboy, control was tantamount to his peace of mind. It was something Leandro and he had rigorously worked on in those initial months after their mother had left. He'd spent hours on the mat mastering several martial arts disciplines.

He had an example from his father's life. He knew that like everything else he'd inherited from him, he could carry a speck of that madness—that devious, manipulative, cruel streak, too.

Control was everything to him.

Stepping out of the shower, Luca walked to the mirror and rubbed it to clear the steam. Hands on the marble sink, he stared at himself.

He looked past the compelling perfection of his features—a face he'd hated for so long—past the now bone-deep mask he showed the world. He had never lied to himself. Self-delusion would have been a welcome friend in all those miserable years.

He was doing this because of Sophia.

He was doing this because he wanted these three months with her.

He wanted to be near her, inside her. He wanted to unravel all the fiery passion she kept locked away.

He wanted to free her from the cage she put herself in; a cage, he was sure, he'd driven her into building.

But this time Sophia knew the score, knew what he was incapable of. She wasn't an innocent who mistook attraction, pure lust for anything else. This was not a marriage like his parents'.

Sophia wasn't some innocent, painfully naive young girl Antonio had handpicked like some sacrificial offering to his father's madness, to further the Conti legacy like his mother had been.

Sophia would never let herself be intimidated or drowned in Luca's personality.

The panic in him calming, Luca breathed out. Excitement filled his veins now.

For the first and only time in his life, the self-indulgent, profligate playboy he'd made himself to be was going to take what he truly wanted. And revel in it.

That he would set Sophia up for the rest of her life and do his part to protect Tina's marriage, *that* was the bonus.

Meet me @ Palazzo Reale Monday 10AM.
Don't wear black. J

The texts came on Saturday night at seven, a whole week after Luca had cornered Sophia at CLG offices. They also sent her soup down the wrong pipe at the dinner table.

Heart pounding, half choking, Sophia had escaped her family's curiosity.

She'd spent the week on tenterhooks. Wondered if she'd imagined the whole episode, if she'd somehow deluded herself into believing that the Conti Devil had proposed marriage.

When she saw Antonio come up toward Rossi's offices, she'd mumbled something to her team and skipped out like a thief.

Her reply—Why?—had gone unanswered. Which meant she'd spent half the night pacing her bedroom, and the rest of it thrashing in her bed.

Monday morning she stood on the steps of the centuries-old building, trying to ignore the curious looks from people coming and going.

She ran a nervous hand over her dress, her only non-black slightly dressy dress. It was a sort of muddy light brown made of the softest linen. Over it, she wore a cream cashmere cardigan to ward off the slightly chilly November air.

With cap sleeves, the dress had been an impulse purchase months ago. It boasted a false buttoned-up short bodice, then flared out into a wide skirt from high above her waist.

The saleswoman had assured Sophia it made her look tall and graceful.

A quick glance in her mirror this morning told Sophia she looked neither tall nor graceful. Nothing could create the illusion when she was two inches over five.

But the thing that had made her groan was that the dress, which had fitted neatly, now sort of hung on her. Like a tent. She'd slipped her feet into five-inch purple leather Conti pumps, throwing caution to the wind.

So what if she felt like her legs would fall off later?

Whipping her unruly hair into a French plait and adding a dab of peach lip gloss, she'd been ready. Her gut twisted into a thousand knots, she had guzzled down two cups of coffee and munched her protein bar on the way over.

Minutes ticked by. Quarter past ten flew by. A couple of old men walked past her, up the steps, and she had a suspicion they were friends of Salvatore's.

Before they could catch her eye, she turned away and checked her phone. She walked up and down the steps, went back into the hall, got a bottle of water then walked back out. And all the while she waited, a sense of déjà vu came upon her.

She'd been waiting, just like this, ten years ago, too. In his bedroom, in his bed. In her underwear, albeit the sheet pulled up to her chin.

Waited for Luca, to tell him that she was in love with him.

He hadn't shown up. Marco Sorcelini had, instead, with a lascivious smirk on his face and his cell phone in hand. Before Sophia could make sense of what was happening, he'd clicked a picture of her. Told her to put her clothes on and go home…

Because Luca Conti had won the bet.

He had seduced Sophia the Shrew, made her fall in love with him and walked away. *Why else would any man touch a woman like Sophia*, Marco had added, *who was neither beautiful nor docile and far too smart for her own good?*

She'd thrown the sheet away, launched at Marco and punched his nose. She'd lived for months in terror that that photo of her would be plastered all over everyone's cell phone. That her humiliation wouldn't be limited to Luca and his cronies.

It hadn't.

The most nightmarish day of her life and it was on repeat again. This time it was her entire family's future that she had trusted him with.

Forty minutes past ten. Frustration and fury scraped Sophia's nerves. Stupid, so stupid, to trust his word. To believe that he'd really want to help her. When everything she'd ever known of him said Luca didn't give a damn about anyone.

Just as she walked down the steps, a great beast of a bike came to a shuddering stop, right in front of her.

Black leather jacket, wraparound shades and a killer, megawatt smile that was like a shot of adrenaline straight to her heart. A small crowd of onlookers whispered behind her.

With sleek grace, Luca pulled his tall form off the bike and handed it off to a valet. Dark shadows, even worse than usual, bracketed his eyes. He looked gaunt, the curve of his mouth almost obscenely lush against the sharp angles of his face.

His jet-black hair gleamed with wetness. He looked like hell and yet, utterly, breath-stealingly gorgeous. The world wasn't a fair place.

He covered the few steps between them, looked her up

and down, leisurely, thoroughly. Took the fabric of her glove between his fingers, frowned and then sighed. A twinkle shone in his eyes as it moved over her hair and her face. "That dress is not only ghastly but loose. And that color is not an improvement on black.

"You have to do better in this department if we want the world to believe we're utterly in love. I do not need extra incentive to tear your clothes off you."

Her fingers clenched tight on her phone, Sophia counted to ten. He wasn't going to reduce her to a screaming shrew in front of the whole city. "You're late. By fifty-five minutes. I…" She gritted her jaw so tight, she was going to need dental surgery. "And you look like hell. I texted you and called you, like fifteen million times. You don't reply—"

"I overslept."

"You overslept?"

"I didn't get to bed until the early morning. And I didn't want to show up here for you all dirty and unshaved."

"You couldn't lay off partying for one night?"

"This whole thing made me nervous."

Her tirade halted on Sophia's lips. Of course he was nervous. Getting married was probably akin to being tortured for him. "Why didn't you just reply?"

"I left my phone somewhere." His long fingers were shackles on her arms. "You're shaking." He scowled. Used to that lazy, amused glance, it made him look dangerous, ferocious. "You thought I wasn't coming."

She braced herself against the concern in his tone. "I was expecting a media crew or at least those society pages social media punks to capture me standing there. Another joke. Only this time, on a much grander scale. *Conti Devil Jilts Sophia the Stupid Idiot… Again!*"

Eyes closed, he pinched the bridge of his nose. A

shadow of strain gave his usually laughing features a haunting look. "That is harsh. I never—"

"You've got to be kidding me. Was there a bet about who could seduce me ten years ago?"

"Si."

"Did you take part in it?"

"Si."

"Did you mean to disappear to Paris with your—" no, she wouldn't call some faceless, innocent girl vindictive names "—*new lover* knowing that I was—" a shudder went through her and she hated how all her strength disappeared when it came to that moment "—in your bed, naked and waiting?" Fresh out of virginity and hopelessly in love... she'd been a besotted idiot.

"Si."

"As long as we're clear, then," she added casually, when she felt like glass with tiny cracks inching around however much she put plasters over it. Somehow, she needed to channel this bitterness, this humiliation, when she was melting for one of his smiles. Because she did.

She melted. She thawed. She burned when it came to this man. She always would, apparently.

A hundred shadows drifted in his usually empty gaze. A vein beat in his temple. He opened his mouth then closed it. Wounded hesitation suited him to perfection like everything else.

Even now, she realized with a sinking awareness of her own foolishness, she waited. As if there could be some other fantastic explanation for the cruel trick he'd played on her.

She sighed and held up her phone. "A text would have sufficed to say you'd changed your mind."

He pulled her wrist up and looked at the dial of her watch. "We're marrying in fifteen minutes."

"What?" Astonishment made her voice screechy. "I... you never told me we were marrying *today*. This morning."

"Why do you think I asked you to come?"

"To submit our documents. I brought my papers."

"All taken care of by a friend."

"The mayor's sister, I assume?"

His gaze flared and she looked away. Damn it, if she didn't keep her pride in this thing between them, she'd have nothing left. Betraying that she knew of each and every woman he'd *dated* over the last decade definitely didn't leave her much.

She turned around and looked at the building with new eyes. "Do you have any contracts for me to sign?"

"Like what?"

"Like a prenuptial, Luca." When she'd have turned, he stalled her with his hands on her shoulders. She heard him take a deep breath behind her. His exhale coated her neck. His body didn't touch her but lured her with unspoken promises.

Now his nose rubbed from her temple to her hair, his fingers leaving scorching trails wherever they touched. "What scent is that? It haunts me sometimes."

"Honeysuckle," she whispered hoarsely, even as she warned herself this was his default. Flirting and seducing was in Luca's genes. "A small American company makes it and I buy it online." She was babbling, the only way to keep her sanity.

"It blends perfectly with your skin." His breath whispered over her cheek. "I can't wait to discover if you smell like that all over."

Liquid heat claimed Sophia, the very fabric of her dress scraping everywhere it touched. She took deep breaths, trying to not sink into his hard body.

He smelled of leather and musk, of quintessential male.

Pleasure and pain, all tangled up in her head. Freedom and captivity, one inseparable from the other. He made her so aware of things she'd forced herself to ignore. Of the thump of her heart, the thrum of her skin, the sudden heaviness in her breasts, the slow, pulling pulse in her sex. Of being a woman who denied herself so many things in the name of being strong. If she'd had a boyfriend, if she'd satisfied her body's demands, maybe she wouldn't have been this vulnerable to him.

Sophia Conti, expert in self-delusion. "A pity you won't," she offered finally, a pathetic sop to a protest. She cleared her throat, as if she could chase away the desperate need. "Please tell me you talked to your lawyer."

"Non."

"Christ, you can't approach this like you do everything else. You should make me sign a contract that what is yours will stay yours."

"I thought you thought me worthless."

"I'm sure just your stock in CLG is worth a lot."

Faint tension emanated from him, his roving hands clenched tight on her shoulders. "I don't care about that stock. Or the company or the legacy."

Something in his tone, a vein of disgust, alerted Sophia. It sounded so discordant, so jarring, for she'd never heard him speak in that tone before. This didn't sound like not caring. It was active loathing that hinted at a depth of feeling she didn't think him capable of.

"It's a legacy, Luca. It roots you to this place. How can you...*hate* it?"

She felt his shrug rather than saw it. "Is that why you want to head Rossi's? Don't let the idea of belonging become more important than everything else."

Faint alarm tripped along Sophia's nerves. *Was that her*

real intention beneath wanting to save her family? Was it an utterly selfish desire to belong?

"Keep your hands to yourself. You're distracting me," she burst out.

The man's hands were forever roaming and roving over her. Even when she was bristling with anger. He touched as if it was as natural as breathing. Sometimes, it was affectionate, sometimes, it was provoking. But always, as if he needed the physical connection.

It was one of the things she'd loved then—being touched by him.

He laughed and continued touching her.

"This is serious, Luca. When we…separate, I don't want any accusations."

"Do you intend to take me to the cleaners, Sophia?"

"It would serve you right if I did."

"There's nothing you could do that would make me end this in a bad way, *cara mia*. Except if you fell in love with me and made a nuisance of yourself."

She laughed. A brittle, fake sound. "That is an impossibility right there."

"Then we're good, *si*? I'm aware that you're placing a huge amount of trust in me. I'm doing the same."

She had no reply to that. In her wildest nightmares, she wouldn't have imagined Luca Conti of all men coming to her rescue.

One hand landed on her shoulder. A finger stroked her nape, between her knot and the edge of her cardigan. Back and forth, up and down, until all of her being focused on that spot. "This is romantic, *si*? Us eloping like this."

She snorted. "No one who knows me would believe I'd elope."

Now the finger moved, snuck under the seam of her dress and traced her shoulder blades. "*Si*, but then I corrupted you with my kisses and my infinite charm and my dazzling good looks. I stole away every bit of your famed common sense, enthralled you. Sounds perfect when you think about it."

She flushed and looked down at herself, at the horrible dress. Would she have dressed differently if she had known? Not that she had anything in her closet that was remotely better or dressy enough for a bride.

No, this was right. Their wedding wasn't a romantic affair. It wasn't even one of those advantageous society arrangements that seemed to abound around her. It had a shelf life of three months, if that.

Her spine rigid from holding herself so tight, she blew a breath. Turned around. "Let's get married."

He smiled then, and the golden sunlight illuminated that gorgeous face. Her breath caught. He hooked his arm through hers and walked up the steps. When she wobbled, one corded arm came around her waist. She felt him look down and followed it.

When he met her gaze, there was such genuine laughter etched in his face that she smiled back. "What?"

"I'm going to take a pair of scissors and rip up all those black trousers you usually wear. You're not hiding those legs again. Not if I have anything to say about it."

They were married fifteen minutes later, in a huge cathedral-like room. Sunlight gleamed through high, soaring windows, dusting everything with a golden glow. Every time she moved, the princess-cut diamond, set in platinum, caught the rays piercing it over and over.

That he'd remembered the rings—for him and her—still shocked her.

Even the impersonal civil ceremony with no personal

vows couldn't seem to dim the momentousness of the occasion.

Sophia couldn't meet Luca's eyes throughout the ceremony. Or anyone else's. Didn't want to see a mockingly wicked smile as if this was just another of his antics, another joke, just another day.

Much as she tried to not attach significance to the day, she'd forever remember it. At least, as her only wedding day.

So the images she had of that half hour were of ancient but stylish furniture, a seventeenth-century tapestry covering one huge wall, luxurious chandeliers, brocade-covered chairs and golden-framed mirrors reflecting back Luca and her every which way she looked—she short and dowdy in her ugly dress, which she promised herself she was going to burn the moment it came off her, and Luca, looking gorgeous and a little roguish in a white shirt and black jeans that gave the best view of his tight butt.

It was a place steeped in history and for someone who'd never been able to afford sentimentality, the hall impressed Sophia. Three months later, or a year later, or even a decade later, this hall would be here, a building that had stood witness to their strange wedding.

Her wedding...to the one man she shouldn't even come near.

The clerk asked for fifteen Euros for the banns license, which Luca didn't have. "My wife is responsible for all matters financial," the rogue added with a glint in his eyes.

The wedding felt both surreal and strangely kooky. As if they were co-conspirators in a reckless game. While the truth was that she was burning all her bridges by trusting Luca.

Her family was going to be excited for all the wrong reasons. Kairos was probably never going to talk to her ever again. Society was going to laugh at her. Even she didn't believe that a man like Luca could fall in love with a woman like her. Why should they?

Suddenly, she couldn't even breathe, the enormity of what she'd done pressing upon her. She was trusting the one man who'd broken the very thing into a thousand pieces with his recklessness.

As if tuned into every doubt coursing through her, Luca wrapped an arm around her. "Trust yourself, Sophia. You made the right decision, for you."

Two of Luca's friends—a woman who worked in the Piazza del Duomo and the mayor's sister, two of his exes, *of course*—stood witness as they signed the marriage license. Neither woman, at least openly, exhibited their shock that the Conti playboy, the man who'd been called a god for his looks, was marrying the short, snarky, shrewish Sophia.

And soon, she became Sophia Conti. A solemn expression on his face, Luca pulled her close and kissed her cheek. Not her mouth, surprisingly, for a man who'd said he was eager to get her into bed.

A tender, almost affectionate caress that brought a lump to her throat.

Waving his friends off, they walked out into the sunshine. It was a gorgeous day for November.

"Let's go," he said then, pointing to his bike.

"No way am I climbing that beast in this dress."

"No way am I leaving my new bride here. Hop on, *cara mia*. I want to get to the Conti offices before they disperse for lunch. I hear they have a board meeting today."

"You want to walk in there and—" she swallowed audibly "—announce what we did?"

"You sound as if we did something naughty. And why

not? I want to see the expressions on my Nonno's face. And Kairos's. And Leandro's."

Sophia wanted to see none of those people. She wanted to go home and come to terms with the emotions bursting through her before she faced anyone else. Once she processed them, she wanted to build a neat little cupboard in her mind and shove them all in there and slam the door.

"Is it necessary to upset them?"

"Stop chickening out, Sophia. You need to stop being scared of them." Which was exactly what she was doing. But for altogether different reasons.

Facing society as the Conti Devil's wife was going to be an exercise in humiliation and agony and a host of other excruciating things. But coward, she was not. With some difficulty, for she didn't want to flash him a glimpse of her underwear, she got on the bike.

With her awareness of the man and an active imagination, she didn't want to straddle anything when he was so close. The leather was supple against the tender skin of her thighs, both indecent and exciting, thanks to her libido.

"*Mio Dio!* Was that black lace and garters?" he asked the moment she settled on the scandalously wide seat.

He sounded hoarse and rough.

"You peeked? You actually peeked?" Outraged, she hit him on the shoulder, got off the bike and sputtered like a woman incapable of forming a coherent sentence. "You... you're the very devil."

He turned to the side, offering her his sharp profile. "You don't think your horribly closed-off dresses work, do you, Sophia?"

Throat dry, it took her a few seconds to speak. "What?"

"You have the lushest curves I've ever seen on a woman, *bella*. Those dresses, all they do is tempt and tease. Didn't you ever wonder why all those idiots made that bet about you ten years ago?"

All those idiots... He talked so glibly as if he hadn't been a part of it. The man seemed to have a selective memory along with a face that would tempt a saint.

And she had never been a saint.

"Because I beat them all in every test we took. Because I proved again and again that I was better than them at everything. And I didn't think they were charming princes like the rest of society did. They—" she swallowed tightly, for she'd never understood why he'd taken part in it "—wanted to see me humiliated."

That whole episode, along with being viewed as prize cattle that he could exchange for an advantageous marriage by Salvatore, everything that was tender in her, had taken a beating.

Before she'd a chance to understand her femininity, it had been crushed. So she had locked it, and any other vulnerabilities, away and continued on.

"All that is true, yes. But they were attracted to you. They thought you were the hottest girl around. They all wanted to be the ones who tamed you."

"Wild animals are tamed," she said in a tight whisper that hurt her throat.

"You can't change the world, Sophia. Men will be men—childish, arrogant and insecure. Any time we see a woman we don't understand, we call her names. All you do by hating the world is make yourself miserable."

"So I should lie down and let them beat me into what they think I should be." Because her mother, Salvatore, Antonio, Kairos, that was what they all wanted to do. They all wanted her to fit into the roles they had for her.

"No, *cara*. You fight, like you always do. You live. You

count your wins. You glory in what makes you stand out and you rub their noses in it."

She smiled, finding the idea intriguing, at least in theory. "And what would these wins be?"

"Convincing the most beautiful man in Italy, *probably Europe*, to marry you, should count as a win, *si*?"

Sophia burst out laughing. He possessed an uncanny knack to make her laugh, at the world and even herself. Like a ray of sunshine in a gloomy, dank cave.

But beneath her laughter, shock persisted, an uncomfortable knot in the pit of her stomach. Every moment she spent with Luca, he tossed her assumptions of him upside down.

He saw and understood far more than the world thought he did.

Even back then, even as he'd seduced her as part of that horrible bet, not once had he tried to minimize her to exaggerate his masculinity. Not once had he called her intelligence and ambition weird. Not once had he told her to be happy with her lot.

His betrayal in the end had colored everything of that time but Sophia didn't remember a time when she'd been so easy with herself.

"You are beautiful, *cara mia*. Enough to make stupid boys do a cruel thing to get close to you."

Was that why he'd taken part in that bet, too? Hadn't he known he didn't need it? She'd been putty in his hands from the moment he'd smiled at her.

She offered a wan smile, far too rattled. "You can make the earth believe it's the sky if you put yourself up to it, Luca. I'm not falling for you."

He sighed, that dramatic, larger-than-life gesture. "Oh, you will, *cara mia*. And you'll love every minute of your descent."

Hands snug around his waist, she hung on for dear life as he took off.

In two seconds flat, wind whipped at the knot of her hair. Her dress rode up to her thighs, and her breasts were crushed against his tensile back.

But for the moment Sophia found she didn't really mind being plastered to him. In fact, she decided to enjoy it.

She decided to call being plastered to the sexiest man she'd ever meet a win.

CHAPTER FIVE

A WWF SMACKDOWN would have had less dramatic effect than when Luca, arm in arm with Sophia, rushed past an aggrieved and bamboozled set of assistants and personal secretaries, and into the conference room on the tenth floor of the Conti offices.

"I thought we should share the good news with everyone in here first."

His grandfather Antonio rose to the bait instantly. His gaze moved from Luca's face to Sophia and then to the way their bodies were flushed together at their sides. A nerve began vibrating in his temple. "What have you done now?"

"Sophia and I got married an hour ago."

"If this is one of your shameless jokes—"

Luca cut off Antonio's building tirade by throwing their license on the table.

Ten pairs of eyes went to the license, scanned it and then returned to him and Sophia.

All ten faces, two assistants and eight board members, including Antonio and Kairos, looked at him as if he had crossed that final line into insanity.

Only his brother, Leandro, didn't exhibit any signs of the panic Luca saw in the rest. But it didn't mean Luca's announcement didn't rattle Leandro. With his autocratic control of his emotions, Leandro wouldn't betray anything until he'd decided on the best course.

Luca decided it was time to make the second, thoroughly satisfactory announcement. "Since my dutiful brother has decided to abandon me and his duties toward the board, I have decided that it is time I claimed my seat on the board and directed its decisions. After all, as someone very cleverly pointed out, it is my fortune, too. And where would my lifestyle be if I didn't have the Conti legacy to live off? I have to protect my assets, push the company in the direction I want it to go." He looked pointedly at Kairos, leaving no doubt as to his intentions.

Also, thwarting all board members who'd done nothing to stop his father's escalating antics felt good. Why hadn't he thought of this before? Luca could see the fear and the shock in their faces. They were terrified that he wasn't joking, that he would repeat history. That he would be another Enzo, and that he would be left to run wild, unchecked.

Luca tapped his knuckles on the glass tabletop, letting the silence thicken with the horror of their thoughts.

Sophia next to him became stiff, as if a pole had been driven into her spine. With the pretense of pushing away at a nonexistent speck on his collar, she reached close and glared at him. "What's going on? They all—"

He stole the words from her in a quick kiss, unable to resist the temptation. He teased and taunted her honeyed mouth with soft strokes, waiting for her to let him in. She was his wife, and damn his romantic soul, he liked it.

He'd never realized what a beautiful, intimate thing that bond could be until he'd seen Leandro and Alex. That it was another thing he could never have—that connection that went beyond anything else. He'd acknowledged that a long time ago, still, his heart raced when he looked at the plain band on his finger.

Fingers on his shirt, Sophia stiffened and then slowly melted into the kiss. He licked her lower lip, an incessant clawing in his gut to own her.

She stilled, blushed and then glared at him again. Her breath was a warm caress against his lips. "You couldn't have done this anywhere else?"

He grinned. "*Non*. I want them all to see I worship at your feet."

She rolled her eyes and he tucked her close against his side.

Leandro sighed. It was that same half indulgent, half disciplinary sound his brother had made countless times when Luca had been up to something new. Leandro hated pretending about Luca. But he had proven countless times that only Luca's well-being mattered.

Amusement flickered in his brother's gaze instead of the fury Luca had expected. Luca grinned, his heart feeling light for the first time in months.

Falling in love with Alex had changed his brother.

"You barely know anything about the business or CLG. And you hate dealing with...*people*, remember?" Next to him, Luca felt Sophia tense, her gaze swinging between him and his brother.

"I said I wanted to take an active role. Not that I would actually do any of the work."

A sort of a cross between relief and fear settled on the members' faces. One of them recovered enough to say, "What do you suggest?"

"My wife, Sophia Conti, from this day will have complete authority to make decisions on my behalf. The lawyers are preparing paperwork even as we speak. Come on, *cara mia*."

When Sophia, wooden and unmoving, only stared at him, he winked at her. Hand on the curve of her waist, he pushed her to the end of the table toward an empty chair. The members of the board watched like it was a movie.

Luca pulled the chair back, seated Sophia and then

stood behind her. "Sophia has seven years of experience working at Rossi Leather. She has an MBA and specializes in risk management and forecasting business trends and marketing. For all legal purposes, she now owns fifteen percent of the Conti stock."

A ripple of shock spread across the room and for once in his life, Luca felt a sense of rightness.

He had known her area of expertise.

He hadn't told her he was giving her complete authority over his stock.

That hadn't been part of their deal. She'd never even imagined...

Eight men—the most powerful in Milanese society— looked at her as if to figure out how she had persuaded/ manipulated the Conti Devil into this.

Damn it, did he really not care what happened to the company? *Or did he trust her judgment and her that much?*

That thought sent her heart thumping against her rib cage.

Sophia somehow managed to smile and nod and accept the congratulations that came her way. Kairos, without looking at her, walked out the minute the meeting was concluded.

She'd understood one thing in the show her new husband had put on.

Luca hated, *no*, despised, his grandfather. The depth of that emotion from Luca, who seemed to fairly breeze through life with no concern and with nothing but surface involvement with everyone, had rattled her.

While Luca's small exchange with Leandro had been civil, too, the bond between them was anything but. There was love between them.

After the depth of emotions she'd seen play out on his

face in the conference room, Sophia wasn't sure she really knew the Conti Devil.

Her gut said one thing while her history with him, quite the opposite.

She had just started looking for him when Luca appeared in the carpeted corridor and pulled her into a small, private lounge that was the size of her bedroom at home.

Cream leather and cream walls greeted her, the quiet luxury of the room markedly different from the business-oriented layout of the rest of the building. Afternoon light poured through the high windows, touching the space with a golden intimacy.

The most surprising thing about the room, though, was a piano that stood in the corner.

And in the middle of all that light, stood Luca, looking like a dark angel in his black jeans and white shirt with buttons undone to his chest. Dark olive skin gleamed like burnished metal, beckoning her touch. The leather jacket was gone.

The devil had intentions. And not good ones, for her mental health. Her body, however, had very different ideas for it was thrumming like an engine ready to take off.

Sophia rubbed her hands on her hips, had to swallow the butterflies in her throat before she could speak. "What is this place?"

"My brother's private lounge."

"It is soundproofed, isn't it?"

"Si." He raised a finger and shook it. "Don't ask me why."

Sophia stole a glance at the door as he closed it behind him. "You have key card access?"

"Si. Why is that so surprising?"

"I thought maybe this was the first time you came into the building."

He shook his head from side to side, making a thick lock of hair fall on his forehead. "No, I've been known to crash here, once in a while. My brother used to be a very hard taskmaster years ago. He's worked for the company since he was sixteen or seventeen. He refused to leave me alone at home."

"Where were your parents?" She'd vaguely heard of a scandal involving their father, Enzo Conti.

"Absent." The shrug that accompanied it seemed far too practiced to be real.

"So, wait, Leandro had this…room built for you?"

"Si."

She looked around the room again, noting the dark, floor-to-ceiling bookshelves. At first glance, the subjects were varied from art to space to the leather industry in Italy. "Wow, all this to just keep you out of trouble?"

"My brother takes his responsibilities very seriously."

"Why do you hate them all so much?"

A shadow flitted over his face and Sophia knew she'd hit the nail on the head. "Will you not move from the door?"

Evasion. If it didn't work, he'd smile at her. Or touch her. Or kiss her. She was beginning to see the pattern. She pushed off the door and casually strolled toward the bookshelves. None of the books were for amateur readers and looked quite worn. *Who did all these books belong to?*

"I thought it was all a joke to you. I still think a part of it is. You're like Puck in *A Midsummer Night's Dream.*"

"A good-looking Puck?"

She ignored his little quip. "You do your little thing and stand back to watch the explosion. But what happened in that boardroom was more than that." She turned around to see him standing close. Instantly, she felt the zing in her blood. The hungry clamor to touch him. The simple need to look at him, study him, to her heart's content. "You let them think you were going to join the board and for all of three minutes, that pack of gray wolves looked terrified. It was kind of funny."

He raised a brow. "Gray wolves?"

She shrugged.

"Why gray wolves?"

"They whiff out their prey's weakness from a considerable distance. They stalk and hunt it until it gives up out of sheer exhaustion. I have seen them all turn on Salvatore these last few months, from the minute things began to get worse, ready to tear *Rossi's* out and keep the good parts. Except Leandro, and Kairos, for his own reasons. Your grandfather leads that pack."

"So the wolves scared you, then?"

Sophia shivered. "Yes. But then I reminded myself that they need me just as much as I need them at this point."

A sense of coiled tightness emanated from him. And Sophia knew instinctually that he was shocked that she'd figured him out. "Why do they need you?"

"To corral you. To keep you amused and away from them." Her fingers shook as she rubbed her temple. Nothing, she was beginning to realize, was simple with Luca. And she'd hitched her already limp pony to his ride.

He touched her then. A mere brush of his fingers over her jaw. Sophia let the bookcase dig into her back, anything to keep her grounded in reality. "Have I ever told you how much I love that clever brain of yours, *cara mia*?"

Warmth fluttered through her stomach. "No. And you are probably the only one."

"I do." Something like pride glittered in his eyes. "And to show my appreciation for it, I'm going to kiss that lush mouth of yours."

She raised a brow. "First, tell me what that was about."

"Is it only me that finds this bossiness of yours hot?"

Another flicker of warmth. Another pocket of heat. "Luca…"

"They had the particular pleasure of seeing my father go off the rails. Now they look at me and wonder if I will do the same."

"Why you?"

"Because I'm the mirror image of him, a carbon copy. The man embezzled from his own company, used his power to prey on women and generally blazed a destructive path through every life he touched. He almost brought CLG to its knees and only then Antonio interfered. He brought Leandro into the company, and together, they ousted him in two years." There was no intonation to that statement. Yet the very bald way he said it sent a shiver through Sophia.

"What happened to him? Your father?"

"He died in jail." A vicious gleam, a dark fire in his eyes that transformed his face. To that of a disconcertingly cruel stranger. "So Antonio waits and watches, as he's been doing for years, to see if I will self-destruct like that, too. He tries to do a course adjust every few years."

Which was why he'd stalked and cornered Sophia. After Luca's latest debacle with a minister's wife, Antonio had been desperate.

But how could anyone think Luca would turn out like his father?

She couldn't imagine Luca ever preying on anyone's weakness. Couldn't imagine Luca destroying anyone's life with such malicious…

What do you call what he did to you ten years ago? the rational part of her whispered. *What he does every day with his life? How much do you really know him?* "You—"

"I think we have had enough talk about bloodthirsty wolves."

Trying to calm her ratcheting heartbeat, Sophia focused her gaze everywhere else but him. "Why are we here?"

"To have a celebratory drink, why else?" He made a show of glancing at his watch, as if he hadn't timed all this with precision. "We have been successfully married for a whole morning."

That was when Sophia noticed the ice bucket with a champagne bottle and next to the bucket, in a cardboard box with a little bow that looked very familiar and dear to her heart, chocolate truffles.

He was seducing her; another warning from that increasingly annoying voice.

She groaned, her mouth already watering as she imagined the dark, rich taste on her mouth. Other disturbing sensations floated beneath. She had told him once that she would sell her soul for truffles.

Countless women he'd seduced and countless little nothings they would have whispered in his ears, flushed from the good sex he gave...did he remember all those details? she wanted to ask. "Keep those away from me, Luca. They are the very devil for my diet."

His mouth pursed tight, as if he was trying to stop himself from bursting into laughter. Which in turn animated the rest of his face.

Mouthwatering chocolate, knee-melting Luca and she— locked behind a closed door.

Ignoring her plea, he tugged her toward him and raised a truffle to her mouth. "A wedding like ours, that sets at least some things to right, deserves a little celebration, *si*?"

Caught in the startlingly deep conviction in his words, his gaze intent on her mouth, Sophia licked her lips.

He groaned then, a deep, husky sound that pinged

through her, leaving pockets of heat all over. "Open up, *cara mia*."

The taste of that melting chocolate exploded on her tongue. A moan she couldn't stop escaped her throat, while his fingers lingered on her lips. Pressed at the soft cushion of her lower lip.

His gaze was hot, hungry. His mouth even hotter as he bent and swiped at her lower lip. A jolt of pleasure traveled through her, so acute that Sophia jerked.

Sinewed arms came around her, pulling her closer. The muscles in his arms clenched under her questing fingers. Air became short in supply. And what was there was coated with the scent of him. She felt dizzy, like she was high. On him.

She licked her lips again.

He bent and dug his teeth into her lower lip. And then stroked the nip with his tongue. Liquid heat rushed between Sophia's legs. His fingers tightened over her hips. "You lick your lips like that, I will think it a call to action."

She tried to wiggle out of his hold. Only managing to press herself tighter against him. "I'm not doing it on purpose."

"I know."

His chest pushed against her breasts. Muscle and sinew, he was rock hard everywhere she touched. What the hell did the man do to have a body like that? With his lazy lifestyle, he should have had a paunch. At least a small belly. Not this washboard abdomen that she wanted to touch and lick and scrape with her teeth.

But she didn't want to let go of him. Not just yet, she promised herself. She didn't want to give up this intimacy with him. This easy familiarity that they were slipping into. The laughter they shared. The way he made her see things about herself she didn't know. She hadn't realized how deprived she'd been of this kind of companionship, how monotonous her life had become.

Maybe there were other advantages to this short marriage of theirs. The zing in her blood, the ache between her thighs, begged her to consider them. She traced the shadows under his eyes, something she'd always wanted to do. "Do you not sleep at all?"

He held her wrist and pressed his face into her hand. Leaned into her touch as if he needed it. Breath whispering like a whistle, Sophia traced the sharp angles of his face. The pad of her forefinger reached his mouth. That mouth, God, that mouth... She had such hot dreams about it.

With no warning, he turned his head, opened his mouth and closed it over her finger. And then sucked it. A hungry, stringent pulse began at her sex, in tune with the pulls of his mouth.

Her skin felt too tight to hold her. The silk of her panties was wet. Rubbed against her inner thighs as she shifted restlessly.

He released her finger. Sophia clenched her thighs closed instinctually, needing friction there.

A dark flush dusted his cheekbones. He knew, oh, God, he knew. He knew where she was burning to be touched. "I'm an insomniac."

It took her several long seconds to realize he was answering her question.

He was an insomniac? "How bad is it?"

"I sleep a few hours every few days."

"That's it? I need at least eight hours every day to feel remotely human. Doesn't that have side effects?"

"It does. But I have learned to live with them."

It made him more three dimensional, more...human. As strange as that sounded. "What do you do, then? In all that time?"

Fingers busily shifted the collar of her dress. His mouth landed on the skin he bared. His tongue licked that juncture, sending hot shafts of pleasure down her spine. "Do you taste like silk all over, Sophia?"

"Yes," she said, completely lost in the magic he wove. She tried to recall some warning, some common sense as to why she shouldn't be in his arms, pressed up snugly against him. With him sucking on random parts of her.

Zilch. Nada. Nothing came up.

Then the diamond on her ring finger glinted, a twinkling ray of common sense. She ordered her body to stiffen, to move away, but it had different ideas. "We can't be doing this. We can't… If you gave me that power over your stock thinking that will make me grateful, thinking I'll happily—"

"Spread your legs and take me inside you?" He was the one who pulled back. "You really think I'd have to pay for sex? I'm not sure who it reflects badly on that you think that, you or me. Or have you truly become as cynical as they call you?"

He castigated her so softly and yet Sophia felt his words like tiny pricks. "Then why?"

In response, he dipped his mouth and took hers again. This kiss was not an invitation or a tease. It was full-on assault, demanding surrender. Almost brutally efficient in the way he slowly but surely made her into a mass of shuddering sensation.

She'd made him angry, Sophia realized beneath the avalanche of sensations. His tongue laved the interior of her mouth, while his hands moved up and down her body, inciting her into a frenzy.

Expert strokes, here and there, perfect pressure, a master of seduction at work. A routine.

His heart wasn't in it. He was seducing her with technique and experience. He was proving a point. She could be a tall, blonde model for all that it mattered to him.

The difference, even as heat drenched her, sent bile up her throat.

"No, Luca, please." She sank her hands into his hair and tugged his face down. "That was moronic. What I said," she finally whispered, her hands molding and tracing the line of his shoulders. "I…have never been able to believe that someone like you could want someone like me."

She didn't want to mention the bet again. It was in the past. But she saw his understanding of it, saw those same shutters come down.

He sighed and instantly gentled. A devil so easily calmed with honesty? A man whose feelings could hurt under that almost impenetrable mask he wore? She wasn't so sure anymore that she knew him.

Across her temple, then over her nose, and then her jaw, he placed soft kisses. "I kiss you because you're thoroughly kissable, Sophia. I kiss you because I can't bear the thought of those lush lips not quivering under mine, of that stout will not surrendering to me. I kiss you because I want to hear that sigh you release when you realize this fire between us is too hot to fight. I kiss you for that moment when your shoulders lose that stiff line, when you melt into willing softness. I kiss you for that moment when you make that little growly sound in the back of your throat, as though you've just realized that you've been a passive spectator. I kiss you because then you take over the kiss, you forget why you should resist me and you devour me as if I was your favorite dessert in the world."

He whispered the last words against her mouth. As if he was infusing her very blood with those tender words.

She sighed.

Then she groaned.

Then she kissed him back with a ravenous hunger. All things he'd predicted. He knew her so well, even in this... It was a faint warning at the back of her mind that dissolved under the influx of such delirious pleasure.

His lush mouth delivered on the fantasies it promised. Hard and soft, sometimes masculine demand, sometimes a tender entreaty.

Vining her arms around his nape, she stretched to reach more of him. He was right; she hated being a spectator. One hard thigh pushed in between her legs, but didn't quite hit the spot.

When she shifted, one hand landed on her thigh, pushed up her dress and then pulled her leg up and around his buttocks.

His thigh moved even farther between her legs. And up. Right against the hungry core of her.

Shamelessly, Sophia clenched her thighs and then moved on his leg, back and forth. Up and down. Pleasure spiraled through her pelvis, building to an unbearable rhythm.

Teeth banged, tongues sucked. Clasping his jaw with her hands, she held him for her delectation. Then she dug her teeth into that carnal lower lip, hard, and sucked it into her mouth.

A growl rumbled from his chest. A wild beat danced in her blood as she realized something had changed between them. Tension radiated from his lean frame. His fingers became more urgent, his mouth harder and hotter.

Playtime was over.

His fingers crawled into her hair, tugged at the clip she'd used to pull it back into a tight knot. The clatter of the clip against the wall where he threw it was a bang in the hoarse silence. Fingers pulled and plumped her hair until it fell in unruly waves around her face.

She forgot what she'd meant to ask him. She forgot what had disconcerted her so much about the scene in the conference room. She forgot why she shouldn't kiss him like this. Only sensation mattered. Only the heat building inside her mattered.

He moved his thigh away and she whimpered. She'd melt into a puddle if he didn't hold her up. Her mouth was stinging, her blood singing; Sophia was so aroused she was ready to beg him to finish it.

He lifted her leg again, pushing away at the ugly dress. Up and up. Until the lace of her garters was visible and then a strip of her thighs. "Sophia." He was panting against her cheek. "This is where you put a stop to it if you don't want to be bent over that table and have me thrusting inside you in three seconds."

Reality came crashing with that crudely worded statement. He'd put it like that on purpose. She growled, a demand and a plea twisted in that animal sound. He laughed, took her mouth with his again.

She jerked away from him, stumbled on jelly-like legs and then reached for him again to steady herself. "No," she said, running a hand over her mouth.

All she wanted was to cry. Her mind felt soaked in desire, frustration. "God, I came looking for you because I wanted to talk." His pupils were dilated, his chest still falling and rising. But he didn't look the least bit put out for being denied the same satisfaction. "I didn't mean to hump you like a dog in heat. You're not angry?"

"I'm in considerable pain, yes…" He sighed "I'm not angry. I know you'd like to believe the worst about me but I do have a little self-control."

"Oh, is there anything I can do to—"

"You can fix your dress and stop offering to help. Next time you offer, I'll ask you to go down on your knees."

O went her mouth again. An instant image fluttered through her brain. Did he ask it of all his lovers? Did they do it because they didn't want to lose his interest?

Personally, Sophia had always thought the act a little subjugating, undignified and maybe even a little painful to the participating woman's mouth. "Do you ask it of all your lovers or—"

"Stop talking, Sophia," he growled again.

Sophia dashed into the attached bathroom. She splashed water over her heated cheeks. His fingers had built her hair into a cloud around her face. She looked soft and feminine and like a woman who lost her mind after two kisses.

Damn it, she had the most important meeting of her life in a few minutes and here she was, climbing all over Luca. He was like her craving for that chocolate truffle. A bad habit she thought she'd beat only to succumb again and again.

He'd suggested she fall. And she was falling gloriously. She thought herself above all those women who threw themselves at him. How bitchily righteous she'd been... If anything, she was even more foolish because she'd already had a taste of him ten years ago.

She'd thought herself beautiful, special to have attracted his attention. And it had been nothing but a bet. "Maybe deprivation will build a little character," she said, coming out of the bathroom.

Could she sound any more naively hopeful, any more sanctimoniously righteous? She couldn't, *absolutely* couldn't care if he satisfied himself with another woman that night.

He was scowling. "We're both consenting adults and have been joined in the holiest of bonds in front of God and man just this morning. You're making us both walk

back out like horny dogs. You have enough character, don't
you think?"

He sounded so pained, so disgruntled, that Sophia burst
out laughing.

It was easy, far too easy, to be mesmerized by Luca's
easy charm. As long as she remembered that there was
nothing of substance beneath. "I scheduled a meeting with
you and Leandro in an hour."

"Your plans for Rossi Leather are ready for Leandro?"

She nodded, barely bracing herself against the admiration in his eyes. "I want to run them by you and Leandro
first before I present them to Salvatore. That way, we're
all in the loop."

How was it that with of all the men she'd dealt with—
CEOs and ruthless businessmen and millionaires—it was
this wastrel playboy that was never intimidated by her?
Who only showed respect for her accomplishments and
her ambition.

Could that easy confidence come from just his looks?
Or was there more to Luca than met the eye?

He uncorked the champagne bottle and poured it into
two flutes. Handing her one, he clinked his against hers.
The bubbles kissed her throat on the way down. She
looked up to find his gaze on her. Rattled by the line of
her thoughts, she said nothing.

They talked of a varied range of topics, sometimes
agreeing and more than once, getting into a heated argument. Only when her watch pinged did Sophia realize how
invigorating and informative their discussion had been.

And how enjoyable.

Throughout the meeting with Leandro and Luca, all
Sophia could think of was how jarringly discordant, how
disconcertingly different this side of Luca was from the
man she'd despised for so long.

CHAPTER SIX

THE LAST THING Sophia wanted, after the events of the last week, was a party.

A party thrown specially in honor of Luca and her.

A party to which every member of the high society of Milan was invited, including men who'd known of her humiliation ten years ago.

A party thrown by her in-laws, the Conti family, which was a minefield of dysfunction—her family seemed so normal even with her differences with Salvatore—she couldn't imagine navigating without setting off an explosion.

The last she'd seen of Luca had been outside the Conti building, six days ago. He'd called a taxi for her after her meeting with Leandro and him and then driven off. The invite for the party came later that night, in the form of a phone call from Leandro's wife, Alexis, her new sister-in-law.

When she'd moaned about attending, Salvatore had warned her that she couldn't alienate her husband's family. *Her new family*, in fact.

To which, she had, quite forcefully and uncharacteristically, asked him if he was that happy to be rid of her. Only silence had remained then. Full of guilt and shame, Sophia had apologized to him and left.

She'd never confronted Salvatore like that. There had never been any need. Since he had married her mother, he'd been kindness itself to her. He'd paid for her to go to University, given her a job at Rossi Leather, provided her with everything she could have ever asked for.

The only thing he didn't give her was his trust when it came to business matters. Could she blame him when it was a one-hundred-and-sixty-year-old legacy that he wanted to protect for her brothers? Maybe asking for him to take such a big risk on her, when she'd never really excelled at the things he wanted of her, was too much?

Maybe things would have been different if she'd been born a Rossi.

At least, she had done the right thing in marrying Luca. Salvatore was delighted that finally he had a connection to the venerable Contis.

Sophia had come to Villa de Conti straight from work that evening, and had been shown into Luca's suite by a smiling Alexis. Aware that she'd wanted to chat, Sophia had claimed a headache and rushed in for a bath.

After her shower, Sophia put on a silk wrapper and stepped out into the bedroom. Her impulse purchases lay in chic, expensive bags on the bed, having left a hole the size of a crater in her bank account. Designer heels lay in another box.

The glittering bags mocked her. She flopped to the bed, feeling foolish now for splurging—when the devil hadn't even answered her texts. *Again.* Was he going to show up tonight?

She'd just rubbed lotion in and put her underwear on when the door opened quite rudely. Cursing, Sophia grabbed her towel just as Valentina, of all people, came into view.

Spine rigid, Sophia preempted the tall beauty, who looked stunning in a long black evening dress. "I'm far too nervous already, so please, Valentina, no theatrics right now."

The younger woman had the grace to look ashamed. "I came to apologize, Sophia." When Sophia remained stubbornly silent, Valentina changed tack. "My brother sent me to see if you wanted help."

"Thank Leandro, but I'm good."

"*Non*, Luca sent me."

The towel slipped from Sophia's hands. "Luca is here? Downstairs?" Her breath ballooned up in her chest.

"*Si.*"

He hadn't deserted her. Just for this evening, Sophia needed him by her side. After tonight, after getting through facing the society that she'd never belonged in, she wouldn't need him again.

"You thought he would not come?"

Curiosity filled Valentina's question. The last thing Sophia wanted was the Contis or anyone else for that matter, to know how little familiarity she had with Luca's lifestyle. "I'm nervous because I know everyone's eyes will be on me and I don't handle attention well."

Valentina's gaze swept over her almost clinically, assessing, and Sophia tugged the towel toward her. "You are hot, Sophia, why do you hide it?"

The question was so matter of fact that Sophia forgot that she was supposed to be angry with Valentina. "Did he ask you to be kind to me?"

"*Non*, I'm not being kind. He did tell me to stop being bitchy to you." The woman didn't mince her words and Sophia was beginning to like her. "You have breasts I would kill for." To punctuate it, she looked pointedly at Sophia's breasts, contained dangerously in a pink bra and then at her own relatively smaller ones, which wasn't saying much because everyone had smaller breasts than Sophia's.

And then Valentina sighed.

Sophia half groaned, half choked.

"I developed very late and even then, they were like apples. Yours are more like…" Sophia wanted to crawl under the bed sheets. "Small melons."

"Please, Tina…stop!" Sophia rubbed her fingers over her forehead, shook her head and then let the laugh building in her chest escape. Tears filled her eyes, her nose, she was sure, was running and her throat and lungs burned. "Oh, how we torture ourselves…I've always been so jealous of your model-like figure, your style and grace. You're like a gazelle, whereas I…waddle like a penguin. Your sense of fashion is…just wow."

Warmth entered Valentina's eyes, transforming her entire visage. "Sense of style and fashion can be…acquired, *si*? But not curves. Unless I go for those silicone implants. But I don't think Kairos will like artificial boobs and there is already too much he…" Stricken black eyes shied away from Sophia's. "I know now that Kairos and you are just friends."

"You confronted Kairos?"

"*Si*. He was angry that I struck you. *But*… I had no business acting like a bitch to you. Not when the problem is between us." Misery radiated from her. "Will you forgive me, Sophia?"

Sophia smiled. "If you help me, yes. Since you're a fashionista who Milan looks up to, can you advise me? I bought three dresses. I don't want them to see a wobbly penguin paired with a strutting peacock. I want to look back on tonight and not cringe." There were far too many cringe-worthy episodes already in her life.

Valentina burst out laughing. "My brother is a peacock?"

Sophia nodded. With a brisk efficiency, Valentina ve-
toed all three dresses in two minutes flat.

"The saleswoman assured me that they are the height
of—"

"*Si*, but she followed your direction to cover up every
inch of skin. What is in the last bag?"

"That one…I picked that one. But it's going straight
back to the shop. I don't know what I was thinking."

Valentina floated through the room, picked up the last
bag on the bed. The knee-length turquoise silk slithered
out in a silken whisper. "This dress is perfect."

Alarm rattled through Sophia. "That was a foolish purchase. It is strapless and too snug and my *melons* will
surely pop out and then—"

"What are you so scared of, Sophia? That people will realize you're beautiful under the hideous clothes you wear?"

"Hey! They're not hideous and—"

"Fine, look like a penguin, then. There will be at least
three women downstairs who have, at some time, been
linked with Luca."

Sophia gasped. "Oh…you play dirty."

No way was she going to be shown up by Luca's willowy exes. Tonight might be a farce, but *she* was going to
be the heroine of the farce.

A thousand butterflies flying in her stomach, she let
Tina do her hair, even her makeup. When Tina pronounced
her ready, she faced the floor-length mirror. Her breath
halted in her throat.

The low cut of the bodice showed the upper curves of
her breasts. Simple beadwork on the bodice caught the light
with every breath she took. The hem of the dress kissed
her knees just so, baring her legs. She turned her foot and
looked at her legs. She did have sexy legs.

The woman in her, the part she tried to hide and ignore

and forget, preened that she looked good in it. Nothing was going to make her tall, elegant or graceful but that was okay. She would continue her diets, grumble about never being svelte but she would also enjoy what she was. No more hiding, as if she was ashamed of herself.

Rub their noses in it...

Her hair, air dried during her chat with Tina, fell in dark waves, softening the strong planes of her face.

Bright red lipstick, brighter than Tina's, made her mouth look scandalously seductive. Like her red lips could somehow balance the rest of her features that she'd told herself were far too stubborn for a woman. "This is too red. It will make everyone look at my mouth—"

"You married the Conti Devil. Of course they will look at you. Why not give them something gorgeous?" She looked Sophia up and down with a strange glitter. "How like my artistic brother to see what you so carefully hide, to see what no one else could."

A cold shiver snaked up Sophia's spine. "Luca is artistic?"

It was Tina's turn to look surprised. "Luca is a lot of things that I can't even keep track of. He works for CLG only to please Leandro. He has a personal..." She threw Sophia a startled glance. "Leandro even calls him our very own mad genius. Apparently, Luca's musical talents have no comparison."

"In a fond, useless sort of way, right?" Sophia asked, her heart thundering in her ears. "He lives off his brother and his family's fortune and dabbles in music, surrounds himself in beautiful things, that kind of artist?"

Her nose high up in the air, Valentina flayed her with her gaze. "That indulgent playboy thing he does—that's only one side of him. Your marriage to Luca, I know that it's an agreement for a few months. That he lets you use him in them. But still you should know that—"

"I'm not using him as much as we're using each other," Sophia interrupted, in prickly defense. Of course, the devil would try to come off as her savior in his account of their deal.

"Luca is not all he seems, Sophia."

Luca works at CLG, just to please Leandro.

Luca is artistic.

Luca was turning out to be more complex than any man she knew.

Sophia halted on the top of the stairs, trying to corral the panic spearing her belly. She tried to let very little in life unsettle her—in that way, she and Luca were alike, although with him, she supposed it was easier, more his natural state.

At least, that's what she'd assumed.

Even taking a couple of deep breaths didn't calm the furor in her veins. She couldn't get a grip on why it mattered this much.

All she knew was that she needed him to be what she and the entire world though him to be. A wastrel, a playboy. A man who cared for nothing and no one.

She appeared at the top of the curving marble staircase like a beautiful thought from his mind come to life. Luca felt a pressure on his chest, as if there was weight there, making it harder to pull a breath. He'd known, and guessed, she would be a revelation.

Oh, but what a revelation she was…

He heard the stunned whispers behind him, like a gathering wave rushing toward the shore.

The gasps, the *bellissimas*, the frantic reassessment of a woman they had all been duped into not seeing. Joy sang through his veins. The same he felt when he finished a piece of music or when he manipulated stock numbers into a pattern, into making sense. Like seeing a piece of art, unfinished and raw, come to life.

His joy in her was possessive and primitive. Suddenly, he didn't want anyone else to see her like this. He didn't want the whole world to see and covet this beautiful creature.

She was his, at least for now. He wasn't arrogant enough to think he'd created her but he'd discovered her, hadn't he? He alone had seen what Sophia was beneath that prickly nature and tough attitude. And tonight, she was a true reflection of the woman beneath—soft and yet formidably beautiful.

He wanted to pick her up, throw her over his shoulder, carry her away to his studio and lock the world away. He wanted to bury himself deep in her, until neither of them could breathe, until he was rid of this obsession with her. Until her mind, body and spirit, they were all only his.

He'd never chased a woman before. They all came to him. That he was chasing a woman who was determined to not be caught by him was perfect irony.

The bold, sensual lines of her body were a feast. The upper curves of her breasts swelled over the strapless bodice, beckoning to be savored. The silk followed the dip of her waist and the flare of her hips, lovingly touching everything he wanted to.

Their eyes met and the world floated away.

Her brown gaze raked over his face, lingering, assessing, almost frantic in its search. A clamor began in his veins as he stood at the foot of the steps and she took each step down.

Shards of light from the crystal chandelier caught at the

white beads on her dress. And glinting brown eyes. They didn't look average or dull right then.

They glinted with a fierce intention.

She looked at him as if…she wanted to peel off all the layers he covered himself in and reach inside the core of him. A shiver traveled down his spine.

As though she'd somehow bypassed the surface sheen of him—his looks, his charm. As though she hungered to know more.

But he couldn't reveal himself to her. He couldn't show the dirty truth of his birth, couldn't show her the devouring hunger for something more than he was allowed to have. Only then would this work. And he was so lust-riddled for her that Luca would have taken even a morsel of Sophia.

By the time she reached the last step, he'd calmed himself down. His practiced smile curved his mouth.

She raised a well-defined brow, all haughty arrogance.

He imagined that was how she commanded her team at work. One raised brow and one blistering remark from Sophia would probably send the staunchest soul scrambling to do her bidding. She wielded it with the same skill now, he thought, as if to start the evening with swords drawn.

All it made him want to do was kiss that brow. And probably her temple. Then that stubborn bridge of her nose. That lush, carnal mouth. Then he would bite, none too gently, on that defiant chin.

A line of fire swept along his nerves at the delicious path he could trace down her glorious skin. Very soon, he promised himself. Very soon he'd have her all rumpled and flushed beneath him, screaming his name. Only he would unravel all that strength she wore like armor. Only he would know the soft, vulnerable woman beneath.

He could have had her that day at the CLG offices but

he didn't want to see her regrets later. He wanted Sophia present and pleasantly ravished when he was through with her. "You look biteable, *cara mia*."

She looked startled at the compliment, looked away then back at him. Had he done this to her? Luca wondered for the millionth time. Had he shattered her confidence so badly?

"Nothing to say, Sophia?" he prompted softly.

"You disappeared for six days, three hours after we were married." Accusation punctured every word. "Even for the short-term agreement that our marriage is—" She bent toward him, her voice lowered to a husky whisper, for she was flushed with awareness. "You can't just rush me into a taxi and walk away. I ate a ton of chocolate and probably gained three pounds in three days. Do you know how many questions I've faced just from my family alone? Salvatore is desperate for your plans for Rossi's."

"But they are your plans."

"Yes, but he doesn't know that." She slowed down her words as if he was a bit slow in the head. Luca had never had so much fun just talking to a woman. "I told him Leandro and you are finalizing them. Damn it, Luca, there has to be some accountability even in this sham. We didn't even talk about where we'd live."

Her whisper caressed his jaw; the honeysuckle scent of her wafted over his nostrils, tightening every muscle and sinew. Acres of glowing skin taunted him. He shrugged, struggling to get a grip on the desire riding him. Hard. "I've never been a husband before, so you have to forgive me. I will check in with you every night at eight. *Si?*"

She sighed, and that made her glorious breasts rise and fall. "Wonderful. Now I feel like your parole officer."

"Will you put me in handcuffs if I violate my conditions, then?" he offered and saw her swallow visibly. "I could not give up control like that for any other woman, *bella*."

Desire shone in her enlarged pupils, a song sung by her hurried breaths. She licked her lower lip, took it in between her teeth, flushed and then pursed it into a thin line. As if she could hide her mouth.

Three hundred people waited for them and he was painfully hard.

Dio, when had lust ever taken control of him like this? Six days and nights he'd spent cooped up in his studio, and he'd still not gotten it under control.

He didn't like needing her so much. He didn't trust himself in this state for he'd never been in such before. He intended to ravish her out of her senses, not lose his own.

"If anyone asks," she said, coming to stand by him, "and by that I mean my mother, we aren't doing a honeymoon because I'm super busy. And you, too."

A tiny sneer curled her mouth every time she talked about his "work." Or lack of it, to be precise. It made him want to pull that snobby upper lip into his mouth and suck on it. He would do it, too.

He was going to need a little notepad to jot down all the numerous things he wanted to do to her. Suddenly, three months felt like a very short time in which to indulge his darkest fantasies with her, to drive her from his blood, once and for all. Especially because the woman was an obvious workaholic.

Urgency laced with his desire now and he ran a brave finger down her jaw. She swatted him away, like he was a fly. "You want her to believe this is a love match."

"Of course I do."

He nodded. "It'll probably break her heart to see her daughter doesn't have a romantic bone in her body."

She rolled her eyes. "Her daughter can't afford a romantic bone. Anyway, we steal all kinds of time during the day to see each other and get up to all kinds of..."

He raised his brows and waggled them. Warmth tinted her cheeks, the brown of her eyes gleaming bronze. Oh, she wanted him, all right.

"Afternoon sex—how delightfully imaginative, Sophia."

"I had to say something when she burst into my bedroom and demanded to know why I wasn't with my beloved husband on my wedding night."

"Why do you live with your parents? Doesn't that curb your nightly...activities?"

"I don't have any nightly..." She clamped her mouth tight, her face flushed. "I...work a lot of late nights and I like to keep track of what's going on with Sal and the company... It's just easier that way."

Again, a pang stole through Luca. Had he so thoroughly crushed her heart that she had no romantic notions left like any other woman?

"I do regret not spending our wedding night with you. Did you wait for me to spirit you away?"

She flushed and it lit a fire inside him. "You're absolutely cuckoo. I can't stay with my parents anymore. Not if I want to have some peace to work in the evenings."

"So move into Villa de Conti. Into my room. Alex and Leandro don't stay here all the time. Neither will I distract you, except when I feel like it. But—"

She hissed. The woman hissed at him. "Where were you? And why do you never answer a single call or a text?"

Luca raised a brow. No one ever asked him where he went and when he came back. Not even Leandro, after he had reassured himself that Luca wasn't going to self-destruct. The novelty of it was amusing and a little disconcerting.

"Here and there," he said, tucking her arm through his. "I can take society only in small doses." Which was more truth than he'd ever confided in anyone. "After the drama in the conference room that day, I needed time to recoup."

"Time to recoup?" she repeated, but with more consideration and less belligerent disbelief this time. Like she was thinking far too much again.

Dio, the woman really needed less thinking, worrying and planning and more ravishing in her life. A good thing he was so committed to it.

"*Si*. But now I'm ready to be your adoring husband." He smiled then and brought her to the huge ballroom.

He frowned as the music filtered through him.

A string quartet was playing. There was dynamics, articulation, wonderful fluctuation to the tempo but no soul to the music, no risk-taking except perfectly executed sharps and flats.

The lifelessness of it jarred through his head. A near compulsion ran in his veins to either yell for the music to stop or to stalk out of the room.

"Luca?" Sophia prompted.

Neither option was feasible, though.

Pasting on his megawatt smile—the one that had once driven a tempestuous young woman to avow love to him in the midst of her own engagement party—Luca turned to her. "Yes, *bella mia*?"

Light brown eyes studied him like he was a fly under a microscope.

Not the effect he intended in that perceptive face. Not even that endearing snort or roll of her eyes. "The music, you don't like it?"

Pure panic bolted through Luca for a second. As if every facade he had built over the years was being ripped away, leaving him utterly stripped of his armor. To face who he was, what he was capable of, in front of the whole world and see the horror he'd seen in his mother's eyes. He couldn't bear that look in Sophia's eyes. "Do you know what is happening with Kairos and Tina?"

"No," she said with an arched look that told him she saw through the ploy. It was becoming harder to pretend with her. Like his mask was slowly but surely cracking, giving her glimpses of him. "We spoke briefly, though."

She offered that tidbit reluctantly as if Kairos needed her protection. From Luca. She gave so much of herself to just a friend. "What did your friend say?" he asked casually, swallowing away the jealousy her friendship with another man aroused.

"That he'll be waiting to offer his support as a friend *when you leave me in pieces*, to quote him. I think Tina is causing major ripples in his life."

The goodwill he heard in her tone for his sister warmed Luca's heart. It confirmed his growing belief that Sophia had only ever wanted Kairos's friendship. "Why do you assume that?"

"Because he said 'We should have never gone near those *Contis*' in a pained voice before he hung up."

Luca laughed. "Good for Tina," he whispered in Sophia's ear and pulled her onto the dance floor.

CHAPTER SEVEN

TONIGHT, SOPHIA DECIDED, as she tried to not search the huge ballroom for Luca like a desperate, clingy wife, she could be a deer. Never a gazelle or a swan, but at least not a penguin—and unlike the last Conti party she attended, this time she was not a skunk.

She also, quite uncharacteristically, decided to put away all the things Valentina had said about Luca into her newly commissioned cupboard in her head. Tonight she wouldn't worry, plan, obsess, hide or hate. Tonight she would take a leaf out of her playboy husband's colorful book and enjoy herself. She'd dance, drink and flirt with Luca, even. Maybe.

It was without doubt the best evening of Sophia's life. Suddenly, it seemed, all of society, the same people that had always looked on her with begrudgingly given kindness wanted to talk to her, invited her to posh luncheons and generally wanted to figure out how she'd corralled the Conti Devil.

Even knowing that Luca had been with half the women there, Sophia met a few women whom she'd love to get to know more. It was as if by lowering her own walls, she could see the others clearer, too.

And with a haunting clarity, she realized how right Luca was. She'd always been different in this strata of society, which in turn had made her defensive. Thirteen, unpolished but streetwise, she hadn't trusted that Salvatore wouldn't change his mind about keeping her; she'd decided from the first moment that she didn't belong there. Instead of risking rejection, she'd built a wall between her true self and everyone else. And then that episode of the bet had given her even more reason to hate them all. A shield, she realized now.

She danced with Luca, who was, of course, a graceful, slick dancer, then with Leandro, who to her surprise, told her she was welcome to come to him for any matter regarding the CLG board. Almost as if he'd been warned by his brother to not offend her.

Kairos was away on a business trip, thankfully.

Then there was Antonio, whom she'd avoided all evening. Sheer cowardice? Yes, but Sophia didn't want him to ruin her perfect evening.

Luca heard the snick of the door behind him and sighed. He'd come into Leandro's study, looking for the legal papers he'd asked Leandro's lawyer to draw up.

Without turning, he knew who it was. He'd been waiting for this confrontation all week. Dreading it. Loathing it.

For his grandfather was quite adept at turning Luca back into that needy, emotional boy he'd been during those hard years. Unable to manage his headaches and his restlessness, unable to sleep.

Cowardly as it had been, hiding out in his studio for a week had an added advantage to it. Antonio never ventured there. For one thing, Leandro had decreed long ago that it was Luca's space—sacred and safe and inviolate. For another, the studio was evidence that Luca had inherited more than just his father's good looks.

Antonio preferred to believe the Contis were invulnerable to anything from simple mood swings to brilliance-induced madness. Even after Enzo's life proved otherwise.

"You cannot give Sophia power over CLG stock or your seat on the board."

"I already have," Luca retorted. So there was at least no pretension to niceties to be had. He grinned; riling up Antonio was a task he'd enjoyed immensely even as an innocent child. "You have hounded us for years to marry. You even picked her as the perfect Conti bride. For the first time in my life, I agree with you. Sophia is perfection."

"You do this now only to mess with all of us."

Trust Antonio to know Luca as well as he did. "Sophia is my wife and has my best interests at heart."

Antonio scowled.

The thought that riled Antonio more than Sophia sitting on the board was a bastard, self-made man like Kairos taking his place at the head.

"Let her be your proxy. That controlling stock of Contis should lie within the family members."

Luca shook his head. "This fixation you have about the glorious Contis needs to be contained, *Nonno*. Haven't you done enough damage in the name of it?"

His grandfather flinched, backed a step as if Luca would attack him physically. Provoked as he'd been, Luca had never done that.

"All I ever did was to make sure your father didn't ruin our family name."

His head jerking up, Luca watched, stunned. Antonio had never offered a defense before. "You knew your son better than anyone. You hushed up so many little things he'd been doing all his life. You should have seen what he was becoming. You should have protected her..." He turned away, breathing roughly, mustering his emotions under control.

"You accept Sophia or you don't." He shrugged. "I've no problem cutting you out of my life, unlike your dutiful grandson Leandro. But she will continue on the Conti board even if I have to legally give her all my stock."

Rage filled Antonio's eyes. "She...married you because I suggested it."

"What the hell are you talking about?"

"Your affairs, your reckless disregard for our name... I was desperate. So I went to her. I thought she was the one woman who could handle you. I offered her a fortune if she brought you to the altar."

Luca smiled easily, more amused than affronted by Antonio's revelation.

Sophia had never hidden the fact that she'd do anything for her family. *Dio*, he knew with a faintly increasing alarm that half his attraction to her was based on that. It was her beauty, inside and out, that enthralled him.

He wanted Sophia untouched by the dirt in his family, away from the unrelenting grasp for power, the manipulations.

He wanted her to be only his, in his moments of light, separate from the dark, self-loathing part of him. But he'd not only brought her into it, he'd made her two powerful enemies already—Kairos and Antonio.

"You give her even a single share of Conti stock and I assure you, you will never see any of it back ever again. She might not be Salvatore's blood but she is as grasping as he is."

Luca couldn't care less, if he tried, about what Sophia would take from him. "Go to hell, *Nonno*. And say hi to your son while you're there."

"I did not offer her up, your mother, like a sacrificial lamb to him, knowing what he was." Luca stopped at the door, knuckles tightening on the knob. Antonio, for the first time in his life, sounded old. Frail. "He married her in secret, just like you did Sophia. He could be even more charming than you, when it pleased him. He claimed he was in love and I allowed it. I thought she would bring balance to his life…calm him. He was happy enough for a while. Your mother… *She married him*, Luca, of her own free will."

It had just struck eleven when Sophia realized she hadn't seen Luca's prowling gait in the ballroom for over an hour. The party was in full swing, champagne was flowing, couples still dancing.

Now she wondered if he'd disappeared. Again.

Apparently, Luca was like a mirage, present for as long as it took to entice and lure. Only to disappear the second you got close.

She had drunk three glasses of champagne with Valentina and her friends. Imagining the calories in three drinks, she'd delicately munched on glazed carrots and fruit from the scrumptious buffet.

The result was that she was mildly buzzed. She walked the perimeter of the huge ballroom, smiling and nodding at people she didn't even know. A woman pointed through the corridor with a perfectly manicured finger and a malicious smile.

Sophia's buzz evaporated as if someone had siphoned off the alcohol from her brain. Strains of husky laughter, of the female variety, greeted her from one open door. Luca's deep tones followed the husky laughter.

Ice slithered through her veins, rooting her there.

Run, run, run. Her brain issued flight responses as if the threat was fatal.

One breath and then another, Sophia forced herself to concentrate on just that. No, it was only her pride that chafed, she reminded herself. It was only sheer disbelief at the man's utter lack of decency. Her heart was stout and uninvolved.

They had no claim on each other, true. He hadn't promised her fidelity, this time or the last. But he wasn't going to show her up as a fool again.

One evening, *Dear Lord*, one evening was all he'd given her and already…he was smarting at the reins? She hadn't even demanded much of him.

She marched into the room, somehow managing to not fall on her face in four-inch heels.

The room was another lounge offering a view of Lake Como. It seemed there was an endless quantity of those at Villa de Conti but not enough distance from his family for Luca. Another fact she'd gleaned tonight. He'd happily offered her a place here because he never was here.

Was there anyone or anything Luca didn't need escape from?

A piano was the focal point of the room and on the bench, with his fingers desultorily playing with the ivory keys, was Luca. A stylish, contemporary chandelier threw patches of light onto his sharp profile.

The notes, though played slowly and haltingly, made up a haunting tune that plucked at Sophia's nerves. At some heretofore unknown place that had become arid from neglect.

A stick-thin blonde sat on his left on the bench, her silk-clad thigh flush against his, leaning over him to reach the keys. Which, from Sophia's angle, clearly showed her lemon-sized boobs—*thank you, Valentina, for that*—rubbing against his upper arm.

Luca stilled, all sleek and wiry strength, but Sophia didn't wait to see if it was in anticipation or in defense. *She'd had enough!*

Refusing to give in to the urge to run and grab the

blonde by her hair, which would give credence to her reputation as a shrew, she walked, sedately, toward the couple so seemingly immersed in each other that they didn't notice her.

"Please take your paws off my husband," she said with a sweet smile that hurt her cheeks. "Also, get out of our house."

The blonde had the grace to look ashamed at being caught out. Sophia fisted her hands, fighting the urge for violence. If *lemon-boobs* so much as smiled at Luca, she was going to lose it.

But the woman, perhaps sensing that Sophia meant business, stood up, slid out with a sort of gliding grace— *another damn swan*—and left the room.

Sophia counted to ten, went to the door, closed it and then leaned against it. Wrenching herself under control. Seeing the stick-thin woman sidling up to Luca… It ripped away her own self-delusions. Her pathetic reassurances.

God, when had she begun lying to herself?

When had she started believing that she was the Sophia that the world saw? How had she believed she could resist this man?

How had she convinced herself that she could take him on and come out unscathed at the end of these three months?

After his talk with Antonio—somehow, his grandfather managed to sink under Luca's skin every time, like an eternal monument to the darker aspect of his life—Luca had felt an overwhelming need to disappear. Antonio had known what his revelation, about Enzo falling in love with his mother, would do to Luca.

Caustic fear had beat a tattoo in his head that he was

like Enzo in this, too, that he was beginning to buy into his own pretense that all he wanted was fun with Sophia.

Had his father married his mother with the best intentions? Had he meant to keep his promise to love her and cherish her? Had he thought he was in control just as Luca thought he was with Sophia?

Had he been aware that he'd become a monster toward the woman he'd loved and yet hadn't been able to stop?

Rattled by Antonio's revelation, he hadn't gone back into the ballroom. To her.

He had not followed the blonde, nor touched her. But he'd been sorely tempted. Here was the way to delineate from the path his father had taken, the only way, it seemed, to retain control of this farce that was already pulling him under…so destructively simple—to touch the nameless woman, to sink into her inviting body and prove to himself that his defenses were intact.

That he was intact.

Only he had looked at the woman and bile had risen in his throat.

Would the ghost of his father haunt him here, too? Was it not enough he'd passed Luca his looks and his madness? Would he now drive him into humiliating Sophia?

Even for a farce, she would never forgive him. And that was one thing Luca couldn't bear.

He faced himself every night in the mirror and only self-loathing remained. He was never alone in his head; he was never alone when he looked in the mirror.

So he'd stopped looking and lived as best as he could. But if Sophia looked at him like that…*non!*

So he stayed. A little weak. A little undone. And a little ragged in his hunger for her. He wanted to be inside her. He wanted to learn everything there was to know about her. In that wanting, Luca realized there was no one else.

No one drove his actions, not stupid bets from which he thought he would protect her; no one whispered in his ears that this, too, was already set. Nothing but pure, scorching desire motivated him. No ghosts of mad fathers or distraught mothers. Nothing but Luca and his desire for her.

He was alone in wanting Sophia, like he wasn't in anything else.

She stood there, plastered against the door. Stubborn chin tilted high in challenge. Luscious breasts fell and rose as she battered at her temper, beating it into submission.

She would not win tonight, not against him, not against her own nature. She was his. The only question was how much she would make him chase her.

But it made sense, that she was different in this, too. That she demanded to be chased, demanded to be won over.

He wanted nothing less for his wife, anyway. Half turned away from piano, he raised a brow. "That was quite impressive. Alex would have nothing on you if you decide to be mistress of the manor, or the estate in this case."

He wasn't grinning, which was strange in itself. She'd have thought he'd love seeing her struggle with her temper. Second, there was an almost somber quality to his expression.

"You couldn't contain yourself for one evening?"

"So the claws are out?"

"Claws are all I have." Damn it, how could she be feeling this sense of betrayal? Had she not truly changed where it mattered?

No, she had. She'd grown a shell to keep the world out while hiding away herself. Even convinced herself that she didn't need or want anything or anyone.

Until this moment.

And she was truly seeing him this time, now that her

own naïveté was gone. Now that she didn't have to hide from herself. "No pretty feathers like your...*numerous friends*. Did you—"

"I have quite the craving for claws, *cara mia*, when they are yours. So stop threatening and start using them."

It was said in a voice taut with challenge. Not mocking or teasing. Shadows moved in his eyes where there had been nothing but insouciance before.

Sophia felt like she'd locked herself in with a predator. Gone was the easy, charming Luca that she could handle, if not admire. This man who looked at her with darkly hungry eyes was not he. He seemed edgier, less controlled. More real.

Back down, a voice whispered. *Back down and walk away.*

Sophia smothered that voice and shoved it out of her head. No force on earth could make her leave the room now. Not now, when maybe, there was a chance she could understand why she was so drawn to him. Why this... madness claimed her so easily when it was Luca Conti.

"I'm a novelty to you right now. But you can't help it, can you?" She couldn't let him bespell her with such words. "You attract women like you were honey and they bees. It's probably coded into your DNA—"

"She. Followed. Me." His nostrils flared. A pulse flickered in his sculpted jaw. Dark fire leaped in his eyes, a lethal warning. "It's a little disconcerting how much the idea of a quick screw with another faceless woman holds no appeal right now."

A sense of coiled danger radiated from him and the woman in her, instead of being terrified, wanted to court that danger. Wanted to sink under his skin and burrow there. Wanted to leave a mark on him this time, like he'd done on her.

Like a moth called toward a column of fire, she went to him. She straddled the bench, uncaring that it pulled the dress to her thighs. That it signaled so many things that she hadn't even realized she was ready for.

The air around them thickened. The party outside melted away. Slowly he moved closer. The masculine scent of him filled her lungs.

"You didn't discourage her. You didn't push her away. You sat there and let her paw you. You didn't act like a man who wants another."

Something gleamed in his eyes, a sudden, violent energy radiating from his frame. His hands curled around her nape and pressed none too gently. The rough scrape of his fingers against her tender skin zinged through her entire body like an electric charge. He dipped his head, and licked the rim of her ear. Arching her back, Sophia closed her eyes.

Deft fingers pulled away her chandelier earrings. Teeth nipped at her earlobe. A surge of liquid desire went straight to the place between her thighs.

Lights and stars behind her eyelids.

The soft tinkle of the earrings as they hit the marble floor threw her a rope toward sanity.

The devil was distracting her and how well. For now, his tongue was licking inside her ear. "You want a claim on me yet you refuse to even wade in?"

"If you're going to make a fool of me again, look into my eyes and admit it."

Her scalp tingled as long fingers sank into her hair and tugged hard. Exposing the curve of her throat to his mouth. Hot and open, he breathed the words against her skin. "You'll not make me feel guilty for something I haven't done."

His fingers were over her bare shoulders now. Stroking

back and forth, up and down, reaching lower and lower over her neckline. Her nipples puckered when he almost touched one on the downward trajectory.

He didn't.

She gritted her jaw hard to keep from crying out. From begging. She was sure that was what he wanted of her. Utter surrender. "Then why can't you just say 'I wasn't going to touch her'?"

She was desperate for him to say he had no intention. But he didn't. Because Luca never lied. The thought of his mouth on that blonde let out a feral anger in Sophia.

"Why set the rules for a game you're too cowardly to play?"

"It's not enough they chase you day in, day out? You can't let one go even when you're not interested?" His hands stilled.

Why couldn't he, for one evening, be hers and hers alone? "Is your self-worth that low? Is it their adulation you crave?"

His arms returned to his sides, abandoning her aroused flesh. He stood up from the bench and walked away. Panic bloomed in her stomach. "I think I've had enough of this drama, this marriage business, for one day."

Denigration, disinterest; it was a slap to her face. Carefully orchestrated to hurt her, to push her away.

There had been such amusement in his eyes that day at the board meeting. But underneath it, Sophia had also felt something else. And when she'd asked him about it, he'd distracted her.

It had definitely short-circuited her brain and stopped her from pestering him. But she now saw it all clearly.

Like an expert writer, he'd controlled the narrative at the board meeting—from their open shock and fear that he might start taking part in the Conti board politics, to suspense for his own shockingly deep reasons, and then, finally, to relief that it would be Sophia who would take his place.

Presented without that convoluted act, they wouldn't have tolerated her presence in their midst, much less welcomed her opinion. But by presenting her as an alternative to him and the mischief he could wreak, he'd forced them to accept her.

Luca was not without control.

Luca was control. He walked it like a tightrope. Every breath, every smile, every word, every gesture, it was all done with a purpose.

"You control what everyone thinks about you." *But why?*

CHAPTER EIGHT

He growled from across the room. This horrible noise that came from his throat, as if he were a ferocious but wounded animal and she the hunter.

She got off the bench and moved toward him.

"Your affairs are always splashed about. There's always some drama at some big party where you behave abominably. The only time one of your affairs wasn't splashed about was with me."

Now his hands were fisted by his sides.

Somehow, that disgusting bet had never reached anyone's ears. Of course, she saw the knowledge of it in those friends of his over the years, taunting and offensive, but no one had actually dared say a word about it to her face. Or spread it around that the chubby geek, Sophia Rossi, had fallen for the devilish Luca Conti.

"Will you give me sainthood now for *not* making a public spectacle of you, Sophia? Are you that desperate to justify this?" The sneer in his voice struck her like a stinging slap.

She bucked against his tone. But she didn't break and run away as he intended. She reached for him and leaned her forehead against his back.

Warmth from his skin radiated through his shirt. Hands shaking, she pulled his shirt out of his trousers. She sank them under it, frantic in her search for bare skin.

Skin like hot velvet, the muscles bunching under her

touch. She moved her questing hands around to his abdomen. Up and down, like he'd done with her. Ropes of lean muscles. And his heart thundering like a ram under her palm.

He was a study in stillness, in tension, in rejection. Every inch of him was locked tight. Another push and he would lash back at her, would break her.

But how could she back down now?

She'd always thought of his looks as the gateway to his arrogance, to his indulgent lifestyle, but now she wondered if they weren't just a mask, hiding so much more than they revealed. Every woman was blinded by his smile; every man wanted to have that natural, effortless charm he possessed; everyone willingly bought into the role he played.

She'd bought it, too, all these years. "You…you perform, Luca. For Antonio, for Leandro, for Tina, for the entire world. You have created this specter of you and you use it to keep everyone at a distance."

He turned and Sophia braced herself for his attack. She was learning him now, learning when there was a hint of the real Luca and when it was the abhorred playboy.

Something changed in his face, then. An infinitesimal tightening of those razor-sharp cheekbones. A thinning of those lush lips. A glitter in those eyes that were always quick with a smile and a comeback, usually laden with sexual innuendo.

He seemed to see straight through to the heart of her—the fears and desires, everything she kept locked away to get through hard life. "You want to have sex with me. Desperately. You crave it and yet, you can't give in to the inevitable. So you look for some redeeming quality in me.

"I shall never be the man for you, Sophia. So, if you are not going to screw me, at least stop pretending."

She blinked, dazed by how much he saw. How accurate he was.

Both of them were right. Both of them saw far too much of the other that no one else saw. And both of them were far too gone to back out now.

He was hers in that moment, Sophia knew. Against his own better judgment perhaps. And the fighter in her reveled in this victory, in wrenching a part of him away that no other possessed.

He could have been with a million women but it didn't matter. Not anymore. She had a piece of him no one else had.

She vined her arms around his waist. Tension thrummed in every line and sinew of his body. His fingers gripped her wrists tight enough to leave marks, intent on pushing her away. And she was the one who calmed now; she was the stronger one in this moment.

"What do you want, Sophia?"

She let her body slowly mold itself against his. "I want you to make love to me, Luca."

His thigh shoved in between her legs, his hands on her hips, pulling her tight and flush against him. He was long and hard and unbearably good against her throbbing sex. The jolt of heat that went through her was instantaneous, all-consuming.

Their eyes met and held. No challenges were issued. No deals were made. There was nothing but will and heat and the desire to burn together.

The neckline of her dress was tugged and pulled, her nipples left knotted and needy. Fingers busied themselves with the zipper at her side now. Breath was fire in her throat. Fever in her blood. The ripping sound of the zipper scraped against her nerves. Cool air touched her breasts and she gasped. Still no fingers where she needed them.

"Interesting." Hoarse voice. Clipped words through a gritted jaw. Muscles under her fingers clenched. Lean body pressing against her suddenly became tense. "No bra."

"Backless dress." Cool as a cucumber she sounded, while she was incinerating on the inside. A breeze touched her skin and she shivered.

"You are like hot silk. I'm going to lick every inch of you."

She closed her eyes and heard him shed his shirt.

Long fingers on her back—gentle, kneading, almost possessive as they pressed her toward him.

Breasts flattened against skin, hot and velvet-soft stretched taut over tight muscles. Nipples rasped.

Hands in her hair held her like that, their torsos flushed tight against each other. His shaft lengthened and hardened against her belly. Her sex clenched and released, hungry for his hard weight. Their breaths rattled in the silence. He took her mouth then.

Soft and slow, his kisses were like honey spreading through her limbs. Roaming hands touched her everywhere, restless and urgent, belying his tender kisses. "Sophia?"

"Hmmm?"

"I should very much like to be inside you now, *cara mia*."

Only now did she focus again on the people a little distance away. Music and laughter. She stilled at the prospect, her pulse in her throat. "Here? Now? They are all... right there."

Fingers tightened in her hair. "Now, Sophia."

It was his way or not. He did this to her on purpose. Pushed her into this corner where she realized how desperately she wanted him. Pushed her past her own boundaries into new territory. Like she had done with him.

He expected her to back off. He expected her to shrivel and hide and ask for the cloak of a bedroom and the dark night.

"Yes," she whispered, pressing little kisses to his chest. Flicking her tongue out, she licked the flat nipple and tugged it between her teeth. She pressed a trail upward to his throat and then closed her lips over his skin. "Here, now."

She felt the shudder in him then. And it was another small victory.

When he turned her, she went. Her will was not her own now. Her body was his to do with as he wanted. "Look at us, *bella mia*," he whispered at her ear.

Sophia looked. They stood in front of a gilt-framed mirror, below which stood an antique writing desk. Two chandeliers cast enough light to illuminate every inch of the huge room.

Light and dark, soft and hard, he lean and wiry and she...voluptuous and flushed, they were different in every way. Skin pulled taut against those sharp features, he was a study in male need.

But she was...she was the one who looked utterly erotic.

No rouge could make her cheeks that pink. Her pupils were large, almost black. Her mouth was swollen, unashamedly wide and seductive. The pulse at her neck throbbed as if someone had pulled at it like a string.

The turquoise silk hung around her hips, baring her breasts. Her nipples were plump, distended and meeting his gaze in the mirror, Sophia felt like she was scorched to the very core of her.

"What do you see, Sophia?"

She closed her eyes, her breath coming in short puffs. "I look indecent. Like everything I want is written all over my face."

"I see a woman whose curves and valleys are as complex as her mind. I see a warrior, a seductress, and I see a woman who hides her heart from even herself."

His words were just as powerful as his caresses. His fingers moved restlessly over her flesh, stopping here and there, pressing and kneading, but never staying. Learning and pressing all over—the rim of her ear, the line of her spine, the demarcation from her waist to her flaring hips, the crease of her thigh, the fold of her elbow...

There were so many other places crying for touch but he didn't touch her there. Her dress slithered to the ground and she stood in just her wispy lace panties. Then those were pushed down, too.

Sophia barely processed it when he turned her and then lifted her onto the table, as easily as if she were a china doll. The wood surface was cold against her bare buttocks as was the wall at her back. Yet, she was burning up all over.

Eyes wide, she watched as he kicked off his leather shoes and socks and then those trousers and black boxer shorts.

He hardly gave her a breath to savor the tall, darkly gorgeous form of his before he stood between her legs. Rock-hard thighs pushed her own wide, baring the heart of her to his wicked gaze. He took her hand in his, kissed the underside of her wrist and he pushed her palm against the heat of her.

Sophia jerked at her own touch.

"Are you wet for me, Sophia?"

Brown eyes widened into molten pools in her face, she looked so innocent.

So pure. So hot. So perfect.

The equation between them was changing and morphing, and all because he had oh so cleverly thought he could control himself. So full of himself, he'd forgotten Sophia was an explosive variable... Joke was on him. Rarely had anyone ever surprised him like Sophia did.

She saw far too much. She didn't tread lightly even in this; she marched in, banners raised, breaking walls down, determined to reach the part he hid from everyone.

It should have sent him running. Instead, here he was.

He was alone, always, where it mattered. It was the only way he could live. But that she saw him, even such a small part, in this moment, he didn't feel alone.

He felt a connection. He felt like someone knew the true him. He was weak enough to want to hold on to that for a little longer. Human enough to want to protect this. Just a little longer, he promised himself. No lasting damage this time, he'd make sure. Only pleasure for him and her.

"What?" she said, all spikes and thorns.

"Take your lovely fingers and dip them into your—"

She kissed him then and swallowed his filthily provocative words. Hard and fast, desperate and a little fierce, until he was deluged in sensation. "If my fingers would do just as well as yours, I wouldn't be here, now, would I?"

Acres of glowing skin, pouty, lush breasts, plump nipples begging to be sucked into his mouth, soft belly and a cloud of brown curls hiding the velvet heat of her. Wide eyes sparkling with desire and curiosity and possession. Such an irresistible combination of strength and vulnerability. So strict even with herself.

She was the most real thing Luca had ever seen.

His lovely Sophia. His lioness, his warrior, *simply his* in this moment.

He wanted to stay in that moment forever. But it could not last. Whatever it was that tugged at them relentlessly could not last. Because he was Luca Conti.

So he did what he did best. He reduced this moment of excruciating intimacy to nothing but animalistic sex. Into nothing but raw heat and primal possession.

"Is it not enough that I'm here, now, Luca?" she finally murmured. Her breath was stuttering. The pulse at her neck throbbed.

"No, I want more, I want everything, Sophia," he whispered, and felt her name move through him like a powerful invocation. "Tell me, did you touch yourself the night of our wedding?"

"Yes," she answered tightly.

"Did you finish?"

"No. It wasn't… I've never before…"

He bent and pressed his mouth to the upper curve of one breast. Her nipple rasped against his chest, taunting him. He gripped the table until his knuckles turned white, his erection pulling up tight against his abdomen.

But there was a keening pleasure in the need riding him hard.

Every inch of him felt alive. Every inch of him felt like a pulse. Denial, even for a few moments, was an alien concept for him. He had so very little, so he reveled in what he could have. He glutted himself on it.

Sexual gratification, once he'd stopped whoring it out for other things he'd needed desperately, was the most uncomplicated thing in his life. But now anticipation was like a drug, heightening every sense, a fever in his blood.

He opened his mouth and sucked on the tender skin. Hard. She was salt and desire and delicious on his tongue.

Nails digging into his shoulders, she convulsed against him. Not pulling away but pushing into his touch. So he did it harder. Her moan reverberated around them. "Touch yourself and tell me if you're already swollen. Take the edge off."

"No." Defiant chin lifted. Demand sparkled in her eyes. And a challenge. His erection lay stretched up against his belly now, engorged and ready. She moved her hands down the slopes of his shoulders to his chest. A pink nail scraped against his nipple. A finger traced the line between his pectorals.

He waited on a knife's edge, his breath bellowing through his throat.

Featherlight and fluttery, her touch made him ache. Everywhere in his body. He felt like that cavernous hungry thing that was his mind had taken over his body now. All he was was desire. As if answering his unspoken request, she touched his painfully thick erection.

No tentativeness, no hesitation, as she wrapped her fingers around the hard length and pumped him, up and down. He thrust into the circle of her elegant fingers and growled. Covered her fingers with his own and showed her how to do it.

"I'm a very fast learner," the sexy minx whispered as she stroked him just the way he liked it. Hands on the wall on either side of her, head bowed down, Luca closed his eyes and let the pleasure wash over him.

Honeysuckle and something of Sophia filled every breath of his. "In your mouth now, Sophia," he demanded roughly.

She would back off now. She hated being told what to do, didn't she? She hated anything that she thought made her weaker or exposed or vulnerable. And of all the people in the world, she'd never bow or bend to his commands—

He tensed as he felt the tentative slide of her tongue over the head.

Dio in cielo, she looked up at him, a wicked smile in her eyes and then her wide mouth closed over the tip of his shaft. His head went back; his vision blurred as he slid into the warm crevice of her mouth.

"Like that?" she whispered when she slid him out, her pink mouth wet, her nudity a luscious invitation.

Challenge and entreaty. Siren and slave. Desire and defiance. He had never seen a sight, heard a sound, more beautiful than her. For the first time in his life, he had no saucy retort, no way to reduce this into simple carnality. How when only Sophia and her wicked mouth would do?

She flicked her silky tongue over the slit and repeated her question. He saw stars, and sky and pleasure so blinding that he couldn't breathe. His hands sank into her hair, holding her in place. He had meant to disarm her; he had meant to somehow bring the chains of this thing between them back into his control.

Instead, he felt unmanned. Distilled to his essence, stripped of his armor.

Sweat dampened his skin as she continued her little ministrations with an eagerness and efficiency that pushed him closer to the edge. There was a fever in his muscles and he found it was he that was shaking now. Coming inside her mouth would be heaven but more than that, he wanted to be inside her, he wanted to see her face when he finished, he needed to drive her to this same…bewildered, out-of-control state she drove him to. He needed to be one with the incredible woman that was cajoling, stealing, wrenching away parts of him.

He pulled her up in a hurry of need, never having felt this sense of urgency, this potent urge to feel and revel. Pressed his mouth to one softly rounded shoulder before thrusting his thigh between hers. Against his muscular, hair-roughened thigh, she was like satin silk, a sweet haven.

"Luca?" she whispered, her eyes impossibly round in her face. The innocent but curious interest in it pounded in his veins.

Dio, was there nothing about the woman he could hold against her? Even in this, she shed her inhibitions, willing to go wherever he took her.

He delved his fingers into her folds to test her readiness. Pink spilled into her cheeks, a spectrum of browns in her eyes. She was slickly wet against his fingers. He stroked the swollen bud there and she jerked into his touch, demanding more. Twisting her chin, he kissed her plump mouth. "First, I need you like this, *cara mia*," he offered, before he took himself in hand and pushed into her wet sheath from behind.

The tight fit of her flesh stroked every nerve in him, a flare of heat pooling at his groin.

Her gasp, throaty and husky, tore at his nerves. Desire and lust, need and something more, everything roped together, all independent flames merging together and setting him on fire.

He met Sophia's eyes in the mirror and Luca believed everything in his life—every ugly thing he'd lived through—was all worth it, if it had brought him to this woman in this moment.

Sophia scrambled to keep a millionth of the wits she possessed, for she didn't want to miss a single moment of being possessed by Luca. She wanted every sense open, for she felt like she was turned inside out, every secret, every fantasy, exposed. In this position, she didn't know where she ended and where he began.

He had made it good ten years ago; even her virginal body huddled under the covers on his bed, had known it. Even as she had refused to let him turn the lights on, look at her in daylight. He'd handled her with tender caresses, reverent touches. However ugly his motives, he'd made seeking and giving pleasure a beautiful celebration, made her body feel like an instrument of pleasure instead of a source of shame.

But this was different. She was not an awkward girl who didn't know what to do with her suddenly voluptuous curves or the sudden, unwelcome, indecent attention from the same boys who despised her guts. She was not ashamed or confused by the demands or the reactions of her body.

Now she was Sophia Conti, the devil's wife, and it had already changed her. For better or worse, she had no idea but it was irrevocable. She owned him in this moment and she owned her sexuality.

Instead of distaste, as her expectations had been about this experience, she felt like she was an extension of him. Or he of her. Instead of shying away, she boldly raised her gaze and met his in the mirror.

Smoothly contoured shoulders framed her slender ones. Dark olive skin, stretched tightly over sinew provided an enticing contrast against her skin. Nostrils flaring, plump mouth pursed in passion, he was magnificent. And so was she, the perfect female counterpart to his masculinity.

Dark fingers moved from her hips, across her rib cage to cup and lift her breasts. He rubbed the turgid peak lightly, then moved to the other one. But even the gossamer touch was too much when she held his hard heat inside her. She clenched her inner muscles, the need primal, instinctual.

He pressed his forehead against her shoulder, a guttural growl coming from the depths of him. He didn't withdraw, but rotated his hips and again, Sophia clenched around him.

Sensation spiraled, inch by inch, until Sophia felt even the jerk of his hot breath against her skin like a stinging caress. They stayed like that, learning each other and testing all the different ways they could move against and with each other, their bodies in perfect harmony, the tension building to an unbearable pitch.

Sophia was afraid she would fragment into a million little pieces if she didn't climax soon. She held on to his forearms and pressed herself against his chest. "Luca?"

He licked the pulse beating frantically at her neck and spoke against her skin. *"Si, cara mia?"*

She arched her spine and pushed back into him, until he was more deeply embedded within her. Voluptuous pleasure suffused her at the hard length lodged inside her. Head over her shoulder, she looked back at him, half-delirious with need. "I'm dying here, Luca."

A quick stroke of his fingers at her clit made her groan wildly. "All you have to do is ask, *bella.*"

She panted, struggling to form a thought. "Please, Luca…don't make me wait anymore. I need you. I need this like I've needed nothing in my life before."

Long fingers gripping her hips with such deliciously tight pressure, he pulled out of her. All the way before thrusting back into her again.

Sophia arched her back, threw her head against his chest.

Her breath came in soft little pants, her channel still trying to accommodate his large size. Every inch of her sex quivered at his stark possession. At the unbelievable pleasure pulsing up her spine. Her thighs shook under her, her knuckles white where she gripped the table.

There was no technique, no experienced caresses. This was raw, real. And so damn good that she thought she'd implode from the inside.

A palm on her lower back pushed her down and she bent, malleable and willing. Like heated clay in his hands, his to do with as he wished. Another hand quested toward her breast, plumping and molding.

Her entire body was like a bow for him. Long fingers pulled expertly at her nipple before moving down, down to tug at the sensitive, swollen bud at her sex again.

He thrust in again, his fingers and his hard length applying counterpoint pressure over her throbbing flesh to his rough, upward thrusts. Pleasure screwed through her pelvis again, nearly cleaving her in half. Sophia sobbed, screamed.

"*Dio*, Sophia," he whispered, before withdrawing and pushing in again.

The intimate slap of their flesh, the slick slide of their sweat-dampened skin, there was nothing civilized or romantic about what he did to her. He was not the experienced lover whose technique and skill in lovemaking was rhapsodized about in silkily whispered innuendoes. He was not the masterful seducer.

With her he was desperate, his thrusts erratic, raw, his need nothing orchestrated. With her, he was just a man who was as desperate for her as she was for him. He took her, savage and uncompromisingly male, and Sophia reveled in it as she climaxed in a wild explosion of pleasure. Fingers roughly holding her down, Luca thrust in a long stroke and then he was convulsing against her, a rapid stream of filthy Italian words filling her ears.

Sophia smiled and decided they were the sweetest words she'd ever heard.

CHAPTER NINE

"MALEDIZIONE, SOPHIA! Stay away from Antonio."

Sophia stilled as Luca, for the first time since she'd known him, raised his voice. He stormed into her brand-new but mostly bare office on the floor newly given over to displaced Rossi staff in the CLG offices in the heart of Milan's business district.

"I have kept every promise I made. What more could you want from that manipulative old bastard?"

Her newly appointed assistant, Margie—Sophia had never had an assistant or an office or even a stapler of her own before—stood staring at Luca, her mouth open wide enough to catch any stray butterflies. The woman had to be fifty and yet, like clockwork, a faint gleam of interest appeared in her eyes and she abruptly straightened out her shoulders, sucked her tummy in and thrust out her meager breasts clad in a thick wool sweater.

Bemused, Sophia turned to Luca. Who was completely unaware of anyone but her in the room. Like nothing but Sophia in the entire world had any consequence to him whatsoever. Whether meetings or parties, whether they were surrounded by a hundred guests curious about their marriage, or just at an intimate dinner with the Rossis— they hadn't socialized much with his family after the party, as if he wanted to keep her separate from them—Luca had the addictive habit of zeroing all his focus on her.

A woman couldn't be blamed for getting used to being

looked at like that. For misunderstanding fiery lust for intimacy, camaraderie for affection. For starting to believe in her own fairy tale that she could tie the charming, incredibly insatiable Luca Conti to herself.

Thick hair disheveled, sporting a stubbly beard along with the constant blue shadows, and dressed in a rumpled white Polo T-shirt and blue jeans, her husband looked like a thwarted grizzly bear. An utterly sexy and thoroughly disreputable version.

Her husband; she was calling him that far too frequently, even if in her head. She was becoming possessive, and she had no idea how to stop.

She sighed, waiting for the stinging awareness that took over her body every time he was near to lapse into a bearable pulse.

Luca, she'd come to learn in four weeks of their all-too-real-feeling marriage, was given to bouts of intense restlessness, which usually signaled that he was going to retreat, from which he emerged a day or two later and then followed furious social activity.

The restlessness wasn't violent or physical as she had learned the night she had found him sitting at the veranda, staring into the pitch-black of the night. It was in his eyes, in the detached, distant way he looked at everything around him, in the long walks he took around the estate as if his energy was boundless. In the warning that radiated from him to be left alone when he was in such a state.

But when he emerged from it, it was as if he hadn't been absent for hours.

She'd hurried back from work one afternoon to Villa de Conti, intensely relieved to see his bike and marched straight into the shower. A wicked glint in his eyes as he watched her, water caressing his hard body. "Please tell me, *bella*, that you came home for an afternoon quickie."

"This is not funny," she'd said then, fighting off his nimble fingers. He'd still somehow shed her of her linen jacket, leaving her in her stretchy camisole.

"Luca, this is serious."

His knuckles traced her nipples, tight and wet against the fabric. "I have a new appreciation for your starchy suits, *cara*. I feel like a kid unwrapping a present every single time I undress you. Only I know the treasure that is beneath."

"We can get help." Her hair plastered to her scalp and her mascara ran down her cheeks. For once, Sophia didn't give a damn how she looked. "I did some research and there are all kinds of new research to beat a drug addiction." It was the only thing that made sense.

To which he had replied that he didn't do drugs, kissed her and then proceeded to show her how *she* could calm him down. He had taken her then, against the wall, under the onslaught of water, with swift, desperate, hard thrusts, his mouth buried in her neck while she had halfheartedly and nearing climax, objected that this was the opposite of calming.

She had no idea what calmed that restless look in his eyes or why he needed to escape.

For a lazy playboy, the patterns of his days and nights were utterly demonic. Her mind reeled at the highs and the lows, at the chaotic clamor that seemed to be his life. She couldn't imagine surviving the erratic quality of his days and nights, the lack of structure... How could he get anything done?

He doesn't do anything, remember? a voice whispered. The shrew, as she had taken to calling that voice, the one she'd developed to distance herself from anything she sensed might make her weak.

But he hadn't once left her hanging.

He'd given her every bit of his attention in numerous meetings she'd had with Leandro and him to reinvent the Rossi brand as a subsidiary of CLG. First she had had to sell Leandro that Rossi was still a household name, prove that it had upped manufacturing standards in the last five years, a project she'd overseen personally. Then she'd shown him sales numbers proving that when it came to belts, men's wallets and other niche leather goods, Rossi was still beating CLG.

"And here I thought you were taking my brother on a ride," Leandro had said drily, pinning her with his implacable gaze.

Once Leandro had come on board, she had taken on Salvatore.

Which had needed a show of support from the Conti brothers—even Sophia had been impressed by the complementary strengths of the brothers, one silent but reeking of power and the other charming but persuasive. An agreement that CLG signed saying it would never do away with the Rossi name *and* endless business proposals, finally convinced Salvatore.

Though he'd grumbled when she'd suggested discontinuing any Rossi products that competed directly against CLG and instead develop a range of more complementary products. Luca had managed to convince Sal in a matter of minutes that Rossi's had sunk because it could never compete with CLG and yet kept trying to, a point she'd been trying to make for several years now.

An official press release said CLG was investing in Rossi's to make their renowned clutches, belts and other accessories, redesigned to meet the luxury standards of CLG and enter the market again.

Sophia had been appointed as the director of overseeing the first production line from design to marketing. An appointment that hadn't filled Sal with confidence until Luca had winked at him and said, "Good to keep some-one from your side in there, Salvatore. You can't trust my brother or Antonio completely."

When she'd thanked him with a kiss on his cheek, he'd grinned wickedly. "I love this whole man behind the woman concept with you, *bella*. Although I like being above and under you, too."

Leandro had watched them with something like shock in those gray eyes.

She'd hidden her face in his chest, her throat danger-ously close to tears, and pretended to find his lascivious comment obnoxious. He'd warded off the emotional mo-ment with humor. As always. But Sophia didn't believe that Luca was shallow anymore.

The truth was that he was weaving himself into every part of her life, into her very being. All too frequently now, Sophia wondered what she would do when he was gone from her life.

Who would she cry to about Salvatore? About the entire species of men? Who would make her laugh? Who would drive her to the edge of ecstasy? Who would hold her in bed as if she were the most precious thing in the world?

She ran a hand over her stomach, as if she could calm the panic. "Hello, Luca. Do you like my new office?"

He pushed a hand through his hair and walked around, his long, sinuous body overpowering the space immedi-ately. Then he turned to her with a frown. "You should have one with a nicer view. Not the one looking at the back alley."

Smarting at his dismissal, Sophia said, "I don't care about the office so much, Luca. Salvatore has agreed to let me pitch the idea for—"

"You should care, Sophia. As long as you act like you

deserve only this much, that's all you get. All these years, you have let Salvatore box you into a position that you were overqualified for. You—"

"I was learning the business, every part of it."

"What is your excuse now? Why are you still pussy-footing around him?"

"Too many things have changed in the past few months. He needs—"

"He needs to hear you say that this is your company as much as it is his. That you're the best thing that's happened to it in the last decade. Have you decided to neatly play in the boundaries you set for yourself, afraid that if you push, he might tell you you're not his daughter after all? Have you decided that is all you could have, Sophia?"

It felt like the ground was melting away from under her feet. Like something she hadn't even seen was ripped open for everyone to see.

Like she was standing naked in the midst of a crowd, her worst nightmare, all her toughness, her strength, her pride, mere illusions. She was that little girl again, desperately pretending that she was not scared at the prospect of leaving the only home she knew. Her throat felt raw. "You don't know what you're talking about."

He reached her then and the tenderness with which he clasped her jaw was enough to break her. She should hate him, this man who saw past everything, but she couldn't. "What will you do when I'm done with you? How will you convince Sal of anything then?"

All Sophia heard in that little outburst was *when I'm done with you*. Her entire world felt colorless, lifeless, in that sentence. "I haven't thought that far ahead."

"Then you aren't much of a planner, are you?"

"Wow, is this how you are when you don't sleep for a few days?"

He ran a hand through his hair in a rough, restless gesture. "No, I'm like this because I found out that you're making secret deals with Antonio. Again."

"*Again?* What do you mean?"

"I know he's the one who put you up to marrying me."

"He told you?"

"*Si.* So tell me what are you doing meeting with him in secret in the middle of the night? Alex saw you."

"So she told on me?"

"She thought I should know that my wife is continuing negotiations with my wily grandfather, *si*. Alex despises Antonio as much as I do."

Sophia knew there was a guilty flush climbing up her cheeks. "I just… I told him to stop bullying Salvatore, and every one else, that's all. He and his gray wolf pack."

The sinuous lines of Luca's face became still. "You did?"

"Yes. It's high time someone stood up to him. He plays with everyone—Kairos, you, me, Tina. Only Leandro seems to escape his clutches. I might have gone a little overboard, I was so angry about it."

"How overboard?"

"I told him if he wasn't careful, I would send him and his pack out of the board with their tails tucked between their legs."

But Sophia had approached Antonio only to ask about Luca, for she knew Leandro could never be induced to talk about his brother. The bond between the Conti brothers, as she'd guessed, was inviolate, for all they were diametrically opposite in temperament.

What haunted Luca? Was it a medical condition? Why weren't the Contis, with all their bloody wealth, doing something to help him?

With each passing day, she felt as if she'd go mad if she

didn't understand what drove Luca. It felt like an invisible wall was already pushing her away from him.

For a man who gave every outward proof of despising Luca, Antonio hadn't betrayed a single thing. Only stared at her as if she was an apparition that had appeared out of thin air. Beyond frustrated, Sophia had vented the anger, the fear that was slowly consuming her from within.

She took Luca's hand in hers, the long, elegant fingers as familiar as her own now. She'd never known this intimacy, this sort of connection with another person, in her life. Not even her mother. Somehow, Luca had become a part of her own makeup. "I would never whisper about Valentina to another soul."

"He told you about Tina?"

He sounded so disquietingly furious that the words poured out of Sophia. "I would never betray your family in that way. I would never ever pull the rug like that from anyone, much less Tina. I know what it feels like to not have a name. To not know where you belong. You believe me, don't you, Luca?"

Luca stared at Sophia, the wistfulness in her tone calming the anger inside. His grandfather really needed to keep his mouth shut. Sensing the wariness in her tense stance, he pulled her into his arms. "You fight so ferociously for Salvatore, I forget you're not even his, Sophia. Tell me more about you."

"There's not much to tell. My English father died before he could marry my mother. She became the village pariah when she found out she was pregnant. She moved to Milan to find a job and to raise me. For a long while, we struggled to make ends meet. She wasn't really suited for any kind of job. So she cleaned houses. Big, posh houses, and I tagged along whenever I could."

"It made you determined to succeed."

"Yes. I wanted to go to college, I wanted a career. Luckily for me, I did well at school. I never ever wanted to have just a glass of milk for dinner. Can you blame my fixation with cakes and pastries? Diets are torture for me, to deny myself food when we didn't have much for so long, my body revolts at the very idea."

He buried his nose in her hair, tenderness enveloping him. "Then why do you?"

"It's okay, I'm coming to realize that I'll never be stick-thin, anyway."

"You're a fighter, *cara mia*. It lights you from the inside out."

"That's what good-looking people say to the ugly ones," she retorted instantly.

They burst out laughing. She hid her face in his chest. It felt as if his lungs would burn if he even tried to contain this.

Dio, what was he going to do with this woman? She made him laugh like no one did. She cast such bright light onto everything she touched. She made him so protective of her, as if that was his only reason in the world.

She made him ache and want with a fierceness he had never known. And the days were dwindling down slowly but surely. Like sand in an hourglass. There was nothing he could do contain it. He had let her see more of him than anyone else.

Every moment he spent with her, he was living an entire lifetime in it.

Everything was becoming twisted, twined together so messily that he wasn't able to keep it separate. Different compartments for different activities, different emotions used in different places, some never to be indulged in; that was his life. There was order in his chaos.

And he didn't know how to stop it. How to harden himself against her. How to remind himself that he could not have her for more than a few weeks.

"When I was thirteen, Mom met Salvatore. He fell in love with her. I wasn't sure he'd want her with me tagging along. So I…" Her voice wavered here and suddenly, a pushing pressure came upon Luca's chest.

He stroked the tight line of her mouth. "What did you do, Sophia?"

"I decided to remove myself from the equation. I packed a bag with two pairs of clothes, took enough money for bus fare, packed two sandwiches and a banana—more than I should have, I know, but I didn't know when I would be able to eat again and I knew Sal would take care of my mom, so I ran away."

Luca's throat felt raw, imagining a barely grown girl disappearing like that. "*Christo*, Sophia! What were you thinking?"

"She needed him more than I did. I couldn't bear to see her like that anymore, shriveling to nothingness, working all hours just to get me through school."

Thirteen, she'd been only thirteen. And so brave. He didn't mistake for a second that it hadn't cost her. That it hadn't left a mark on her. That it hadn't changed her in ways even she couldn't see.

Seeing the best or worst of yourself at such a young age, it set a precedent. Now she thought it was up to her to solve her loved ones' problems.

How could Salvatore not see how precious her loyalty was? For the first time in his life, Luca offered what he always took. What he craved like he did air. Comfort, touch, companionship. That she'd revealed a part of herself, a part he was sure no one knew, made him feel as if he had gained a treasure.

Hooking his hands on her hips, he pulled her into his lap on the settee. She jerked first, as if to reject the embrace. "Sometimes, I dream the bus left with me in it."

"You're here, *tesoro*. In my arms."

Something fierce rose inside Luca. He would ensure she never had to do something like this, he promised himself, that she'd never have to sacrifice her happiness for the sake of her family. He'd look out for her.

Her thighs bracketed his as he enfolded her within his arms. He nuzzled her hair, needing to touch her as much as she needed it. Settled as she was snugly against him, it wasn't lust that she invoked in that moment. But something far more tender, and rooting.

"What happened then, *cara*?"

She inhaled noisily. "They both came after me. Mom said she didn't want a man who didn't accept me, too. Salvatore went on his knees in front of me, I mean, can you imagine the scene? Rough, abrasive Salvatore being gentle... He looked me in the eye and told me he was my father from that day. He's always been kind to me."

Luca's respect for the man rose. "Except when he arranged your marriage."

"He's traditional. He thinks women, including his shrewish daughter, need to be protected. I was ready to marry whoever he pointed at. Only the man he picked found out that I'd given up the prize to you and refused to marry me. At least, he never told Sal why." Uncertainty threaded through her tone, her soft body tense in his arms. "It was you, wasn't it? You warned them all."

Suddenly, it felt like the most important thing in the world to Luca that Sophia didn't think him cruel and heartless. Or shallow. Or a useless waste of space. Or a man who was incapable of caring. All the things he'd made himself to be became an unbearable burden when it came to her.

"If I had known what Marco intended, I'd never have sent him there. I…"

That she burrowed into his arms instead of withdrawing, his breath seesawed through him. She felt like warmth and generosity, strength and softness, the woman placed in the universe, it seemed, to balance him.

Forehead tucked into his neck, she hid her face, but the quiver in her words was still there. "Why did you take part in that bet? I can't just believe you could knowingly take part in someone's humiliation. At least, tell me it was that dumb need to prove yourself among them. Tell me I was incidental, Luca and not the—"

"Hush…*cara mia*, it was nothing like that. Believe me, I…I never meant to hurt you." When she became stiff in his arms, he forced her to meet his eyes. For once in his wretched life, to show the truth, instead of hiding behind shadows. "When I heard about the bet, I was furious. But there was no way to dissuade that lot. So I joined in. Only to protect you from their stupid ploys. Instead, I got involved with you. Those weeks we spent together… It was incredible.

"But I was barely a decent man, Sophia, much less worthy of you. I had to end it. So I told them I had won the bet. Marco was supposed to see you, and then walk out quietly. But that scoundrel humiliated you. You were never supposed to know about the bet.

"When I found out what he did, I smashed his cell phone. Warned them I didn't want to hear your name again on their lips. I knew you would be cursing me to hell, which was for the best."

CHAPTER TEN

FOR A FEW SECONDS Sophia felt dazed.

He'd meant to protect her. Knowing that he'd fallen for that indescribable pull between them, she felt light. As if the invisible boulder of shame and humiliation and self-doubt she'd been carrying around her neck for a decade had been lifted away.

It didn't matter that he'd ended their relationship like that. It didn't matter that he'd run away with a lover, in an effort to sever whatever they had shared.

It only mattered that those weeks had been special to him, too.

"I did for a long time," Sophia replied. Had a woman ever been so happy to find out the real reason of why she'd been dumped? But then their whole relationship was strange. "I cursed you, and for a really crazy period there, I even considered having some voodoo done on you. You know, have your manhood shriveled or some such."

"Manhood?" he said, the word full of mockery.

She could feel her cheeks burn but for the life of her she couldn't say the *p* word. "Fine. Your instrument of pleasure."

He laughed. She loved making him laugh. It was quickly becoming the most favorite thing about herself. Second in that quickly growing list were her previously hated breasts. Anything that could fuel those dark fantasies he kept whispering in her ear proudly earned that place. "Your mighty sword? Your shaft of delight?"

Tears rolled down his cheeks and he pulled her on top of him until she was straddling him. "Say it, Sophia."

"I don't want to."

"You prude."

Her chest hurt for the laughter bursting through her. "I'm a liberated woman who has no qualms about her sexual needs. Now, go back to the house, pretty yourself up and be ready to satisfy me when I come home tonight. See?"

"You're going to pay for it."

"I'm not a prude."

"Then say it."

"Luca, that word is so clinical and dull for the fantastic, mind-blowing things you do with it. I will not call the most awesome thing in the world that horrible name."

The most debauched man on the face of the earth blushed then. His nostrils flared, his mobile mouth pursed and there was such delight in his eyes.

Sophia giggled.

He hugged her then. Tightly and like she were precious cargo. "You, *cara mia*, are going to be the death of me."

His hands reached for her shoulders again and Sophia exhaled in shuddering relief. Suddenly, she couldn't imagine going another minute without his hands on her. With urgency that was part desperation and part fear, she kissed his mouth.

"Just stay away from Antonio. And Kairos and Leandro, too, for good measure. I don't trust any of them."

"Not even your own brother, Luca?"

"Leandro will not harm you, true, but he's the master of manipulation. I don't want to take a chance."

She traced the bridge of his nose with a finger, warmth

settling in all the neglected pieces of her soul. "You're doing that thing, Luca. That thing that I love you for not doing."

Luca was sure his heart had stopped for a second. "What is it?"

"Other than what you're doing now?" the minx whispered saucily against his mouth.

He laughed. "What is the other thing, then?"

"You never used to tell me what I could or should do. You only used to say *get on with it, cara mia.* Now you are like the rest of them. You want to change me."

If there was ever a warning put so perfectly, Luca didn't know what it could be. He was becoming someone else with Sophia. He had had so many lovers and he'd never been possessive of anyone.

And yet, with Sophia, the urge to protect, to possess, was primal.

He knew why, too. She made him like himself. Gave him a different definition. Beyond what he'd been predetermined by genes and history.

He saw someone else when he looked in the mirror these days. He saw the man Sophia saw. The man who evoked that slow but saucy smile when her gaze flicked to him across the boardroom, the soft flush that dusted her cheeks when he passed by and made sure he touched her amidst a crowd, the man who gave her that flushed and well-loved look when she came, the man she'd held tight when she was finally on her way to saving Rossi's from sure ruin.

The man she looked at with such fierce protectiveness when she thought he didn't know. The man she kissed when she thought he was finally asleep after seeing him walk around like a ghost. Just for her peace of mind, he'd pretended a couple of times, stayed with her until the worry for him cleared from her brow.

It was addictive, exhilarating, how she made him think of himself.

"I would never change you, Sophia. But Antonio has a habit of ruining things. And I won't always be here to shield you from him or his pack."

That was what had bothered him since Alex had told him. In his reckless need to have her, he'd made her a lot of enemies and robbed her of her one true friend.

"Then why not tell him that my advisory capacity for your stock is only temporary?"

Because he didn't mean for it to be. The idea took root, digging deep.

"Luca…"

"Now for the real reason I came here," he said, filling his hands with her breasts.

She laughed, her eyes wide, her breath already erratic. A voluptuous Venus. "Margie—"

"Margie cleverly disappeared."

"Luca…this is my first week working with members of CLG, in a new office. Your brother, your grandfather, they all work here… We can't just…"

"The question is…do you want me, *cara mia*?"

"Yes. I'm a little ashamed that I always want to say yes, Luca. It's setting a bad precedent between us, isn't it?"

"There's nothing to be ashamed about, *tesoro*. We… Our bodies were made for this…" He snuck his hands under her blouse and reached the hard tip. Lifting one lush breast, he took the nipple in his mouth through the silk of her blouse. He bit on the distended tip and suckled.

A moan fell from her throat. She muttered something filthy. He'd never been so hard and so amused at the same time.

Luca pulled her skirt up, thanked the man who invented

thongs and touched her between her legs. She was utterly ready for him.

He pushed his fingers up and down the crease of her folds, played with the swollen little bud there, keenly aware of every hiss of her breath, of every shift in her body.

"Oh, Lord…" Tiny shivers shook her frame. He buried his face in one shoulder and tasted the salt of her. Sweat made her skin soft and damp.

"I wish you would say my name. It is *my* fingers deep inside you." He hooked his fingers and swirled them in tune with his words.

She rewarded him with a groan that sent a flare of heat over every inch of him. His erection pushed against his trousers. "Oh…you…*arrogant, conceited*… Luca…I need…"

He took the tender skin between his teeth and suckled while he penetrated her lush heat with two fingers. She convulsed against him, pushing her wetness against his fingers. "What do you need, *cara mia*?"

"You. Inside me. Now."

Lifting her up, he unzipped his trousers and freed himself.

Cheeks flushed, irises dilated, wide mouth bee-stung, she took him inside her. Luca felt a deeply primal satisfaction as he glided deep into her invitingly slick heat. Like a glove, her flesh closed around him and his head went back with a groan.

Her hands in his hair, Sophia stared at him with a startling intensity.

For a few seconds, they stayed like that, unmoving, gazing into each other's eyes. Just reveling in the beauty of the moment, the raw intimacy of it.

He didn't shy away from it. Neither did she. And Luca

knew it was getting out of hand. This was not merely good sex. This was not even just fantastic sex.

This was Sophia and he creating something special, something he'd never known before. The sum of them becoming more than their individual selves.

She kissed him tenderly, as if she was aware of what the moment meant, too. As if she, too, was shaken by the wild beauty, the palpable magic of it.

And then because they were so desperate for each other, because they were greedy for what they could give each other, she moved over him.

That first slide of friction was unbearably good.

"Rotate your hips on the way down," he ordered hoarsely.

"Your wish, *my master*, is my command." Hands tight on his shoulders, she did as he said. The movement rubbed her breasts against his neck and chest, rubbed him against the slick folds of her.

"Oh, Luca…"

Loosely holding her hips, Luca let her set the pace. "I know, *cara mia*." Measly words for the fever spiraling in their blood.

Confident now, she moved faster.

Tense and fluid, demanding and supplicant. Her moans became keener, louder, signaling she was getting closer to the edge. When she arched her back on her way down, he took her mouth with his, swallowing away her cry. Not to mollify her, but because he didn't want anyone else to hear how she sounded in the throes of falling apart.

She was his, her cries, her moans, her sensual demands and her husky whimpers, *all his*.

He thrust up, fast and hard, as her muscles milked him. Climax beat at him in relentless waves, a fire breathing through his veins. Sated and in good terms with himself

and the world, he wondered why in hell their marriage
had to be temporary.

What was the harm in continuing like this?

They both knew what the score was. Maybe this was
his chance at companionship. He was so tired of waking
up with women he had no intention of knowing. Never
standing still. Even if she only knew a fraction of him, it
was still more than anyone else did.

He pushed damp hair away from her forehead and
pressed his lips to her temple. She snuggled against him,
and Luca, for the first time in his place, felt completely at
peace with himself.

CHAPTER ELEVEN

SOPHIA WOKE UP with a start, something sinuously haunting seemed to have lodged in her veins, and peered at the unfamiliar surroundings. This was not the high, luxurious bed that she had taken to falling into in exhaustion the past month. The walls were not the pale cream, the drapes not the sunny yellow that Luca pulled away a couple of times, calling her a lazy cat. No great Conti wealth peered down from paintings on walls.

This was not the bedroom in Villa de Conti where Luca had joined her at all hours of the night in the past month—once it had been 3:00 a.m. and she wasn't sure who was more shocked, she, to see him emerge buck naked and dripping wet from the shower, or he, to see her sneak into the bedroom with her laptop and a sliver of red velvet cake from his niece Izzie's birthday party.

What had followed had been a crazy night of cake, champagne, a wet Luca and the bed.

Here, the walls were bare and the general impression of the room was utter chaos. The bed on which she lay was the only surface not covered in books and loose paper. Realization came slowly to her sore, sated body—this was Luca's studio. The only familiar thing here was the unmistakable scent that their bodies created together—the scent of sex and sweat and raw intimacy.

When she hadn't seen Luca in a week, nor heard a word, she'd invaded Leandro's office, demanding to know where

Luca was. With each passing day that she hadn't seen him, a frenzy of fear and worry had built inside her.

Kairos had been defeated in his pursuit to be CEO of CLG, leaving the position empty, and wouldn't even talk to her. Rossi's financial future looked better than it had in a decade. And Luca had thoroughly ravished her, his eagerness and passion chasing away her own inhibitions, not that she'd need much persuading once she'd seen past his facade.

Now that all his goals had been achieved, was he done with their marriage? The memory of how easily he'd walked away last time—whatever the reason—wouldn't leave her alone.

This time, she wanted him to say to it to her face.

She wanted closure if he was ending this. But more than that, she had enough of the game he played with the world. She wanted to face the real Luca. She wanted the truth of him, a part of him that no one else knew before she let him finish this.

Grudgingly, and with warnings, Leandro had driven her to the high-rise building that was only a few miles from the Conti offices. He'd accompanied her to the door.

If Luca had been shocked to see her standing on the threshold of his apparently inviolate space, he'd hidden it quite thoroughly. Naked torso and blue jeans molded to hard thighs, he'd sent her heart thudding. Dark hair all kinds of rumpled and a gaunt, introspective set to his features that she'd come to recognize as a need for solitude, he looked utterly delectable.

Arms folded, Leandro waited and watched them, a faint tension emanating from him. He didn't know what Luca was going to do. With her, she'd realized with a sliver of alarm running up her spine.

But even the thought that Luca could harm her was ludicrous. Strip her armor and distill her to the core of her, yes. Hurt her with reckless or cruel intent, no. She was as sure as the wild beat of her heart in her chest, like the flutter of a trapped bird.

"Hello, Bluebeard," she'd tossed at Luca then with a manufactured sauciness, and ducked under his arm, refusing to give him a chance to turn her away.

She didn't care that he hadn't even sent her one of his teasing, quirky texts in a week. That he didn't want her infiltrating whatever it was that he guarded so fiercely. She didn't care that in a matter of weeks he wouldn't want her in his life.

Already, there were warning signs. At least once every day, he reminded her the days were counting down, a calculating look in his eyes. Afraid that that one question would start a conversation she was in no way prepared for, she'd evaded him. She didn't care that slowly her heart, her emotions, her very soul, were slipping away from her. That she had lost all rationality about this thing between them. That for the first time in her life, it wasn't her career or her family's future keeping her up at night.

That had been at seven in the evening. He'd closed the door and turned to look at her, a devouring light in his eyes. Slowly relief gave way to other uncomfortable emotions—awkwardness and anxiety. They stood there staring at each other, both aware that a line had been crossed.

She didn't say, *you didn't call in six days.*

He didn't say, *you're acting like a clingy wife.*

When he reached her and cupped her jaw, she'd almost wept with relief. "You look exhausted."

She'd leaned into his touch, too far gone to even think of hiding her need for him. "Didn't sleep much the last few days. I don't know how you do this all the time."

His fingers covered her nape; his nose rubbed against her jaw. "How did your proposal go?"

She smiled against his shoulder, the familiar scent of sweat and soap and skin anchoring her. "It went very well." Nuzzling into his skin, feeling the thud of his heart under her hands, only then did the clamor in her blood calm. "With you on my side, I can even achieve world domination."

"Bene."

He'd picked her up then, as if she weighed nothing, and declared they'd go to bed. For sleep, first, and then other things that they both were in desperate need of, he'd declared throatily against her hair.

The scrape of her skin against the soft cotton told her she was still utterly naked. Instinctively, she pulled the duvet up toward her chin and turned to her side.

The pillow didn't even bear an indentation—he hadn't slept at all. Whereas she'd been thoroughly wiped out. Like a possessed man, he'd driven her to the edge again and again. He'd always been playful before, even when he'd made her do the wickedest things.

Laughter colored everything they did. Even when they were hungrily going at each other like rabbits. He said the funniest things and found her no-nonsense outlook humorous. Except tonight.

A price, he'd said, scratching his stubble against the tender skin of her inner thigh, when she'd begged him to stop. She had to pay a price for coming to Bluebeard's lair. And even with his wicked mouth at the core of her, and her throat raw from screaming his name, Sophia realized she'd already paid a price.

A crisp breeze flew in and she shivered, the last remnants of sleep chased away. Her eyes adjusted to the darkness punctured by the moonlight through the floor-to-ceiling glass doors. Wrapping the sheet around her, she walked to them and peered through.

It was pitch-black, the darkest time of the night, just before dawn.

She went into the bathroom, washed her face. Sneaking into his closet, she found a dress shirt and pulled it on over her underwear.

That was when she heard it.

The strains of music. That same tune he'd played haltingly, almost lazily, that night of the party. *It* had woken her.

Heart beating a thousand times faster, she went, her entire being tugged as if by a rope. Just as she reached the door and pushed it open, the music stopped.

No, no, no.

Like a wisp of smoke she'd been chasing for hours in some deep, dark forest but forever lost now. Only an echo of it lingered, in the very stillness of the air, in the loud thud of her heart.

"Play it again," she demanded, leaning against the wall, her voice loud and uneven.

Skin stretched taut to stiffness over muscle, his bare back was a map to his mood. His hands still on the keys, he didn't turn around. "I didn't realize you were awake."

Sophia walked a couple more steps into the room and halted. An urgency was building in her, as if she was at a crossroads that would change her life. "You gave it your best shot to wear me out, I know. What did you think to do once I fell asleep? Smuggle me out of here? Drug me and take me back?" For the life of her she couldn't keep the accusation out of her tone. "Even you, with your unending energy and libido, can't keep me in that room forever."

He turned and leveled a look at her over his shoulder. "You're developing a sense for drama."

"Dramas and masks are your forte."

He raised a brow then. Masculine arrogance dripped from the lazy gesture. Her breath held, Sophia waited, for he could rip her apart in that moment. It was the same look he'd worn when she'd said he thrived on control. He would have decimated her then, too, but Sophia had backed off. Stalled him by offering herself up.

Only a few steps between them but it could have been an oceans-wide chasm. A stranger looked back at her. Not the one who laughed with her. Not the one who'd moved inside her like he was an extension of her own body.

She stayed at the door, afraid of breaking whatever tenuous thing had built between them. Afraid that if she walked out the door tonight, it was all over.

"Please… Only once. I…would give anything you ask of me to hear it once."

Something akin to shock flashed in his eyes.

She forced herself to smile, to act as if her heart wasn't rearing to leap out of her chest. As if she weren't standing over some abyss, ready to fall in. Fear and hope twisted into a rope in her belly.

"I…have never played for anyone. Not even Leandro and Tina."

"I don't give a damn. I want to hear it."

He didn't blink at her outburst. He didn't reply. He just turned back to the piano. Silence reigned for so long that Sophia was sure she had lost.

But then long fingers moved on the keys. The tension melted from his shoulders and back. He became fluid, an extension of the instrument. He forgot her, Sophia realized. There was no one but him and the tune that flew from his fingers.

Slow, haunting, full of a soul-deep pain. It continued like that, sneaking insidiously into every pore, every cell, until Sophia felt the haunting desperation as her own. It was gut-wrenching, visceral, with a swirling motif turning back on itself again and again, as if it couldn't free itself of its tethers. As if it was choking but still couldn't escape.

Until a different note emerged and almost disappeared. She tensed, wondering if she was imagining it. If it was her own audacious hope that she was hearing in the music.

But that note emerged again, like the crest of a wave, like the brilliance of light in a darkened corner. Again and again, until the haunting pain was slowly being washed away by the tremulous hope. The tempo picked up, now the notes of pain and fear being lost among the high notes. It rose and rose until nothing but hope remained. Even that hope was tentative, fragile, a jaggedly painful life but still it glittered.

The high note held and held until it soared like a bird in the sky, stretching every nerve in her tight.

Sophia sank to the floor, her body shuddering at an avalanche of emotions she couldn't even name. Her knees and hands shook, tears running a blistering path over her cheeks.

She felt transformed, like she herself had risen from the ashes, painfully new but full of hope. The beauty of the composition was an ache in her throat. For several minutes—or was it aeons?—she stayed there on the floor, her heart too full to feel anything.

Slowly, her heartbeat returned to normal and the contrast of the silence that descended was deafening. Like the silence a storm left after its destruction.

Luca stayed at the piano. She'd never seen him so remote, so distant, almost as if he stood at the edge of civilization instead of being the charming lover pursued in droves by women.

She pushed herself to her feet. Today she would heed

his unspoken warning for she felt like a leaf that could be blown away by the wind. She couldn't laugh if he told some slick joke. She couldn't bear it if he became that… that travesty of an indulgent playboy when that astonishing beauty, that incredible music, resided in him.

For once, she didn't feel victorious for being right. She felt nauseous and furious and frayed at the edges.

"What did you think of it, Sophia?"

His question stilled her hand on the door. She looked at the dark oak, unwilling to face him. How could he contain so much inside himself? How had he bared a part of him but ripped away something of her?

"It was…interesting," she replied. There was no word that could do justice to that piece of music. All she knew was that she needed to get away from him before she did something stupid like bawl over him…or rage at him with her fists. Was this what came out of those periods of restlessness, those times that he disappeared?

It was like that piece of music had broken open the cupboard in her head and all she could see, feel, were messy emotions roiling in and out of her. She was spoiling for a fight, a down and dirty match. She felt a huge wave of emotion building inside her, battering at her to burst out.

"Interesting?" he said, and she heard a sliver of laughter in that single word. "I think that's the first diplomatic thing I've ever heard you say."

She turned and faced him.

He looked like the same Luca who'd mocked her three hours ago. The same one who had fed her strawberries and cream while she'd worked on her laptop, the same one who'd brought her pots of tea and pastries when she'd worked into dawn. The same man who had licked and stroked her to ecstasy as if it were the one and only reason he was put on the planet.

But he wasn't the same.

She didn't know him at all.

Slowly, she realized what he was telling her. What his slick smile was about—an invitation to join him in the parody he carried out every day. Nausea welled up inside her.

"Whose composition is it?" she asked, giving him a chance, giving him a warning of her own. "It sounds… classical."

He smiled then. And instead of charm, she saw condescension. Instead of genuine amusement, she saw smugly bored arrogance. Instead of miles of charm and insouciant wit and reckless antics, she saw pain and utter anguish and a thin flicker of hope. Instead of a man who went through life in pursuit of reckless pleasure, she saw a brooding, dark stranger.

Like she was at a reproduction of Dr. Jekyll and Mr. Hyde.

"Do you know classical music, then?"

Look at them, holding a conversation as if they were on a first date. Thrusting and deflecting as if there wasn't a storm gathering around them.

She shrugged, preparing herself for the fight. He knew nothing of her if he thought she would back down now. "There were a few months there after my mom and Sal married where he thought I required a little polish. It was a bleak time. There was a piano teacher, ballet classes and even an art teacher. Penguin me and ballet, can you imagine?"

"If you call yourself a penguin one more time, I shall spank you."

"I also now see why Tina was so amused when I called you a peacock."

"What am I, then?"

"A panther."

"Why?"

"Its spots are in plain sight under that black coat. It is more vulnerable than any other jungle cat for, however much it tries, it can't blend in like the other ones. It automatically stands out."

He stood like a statue, with his hands behind him. The man she had thought couldn't be still in any way, the man she'd thought lacked any depth. What a laugh he must have had all this time...

"But we were talking about music, weren't we? I practiced for hours and hours, determined to be the perfect little princess to please Sal. Even though my strength lay in numbers. Mr. Cavalli said I was brilliant with technique, but I played without soul. That for me it was just a means to an end." How right old Mr. Cavalli had been.

Music, music like Luca played, just was. It defied paltry human parameters. It defied night and day; it defied constriction or boundaries. It defied definition of any sort.

"Like a piece of flaky, buttery pastry, he'd say, only without the warm, sugary goodness in the middle. It was such a good metaphor, I was completely horrified and quit. So, yeah...I do know a bit about music."

And before she could regulate the words, they shot out. Like pieces of jagged rocks shattering the carefully constructed glass wall around him. "It's yours, isn't it, Luca? You wrote that piece."

CHAPTER TWELVE

THEY'D HAD SO LITTLE time left. A handful of moments. Of laughter and making love. Of late-night feasts and frantic early-morning sex. He was going to pack so many things into that time. He was going to persuade her the best way he knew to extend the duration of their marriage.

To however long it would take for them to get each other out of their systems.

Now they had nothing.

It was over.

Luca felt a strange kind of relief on one side. That it was all over. The end of things was something he was infinitely familiar and comfortable with.

Hiding in plain sight had never been harder than it was with Sophia. She clawed and ripped, cajoled and kissed her way to the core of him. The rational part of him that reminded him whose son he was and how he had come to be took a beating at her hands.

You are Luca Conti, it shouted in an eternally tireless voice, forever reminding him what he should and shouldn't have. It grounded him. It balanced him.

Then there was the second half. The part that he had never made peace with. The part that craved and gobbled up everything and anything, that demystified the most complex puzzles for him in a matter of seconds.

He'd always thought of it as a yawning blackness, forever hungry.

There was beauty in it; there was intellect in it. And above all, it just was.

And it was that part that was thrashing, wild with grief, already mourning the loss of this woman. The woman who above everyone else had seen and identified it. The woman who promised friendship, companionship, acceptance with her words and demands.

But Luca had a lifetime of practice suppressing this part of him. Or at least ignoring it just enough. Pretending that it didn't exist had only pushed him even more toward the edge. Like Antonio had done with his father.

So instead, he had compartmentalized it. Like a wild dog that was fed just enough from time to time to keep it compliant, to keep it tethered.

He felt Sophia's hand on his flesh and realized how cold he was. Or maybe that was grief, too.

"Luca?"

Turning toward her fully, he answered her. "It is my own. I finished it this last week. Which is why I didn't call you."

Her beautifully intelligent eyes flared then steadied. "A week?"

"Si."

"You don't sleep or stop until you finish it."

He shrugged.

Now the truth lay between them, a dark specter.

He could see that she hadn't expected him to agree. She had guessed it but there had been a small hope that it might not be true. That he was the waste of space she thought him rather than…*whatever freak of nature* he was. It was the same realization he had seen in his mama's eyes for years before she'd left.

The tremulous hope that his last episode of restlessness and headaches and the furiously written music was all just a one off. And the crushing sense of defeat as she realized that he was just like his father. Not just in form but in his mind, too.

As if that wasn't unbearable enough for her.

With Sophia, however, that bucking lasted only a few seconds. He saw, with a strangely detached fascination, the moment she faced the disconcerting truth and accepted it. Her shoulders squared. Stubborn chin lifted, ready to march into battle.

He laughed then. And because he was so weak, and because he had trapped himself without a way out, he hauled her toward him and kissed her. He, the creative genius with an IQ off the charts, he had thought himself so clever. He would seduce her, he would steal a part of her and then go on his merry way. Or he would take and take of her but give nothing of his own self.

What an arrogant fool he was…

At the back of his mind, furious panic was setting in. Like a gathering wave of blackness that would rip him apart. It sent his heart thudding so loud that he could feel it in his throat.

His lips on Sophia's became more demanding, rough, desperate. He wanted to sink under her skin and never emerge. He wanted to drown in her forever. He'd barely breathed the pure, shining wonder that was she before she pushed him away. Wiped her mouth with the back of her hand.

"Is my touch already that distasteful, *cara mia*?" he retorted, unable to keep the ugly jeer out of his tone. Unable to not slide a little into the quagmire of self-pity.

This was what happened when he forgot who and what he was. *Dio*, he became a wounded, raving dog. And if she didn't leave soon, he would take a chunk out of her.

"What?" She glared at him first. Then her eyes lost that

glazed look, her mouth became a purse of displeasure and then she shook her head at him. "You kiss me and I lose all rationality, all common sense. I will not let you sex me up and send me on my way again, with a pat and an orgasm."

Something in him calmed at the matter-of-fact tone. As long as she didn't loathe him, he could still keep his dignity even as he ended the one meaningful relationship of his life. He sighed, folded his hands and leaned against the wall. He would last through this, too. He always did. "Sophia, you are making a big—"

"You cheated me, again. You—"

He laughed. "Even you couldn't rise above making this about you, could you?"

She flushed. "I was just warming up. Your entire life is a lie."

A shaft of anger pierced him and he welcomed it. He never lost his temper, as a rule. There was enough unpredictability in his head and he ruled the rest of it with a tight leash. Trust Sophia to provoke that, too. "My life is what I need it to be."

"And why is that? This is not the dark ages to fear… talent, *no…talent* is such a lukewarm word, isn't it?" Her entire body bristled with the force of her words. "To fear such beauty, such…genius, whatever else it is accompanied by. You can't just…throw it away like this. My God, what is your brother thinking?"

His faith in her wavered then, at the strange light in her eyes. "My brother thinks I have enough problems to deal with without pursuing fame and recognition."

"Fame and recognition, Luca? That's not what I mean. There is such beauty in your music, such pain and hope…" Tears filled her eyes and swept down. "I…I just wish… Looking at you, at the perfect foil your looks and your charm provide you, I can hardly believe it.

"Until I close my eyes and that music moves through me. Then I open my eyes and I see you. All of you."

The sight of Sophia's tears unmanned him like nothing else.

"Why have you made your life into such a travesty? How can you bear to contain all that and breeze through life as if you were nothing? You have made a joke out of a gift—"

It came at him then, fraying the edges of his temper. Anger and self-loathing and utter helplessness. He stepped away from her. It was the helplessness that flayed him. Always. And he knew Sophia wouldn't stop until he laid himself bare in front of her. Until he stood there in all his utterly powerless nakedness. Until he satisfied her, too, that this was all he could be.

"I've never had a choice to be anything else. I do not believe it is a gift."

He saw her blanch then. "The headaches and the insomnia… I'm sure they make it very hard. But you said yourself—"

"You're not listening, Sophia. My father was like this but violent. Antonio neither helped him nor controlled him, with the fear of the Conti name being dragged through mud. Enzo ran wild, buried those headaches in alcohol and drugs. He became abusive. And when my mother told him she was leaving him, he…lost it. He…" His voice broke here, and Luca felt like he was a jagged rock, full of painful edges, never changing. "He forced himself on her. And you know what she had as a result? Me, in his image, every which way."

There it was, his shame. The very cause of his existence. A mass of ugliness shrieking in the room with them.

Acid burned through his throat. He wanted to sink to his knees and cry as he'd done the day he'd found out. He wanted to throw himself into her arms as he'd done once with his brother. He wanted to…take Sophia and bury himself in her sweetness; he wanted to escape in her arms one more time.

But he would not give in to any of those urges.

To not rail at something he could not change, to not become what his father had, that was in his hands. It was his choice to make.

So he stood there, bending and bucking at the fresh grief that tore through him with vicious claws, but refusing to break. For it had been years since he had felt the loss of the freedom to be anything else. But she made the grief and the loss fresh tonight.

Sophia made everything hurt again, ravage him. Everything was excruciatingly raw again.

Her face had lost all its color; tears filled her eyes and overflowed. Luca held her gaze, locked away his own. Crying had ever only made his headaches worse and all his pain was reflected in her clear gaze, anyway.

She didn't utter platitudes. She just stood there unflinching, absorbing everything he threw at her. As if his pain was hers. As if she would stand and fight for him, too. As if he, too, had been accepted into that band of people she loved and protected so fiercely… He had never wanted to belong to someone as desperately as he did then. Never wanted to put himself in another's hands so much.

He never wanted to believe that he could have loved so much.

He weakened then. Almost broke. Until he started speaking again, until he reminded himself. "He was a monster to her. And every time she looked at me, *Mama* broke inside a little. And then I started having these bouts of restlessness, these…episodes. In the beginning, I was barely rational through them. They terrified her. *I terrified her.*

In the end, she walked out. So do not dare to tell me that it is a gift I should celebrate or rejoice. Or share with others. Do not presume to tell me how I should live my life."

He thought he was like his father. That wasn't just Antonio's fear.

It was Luca's, too.

But Luca, unlike half the thickheaded men she knew, was also extremely self-aware, was so much in touch with his emotions. He had to know he was nothing like his father. That he would never hurt anyone.

"Did you ever get violent like him?" she asked, still processing everything he'd told her. He looked remote, painfully alone. This was his cross to bear, she could see. This fear was the invisible wall she'd been throwing herself against.

He shook his head. "No. I... When I was too young to understand, Antonio thought I was just being a boy. But my brother, he understood it. He would never leave me alone, night or day through it. Headaches, or insomnia, or madly scribbling notes on paper, Leandro stayed with me like a shadow. He...helped me develop self-discipline, told me again and again that just because I was a genius that didn't mean he would be my servant. But he became more—he became mother and father and friend to me."

Sophia smiled and nodded, a little of the pressure in her chest relieving. She would kiss Leandro when she saw him next for what he had done for Luca. But there was also panic building inside her. A sense of cavernous loss and a chasm of distance between her and Luca that she couldn't cross. "Then you're nothing like him, are you?" She heard the crack in her tone then. The desperation.

But none of it touched him. "You're a foolish woman if you think I'm not. After everything I just told you."

Standing helplessly there, Sophia realized it then.

That he was like his father was not a fear. It had become his shield against more hurt. More rejection. It was his reason to separate himself from everyone, his reason to loathe himself.

What else could a mere boy do to protect himself against the violent image that he'd been brought into life through such a horrible act? Against a fate he couldn't change? And what torture to be always reminded of it, again and again, of the man who'd wreaked that destruction, to have no escape from it?

Something so beautiful, but tainted in ugliness. Much as she pitied his mother, Sophia was filled with a powerless rage. "She should have protected you. It was not your burden to bear."

For it was nothing but a burden. An unimaginable one. Every inch of her flinched when she imagined how trapped he must feel always. How much he must crave escape from himself…

"How can you blame her of all people?" He was blazingly furious now. But Sophia much preferred him like this instead of that cold smile he'd given her earlier. She preferred the wild, unruly part of him, the part she was sure he hated. "She was innocent in all this."

"So were you!" she yelled, fresh tears pouring out of her eyes. "She could've been stronger for you. She… It was not your fault. None of this is."

"I'm aware of that. You think I have been punishing myself all these years? Do you see the life I have lived?"

She wiped her cheeks and smiled. "No, and I think that is your greatest accomplishment, isn't it? Not that beautiful piece of music. Not whatever mysteries your genius mind can solve. Not the big joke you play on the whole world. You laugh through life, you strut through it, you don't make any apologies for the way you do it…" She was laughing a little and crying a little again. "You…*live it so gloriously, Luca.*"

Her chest constricted, every inch of her yearning to hold him to her, to mold him with her fingers. To feel that hard body against hers and tell him that he was loved. That he was the most glorious, wonderful man she'd ever met. That he'd filled her life with courage, and laughter and love these past months.

That he was better, more than any man she'd ever known.

Genius or not, Luca was generous, kind, magnificent. But now that she knew the reality of him, now that she had heard his music, there was no escape. Her fate was tied to his.

She had toppled into love and it was exactly as she had feared. Her knees were skinned, her body bruised, her heart already taking a beating. And after all her careful maneuvering through it, after being strong for so many years, he was going to rip apart the very fabric of her life.

For there was no light in her world without him. No laughter, no joy, no color. She was nothing but the drab, colorless, staid Sophia.

His poisonous hatred about his genius, his self-loathing, it all stood there like a dark, forbidding stone wall that she couldn't climb, much less conquer. An almost tangible thing rushing him away from her, blocking her. "You live this life you've been given, Luca. I can't help but admire that."

Something flashed in his face then—relief or peace—and she thought it might be a small chink in his armor. A tiny crack in that impenetrable wall. "Then we are in agreement, *si*? Because I thought we could make this a more permanent arrangement. With some ground conditions."

The offer was made with a tease, a lighthearted tone. But it was full of wretchedness, too. For he also knew what it meant if she hated the other part of him. If she agreed it was a shame to be hidden away because now she knew where it came from.

She could see it all in his face, she understood his complex mind so well. Not now, but eventually, he would hate her a little for what he was already doing, too.

She was damned if she did and damned if she didn't. Despair gave way to anger. How dare he decide their fate like this? Who had given him this right to govern her joy? "No, we're not in agreement. I will not hate, I *can't* hate something that is part of you. Like you do. I won't pretend. I can't look at you and not see all of you. The masks have come off—there's no going back, Luca."

"I didn't realize you have a love for such melodrama."

"Drama? You think I choose this any more than you choose to be what you are? I accept the part of you that flitted from woman to woman all these years because you thought that was the only kind of connection you could have. So I must accept this, too. Please, Luca." She reached for him then. "Don't you see I understand?"

He stiffened, his features haunted. Pain was a live thing in his eyes then. "You see me as broken now, and I can't stand it. I have never pitied myself and neither will you."

Her own fury rose, fueled by fear. Why wasn't he seeing what he meant to her? She wasn't the sentimental sort; she didn't know how to make big declarations. She didn't even understand half of the riotous emotions coursing through her right then. All she knew was this: they could not end that night, not over this. "Do not presume to tell me what I feel about you, then."

"I have given you everything I'm capable of, everything I have, Sophia."

"I have found that place, Luca, the place where I want to dwell. By your side. Just don't ask me to pretend like I don't know the true you now. I can't unsee you. I can't unhear that music…" But even as she said it, she knew nothing would change his mind.

His beliefs about himself were bone-deep, a disease that would steal him away from her. He would never accept himself. And he would never accept what she felt for him.

He had not left her with an illusion of her strength, either; he'd left her nowhere to hide. Reckless, he'd ripped it all from her and now she had nothing to fight him with.

Such powerlessness flew through Sophia's veins that she wanted to throw something at the wall. She wanted to beat her fists into something and feel the crunch of bones.

But she did nothing like that. Sensible as always, she realized the futility of a violent tantrum. There was nothing to do but wait and hope that he would let her in again. That years of deeply held self-belief might shift.

She reached him and laid her hands on his shoulders. Her fingers moved over the slopes of his neck, the jut of his collarbone, the warm, taut stretch of skin over muscle.

He didn't reject her touch. He didn't return it, either. The man who always, *always*, touched her as if he couldn't bear it otherwise, who had taught her what it was to touch and kiss and learn another, didn't touch her now.

Head bowed, he stood there like a statue, a warm, wonderful man who'd all but ripped a vital part of himself and kept it away.

She kissed first one cheek and then the other. Masculine and sweaty, the scent of him made her blood sing. The clench of his muscles as she wrapped her arms around his naked back… She was aware of every breath in him as if it were her own. Finally, she clasped his cheek and kissed his mouth. Poured every bit of her into that kiss. "If only you would give me one chance—yourself, one chance—Luca. Give this thing between us one chance…"

Sophia turned and left his studio. His world. And a huge part of herself with him.

It took Sophia three weeks and a clip of Luca dancing with a seminaked burlesque dancer in a night club in Paris—circulated by Marco Sorcelini—to realize Luca wasn't coming back.

When she'd discovered from Leandro that Luca had left not just Milan, but Italy, the morning after that painful night, something inside her had frozen. She had packed it all away, told herself that he needed time to figure it out, to stop running. After all, the fear that he could be like his father, the ugly truth that he should have never had to face, that isolated lifestyle he'd made into an art form, had a decades-deep grip on him.

It had been his shield against more rejection, against pain.

How could he let go of those beliefs just for her? How could she expect him to, after knowing her for only a few months?

Interestingly, it was a discussion prompted by her step-father that had torn the blinders from her eyes.

Sophia had returned from work at almost eleven when she'd seen Salvatore waiting for her in the study. Knowing that she couldn't indefinitely avoid her parents' concern, she'd joined him. She was exhausted, sleep-deprived and she'd caught the first hint of the rumors about her record short marriage.

No one woman could keep the Conti Devil…
Conti Devil seeking new distractions…
Conti Devil flees Italy and his marriage…

Her cheeks hurt from the number of times she'd tried to keep her expression calm.

Salvatore offered her a glass of water and peered at her patiently while she finished it off. "Sophia, have you decided what you're going to do?"

"About what, Sal?"

His dark brows had gathered into a frown. "About your marriage. I think it is better for you and Rossi's if we see a lawyer immediately. Now, I have—"

Wretched fury burst out of Sophia. Her whole adult life, it was all she'd heard about—the Rossi Glory, the Rossi Legacy. "Is Rossi's all you care about?"

Salvatore blanched. "*Non.* I worry about you, too, Sophia. But after years, Rossi's is benefitting from the Conti family's influence and it is better to separate your marriage from the business as—"

"Christ, Sal! Rossi's is not thriving because of Leandro or Luca or the great CLG. But because of me! I'm the one who turned the company around. I'm the one who…" Shameful tears blocked her throat; Sophia looked away from him. But the tears had also released her fear.

She had had enough of lying down and taking what she was given. Tired of fighting for a place without actually demanding her due. Like a faithful dog happy with scraps.

That infuriatingly slick charmer had been right in this, too.

Looking thoroughly befuddled, Salvatore took her hand in his. "I have loved you like you were my own—"

The dam broken, Sophia snatched her hand away. Words were so easy. Staying behind lines, worrying about Sal's fears, justifying Luca's past as reason enough for his current cowardice… It was all so easy. "Do you truly, Sal? Then why not trust me with your great Rossi legacy? Why have you never considered me to be your successor? After all, I've worked damned hard to be here. I'm the best thing that's happened to the company in years."

And just like that, Sophia fought her own insecurities, ripped away the cocoon of self-delusion she'd built for herself. Even then, guilt about her family and her love for this abrasive but inherently kind man almost took her out at the knees. "I have only ever worked to make Rossi's whole again. It is my company as much as it is yours. But unless you see that, unless you give me the role I deserve, I quit, Sal. Tonight, now. Consider this my official resignation."

Sophia had barely turned around when Sal stopped her. Her tears ran down her cheeks, a testament to what the cruel Luca Conti had done to her again.

Hands on her shoulders, Sal lifted her chin, quite like he had done when she had been thirteen. Black eyes filled with regret and concern and a gruff sort of tenderness. "You will forgive an old man his old prejudices, *si*, Sophia? You are right. You are and have always been stronger than any son I hoped for. Rossi Leather and its future, they are all tied to you. You are its future, *bella*. Forgive me, *si*?"

When he pulled her into his warm embrace, Sophia broke down into shuddering sobs. She cried for herself and for Luca, wondered if he would ever come back.

That night, desperate for a little connection to him, Sophia packed a bag and went back to Villa de Conti at the stroke of midnight. If Leandro and Tina thought her a little mad, they didn't betray it by word or look. Her throat had filled with tears when they had silently stood in support while she wandered through Luca's room like a wraith.

He'd given her everything—a chance to save Rossi's, an opportunity to explore her potential, a new family that somehow seemed to love wholeheartedly despite their dif-

ferences, and more important than anything else, her belief in herself.

What was she supposed to do with all the riches in the
world when he wasn't there? What was pride when her
heart itself was broken?

She lay awake in the bed she'd shared with Luca countless times and cried again. It was time to face another truth.

Her foolish belief to wait and hope that Luca would let
her in again was nothing but sheer cowardice. The deep
freeze that seemed to have settled around her heart ever
since that night, her self-possession, her brittle calmness
in the face of the rumors flying about Luca dumping her
after three months of marriage was nothing but docile acceptance of his decision. A habit that was as embedded in
her, it seemed, just as Luca's fear was.

Instead of fighting and scratching and kicking her way
into his life, she hid beneath her fake strength. She had
even started withdrawing from society, afraid of facing
their pity, or scorn or both.

She'd done this the last time, too. Instead of confront-
ing him, she'd quietly slipped back to her life, accepting
his decision. Not this time.

Not when she knew that the kind of intimacy and connection and laughter that she and Luca had shared came
once in a lifetime. Not when she knew they were made for
each other. Not when there was so much love to be filled
in both their lives if only…

If she had to break Luca to make him face himself, face
Sophia and her love, she'd do it. If it was destruction he
wanted, she would hand it to him. She would shatter every
pretense he'd carried out, rip apart every lie he'd weaved
around himself.

And maybe when there was an end to all the things he

clung to, an end to the farce, an end to life as he knew it, maybe then they could have a new beginning.

But one thing was sure: she wasn't giving up without a fight.

CHAPTER THIRTEEN

Two months later

LUCA WALKED INTO the high-ceilinged breakfast room of Villa de Conti and stilled. Shock rippled through the room, a tangible tension in the air. His family looked up at him— relief the more prevalent of emotions flitting across their faces.

"Where the hell were you?" Leandro shouted across the vast room, his legendary self-control absent. "*Dio*, Luca! You could've been be lying dead in some part of the world for all we knew."

"*Papa*, you're shouting and swearing," Luca's seven-year-old niece, Izzie, piped up.

Luca raised a brow at his brother. "If I die, you would hear."

"We know you're not dead." This was Tina. "You made sure we all knew what you were up to."

Something in her gaze caught Luca and for once in his life, he shied away from his little sister. Had he changed or she?

Izzie lifted her arms to him. "I missed you, *Zio*."

Here was another one of the female variety from whom he'd never been able to hide. He lifted her from the break-fast chair and buried his face in her sweet, strawberry-scented hair. Something loosened in his gut.

Small arms clutched his neck tightly. He pulled her tiny

hands from around his neck, kissed her cheek and put her back in her chair.

His sister-in-law, Alex, was next. Usually, Alex, who was slender and willowy, coming at him was like holding a bouquet of dainty summer flowers. Pleasant and leaving him with an utter sense of well-being, of deep, unwavering affection. Of the innate goodness of life.

Heavy with pregnancy, when she threw herself at him today, though, Luca wavered on his feet and smiled. Her grip was just as tight as her daughter's around his neck. "You worried the hell out of all of us. Are you well, Luca?"

A lump lodged in his throat and he nodded.

What a fool he'd been... He'd denied a part of himself for so many years. And in the process, denied himself so many good things, too. He kissed Alex's cheek soundly, knowing it irritated Leandro. "You still won't run away and marry me, *cara*?" He said it loudly and saw the scowl on his brother's face.

Alex pulled back from his arms, ran a shaking hand over his cheek and laughed. "Bigamy, I believe, is a crime in Italy, too, isn't it?"

And just like that, the pressure on his chest returned.

Dio, he felt like he walked around with a permanent boulder on his chest. Or he was developing some serious heart trouble. Personally, he preferred the second. At least he could get it treated.

But no such luck.

He was in the peak of his prime, a physically perfect specimen of mankind. Although, lately, he'd begun to loathe himself less for what was inside, too.

He kissed Tina's cheeks, leveled a cursory nod at Antonio and sat down.

The scent of coffee and pastries filled the air, the tinkle of coffee cups and cutlery discordant in the awkward silence. Izzie finished her milk and toast, hugged him again, sought reassurance that he wouldn't disappear again and left the room.

Luca waited, his breath pent up in his chest, his fingers not quite steady.

They were looking at him, and then shying away. He put his coffee cup down so hard that half the coffee sloshed over his fingers. "I haven't gone mad, so everybody can breathe easier." Only the frown on Antonio's face relaxed.

He had to give his dear old *Nonno* some points for constancy—always a little afraid for Luca.

Leandro shrugged. "I never thought you would."

All his brother had ever done was tell Luca that he had a choice to be like their father or not. But Sophia had showed him that the choice was not just to be different from his father. But he had the choice of accepting himself, too. Of being happy in his own skin.

"Destroy every chance at any happiness you could have, like I almost did? *Si*," Leandro continued. "Fall into some kind of mad abyss and froth at the mouth? *Non*.

"What Enzo did or was, what resides in you, that is not our legacy, Luca. What we do with our lives, is. Aren't you the one who told me that?"

His throat full of unshed tears, Luca nodded. And then he asked the question that had been tormenting him all the way through his trek through the markets in Marrakesh. Through the deserts of the Middle East and the cold winter of Prague.

Through endless parties and long lonely nights even in the midst of crowds. Because Sophia was right. His mask was off and he was tired of pretending that he was worthless. He was tired of acting as if what he had was enough.

For years he'd made an art form of running away from himself. But he couldn't run away from Sophia and his thoughts of her. He couldn't run away from the man she made him to be, the man she thought him to be.

"How is she?"

There, he was bare naked again. With no place to hide, no mask in place to retreat behind if it hurt. No shallow facade to reject before being rejected. It was not a feeling he was going to get used to anytime soon.

"Ask her when you see her."

"Why am I seeing her?" He wanted to, desperately. But for once in his life, he didn't know what he was going to say. All his charm, his quicksilver mind, nothing really helped when he lay awake for long hours wondering what he would say to her.

How he would beg.

"She's taking you to the cleaners," Leandro added with quite a relish.

It would serve you right if I took you to the cleaners.

The shock on Luca's face deepened his brother's smile. "Her exact words. She wants a huge divorce settlement."

Divorce? She was talking divorce? Had she decided he wasn't worth it, after all?

Luca's heart sank like a stone, leaving a gaping void in his chest. Had he self-destructed, then? Had he become that self-fulfilling prophecy? Had he lost the one woman who'd loved him despite the fact that he hadn't deserved it? And he couldn't blame it on what Enzo had passed on to him. No, this was all his doing.

Merda, was it all over already?

"I told you to give her my share of the Conti stock," he offered numbly. Suddenly, his world felt emptier than it had ever been before.

This blackness, this yawning stretch in front of him, this was what would break him. His love for Sophia, that was the only thing that would knock him out at the knees, he realized now. Not some pre-decided genetic sequence. Not a lack of control.

Living without Sophia's love, returning to the meaningless, empty tomb of his life, would send him to madness.

"To quote, 'It costs him nothing to give it away, that bloody stock.' She doesn't want it, Luca." When Luca glared at him, Leandro shrugged again. "Don't shoot the messenger. You left me here to deal with her and she is on a warpath. She wants your personal fortune, your studio, even your countless pianos. Apparently, everything you have ever hidden, everything you have ever made through your *genius*, she wants it. And your antics all over Europe with all those women, you have given her lawyers enough rope to hang you with."

Why say no to CLG stock when it would give her a seat on the most powerful board in Milan? When it would mean the culmination of all her dreams?

She had him utterly baffled, more than a little disconcerted, and he was supposed to be the genius. *Did she hate him so much, then?*

He hadn't left her any other choice when he had left Milan in the dark of night, when he'd made sure tales of his escapades had reached every big media outlet that had chased him. His cruelty haunted him now.

Dio, what had he done?

Leandro wasn't quite finished.

"She has discovered, *to her delight*, her words again, that you're a millionaire a hundred times over. 'Your dear brother is full of little secrets, isn't he?' Her lawyers are quoting 'emotional distress, spousal abuse and abandonment of marriage' as grounds for divorce. Even society's sympathy lies with her. Sophia Rossi is not only clever, she's extremely resourceful."

"What the hell do you mean *society*? This is between me and her."

"No, it's not. It is a scandal now, another Conti spectacle like the last one…like Enzo started. Alex and I can't step out without being hunted by the media. Sophia and Salvatore are talking about *your separation* to everyone who will listen. There was a featured article last week that hinted you were the mastermind behind the innovative waterproof sole technology we use in Conti pumps and those gravity-defying metallic stilettos that made us big globally."

"Huang?" Luca said. "She spoke to Huang."

Leandro nodded. "They are all speculating what you've been up to all these years to have made so much money. They are all questioning your behavior all these years, wondering if you're like Enzo. She made you a person of interest to every rabid newspaper, every network station. I…I can't control what they get their hands on, Luca."

Wave after wave of shock barreled at Luca. Now he understood the gravity in his brother's voice, the concern in those gray eyes.

If someone found out about his birth, if they knew that the same hungry cavern dwelled in his mind, too, the same fear and distaste he saw in Antonio's face would appear in everyone's…

He put his head in his hands, his breath sawing through his throat. Was this all just to hurt him as he had hurt her? Would she reveal the circumstances of his birth, too? Would she make the world think him a shame, as he'd thought of himself for so long? Would she—

"*She is outing me.* She's telling the world who I am," he said, his stomach clenched so hard he couldn't breathe.

Leandro finally leaned back in his chair. "I believe so. Nothing I could say would convince her otherwise."

Luca groaned, the sound coming from the depths of his soul. The groan morphed into laughter that made his lungs burn. He felt like he was caught by an eddy, tossed around this way and that. He laughed until there were tears in his eyes and he was shaking, shivering with relief, with the release of fear and so much love that he couldn't even breathe.

Hands on his temples, he ducked his head, waiting for the dizziness to abate. Tears poured down his cheeks, and he wiped them with shaking fingers.

With his breath returned the image of Sophia that had tormented him for months.

Sophia with her heart in her eyes, her body shaking violently as she kissed him and told him that she accepted all of him. That all he needed to do was give them a chance, a real one.

Sophia, who would not take defeat lying down. Sophia, who fought to the last breath for the people she loved. "Please tell me you did not threaten or manipulate my wife in any way?"

Something flashed in Leandro's gaze. Leandro seemed to have frozen as if he could not believe it. As if it was impossible that Luca had finally, irrevocably fallen in love. "She has also already turned around Rossi's stock. According to some of my sources—"

"Your sources?" Luca demanded. "You are having her watched? Guarding your company?"

"I was worried about her, Luca. So is Salvatore. She works like a demon, she... The news about you that has reached us, she...she has not been the same. Salvatore appointed her CEO of Rossi Leather.

"Her idea for a flagship design store in the midst of Milan's fashion district made the CLG board salivate. The store will display every new product line weeks before they actually hit the market. It will become the center of every designer event in the city. But she fought for her stepfather like a lioness, said it was her family's legacy and they finally voted to call it *Casa Rossi*. Ten designer brands, including Maserati, are going to be part of her inaugural event tomorrow night."

Despite fear beating a tattoo in his blood, Luca nodded. He had no idea if Sophia would take him back, but he meant to spend the rest of his life begging, hounding her, chasing her, generally turning her life upside down. Like she had done with him. If he had to spend the rest of it on his knees, naked and shivering, he would do it.

If he had to spend the next hundred years waiting for her forgiveness and her love, he'd do it happily.

"I have never met a woman quite so ferocious," Tina added with no little pride in her voice.

Ferocious and funny and far too softhearted, the woman he'd fallen in love with was too good for him. "You take her side over your gorgeous brother's?" Luca threw at Tina.

"Since I have discovered that my brother is a donkey's behind, *si*." Tina waited for Leandro to stop laughing, a serious light in her eyes. "Since she has done me the favor of telling me the truth. Since she's the only one who treats me as a grown-up woman and not a commodity to be protected or controlled. Or used as a bargaining chip in blackmail."

Instantly, all humor evaporated from the air. Tension rippled across his shoulders and he saw the same in Leandro's face. Anguish danced in his brother's face and for his sake, Luca hoped Tina would forgive Leandro.

She threw the last words viciously at Antonio, her voice breaking. Antonio, whom Tina had loved so unconditionally, had the grace to look ashamed.

"What truth?" Luca finally managed to say. It seemed

Sophia had left no stone unturned in opening their family's vault of secrets.

"That I am not a Conti. That my father was a poor chauffeur *Mama* fell in love with after she left you and Leandro. That my older brother, the Conti Saint, set up my marriage to Kairos because he thought I would fall apart if the truth ever came out and a powerful, handsome husband could make up for it. That my second brother, the Conti Devil, married her to keep my power-hungry husband from breaking my heart. I think I prefer your way, Luca. If I had to choose between one of you manipulating my life as if it were a chess board."

"Tina, *tesoro*, I'm so—"

Tears rolled down Tina's cheeks as she cut off Leandro. "I'm not angry, Leandro. At least not anymore, now that I have had time to recover from the shock. All you and Luca have ever done is love me, *si*? You could have hated me for *Mama*'s abandoning of you. You could have left me to my own fate when she died. I am your sister and nothing could change that. But I look at Sophia, I look at the state of my marriage, and I realize what a naive fool I am. I am leaving Kairos. And Milan." *She was leaving them both.*

Luca reached her the same time Leandro did. He held her tight while she sobbed. Luca had never been more proud of his little sister.

Fear danced in Leandro's eyes, and Luca shook his head in warning. His brother's job for years had been to protect Luca and Tina. But it was Tina's life now.

Luca kissed her cheek while Leandro compulsively said, "Where are you going? Will you stay with friends? You will tell us if you need help, *si*?"

Tina laughed at Leandro and hugged him tight. "I am an adult, Leandro. I can take care of myself. You're to stay out of this thing between Kairos and me. But *si*, I will keep in touch, although only if you tell me what state Sophia leaves Luca in when she's through with him."

A weight lifted from Luca's chest and he hoped Tina would find happiness in her new journey. He found himself frantically praying to a God he had only ever hated before.

"You're a genius, *si*?" she said to him, exaggerated doubt in her teasing tone.

Luca nodded.

"Then, *per piacere*, do not lose the most wonderful thing to ever happen to you."

Casa Rossi, the first major designer store of Rossi's after its reinvention and the lounge bar on Piazza San Fedele, glittered on its opening night. Creamy white carpet and sofas, with different designer pieces from every noted brand on the shelves, made the space an intimate, exclusive event.

Pink champagne flowed freely, designer-clad men and women walked around and talked and got noticed by people they wanted to be seen by. More than a few people had approached her. Sophia had no doubt it was more to feed their own curiosity than anything else.

Because she'd dragged the venerable Contis into an out-and-out war. She refused to let Luca hide. She had been terrified when Leandro had come to see her but refused to back down.

Already the list of people who wanted to be invited to the next event was growing exponentially according to her assistant. Sophia had quickly looked through and struck off some of the men who'd called her quite a range of names over the past few years.

She adjusted a buttery-soft white leather clutch, still amazed at the success of her idea. Where Conti Luxury Goods entered, the entire range of companies who had once turned away from Rossi's joined in. The gray wolves were all walking behind her now, like domesticated dogs, following the line of meat to Rossi's.

Luca would so totally get that, she realized with a laugh. She'd have to tell him and then they would make fun of… And just like that, the painful knot in her stomach returned.

Two months since that night. She'd been pitied, smirked at, laughed at, that she had thought herself good enough to take on the Conti Devil. She'd turned her very life into a circus, herself into a cheap act for him. To make their marriage, its failure and Luca the focus of every rabid gossip in Milan.

Already, so many things had come out about him. Luca had to face himself. Accept himself. Only then was there a chance for them…

Having given up even a pretense of pride, which was all she had these days after making such a thoroughly public and humiliating spectacle of herself, of manipulating everything to lure him out, she'd begged Tina to tell her if she'd heard anything from him.

Hysterical that their fates had reversed. Now Tina was the stronger one, the one who told Sophia her brother wasn't worth it while Sophia became a shadow of herself.

She lay awake at night, aching in mind and body, worked like a demon during the day…and it was taking its toll on her. This…faith in him, in her, in their love, the laughter they'd shared, it was burning out now.

What was she going to do if he never returned?

And then she heard it, the soft strains of music coming from the lounge bar beyond the foyer. It had a piano but she had actively looked away from it, for it had the power to send her to her knees now.

This was what he'd made of her. She, who had never been afraid of anything, was now scared of pianos, and music, bikes, the streets leading to the Piazza del Duomo, and couldn't look at chocolate truffles without breaking down into sobs.

Suddenly, a strange silence replaced the soft chatter. And in that silence came that music again, the point in that vicious circle where it was trapped. Sophia felt like she was living the song.

Heart in her throat, she walked to the lounge.

There he was. He sat at the piano, his head bowed, his fingers flying over it. White shirt and dark trousers, hair wet and gleaming, shoulders fluid. Soft pink light filled the room, casting flashes of light on him. Teasing and taunting her. Driving her utterly mad.

Sophia blinked.

It had to be one of her feverish dreams in which she heard that tune again and again, in which she saw him look at her with that hunger and desire, in which she felt his hands on her, holding her, touching her, driving her out of her own skin. In which she saw him poised over her wet sex, his expression one of utter reverence and wicked desire.

She could feel him between her legs now and she clutched her legs closed tighter.

Her heart thumped. Her breath stuttered. She felt feverish. Tears threatened to spill over. She leaned against the far wall and closed her eyes. She was so cold, exhausted. Like she was breaking apart again and again.

And then the tune rose to its pinnacle, hope and life twisting together.

"Stop, please," she yelled. It did.

A frisson went through her and then she felt him in front of her.

His warmth. The scent of his skin. The air charging around him.

Her eyes flicked open.

Dark shadows under jet-black eyes. Wide, wicked, sensually carved mouth. Blades of cheekbones. Perfectly symmetric planes of his face.

The most beautiful man she had ever seen.

The man she loved beyond bearing.

She extended her arm, fluttered her fingers over his cheek. Ran her thumb over the sweep of one cheekbone and then over the defined curve of his upper lip. Her fingers kept sliding away from his face, so violently was she shaking. She felt his fingers clamp her wrist and hold her hand there against him, leaning into his touch.

She felt the pulse in his neck against her hand, frantic and hurried.

She felt his breath on the back of her palm, frenzied and rough, as if he had run a great distance to find her, instead of prowling from one corner of the room to the other.

She felt him, all of him and she shuddered violently. Her heart slammed against her rib cage.

He *was* standing before her. He was finally here. He had returned.

Sophia drew her hand back and slapped him across the cheek. So hard that his sculpted jaw went back and shock jarred up her arm. The sound of it reverberated in the silence, propelling her out of her nightmarish state. "Leave me alone," she whispered, her voice on the verge of breaking.

He didn't move. Didn't utter a word.

Only gazed at her with glittering eyes. Even in the pink light, Sophia could see the mark she'd left on his cheek. Desperate, panicky, words came and fell away from her lips.

Please stay. Please want me. Please love me.
Please don't ever leave me like that again.

No, she wouldn't beg.

She made to push away from him but he moved faster. Trapped her against the wall, his arms bracketing her on either side. He said nothing, though, only stared at her, held her like that as if he was completely complacent in that position. As if he was content to hold her in place and gaze at her for eternity.

She kept her gaze at some far point in the distance. If she stared into those eyes, she would break permanently.

"Will you not look at me, Sophia?"

"I hate you. I…despise you. You…are exactly what I always thought you were," she spat at him, her dignity, her self-respect, everything in tatters. Her strength nothing but a shadow in the face of her love for him. "A heartless bastard who can see nothing past his own bloody genius, nothing past his own demons. You were partying with your… damn groupies while I…I…" And then she fell against him, hate and love inseparably twining into a rope, binding him to her. "If you kissed a single one of them, Luca, if you have even touched one with a long pole…I'll kill you with my bare hands." Only then did she raise her eyes. He had never lied to her, but this… She needed to see the answer for herself. "If you so much as… This is over. We are over."

"*Non, cara mia*. I couldn't even look at another woman. I…was a bastard. For those first couple of weeks, I wanted to make sure you hated me. Your words that night, they haunted me. They hurt me. They mocked me. I thought I would give you all the reasons in the world to hate me. I thought I would shake that resolve in your eyes, show you what I truly was.

"But, *Dio*, I couldn't go through with any of it. For the first time in my life, I realized what I had lost and that it had nothing to do with being my father's son. That it was

I that was ruining my life with my own actions. I promise, *cara*, I could not look at another woman but you."

Something small and tenuous built inside Sophia again. Hope had never terrified her like that. "I did hate you. But I couldn't shake off that faith in us. Is that what love is? This blind, illogical, irrational faith in the man who tears you apart so recklessly when all you've done is love him? I have no more, Luca. I'm done loving you."

He shuddered around her, like a flash of lightning in the sky. His lean body jerked and settled around her again. "You did all this to make me face myself. You would give up on me now?"

She felt his hands move through her hair, his nose buried in it, her name a mantra on his lips. He held her gently as she sobbed her heart out. Two months of tears, two months of fears...two months of staying strong for him. "Sometimes, I feel like you have taken everything from me. Like a bus carried me away from everything that I loved. Like I will never breathe properly again. Like I will never be free again.

"I hate being in love. So much. I... It hurts so much."

"Shh...*tesoro mio.* Shhh...please, Sophia. No more. I can't stand the sound of you crying." She heard the tension rise in him, too, heard the catch in his voice as if he, too, was breaking down.

He pushed away her hair from her forehead, wiped the remaining tears from her cheeks. Gently, oh, so tenderly. "I...ran so far, so fast, that night. But you...you were already a part of me. You... Everything was so colorless, Sophia. Even music could not soothe me. And then I saw myself. As you saw me. And I realized this life that has brought me to you, I could never hate it. *Ti amo, tesoro.* With every breath in me. Will you let me love you, Sophia?

Will you give me the chance to be the man you deserve? I swear, *cara mia*, I will never hurt you again."

Sophia threw her arms around his neck and held him tight. Breathed in the scent of him. He was solid and male around her. "Yes, please, Luca. Love me. Spend eternity with me." He breathed a sigh, relief maybe, and held her tightly back. She gave herself over to Luca's love. Her heart was his already.

EPILOGUE

Three years later

"I'VE BROUGHT SOMEONE to see you, Mrs. Conti."

Sophia whirled around at that voice so fast that her head spun, her heart climbed up into her throat. She had seen them only this morning before she left for work, but her heart still ran away from her at the sight of them.

It was only three weeks since she'd returned to work after a six month maternity leave. But she missed spending those lazy mornings in bed when Luca would bring their bawling bundle into their bedroom and all three of them would cuddle, play and sometimes just fall into exhausted sleep after a cranky night.

Luca stood at the door, with the baby basket in hand, wicked mouth curved wide in a smile.

Her assistant, Margie, was faster than Sophia in reaching the new arrivals. She took the precious bundle instantly away from his father and cooed over him, before Sophia had even managed to breathe normally. "You're lucky, Mrs. Conti," Margie said in between the baby gibberish she spouted to their seven-month-old son. "You've got the two most gorgeous men in Italy chained to you."

Sophia looked at her beaming son, gave him a cuddle and a quick kiss before Margie stole him away from her again. "I do, don't I?" Laughing, Sophia met Luca's gaze.

White shirt and blue jeans hugged her husband's lean figure. Blue, ever-present shadows under his eyes. Stubble on his jaw, because he wouldn't have found time this morning to shave. He looked thoroughly disreputable, for once, the very image of the crazy genius he was, and heartbreakingly gorgeous.

"You left without saying goodbye this morning."

Her heart still racing, Sophia sighed. "You looked dead to the world." She knew how little sleep he managed.

"Yes, but I don't like you leaving for the day without kissing me goodbye."

Reaching Luca, she threw her hands around him while he took her mouth in a fast, scorching kiss full of frantic hunger. The same desire flooded her limbs and all she wanted was to steal away with her man for an afternoon of pulse-pounding sex, like they hadn't indulged in a while. Her sensitive nipples peaked when he stroked inside her mouth with erotic expertise that to this day stole her breath. That made her want to be just this wanton creature who made the sexiest man rock hard, and forget all her other roles—daughter, aunt, CEO of a multinational company and even a mother.

Pulling back slowly, he sank his fingers into her hair. Eyes glittered full of wicked invitation. "Take the afternoon off," he said, mirroring her very thought.

Sophia kissed him and drew back quickly before he could ensnare her again. "Even if I did, what about your son? He gets crankiest before his afternoon nap, remember? Takes after his father, the devil."

"He's an angel. Just look at him."

Dark-eyed, dark-haired, with a charming toothless grin, Leo was a mirror image of his father. The look in Luca's eyes when he had held their son for the first time had almost crushed Sophia's heart.

There had been fear, and wonder and hope and so much love. He had lifted the squalling infant in his arms so tenderly, tears running down his cheeks. And then he'd met her gaze. "He looks like me," he'd said then, a sort of helplessness in his voice. As if it broke his heart a little, all over again. "*Dio*, Sophia, what if he…he is like me, too?"

Luca's scars had healed, but not vanished.

Sophia had been crying, too. But she had stayed strong for him. She'd clutched Luca's free hand with hers and squeezed tight. "Does it matter who he looks like when we love him so much? He's a piece of our hearts, isn't he?"

It had taken them only twenty-four hours, however, to realize their son, notwithstanding his cherubic looks, had the temper of the very devil. Within two days he'd reduced Sophia to hysteric tears and a dark fear that she couldn't even calm her own son.

Packing them into his Maserati, Luca had driven them around all night, lulling them both into frantic sleep. The next night it had begun all over again. Until Luca had started playing the piano.

Only those two things calmed Leo enough to sleep every night now.

The smallest disruption to his schedule, and Leo was known to scream at decibel levels that could rupture unsuspecting eardrums. A thing that seemed to endlessly amuse his two cousins, the perfect little girls they were. "Why couldn't I have a beautiful little doll like Izzie or Chiara?"

His arms around her, Luca nuzzled her neck. "You know what we could do if you want a girl, *cara mia*."

Sophia snorted. "No way. I haven't even lost half the weight I've gained. I wish men gained weight when their wives got pregnant. It's not fair that you…you continue looking like you do while I look like a baby elephant."

"Watch that mouth. That's my lovely wife you're talking about." He pressed a kiss to her temple, reverent and tender. "I love you just as you are, Sophia. I wouldn't change a single thing about you. I would change everything about my past, everything about myself, to prove it, if I could."

The regret and pain in his tone was like a lash against her skin.

He accepted her for everything she was, flaws and all those little eccentricities, and she loved him, too. That she'd hinted, even unknowingly, at denying him that same acceptance was anathema to her.

"Si," Sophia whispered urgently. A shiver went through her and he held her tighter. "I do. And I trust you, Luca."

Even to this day, she woke up sometimes in the middle of the night, saw him next to her on the bed, usually hogging all the sheets and pushing her to the edge of the bed in his need to hold her tight, and wondered at how much this gorgeous, beautiful man loved her.

And how deeply and how completely. The wonder in his eyes when he looked at Leo and her every day, it humbled her.

"Did you really want a girl, Sophia?"

Sophia locked her hands on top of his, settling into his arms. "Not really. Although I do worry sometimes."

"About what?"

"I think of the future, and I'm sure I'll dread mornings where I have to leave you two at home and walk away. I imagine coming home to a disaster zone."

"Are you saying I'm going to spoil our son?"

"I know you're going to spoil him rotten. And I'll have to be the strict one."

He nipped at her shoulder, his lowered voice a caress. "But you do strict so well, *bella mia*."

Melting on the floor of her office was not an option so Sophia snorted instead. "I see that you're not even saying no."

His hands tightened around her waist, pressing her into his front. The length of his erection was a brand against her back. Her mouth dried, a rush of wetness pooling at her sex.

Sophia caught the moan in her throat, thanking Margie for discreetly walking away with their son to her private sitting area.

In the short time she'd been back at work, Luca and Leo's visits to her workplace were already the highlight of the day for all the women in the office. Everyone wanted to hold her son, and everyone wanted to see Luca—the infamous playboy turned devoted husband and doting, stay-at-home dad—tease, taunt and make their strict boss blush. Or so Margie had told her when Sophia had asked why there was always a rush on their floor during lunchtime.

"I have asked Alex if she'd watch Leo tonight," he said now, swiping that clever tongue over the very spot he had dug his teeth into at the crook of her neck. "She said yes. She also said she was surprised that it had taken us this long to ask her. She *also, also* said she would be keeping tabs, that the minute she hears that Leo's sleeping better, she expects us to take Izzie and Chiara. Even if we have to rip away the little one from my brother's hands."

Sophia laughed. Leandro was so protective of the girls that it took all of Alex's energy to ensure they had the freedom that little girls needed to run around and express themselves.

On the opposite end of the spectrum was her husband,

who praised their little boy for his perfect aim when he threw his bowl of mashed peas across the room like it was a soccer ball. Luca had converted a whole room in his studio into a kid-safe playroom for Leo, who even as a seven-month-old challenged himself into how destructive he could get each day.

"The whole night? Is he ready for it, do you think?"

His fingers laced with hers, he held her tightly. "He is. Are you?"

It was both alarming and a little guilt-inducing to see how easily Luca had taken to fatherhood. He loved doing everything from morning to night without a single complaint. His energy, it seemed, was boundless.

He had watched Leo the whole night for weeks, only bringing him to Sophia for feeding. While Sophia had struggled, Luca had decided it was the perfect cure for his insomnia.

"I know that right now, you know more about his habits than I do, but I thought maybe—"

"Shhh, *bella*. Didn't we talk about this? You've got nothing to feel guilty about. I love looking after him. I love bringing him to visit you here. I love seeing the glow you get when you work your ass off and you make a win in this world. This is our family, Sophia. Our life. This is what works for us. You've worked so hard to get here and it's not like I'm ever going to work a nine-to-five job."

"Yes, but I'm worried that you're not getting any time to yourself. And that you'll probably resent me sometime in the future, or think I'm not—"

"I love you. All of you. The woman who bawled like a baby when she held our son the first time, the woman who told her stepfather, in an uncompromising tone, that she and only she, could run Rossi's the best, the woman who resurrected Rossi's from its broken state, the woman who fought for me like a lioness, the woman who cries every time I play the piano.

"And that woman, that is who I fell in love with. That is who made me see a future full of love. Don't you dare change on me now, *cara mia*.

"I'm aware every minute of every day that I have this happiness, this love, this family with you and Leo because you're who you are. I adore you, *cara mia*, more every day."

Tears pricked at Sophia's eyes, a lump in her throat blocking any words from coming out. Even if she was capable of them with her heart swelling in her chest. She turned and buried her face in his chest.

God, she loved him more and more each day, too. And sometimes, the depth of that love, the power it gave him over her, the possibility of her entire life falling apart at his hands…it choked her, too. That fear was becoming less frequent, though.

When Luca loved, as she'd learned in the last three years, it was with such unerring devotion, it was with such absolute giving, that it filled her with awe.

She squeezed him for all she was worth. "Okay, you and your son have to get out of here if I'm going to take the afternoon off."

Desire glinted in his eyes. *"Si?"*

"Yes, but not for what you're thinking."

"What, then?"

"Shopping," she whispered against his mouth. She stroked her tongue into his mouth and pressed herself against him. His erection was a long, hard length against her belly. Darts of desire shot straight down to her pelvis. "I need new lingerie. Lots of red and black lace, I'm thinking, and those stilettos that I hear are new in the market."

He groaned and leaned his forehead against hers. He was breathing hard as if he'd run a mile. "I guess I should shave, then."

She ran a hand over his jaw, loving the bristly texture against her palm. "No, no shave," she whispered at his ear. Laughing, he hugged her one more time and Sophia thought life couldn't get any better.

* * * * *

LET'S TALK
Romance

For exclusive extracts, competitions
and special offers, find us online:

- facebook.com/millsandboon
- @MillsandBoon
- @MillsandBoonUK

Get in touch on 01413 063232

For all the latest titles coming soon, visit
millsandboon.co.uk/nextmonth